Ash curle  and wrapped up in the scratchy blanket. *If I ever get out of this place, I'm going to proposition Hawk and tell him once and for all how I feel about him. I'm going to tell him, I think about him night and day. How I long for him to hold me in his arms and to kiss me senseless. Now if only he could find me.* Still feeling weak from the drugs, weariness overtook her, and she slept focusing her thoughts on Hawk.

Even in her sleep, Ashlyn could sense the air around her humming with energy. Her mind was consumed with Hawk, and she unwittingly connected to him. Reaching deep, her concentration intense, she begged him to help her. A feeling of warmth filled her, and her nose twitched when she caught a whiff of Hawk's woodsy, masculine scent. Without warning the door to their link was suddenly slammed shut, and Hawk was forcibly ripped from her mind. Waking with a start, Ashlyn bolted upright.

"Dear Goddess, I actually felt him!" she exclaimed, in shock. "But how?"

Ash sensed the loss immediately. There had always been a connection with Hawk, but this was something altogether different, something stronger, something, much more. Hope flickered inside her. Now, if only she could do it again.

The House of Fire

by

M. Goldsmith
and A. Malin

Guardians of the Elements Series

The House of Fire

COPYRIGHT © 2018 by Melissa Paticoff and Anita Plutner

Cover Art by *Debbie Taylor*

The Wild Rose Press, Inc.
PO Box 708
Adams Basin, NY 14410-0708
Visit us at www.thewildrosepress.com

Publishing History
First Fantasy Rose Edition, 2018
Print ISBN 978-1-5092-2003-8
Digital ISBN 978-1-5092-2004-5

Guardians of the Elements Series
Published in the United States of America

Dedication

To our family and friends
for their love and support throughout this adventure.
We love you.
~Melissa and Anita

Chapter One

Ashlyn

The sounds of clanging tools, shouting, and organized movement rose in the air from the Village Square below. The chaotic excitement drifted upward in the pleasant spring breeze reaching the South Tower's Atrium. Ashlyn stood in front of one of the massive cutout windows. Fighting the gentle wind, she repeatedly swept long red curls out of her eyes and mouth. Leaning over as far as she was able, she peered down losing her grip momentarily before catching herself. White knuckled, she took a deep measured breath to slow her racing heart.

"Chill out, girl. You are Ashlyn Woods, Guardian of The House of Fire. You can handle a little ceremony and festival."

Her Fire responded to her little pep talk with a sudden rush of adrenaline coursing through her body. From deep within, she felt the precursory warmth spread as her Fire surged to the surface. Flames licked along her arms and down to the tips of her fingers. As if her years of developed control hadn't existed, Ashlyn's Fire fought her. An imbalance was creeping its way into Ash's powers. Her Fire swelled and receded of its own accord. It taunted her, and she had never felt so disconnected in her life. She truly hoped it was because of all the excitement churning throughout the small village of Aether and that things would return to normal soon.

Ashlyn focused on the reason for the festival; the newest addition to Aether's House of Fire. Nearly eighty-five years had passed since the birth of a new Fire Guardian, and she was dizzy with nervous excitement when she held the infant for the first time. Closing her eyes, Ash recalled their meeting just days ago.

****

A tuft of red hair peeked out from under the blanket swaddling the newborn. Ash loosened the wrapping to find the baby's tiny hands. They were clenched in tight fists even as the infant brought one to her perfect pink lips.

Softly, Ashlyn spoke, "Well, little one, I sure hope you're going to stay this sweet forever."

Stroking the infant's cheek, Ash looked into her eyes and felt an instant connection. A delicate little hand stretched up, and Ashlyn finally caught a glimpse of the prominent birthmark which proclaimed the newborn's status as a Fire Guardian. Her palm was etched with a bold triangle pointing upward toward her fingers. The mark resembled a brand. Deeply embedded in the skin, the impression gave the appearance of having blistered and healed in a blush tone.

As was her habit, Ashlyn absentmindedly traced the outline of her own Guardian mark. Head spinning, heart pounding, Ashlyn tried to quiet her rioting emotions. Feeling a bit overwhelmed, she returned the baby to her bassinet. The birth of this child was certainly a cause for celebration, but Ash had been consumed with a strange uneasiness closing in on her.

****

As her hand made contact with the Vessel of Fire, Ashlyn was pulled away from her thoughts. The Vessel was one of the four representations of the Elements which guided her people: Fire, Water, Air, and Earth. She ran her fingers along the rough surface of the hollow, concave container made of ancient stone. The feeling warmed Ash, and she focused seeking balance. The Vessel stood proudly on a raised pedestal housed in the center of the Atrium. The eternal flame from within its confines blazed luminously and cast a dazzling glow on the surrounding area. It could be admired from down below yet was impossible to reach and protected by powerful magic. Only the symbol on a Guardian's palm could admit a person to the chamber.

All Guardians shared symbiotic relationships with their corresponding Vessels. Each Guardian channeled the Element's power further enhancing her own gift through it. Placing both of her hands on the Vessel, Ash addressed the Flame. "All right now, we can do this together." Closing her eyes, she concentrated on the Vessel. Ashlyn chanted softly, "Balance." Her own Fire answered with a burst of intensity.

Chimes sounded loudly pulling Ashlyn out of her reverie causing her Fire to escape back out of her reach. Rolling her eyes, irritated, she grumbled. "What now?" She turned on her heels releasing a breathy sigh. "It's definitely going to be a long few days." She stomped to the door and then raced down the stairs.

Ashlyn was relieved when she saw Sol, her mentor, standing by the door. Sol stood tall in her usual elegant manner. She had the characteristic red hair of a Fire Guardian and glowing golden eyes. Her hair was straight, cropped short, and a deep shade of auburn. Her soft-spoken confidence always put Ashlyn at ease. Sol embraced her with a smile.

"It's time for us to talk. I wanted to make sure you were ready for the ceremony tomorrow."

"Ready as I'll ever be, I guess. It's strange to think I'll be the teacher now. We both know how…um…impulsive, my mother would say, I was when I was young."

Sol chuckled. "Well, you certainly put my patience to the test. I'll never forget when your powers began to emerge when you were young, and you set Hawk's pants on fire for teasing you. I knew I had to scold you, but inside I was laughing for a week."

Ashlyn slipped into the vivid memory allowing it to wash over her and fill her up.

****

She had held tight to Laurel's hand as they skipped their way to the playground at recess. The two best friends wanted to get to the spinning merry-go-round first. They took off giggling, racing to the spot where their prize stood. Skidding to a halt just short of victory, they spotted three boys taking turns spinning each other madly at dizzying speeds. "Hawk Crane, Quill Robbins, and Kai Sanders, of course," Ashlyn mumbled, in an irritated tone.

"Come on, let's go play somewhere else." Laurel kicked the dirt beneath her feet staring at the ground. "Those boys are bigger than us, and they play too rough."

"No way, we called dibs yesterday. I'm going to ask them to give us a turn. It's only fair."

Ashlyn and Hawk's families had been close friends

4

her entire life, and as very young children the two had always been inseparable. Ash barely possessed an early childhood memory that didn't include the Cranes. Though lately, Hawk had been acting strangely toward her, distant, yet too close, all at the same time. In the mind of a ten-year-old it was a difficult thing to understand. Only weeks before they had been climbing trees and playing together. Then suddenly, Hawk had become surly and argumentative. As they approached the boys, Ashlyn felt Hawk's stare penetrate right through her. It was unnerving to say the least, and her Fire tingled deep inside her. Her Flame sought out something Ash didn't recognize, or even comprehend, so she shook it off.

"Hi guys, we'd like to take a turn on the merry-go-round, please?" Ashlyn asked, politely.

"We were here first, so too bad on you." Quill responded by sticking out his tongue at the girls.

Ashlyn's hair started to release smoke, and tiny sparks glinted from her fingertips. She felt like a lighter repeatedly getting flicked on and off. Sol had been helping Ash practice her control for several weeks, but discipline and restraint were not her strong suits. Anytime she was startled, upset, or excited, her Flame burst forth.

Ash crossed her arms over her chest and stuck out her chin. "You better give us a turn, or you'll be sorry."

"Oh, please, what are you going to do about it...Sparky? Your mom, told my mom, you can't even control your stupid Fire. She says you can't even light a match." Hawk laughed and turned to his friends. "Watch out guys, or Sparky here is going to set you on Fire."

5

Smoke continued to rise from Ashlyn's hair lifting it as if caught by a swift breeze. The sparks at her fingertips erupted into flames spreading down her arms and danced about as they gained more momentum. "Take that back, Hawk Crane."

"Or what, Sparky? Going to go tell on me?"

Before Ash realized what was happening, her Fire shot out in a rush from her hands and soared toward Hawk. He turned to move out of the way, but Ash's Flame caught the back of his jeans setting them alight. Quill and Kai howled with laughter, as Hawk rolled on the ground trying to douse the flames.

Remorse and guilt spread through Ashlyn. "I'm so sorry, Hawk. I didn't do it on purpose. Are you okay?"

Hawk had furiously patted the back of his pants as he glared at her. "Stay away from me, Ashlyn."

****

Ashlyn's mind came back to the present, as the memory slowly drifted away.

"Where did you go off to?" Sol asked.

"Sorry, I was just remembering the way things used to be when Hawk and I were young. No one pushes my buttons the way he does. He's kind of quiet around me now, but I know he watches me when he thinks I'm not looking. Not in a scary stalker kind of way, it's just like a weird connection or something. I don't know. I'd hoped as we grew up things wouldn't be so awkward between us. But it is what it is, I guess."

The feeling of being both attracted and repelled at the same time lingered between them. Ash couldn't deny feeling compelled to seek out Hawk whenever he was near. She couldn't help thinking about how handsome he was. He had been tall as a teen but

6

nothing close to his six foot four-inch height today. His long black wavy hair hung to his broad shoulders. He was well muscled and possessed the most beautiful dark eyes she had ever seen. Ash's senses became heightened around Hawk, and her body sent her strange signals whenever he was near.

In fact, the other day when the Protectors had been training, she found herself staring. The massive expanse of Hawk's bare chest, toned, with pure muscle covered in bronzed skin, called out for her touch. With a visceral reaction, her gaze connected to his incredible form. She stood glued to the spot drawn in by a myriad of sensations. Warmth gushed through her, and tingles traveled down her body leaving her feeling aroused and unsettled. At times, Ash thought he also felt the intensity of the link between them. As if Hawk could somehow read her thoughts and sense her presence, he looked up to meet her gaze. Ash felt his hands stroking her hair, yet he remained standing at a distance. She shuddered and brushed away the uneasy memory. Ash needed to stop daydreaming about her secret crush and focus on what was happening in the here and now.

"How am I going to do this, Sol? I'm not you."

"You don't need to be anyone but who you are, my lovely Ash. You are wise and strong. This baby is lucky to have you as a mentor. And remember, I'm always here for you."

"Thanks for saying that." She felt heat rising in her cheeks, knowing they were turning bright pink. "My powers have been a little wonky lately. I guess it's just all the excitement around here. I have a really strange feeling I just can't seem to shake."

"What do you mean?"

"I'm not sure I can explain it exactly, it's just this feeling, a sort of foreboding. Oh, I don't know what I'm saying. Just ignore me."

"What do you mean about your powers being wonky? You know as Guardians, our Fire has a will of its own. It will always try to warn you and protect you. You need to maintain balance and control. You need to connect."

"You know how hard I've worked on my control, and it's usually excellent. But lately, I can feel the flame within me always so close to the surface even when I try to call it back. And other times, I can't seem to bring it to the surface at all. It's like being a teenager all over again."

Ashlyn had the appearance of a young woman approximately twenty-five years of age. In actuality, she was soon approaching her eighty-third birthday. Her people lived an inordinately long time due to their kinship with the four Elements; Fire, Water, Air, and Earth. They were each strongly connected to all of the Elements, but most individuals were more dominantly united with a singular Element. Though infrequent, some people, like Hawk, were linked to more than one Element.

As the Guardian of Fire, Ashlyn's powers were incredibly potent. She worked all of her adult life to subdue her emotional nature in order to gain mastery of her Fire. It was a constant struggle for Ash. Her gift was a great deal stronger than any of the other members of the Fire community. Although some of the people in The House of Fire exhibited a small amount of control over fire, none could match the powers of a Guardian. It was rare for a person to be able to create fire but not as uncommon to be able to influence it once it was already ignited. Ashlyn's powers and abilities surpassed those of all previous Fire Guardians.

"Try not to worry too much. I'm sure it's just all the commotion going on around here making your powers a bit unsteady. I understand better than anyone the pressure you are feeling right now. I have faith in you, Ash. You'll be wonderful, and everything will go smoothly at the festival tomorrow including the ceremony."

"I'll try to relax, but I think it's going to be a lot easier said than done."

"You just need to rest. I'll stop by in the morning and walk over to the Village Square with you. The Elders want to talk to both of us before the ceremony tomorrow night."

"Ok, sounds good."

Sol left her with a quick hug and headed toward her own home just behind the South Tower. Ashlyn collapsed on the couch and closed her eyes. Her mind raced with thoughts of tomorrow's ceremony and her pivotal role. When darkness fell the next evening, Ash would stand before all of Aether and pledge herself to the new baby Guardian.

The sun was beginning to set and the sky was alight with brilliant reds, yellows, and oranges; reminding her of Fire. Allowing her mind to wander, Ash forced thoughts of tomorrow and its significance away. Finally, she dozed off. Her dreams were troubled. She dreamt of being chased.

****

Hawk

Hawk's gaze automatically focused on the top of

the village's South Tower while he stood transfixed from the Square below. He admired Ashlyn as she stared down from the grand windows. Irresistibly beautiful and very shapely, she stood tall. Her hair, the color of fire, was long and reached almost to her waist. As he watched it dance around her face, he imagined what it would feel like to touch, or better yet, to wrap the soft-looking strands in his fingers. Her fiery curls always seemed a bit unruly just like Ashlyn. Her eyes were enchanting; a glorious golden color, and they appeared to see all, especially him. Yet, he saw her, too.

Lately, Hawk sensed an unusually pensive mood from Ash. When he thought about it, maybe it should have been strange to him to feel Ashlyn's thoughts and moods, but it seemed natural. The many hours he'd committed to dreams of Ashlyn soft in his arms did, too. She had captivated him even when they were very young. It wasn't simply her beauty, it was an inexplicable magnetic pull. Just the other night, he'd been walking by the back alley which led to the café, when he felt it.

****

Compelled to go in a direction deviating from his norm, Hawk was forcibly drawn to the café's little-used rear entrance. Just as he was about to ask himself why he was back there, it suddenly became clear. He turned to head inside and bumped into Ashlyn coming from the other way. Their collision had her teetering and Hawk's hands automatically moved to her hips to steady her. He stepped aside to let her pass, but she countered simultaneously forcing their bodies tighter in the confined space. The smell of cinnamon filled his nose as he breathed in Ashlyn's scent. Her breasts pressed up against him, as they both attempted to maneuver out of each other's way. Instantly, the air around them crackled, and Hawk couldn't control the urge to pull her even closer. He leaned in, his mouth a breath away from hers. They were so tightly connected he could feel her heartbeat in a rapid staccato, its rhythm matching his own. The air around them swirled with electricity and jolted through him, throwing him off balance. At that moment, Hawk and Ashlyn were completely in sync. She seemed as overwhelmed by their connection as he was. They synchronously pulled away from each other. Before Hawk could even speak, Ashlyn had fled back down the alleyway into the night.

****

Two strong hands shoved him from behind, and Hawk staggered forward. The sounds of snickering escaped someone's lips, as he regained his balance. Turning, he discovered his best friend, Quill, doubled over laughing. Any attempt to maintain his composure was completely gone now. Hawk rolled his eyes. The two had been best friends for as long as he could remember. They grew up next-door to each other, and their families had always been close. Nobody knew Hawk better than Quill.

"What the hell, Quill?"

"Sorry, buddy, couldn't help myself. Hmm. I wonder what you're staring at up there?"

"Oh, shut up!"

"Could you be any more obvious with your gawking? People are going to notice the way you obsess about that woman. I know she's *hot,* but you better control yourself unless you want all of Aether talking about you."

"I know you're right, but there's always been something about her—"

"Yeah, there's something about her all right. Ever since we were kids, you had the *hots* for her. She obviously had them for you, too, remember when she set your pants on fire." Quill tried, but failed to contain a chuckle from escaping. "I told you not to tease that girl. She may be beautiful, but she has a sick temper."

"Hey, it's not my fault Ashlyn had no sense of humor back then."

"You have to admit it was actually pretty funny watching you roll around on the ground trying to put out the flames." Quill bent at the waist, laughing. "You did kind of deserve it for teasing her all the time. Hopefully your flirting skills have improved now that we're not kids anymore. Just show her the old charm. I know it's in there somewhere."

River, the lead Protector, yelled from across the Square. "If you two kids are done chatting over there, do you think you can help us move some of these tables and benches? We still have a lot to get done around here to be ready for tomorrow."

"Sorry, River," Quill responded. They walked over to join the rest of the Protectors who were helping set up for the festival.

The Aetherians really knew how to celebrate and the excitement was palpable. The village was located in a secluded rural area with its nearest neighbor more than thirty miles away. Their concealment from the outside world created the need for the villagers to make to their own fun, and they relished any opportunity to do so. It was rumored the village was cloaked in magic, and rarely had ordinary humans managed to penetrate its borders.

The Village Square had been created with a beautiful mosaic compass rose at its center directing the villagers toward each of the four Towers. The Fire Guardian and her family lived in the South Tower. The West Tower was occupied by Water, the East by Air, and the North by Earth. Cobblestone pathways led out to each of the four Towers. The grand structures stood four stories tall and were identical. They were timeworn but still majestic. Built solidly of ancient looking stone and mortar, they had the appearance of small castles. Each had a magnificent open-air Atrium at the top which housed the Vessels of the Elements. Aether's Square expanded outward to include a school, Medical Center, Council Chambers, Protector's Headquarters, and a few select shops. Family homes were built outside the Village Square overflowing into the wooded areas alongside and behind the Towers outside the village proper.

Hawk and Quill both grunted as they hoisted a huge table over to where the others were being placed. Tomorrow, at the celebration, every surface would be covered with a variety of delicious food contributed by the villagers. Following the ceremony welcoming the new Guardian, there would be music, dancing, eating, and some drinking, of course.

Huge casks of wine and beer were rolled in and placed in close proximity to the head table. Ashlyn, her family, the Council Elders, and the new Guardian's family would sit in the place of honor. Dozens upon dozens of other tables were also placed in every available open space throughout the area. Benches were set up around the Village Square's center, arcing around on all sides of the compass rose, where the ceremony was to be held. All of Aether's residents would be in attendance for the ceremony and the festival following.

The birth of any child among the villagers was thrilling to the people. Many couples were never able to conceive children, and if they did, they usually had only a single child. The Elders believed it was the God and Goddess' way of controlling Aether's population due to its people's longevity. Inhabitants usually lived for hundreds of years and were not often prone to common illnesses found among ordinary humans.

The oldest members in the community usually suffered a slow and steady waning of power until they were diminished to the point of appearing typically human. Eventually, these individuals never awoke from slumber and were believed to transition to a place of tranquility; a metaphysical existence, known to the people as Arcadia. In a world without physical boundaries, the Aetherians continued on in a mystical, spiritual, and boundless manner. Passing on to Arcadia was celebrated among the people.

Hawk recalled his grandmother's Passage Ceremony, a touching ritual held whenever a soul left the Earth in search of Arcadia. Just this past fall, the entire community had gathered by Aether's Grand Lake for the service.

****

Wrapped in a cotton cloth, having departed the Earth a mere two days ago, she had been set atop a platform surrounded by wood. Breathing in deeply, Hawk's nose instantly recognized the smell of the freshly cut timber. His grandfather stood before the entire village and spoke about their wonderful life being Joined together, as Kanti and Adara. He spoke with pride when he described how devoted and kind she'd been throughout her life. Following the speech, Ashlyn, as Fire Guardian, set the remains ablaze. A bittersweet feeling filled Hawk. He watched as his beloved grandmother was reduced to cinder. Her ashes were divided among the other Guardians. The Water Guardian dispersed the embers into the lake, the Air Guardian scattered the ashes to the wind, and the Earth Guardian combined her ashes with the soil. In this manner, she was eternally linked with all four Elements. It was then believed she had passed onto Arcadia.

****

The only time the citizens of Aether mourned a loss was when someone was taken prematurely. Aetherians were far stronger than ordinary humans. Although they were not immortal, individuals healed faster and were resistant to human disease. The race was still susceptible to traumatic injury due to accidents or attack. Occasionally, injuries were sustained that were, too great for even an Aetherian to recover from. Therefore, all life was cherished by the people of Aether and still held a sense of fragility.

Tomorrow would be a unique and memorable day for the entire village. Celebrating new life, especially that of a Guardian, was monumental. The younger generation had never witnessed the dazzling ritual of the Fire Guardian ceremony. Hawk was anxious to experience it for himself, as he was just a baby the last time this ceremony took place. Hawk, the other Protectors, and volunteers worked diligently to finish the preparations before the sun dipped down in the sky.

****

Ashlyn

Large faceless men dressed in black continued to pursue Ashlyn no matter how fast she ran. She sprinted between the trees in the densest part of the forest beyond the houses of Aether's village. The ground rushed by under her feet making her feel dizzy. Her lungs burned, and her legs felt heavy. Her panic rose, as she attempted to call her Flame to the surface. Her eyes darted about the forest, searching. She needed to protect Aether from this legion of faceless men. Tiny sparks burst from her fingers, as she attempted to set a series of small controlled fires behind her. If Ash's Fire was too sizable the entire village could be in jeopardy.

She raced around trees, rocks, and large branches which created an obstacle course in her path. The faceless men continued their pursuit relentlessly. Terrified, panting, heart pounding, Ash pushed herself to run even faster as bullets whizzed past her. She could sense them gaining on her. Finally, Ashlyn stopped, regained some of her composure, and turned toward her attackers as her entire body was engulfed in flames.

The next thing she knew, her mother, Rowan, was shaking her. "Ash, wake up. It's just a dream. You're safe here at home." Her mom smoothed Ash's hair back from her face.

Ashlyn woke from her nightmare breathless and soaked in sweat. It took her a few moments to realize she was free from danger and in her own home.

Her father, Mica, barreled into the room seconds later. "What's going on? Are you okay, sweetie?"

"I'll be all right in a little bit. I had a dream that felt

way too real. It was terrifying. I can't stop shaking."

She confessed the frightening details of her nightmare to her parents and attempted to control the trembling in her hands. Mica went to the kitchen and returned with a glass of water.

"Here, sip this slowly. It will help."

Ash took the glass from her father, shaking so badly the contents sloshed over the sides. Mica wrapped his strong hands around Ash, steadying her.

"Thanks, Dad," she said, leaning on him for support.

Her parents had always been her greatest source of comfort and encouragement. Ash knew how fortunate she was to have them as her champions throughout her life. Her parents shared the most loving and warm relationship of any Adara and Kanti she had ever witnessed. She longed to share the beauty of that kind of love with someone. The only man who ever came to mind when she fantasized about love and a Joining ceremony was Hawk, the beautiful Protector who dominated her thoughts. Ashlyn was convinced Hawk sensed their connection as deeply as she did. The chemistry and sexual tension between them grew more and more over the years. The constant ups and downs felt like being on a teeter totter in perpetual motion. She wondered if perhaps it was her role as the Fire Guardian that made him leery of a relationship with her, or maybe, it was Ashlyn herself? The sound of Rowan's voice had Ash tuning back in.

"Are you sure you're okay, Ash?"

"I'll be all right, Mom. I'm just a little freaked out by the nightmare. You know I've been having some trouble with my powers recently. I think the combination is honestly too much. With the ceremony tomorrow and all the pressure involved, I feel like I've gone absolutely haywire."

"That's perfectly understandable considering the momentous event taking place around here." Mica held her closer.

"Your father is right, honey. Try to take a few deep breaths."

With hands that still jittered, Ashlyn slowly sipped the water. Condensation dribbled down the sides of the glass. She focused on the tiny cascading droplets of water instead of her nerves. She placed the glass on the coffee table in front of her and took a few deep measured breaths.

"Better?" her mom asked.

"Getting there, thanks, guys. I feel like such a baby. I'm sorry I scared you."

"Don't be silly. You've had a lot on your mind the past few days. It could happen to anyone." Mica reminded her.

"I'm going upstairs to take a bath. That always makes me feel better. I'll see you in a little while."

Ashlyn gingerly made her way up the stairs to the sanctity of her bedroom suite. She gripped the handrail tightly for balance, her legs still shaky. Once she was alone in her room, Ashlyn hopped up onto her elegant four-poster bed. She sat on the end dangling her feet the way she had when she was small. Swinging her legs, like a metronome keeping a rhythm, always had a calming effect on her. She knew it was an odd sort of meditation, but she never questioned its effectiveness.

After she felt a bit more centered, Ashlyn entered her private bathroom. She loved this space. The room was large. Beautiful earth toned tile mixed with natural stone warmed the expanse. An enormous raised tub with a lovely surround housing an abundance of candles took up one corner. Two sinks with a spacious countertop for all her personal items filled an entire wall. The spa-like bathroom also boasted a generous shower with a bench and multiple sprays. The toilet was enclosed in a separate water closet.

The faucet let out a little squeak when Ashlyn turned it to fill the tub. Waiting for the water to rise, she delicately touched the wicks of each candle with the tip of her finger setting them alight. Reaching for the light switch, she set it to dim. With a flourish, her clothing piled up on the floor as she undressed. Climbing into the tub, she allowed her Flame to come forth when her toes hit the surface. Steam rose from the basin as she sank into the heated water.

Ashlyn sighed, settling in, enjoying the sensation of the luxurious bath, but she couldn't block out the disturbing images from her nightmare. She forced her thoughts to travel to the one thing guaranteed to always help distract her; Hawk Crane. Ash's mind took hold of a memory from long ago and had lingered in its depths.

****

It was a warm summer night. Laurel had convinced her they should sneak to the Grand Lake at midnight and go skinny-dipping. Usually, it was Ashlyn pushing Laurel to act more impulsively, but since Laurel started dating Kai Sanders, Ashlyn was seeing a whole new side to her best friend. Only two years after finishing high school, Laurel was hyper focused on becoming a teacher, and Ashlyn was deeply immersed in her Guardian training. Letting loose seemed like a great idea at the time.

The night was still, the sky cloudless, with the most beautiful array of stars shining brightly above them. In silence, they stood by the water's edge and removed their shoes and clothing. Of course, Laurel's were folded neatly in a pile while Ash's were strewn across one of the large rocks lining the shore. The moist sand squished between her toes as she stepped into the cool water. Diving deep, the momentary freedom from responsibility felt like heaven. Surfacing, she was stunned to hear male voices on the beach. As if by instinct, Ash reached out and sensed Hawk before he came into view. She stayed quiet and listened to the sound of his voice which settled low in her belly.

Ashlyn's thoughts were jumbled in her head, *This is crazy...freaking out here...this is Hawk, we played together when we were children...please don't notice me...oh my god, I'm naked...I'm so going to kill Laurel...where did she go...I bet she planned this whole thing.*

Shrieks of laughter and splashing rang out loudly in the quiet darkness breaking the peaceful spell she had been under just a short while ago. *Guess Kai found Laurel.* Ashlyn's mind raced. *Now where did Hawk go? I know I heard his voice.*

A few moments later, a break in the surface nearby startled Ash, and the water around her steamed as her Fire emerged. Ashlyn called her Fire back the way she had been practicing and regained control.

Hawk's low husky tone reached out to her in the darkness. "Ashlyn? Is that you? Kai is a dead man. He told me it would just be the guys tonight."

"Yes, it's me. I think Laurel and Kai are trying to

do a little matchmaking here. Sorry."

"Why are you sorry? You didn't plan this, did you?"

Appalled at the thought, Ash's voice rose an octave. "Of course not! Do you think I want to be out here naked with you right over there?"

A rumble of laughter rose from deep within Hawk's chest. "Okay, Ash, tell me how you really feel. Am I that awful?"

"No, no. That's not what I meant. It's just, well, you're, you," she said, tripping over her words. "I'm sorry, Hawk, this is just way too weird. Honestly, being near you freaks me out sometimes, especially when we're alone." She exhaled deeply.

"It's all right, Ash, really. I always have appreciated your blunt honesty. My bruised ego and I will just swim away and leave you alone."

"Please, wait. I don't mean to sound so harsh. I'm just confused. You confuse me."

"Me? What have I done? I haven't teased you since we were kids. I never bother you—"

"No, you don't bother me. You just ignore me, but there you are inside my head anyway… Ugh! I'm not explaining this right… I'm sorry. I'll go; please, turn your back while I swim away."

"Ash, wait, please. What do you mean I'm in your head?" He pulled her gently by the arm.

Their chests collided in the wake. Ashlyn gasped as her nipples responded. As if driven by force, her hand reached out involuntarily and stroked Hawk's bare chest. His eyes closed, and Ashlyn couldn't decide if it looked like agony or ecstasy on his handsome face.

Quickly, she pulled her hand away. "I'm sorry."

Touching Hawk, even in such a simple way, sent a rush through her body and her mind reeling. "I can't deal with this; I have to get out of here. I'm sorry, Hawk."

Ashlyn had turned away from him, dove back under the water, and headed toward the shore.

****

With a shake of her head, Ashlyn's thoughts returned to the present. Even after all these years of the constant push and pull between them, Ash was sure of one thing; she was still unsure where Hawk was concerned. Except, when it came to her feelings of attraction, of that she was certain. She ran hot in every way when Hawk was near.

She closed her eyes and visualized him standing before her in all his splendor. He lowered himself into the bath to join her. As she imagined his strong arms encircling her, she could practically feel Hawk drawing her back against his chest. When she envisioned his large body pressed tightly against hers, she became energized and aroused. Ashlyn couldn't help but dream of what it would be like if they were actually together.

Looking down at her wrinkled fingers and toes, Ash decided to leave the cocoon of the warm bath. Already dripping on the floor, she squeezed the excess water from her hair before grabbing a towel. The toasty terrycloth smelled like fresh laundry, and she wrapped herself up. Once in her bedroom, she yanked open the door to her walk-in closet and pulled on a pair of her favorite cozy sweats with a long-sleeved T-shirt.

Pacing back to the bathroom, she tossed her towel on the growing pile of dirty clothing collecting on the floor. Frowning when she stole a quick glance in the mirror, she snatched her hairbrush off the counter.

Yelping, she ran it through her hair attempting to tame her mass of wild red curls. She blew out a breath. "Good enough, I guess." When she reached the doorway to leave, she turned back and gestured with a slight wave of her hand. All of the candles extinguished in an instant.

Tantalizing smells wafting up from the kitchen brought her back downstairs to join her parents. Rowan was an amazing cook, and Ashlyn realized how hungry she was when her stomach growled loudly.

Mica laughed at the sound. "I guess someone is feeling better and definitely hungry."

"Ha-ha, I haven't eaten all day. What are you making over there, Mom? Do you need any help?"

"I'm all set, thanks. In fact everything is ready," Rowan said.

They took their seats as her mom set a giant bowl of pasta with shrimp in a rich-looking sauce, a side of roasted broccoli, and garlic bread on the table. It all looked and smelled fantastic causing Ash's stomach to rumble noisily once again. They all burst out laughing lightening the mood considerably.

"I texted Laurel. I think I'm going to take a walk over there after dinner. I could use a little girl time," Ashlyn mentioned. Her best friend was an easy-going person in contrast to Ash's intensity. She was calm and levelheaded, where Ashlyn was passionate and excitable. Their opposite natures were always a good balance.

They finished dinner keeping the conversation light and with no mention of her disturbing nightmare. Ashlyn helped her dad clean up the dishes while her mom packed away the leftovers. When everything was in order, Ashlyn grabbed a sweatshirt off the coatrack by the front door.

"I'll probably be home late, so I'll see you in the morning. Don't wait up for me."

Laurel lived far beyond the North Tower at the very edge of the village deep into the woods. Her family was of The Earth and loved to be near the forest. The Green family had occupied the same house for many generations, and Ashlyn loved spending time there. There were some people among the citizens of Aether who were intimidated by Ashlyn's power and role as Guardian. At the Green's home, she always felt welcome and was simply one of the family. It was comforting to belong rather than be on the periphery. As she made her way, the crisp spring air chilled her slightly as the wind whipped her hair around her face. Ash zipped her sweatshirt up a little higher and picked up her pace a bit.

Knocking on the door, she entered without waiting for a response. Her friend was stretched out on the sofa reading a magazine. Laurel was a stunning woman with long, straight mahogany colored hair. Ashlyn thought it always looked so shiny and perfect whereas hers was wild and unruly. Laurel was petite with beautiful olive-toned skin. She had almond shaped, chocolate brown eyes that reflected her nurturing temperament, which was probably why she was the most popular teacher in the village's school.

"Hey there, stranger, long time no see." Laurel waved.

"Hi there, my friend. Thanks for hanging out with me tonight. I really need your calming influence," Ash said.

"Yeah, you're definitely looking a little lost tonight."

"Ha-ha. I'm not lost, just a little anxious I guess. Want to take a walk with me?"

"Sure, hon. Let me just grab my shoes, and a jacket and I'm all yours." Laurel returned moments later. "If it's not too late, do you want to grab a drink at the Pub after our walk?"

"I'm not sure if one is going to cut it. Do you think the pub has an IV pole I can hook up to some vodka?" Laughing, they retreated to the back porch where Ashlyn embraced Laurel with a tight, emotional hug.

Laurel returned the gesture. "What's wrong, sis?"

Talking a mile a minute she blurted out, "I'm a wreck, my powers are wonky, I had a horrible, crazy nightmare, not to mention I think I'm in love with a man who I can't seem to get close to and—"

"Whoa there, just calm down. One crisis at a time, please. Let's take a walk and you can tell me all about it."

They stepped off the porch and headed down one of the many paths into the woods behind the Green's house. Even though it was quite chilly, it was an exquisite night to be out in the forest. Most of the trees were filled with leaves again creating a canopy above on the crisp, cloudless, early spring night. The nearly full moon shone brightly through the openings between the trees forming tiny spotlights on the ground as they strolled along. They meandered onward in silence for a while, the only sounds were the dead leaves crunching under their feet and the whistling of the wind.

Heading off the path as they wandered farther into the woods, Laurel finally spoke. "Are you a little more relaxed now?"

"Yeah, thanks for always getting me and knowing what I need."

"That's what best friends are for. Why don't you pick one neurosis and spill it, sister?" Laurel said, trying to lighten the mood.

"I guess it started last week when the baby Guardian was born. My powers have become completely out of control, like when we were crazy adolescents. My Flame either keeps surging to the surface and I can't seem to call it back no matter how hard I try, or it won't come out at all. I just keep having this awful feeling in the pit of my stomach."

"I know you, Ash, I'm sure you're nervous about living up to the Elders expectations. The powerful Ashlyn Woods, keeper of the Flame. Give yourself a break. You may be the Guardian of Fire but in your heart, you're just as vulnerable as the rest of us."

The loud snapping of a twig behind them pulled their focus from each other and their conversation. It had been pretty quiet and they hadn't noticed any animals in the area when they were hiking along.

"Did you hear that?" Ashlyn asked.

"Yes, it was probably just an animal."

"I don't know about that. Maybe we should head back toward home. We've gone much farther than we usually do."

As they turned to head back in the opposite direction, they heard more branches breaking and a heavy rustling. Ashlyn whispered, "I have bad feeling about this. Let's hurry!"

The two women started to move more and more quickly until they were almost jogging. "I still hear it. I think it's getting closer. It's definitely getting louder. Come on, let's run." Ash gently tugged on Laurel's hand encouraging her to move ahead, as nervous knots tightened in her stomach.

"Calm down. I'm sure it's nothing." It seemed to Ash, Laurel was trying to reassure herself, as much as Ashlyn.

Just a short distance ahead there was a large gap between the trees allowing the light of the moon to shine luminously down. There, underneath, stood a dark figure with a gun pointing directly at them. Laurel screamed, and Ashlyn turned toward her friend with the realization this was her nightmare come to life. She grabbed Laurel by the sleeve urging her to flee as she felt something whiz by her cheek. They charged through the forest sprinting at top speed.

"Run, Laurel!" Ash yelled.

She could feel the presence of the stranger in black closing in on them. Ashlyn knew she needed to get her friend to safety. Laurel's powers were limited. She could create only modest vibrations in the ground, not enough to cause any real damage. Laurel charged ahead with graceful movements, barely winded.

Ashlyn was in her dust, pumping her arms and legs to keep up. With her heart beating loudly in her ears, Ashlyn called her Flame to the surface but like in her dream, she was feeling powerless. Fear pulsed through her an invader in her own body. The muscles in her legs protested and she felt herself slowing slightly.

Her friend continued to forge ahead, and Ash could tell Laurel didn't realize she was beginning to lag behind.

As Laurel zigzagged through the trees, three more

men dressed in black with masks enshrouding their faces, lurched toward them. Ashlyn made the decision to change direction in order to lead them away from Laurel.

Just then, Laurel glanced over her shoulder and noticed Ashlyn was no longer behind her. "Ash! No! Don't!"

She shouted back, "Keep running, Laurel, get help. I'll be okay!"

Her plan worked, because the three additional figures turned to pursue Ashlyn. Only their original attacker seemed interested in chasing Laurel.

Ashlyn attempted to control her emotions in order to call her Fire to the surface. Her fingertips sparked, and she set a few small fires off behind her. Projectiles continually brushed by her getting closer and closer. She took cover behind an ancient looking tree its girth shielding her.

Pausing momentarily, she breathed in deeply attempting to regain her composure. Ash sensed the heat rising up from within her and willed her Fire to the surface. With an audible whoosh, her entire body ignited in a burst of flame.

Ashlyn faced the three figures from her nightmare with renewed vigor, as her body remained engulfed in flames. They stared at her while backing away, shocked, and dumbfounded. Arms outstretched, she prepared to launch her Fire, when without warning, she felt a sharp stab in her shoulder blade. Ashlyn pivoted around to identify a lone man standing behind her.

Anger bubbled up. "I'm going to incinerate you!" A warm rush flooded her cheeks. Ashlyn attempted to project her Flame toward the cloaked figure. Suddenly, her limbs felt heavy, and her arms fell uselessly to her sides. The power of her Flame gradually ebbed, until it was completely extinguished, and she fell to the ground in a lifeless heap.

Chapter Two

Kai

Kai Sanders sat at his desk in Aether's Medical Center. When he couldn't sleep, Kai often came in to work. Insomnia plagued him on a regular basis. He massaged his temples with the tips of his fingers attempting to relieve the ache in his head. Perhaps it was the pressure of being Aether's only actual medical doctor. It had taken many years for Kai to get permission from the Elders to attend medical school, and he took his position very seriously. In fact, being a doctor was his entire life.

It was a quiet morning since the Clinic wasn't due to open for several more hours. Kai expected it to be completely empty with the festival and ceremony taking place this evening. He planned to close the Clinic early so he and his staff could attend. He knew his best friends, Hawk and Quill, would force him to have a drink afterward, or knowing Quill, way more than one. Kai worried if he got carried away and an emergency popped up, he wouldn't be of much help.

Many people in the Water community had a natural gift for healing, but the Sanders family had been healers since the beginning of the people's history. They were compassionate, kind, and understanding making them remarkable practitioners.

An endlessly curious child, Kai trailed his parents

constantly in the Medical Center. He was a tiny sponge attempting to soak up every bit of knowledge. For as long as he could remember, he wanted to continue on in the Sanders family tradition as a healer.

Endowed with a special power, Kai demonstrated the ability to touch individuals and sense their physical condition, however, not without consequence. Through this connection, their pain invaded his body. Over many years, with practice and training, he learned to control his ability. When necessary, he could bring forth his power. This was a rare gift even among other healers in the Water community.

Shivering, Kai retreated back in his mind to a time which transformed his life in every way. He had been forced to use his gift to reveal the most devastating news. It was hard to believe the tragic events and their aftermath had happened more than fifty years ago. He remembered every detail as if it were yesterday.

****

"I wish everyone would get off my back about working in the Clinic too much," he said, to his friend. Kai turned back to file charts in the cabinet behind the reception desk. "Now it's not just my parents, but it's Laurel, too. They keep saying I need to spend more time socializing." Thankfully, he had Hawk and Quill to push him to get out more often. Laurel, on the other hand, tempted him away from work in a very different way.

A thunderous crash followed by desperate shouts from the Village Square ceased any conversation. Kai rushed to the front door poking his head out to see what all the commotion was about. There was a person sprawled out on the ground in front of the village's market with a ladder beneath him. He shouted into the Clinic for someone to get a gurney quickly, and that he needed a team to help outside immediately. His father, Rayne, and two assistants, came racing out.

"Hurry, Dad, it looks like someone took a pretty serious fall off a ladder by the market."

Kai ran to make certain everything was prepped and ready in the trauma room they used for just such emergencies. Their Medical Center contained many medicines, ointments, and creams developed by the healers, using nature's bounty, as they called it.

The team burst through the Clinic doors sprinting in with the patient on a stretcher. Blood was flowing heavily from the victim's nose and ears. His face was unrecognizable with significant swelling already present, and his left leg appeared contorted. He remained unmoving as they wheeled him into the trauma room.

"It's Storm, Kai." Rayne's voice quivered. "He was repairing something on the market's roof when the ladder slipped from its footing."

Storm was Kai's sixteen-year-old cousin, and they shared an extremely close bond. The kid had been bouncing off the walls with excitement after landing an after-school job working for the village's construction crew. It was unnerving to see the vibrant teen, comedian of the family, who loved working with his hands, lying motionless. Kai's face dropped, and his mouth hung open. The severity of Storm's injuries were overwhelming.

"We need to get word to Uncle Burke and Aunt May. And, Kai, hurry. It's really bad."

Kai returned shortly to find his father in the trauma

room with several assistants crowded around treating Storm's various injuries. He was clearly still unconscious. Rayne was touching Storm's belly concentrating on his examination. Several different x-rays hung from the light box on the wall; one displayed a severely broken leg, another a fractured skull, and one showed completely shattered facial bones.

"Dad?" Kai said, getting Rayne's attention. "How is he? Burke and May are here. They're waiting outside and are very anxious to come in and see him."

"I need you to come here and help me first. Come and touch his belly. It's quite distended and firm to the touch, and I'm not exactly sure what's happening inside. I know how hard this is on you, but Storm needs you."

Kai approached the bed. "I can feel the pain every time I place my hands on someone and try to see inside."

"I know, son, but I'm not sure what else to do. I'm almost certain he is bleeding internally. That, along with the fractured skull and leg, not to mention the severe facial trauma, he is just not healing the way we usually do."

Kai placed both of his palms on Storm's distended, tense belly, took a cleansing breath, and closed his eyes. Images flashed in his brain as the extent of Storm's injuries revealed themselves through Kai's gift. A tremendous jolt of pain exploded inside him halting him in place. His face dripped with sweat, and his body shook. Rayne pulled him back by his shoulders and turned Kai to face him.

"Well? What did you see?"

"Oh, Dad." He hung his head choking back tears.

"It's his liver and spleen. They're a mess."

"I was afraid of that. I guess we just have to treat what we can and hope his body takes over to heal the rest." Rayne instructed his team to set the leg and clean Storm up as he went out to see his brother and sister-in-law, with Kai trailing close behind.

May wept quietly on Burke's shoulder as he comforted her silently. Burke jumped to his feet as soon as he saw Rayne approaching from the corner of his eye.

"Rayne, what's happening? How is he? Can we see him?" Burke said, in a rush.

"You can see him in a few minutes. They're setting his broken leg right now."

Looking relieved, May said, "Thank the Goddess it's just a broken leg. I thought something really terrible happened to him." Her relief was short lived when she read the expression on Rayne's face.

"I'm so sorry, May, but the leg is the very least of it. He has a fractured skull, severe facial fractures, and is bleeding internally. He is still unconscious and doesn't appear to be self-healing. I'm afraid there might be too much damage for his body to repair. We will have to wait and see and pray. There is nothing more I can do for him right now."

Catastrophic accidents and attacks, being a rarity among the citizens of Aether, left the people with a limited capacity to deal with helplessness and loss. Most injuries were easily treated and individuals generally recovered quickly due to their innate powers of regeneration. Kai felt paralyzed in his inability to revive Storm. His full of life sixteen-year-old cousin was most likely going to die, and Kai acknowledged he was powerless to stop it. His mother found him standing in the hallway a short time later.

"Mom, I feel so useless. We need to do something. The humans have surgeons who could help him. Can't we take him to a human hospital?" Kai begged.

"I want to say yes, of course, but this has come up before and the Council felt it was too much of an exposure risk. We're simply too different from them, Kai. Our blood is not the same. We don't heal the same way. The humans would know, and that would leave us all vulnerable. Human curiosity is a very dangerous thing."

Rayne joined them a short while later in the hallway. He looked pale, haggard, and wore an expression of complete devastation.

Kai began to pace. "This is absurd. We have to do something, Dad. We can't just sit idly by and watch Storm die."

"I'm so sorry, Son. You know I love Storm as much as you do, but there is nothing in my power that can be done."

"Well, there is something I can do. I want to become a surgeon. We may not be able to help Storm, but I can't bear to see this happen to someone else. I want to petition the Council to go to medical school."

The monitor's alarm from within the room blared loudly, and they hurried inside where Burke and May stood vigil over their son. Storm's face was swollen, and his features were obscured making him appear almost alien. His head was wrapped in a dressing covering his entire skull. With red, puffy eyes, tears poured down May's face. Burke remained more stoic and looked lost in shock. They turned when they saw the rest of their family enter the room.

May grabbed Rayne's sleeve and looked up at him. "Please, help him."

Rayne's voice cracked as he hung his head dejectedly. "I'm so sorry, but it is beyond my capabilities. I would give anything for the gift to heal him."

A harsh alarm droned shrilly as a flat line flashed continually across the screen. Rayne walked over to it and switched it off. "He's gone." Tears welled in his eyes.

May dissolved into heaving sobs, and Burke held her closely with tears streaming down his own face. Kai and his parents clung to them desperately, utterly crushed.

A short while later, they moved Storm in order to prepare him for his Passage Ceremony. Word had already begun to travel throughout the village of the tragic loss of Storm. A somber mood spread all over Aether. People reflected on the passing of such a young and vibrant person.

Rayne and Kai headed over to the Council Chambers located on the other side of the Village Square. The gray stone building, though somewhat simple in appearance, evoked an authoritative air. Perhaps the Elders housed within its walls gleaned extraordinary respect because their gifts held incredible power and strength. Aether's delicate balance was pieced together by many moving parts, and the Elders were an integral component.

The Council Elders consisted of the oldest living former Guardians from each of the four Houses, as well as the oldest living Protector. All of the past Guardians sat on the Council itself as well as three of the senior most Protectors. The Elders governed the people. The remainder of the Council supported them and served as a voting authority when necessary.

When Rayne and Kai entered the reception area, they were immediately met with a sympathetic look from the woman behind the desk. Clearly, word of Storm's demise had reached the Council already.

"Are the Elders available? We request a few moments of their time if it's possible," Rayne said.

"I'll check if you give me a minute, but I'm certain they will see you both." She rose from her seat and went into a nearby room closing the door.

The receptionist returned shortly and escorted them into a spacious conference room. There was an immense table that reminded Kai of a corporate office. He almost laughed at the absurdity of the setting; a group of people averaging in age of about four hundred and fifty years, in a room much more suited to a company of high-powered executives. The Elders were unquestionably endowed with tremendous power and were held with the utmost respect and esteem.

A door at the back of the room opened pulling Kai from his musings. The Elders entered and took their seats at the table gesturing for Rayne and Kai to do the same. He had almost forgotten what an extraordinary group the Elders were until his heart pounded and his palms moistened.

There was Raven, who was of The House of Fire, a tall, lean woman whose red hair had gone to mostly white. She still stood erect and carried herself with an air of strength and grace. Bey was of The Water. She was a beautiful woman with eyes the color of the sea and still vibrant golden blond hair that flowed long down her back. Coro was of The House of Air, a tiny woman with a sharp wit and even sharper tongue. Kai found her to be endlessly amusing. Vale was of The Earth with wavy jet-black hair and sparkling emerald green eyes. A curvaceous woman, with a fuller figure than most in Aether, Kai knew she must have been simply stunning in her youth. Finally, there was Bear, the Protector, who at over four hundred years old was still an intimidating and imposing figure. He wore his name well, about six feet four inches tall, with shoulders as wide as a Mack truck. Bear was not a person to be trifled with.

Rayne greeted the Elders with a slight bow. "Thank you for seeing us. We greatly appreciate your time."

"Welcome, Rayne and Kai. Please let me speak for all us in saying we are devastated by the loss of your nephew, Storm," Raven said.

"Thank you very much. We appreciate the sentiment," Rayne replied.

Kai stood, drumming his fingers on the table. "Storm's passing is relevant to our reason for being here. Do you mind if I speaking freely?"

Coro answered, "Please, by all means speak your mind, young man."

"The loss of Storm is one all of Aether will suffer, not just our family. The feeling of helplessness among the healers is profound. The human world has surgeons who might have been able to save him with knowledge and skills we simply do not possess. I am imploring you to allow me to attend medical school, so I may prevent such tragic loss from occurring in the future."

"We were just discussing this sorrowful event

before you and your father arrived," Bear said. "We understand your desire to help the entire community in light of this tragedy, but there are some obstacles we must consider. Not everyone in Aether believes we should progress forward with scientific and technological advancements. Some people feel the Elements should be the community's sole focus. In addition, the nearest medical school is too great a distance for you to travel to and from each day. You would have to live away from home. Human curiosity can be a danger to our kind. Living among them would present a great challenge to you, Kai."

"I've already proven I can handle myself with the humans. I graduated from college not very long ago, and I encountered no difficulties. I understand them. There are many others who work outside the village every day. I'm certain I can protect our people." Kai clasped his hands to his chest. "It's the 1960's, not the 1860's. It's imperative I gain these skills and knowledge to prevent this kind of loss from happening again."

"Why don't you both step out for a few minutes and let us discuss this matter? The safety of the people of Aether is of paramount importance to this Council. I assure you we will impartially examine all sides of this situation and resolve this issue with haste," Vale said.

As Rayne and Kai proceeded to the exit, Kai turned back. He could feel the flush of his cheeks as he burst forth with an impassioned plea. "Please, let me do this for the people. Let no family suffer this kind of unnecessary loss again. I appeal to your great wisdom. Thank you for your consideration."

Kai paced nervously the entire time they were

waiting while Rayne sat stiffly, unmoving. The silence between father and son filled the air like a heavy, thick fog. Kai could feel it weighing on him. A nearby grandfather clock loudly ticked away the minutes while they waited for the Elders. Kai wasn't sure how much time had passed, but it felt like days to him. Suddenly, the door seemed to open of its own volition reminding Kai of the immense power contained within the walls of the Council Chamber. They entered, and Rayne returned to his seat while Kai remained standing.

"Please be seated, young Kai," Raven said.

Reluctantly, he took a seat and inhaled deeply, trying to relax. "Please, what have you decided?"

"You should know the decision was not unanimous. However, the majority of the Elders believe we should protect Aether by following the old ways and using the Elements and nature to guide our people not modern technology. I am afraid we are declining your request at this time. You may, of course, present your case to the Elders again in one year's time. For now, we believe you need to grieve the loss of Storm. May the God and Goddess be with your family during their time of sorrow," Raven said, clearly dismissing them.

Rayne quickly ushered Kai out of the Council Chambers before he exploded in front of the Elders. Once they were outside, Rayne loosened his grasp on Kai's arm. Rage seeped through every pore in Kai's body. He pounded the wall behind him drawing blood from his knuckles. "How can they say no? I don't understand."

"Kai? Oh my god, look at your hands!" He turned to the sound of his name. Leaning against the building, Laurel stood with a pained expression on her beautiful face. "I just heard about Storm. I'm so sorry." Tears pooled in her eyes. "Are you okay?" Taking a few steps toward him, she tried to wrap her arms around his waist, but Kai pulled away.

"No, I am not okay. Storm is gone, and the Elders denied my request to go to medical school." His volume escalated to the point of shouting. "They won't even listen to reason. I have to wait a full year before I can try to convince them to change their minds. Their paranoia toward the humans and technology is going to destroy Aether."

People from around the Village Square were beginning to stare. Rayne stepped in and forcibly took Kai by the shoulders. "That's enough, Kai. You're upset. We all are, but the Elders have a point. Sending you away for so long would be a tremendous exposure risk. They're just trying to keep everyone safe, including you."

"I don't care what they say. I'm going to the University library every day, and I'm going to teach myself as much as I can until those stubborn old fools change their minds."

"Kai, please wait. Don't do anything rash. Your father is right; you're just emotional right now. Give your anger some time to subside. I want to help. Please let me help you." Laurel offered with outstretched arms.

Kai, frozen in place, couldn't bring himself to retreat into the warmth of Laurel's loving embrace the way he wanted to. His heart hardened on the spot. He was truly broken. "I'm sorry, Laurel, but no one can help me. I have to dedicate myself to this, for Storm and for everyone in Aether. I won't give up on this, ever."

Laurel's voice quivered. "And what about us, Kai? Are you going to give up on us?"

"Really? That's what you're thinking about right now? Us? What about Storm? This is no time to be selfish. How can I be happy, have everything, when Storm is dead? How is that fair? I love you, Laurel, I'll always love you, but I have to do this right now."

Without uttering a word Laurel walked over to Kai and kissed him on the cheek. Then, she turned away and walked off without looking back. He felt the moisture from her tears on his face, but he couldn't bring himself to care. His senses had gone numb.

Rayne finally spoke, "Son, I'm afraid you may have just made the biggest mistake of your life."

****

Laurel

One more shot rang off before Laurel's tormentor turned his attention away from her and toward the bright flash just off in the distance. The ground shook beneath her as he bounded off with heavy footsteps toward his men. She registered a burning pinch in the back of her leg but continued to charge ahead. Sweat dripped down her back, and her legs felt shaky. She'd never forget the look on Ash's face as she led them away. "Oh, dear Goddess, please, I need help!"

After putting a short distance between herself and the masked strangers, Laurel paused momentarily as the world around her spun. Listless, weak, her limbs heavy as though she was stuck in quicksand, she stumbled perilously unable to maintain her balance. Tripping over a downed tree limb, she tumbled to the ground. Branches and brambles snagged her clothing keeping her down, holding her captive. Unable to move, her last coherent thought was of her friend.

Laurel struggled to rouse, her eyelids so heavy they felt as though they were sealed shut with super glue. Her entire body shivered uncontrollably. Absolutely numb from the cold, she wondered if she had left her bedroom window opened last night. The air had a nebulous quality to it; everything was obscured, clouded. Weak and dizzy, her limbs felt like they weighed a ton. Groaning, she bore down attempting to lift her arms and legs to no avail. She gagged as waves of nausea ebbed and flowed through her. Momentarily, she entertained the idea this might be the worst hangover in history, but she didn't remember drinking with Ashlyn last night.

From within her fogginess, the frightful events of the night crept into her consciousness. Had she and Ashlyn been hunted by masked men? Did Ash try to save her? She attempted to reflect back on the cryptic memories flooding in and out like an interrupted electrical signal. Was there a flash of light? Her thoughts were terribly muddled, and she remained unsure as to what was real and what was simply imagined.

Her subconscious took control thrusting her into a world of disjointed memories. The image of a strikingly beautiful man, with golden blond hair and aquamarine eyes, flashed in her mind. It was Kai. On his left cheek he possessed an adorable dimple which added a boyish look to his otherwise masculine face. Tall and fit, he worked his well-proportioned frame naturally. Each time she blinked, a new perspective of the complicated man projected itself before her. Kai's face, with emotional anguish deep inside him, lost. Joy, pure and beautiful, etched into his handsome face. Passion, hot and fiery, consumed with lust.

Though they tried, things were never the same for them again after Storm's death. Laurel knew Kai had pushed her away to add to his own pain and guilt over not being able to save Storm. She thought she'd moved on, but Kai was always present even if he remained out of reach. It was odd, whenever she and Ash went to the café, or the pub, Kai and his squad were always nearby, watching them. As much as she didn't want to, Laurel still got butterflies in her stomach every time Kai looked at her. She longed to feel his hands on her, but her heart had been crushed. She still loved him but holding onto her memories of her time with Kai would have to suffice. He was a broken man.

Soon, the images and her memories grew hazy. She wanted to stay with Kai to keep him in her mind, but the force of the sedative was too strong. Fighting against the pull of the powerful drugs, Laurel finally succumbed. Even her mind could no longer resist the urge to retreat within herself and blackness claimed her.

****

Kai

Pounding in a rapid staccato on the Clinic's back door made Kai's ears perked up. He faintly made out the voice of woman; she was pleading. "Hello? Please, help us!"

He rushed to the door and swung it open revealing Laurel's parents. Holding an unconscious Laurel in his arms, Canyon was red faced and sweaty looking. With unshed tears in her eyes, Zarina looked frantic. When Kai took in Laurel's battered appearance, he knew his face must have gone ashen.

"Bring her right in here, Canyon." Kai led them directly into the nearest treatment room.

Canyon placed Laurel gently onto the exam table with a heavy sigh. Zarina appeared next to the table and delicately brushed the hair from her daughter's face. Laurel's eyes remained closed. Her body trembled even in her lethargic state.

Kai quickly began to examine her. "What's going on? What happened?"

"We have absolutely no idea. We haven't seen her since she went for a walk with Ashlyn late last night." Canyon faltered. "I woke early, and it was still dark out. I realized Laurel never came home. I got worried, so I walked into the woods. I'm not really sure why. I don't know what I expected to find. I just had this horrible feeling I needed to look for her..." His words trailed off. Then, shaking his head, Canyon continued, his voice clogged with emotion. "I-I found her in the woods. She was shaking violently, and she was covered in blood. I thought we were going to lose her—"

Zarina chimed in, "but we didn't lose her, and Kai is going to save her. And don't forget about this, Can." She produced what looked to Kai to be some kind of tranquilizer dart and handed it to her Kanti.

"This was embedded in the back of her leg." Canyon passed the dart to Kai who glanced at it before placing it on the counter.

"You've got to help her. Dear Goddess, why is she shivering so?" Zarina's eyes filled with tears.

Canyon put his arm around his Adara. "She's going to be all right, honey."

Pulling out several blankets and tucking them securely around Laurel, Kai's hand gently brushed against her soft skin. He needed to remind himself he was her doctor, and she no longer belonged to him.

"Looks like she has mild hypothermia. Her other injuries are minor. I'll clean and dress those when her temperature regulates. I'm not sure what's in this dart or if that's what caused her unconsciousness, but I'll do a CAT scan just to be sure. Let's just get her warmed up a bit."

Kai picked up the offending object and rolled it between his fingers examining it more closely, and held it up to the light. "But where did this come from? It's just so odd. Why would anyone want to hurt Laurel?" He pulled out his phone and then refocused on Laurel's parents. "I'm just going to send my dad a text to come and give me a hand here. We'll figure this out; try not to worry too much." Even as his fingers tapped the screen, he kept a watchful eye on Laurel.

Zarina continued to stroke her daughter's hair. "Come back to us, baby. Tell us what's happened to you," she whispered.

"Maybe I should check with Ashlyn and see if she can shed some light on any of this? I know it's still really early, but I want to call. What do you think?" Canyon asked.

"Call. Call now. They'll want to help," Zarina reassured.

Kai interjected, "It's a good idea, Canyon. If Ash was the last one to see her, she may know something. Come out in the hall with me, and we'll call her together."

He watched on as Canyon punched the numbers into his cell. Poor guy, his hands trembled, and Kai took the phone from him putting it on speaker.

"Thanks," Canyon said, with a sad smile.

Rowan picked up on the second ring with a groggy voice. Kai listened in as Canyon explained the situation. He could hear muffled talking and then a few minutes later Mica's booming voice came over the line. "Canyon, Ashlyn isn't here. Her bed hasn't been slept in. We're just throwing on some clothes, and we'll be right there."

Rowan and Mica arrived a few minutes later. Kai and Rayne were standing in the doorway to Laurel's room talking to her parents who stood just outside. Rowan ran and embraced Zarina. Mica and Canyon shared a brotherly hug.

"Kai was just about to fill us in on Laurel's test results. Go ahead, Kai, what's going on?" Canyon said.

"She's stable, and the CAT scan was negative. A CAT scan machine indicates abnormalities with organs, soft tissue, bones, and can even illustrate collections of fluid. Laurel's scan was clear. She is out of danger, but the question remains; why she is still unconscious? Her body's self-healing ability is not kicking in. Our best guess is the dart contains a drug we aren't familiar with. I'm going to run some tests. I'll get to the bottom of this, I promise. Hang in there."

"I think we should go talk to the Elders right away. We need to find out what happened to Laurel. And it's urgent we find Ashlyn," Rayne said.

"I agree. I'll go with you, and I think you should come, too, Canyon. We need to get on this right now before too much time passes. Our daughters' lives may depend on it." Mica rushed toward the door.

"Okay," Canyon agreed and turned to Zarina. "I'll be back soon, honey. You and Rowan stay with

Laurel."

"Hurry back and let us know what the Elders have to say," Rowan said. Tears pooled in her eyes as she pushed them all toward the door.

Chapter Three

Ashlyn

Numbness inched its way up Ashlyn's body until she was depleted, and the last remnants of her Flame were squelched. The charred vestiges of her fire-consumed clothing irritated the inside of her nose. Barely a whisper escaped her lips when she tried to speak. Her eyes darted around frantically taking in glimpses of the men in black. Confusion hung heavily over Ash's mind. She felt restrained both mentally and physically. Deep male voices surrounded her, and she tried not to panic, but she was reduced to an unmoving heap. The chill in the air settled deep in her bones.

"Hey, check her out. I'm gonna get me a piece of that ass."

"Ya gonna have to wait in line, dude. Nice of her to take her clothes off for us."

"You morons will do no such thing. The Boss wanted whichever one of them we found unharmed. That includes you laying off the goods. You, go get me a blanket from the van, and make it quick. You two, do a sweep of the perimeter and make sure it's clear. We've got to get out of here now."

Ashlyn could feel the stranger's warm breath on her skin as he bent low to speak directly into her ear. The man's face, a study in horror, appeared scarred and distorted. Only a thin whoosh of air exited her mouth when she tried to scream.

"My men may be idiots, but they're right about one thing. You are a fine piece of ass," he said. Slowly, he dragged a finger down her spine sending waves of nausea through her. "You're coming with us, Firecracker. When the Boss is done with you, I'm gonna take what's left." He stood back up to his full height looming over her. Then, he drove his booted foot directly into her flank, her ribs throbbing in protest.

The blackness of the night's sky hovered menacingly above Ashlyn. One of the men returned with a gray blanket and dropped it on top of her. The cold spring air penetrated the thin material. The damp ground was frigid against her bare skin, and the chill seeped in, bone deep. Even though it wasn't protecting her against the bite of iciness, she was relieved to be covered up. Ash hoped it would distract the men from her nudity, but the whispered promise of the dark stranger invaded her thoughts.

"What now, Devlin?" one of the soldiers asked.

"We're going to move out as soon as the others clear the area. Let's head back to the van. I'll take the girl."

The man called Devlin took hold of Ashlyn and the blanket together, easily lifting her into his arms. She fought the urge to vomit as everything around her spun from the sudden movement. Her head pounded, and her side ached from his kick. She was completely vulnerable in this state. Ash knew she needed to fight back or else she would surely be taken from her home. Determination and despair mingled as she attempted to move her fingers. Her forefinger gave a slight wiggle, and she dug deep searching for her elusive powers.

Concentrating, she called to her Fire, but not even a spark came to the surface.

The jostling and harsh treatment continued as they approached a black van with no windows. Ashlyn heard the voices of the other men, and her stomach dropped when she caught a glimpse inside the back of the van. Shelves and cabinets filled with boxes and other items lined the perimeter of the interior. A stretcher like the ones in the Medical Center dominated the space, except this one had chains with cuffs by the head and the foot. She knew if they got her into that van it was over for her.

Ash called on her inner strength shouting in her head. *You are a Guardian! You are of The House of Fire! You can do this!*

As Devlin endeavored to lift her into the van, a burst of adrenaline rushed through her body. She kicked out her foot connecting with his groin.

"Ugh!" He grunted out in pain instantly dropping her in the doorway.

The tips of Ash's fingers slipped off the edge of the van's threshold. She flailed awkwardly grasping for anything within range to brace herself. Inadvertently, she plucked a small box off one of the shelves. Too weak and uncoordinated, her momentum slammed her to the ground. The impact bounced the box from her clumsy grip and was it thrown under the vehicle. The package was quickly forgotten when pain radiated down her shoulder, pulling her focus.

Devlin yelled to his men, "Get me a syringe and one of the ampules in the box marked with a red *X*. Now!" To Ash, he spat, "You're going to pay for that, bitch!"

He grabbed her roughly with a needle in one hand manacling her, digging into to her flesh. Ashlyn searched deep within to call her Flame to the surface. Sparks discharged from her fingers. They were faint, but she knew she burned him, even as she felt the needle pierce her skin.

"Night, night, Firecracker, see you on the other side," Devlin condescended.

"F-f-f-ry you," Ashlyn sputtered, before blackness overcame her.

****

As she gradually began to rouse, Ashlyn wondered why her head pounded like the rhythmic beating of a drum. Struggling to open her eyes, a burning brightness flooded Ash's vision as though someone was shining a flashlight directly into her retinas. She slammed her lids back down. Wave after wave of nausea rolled over her, and she fought the urge to vomit by breathing deeply. Suddenly, she was swamped with chilling memories of being chased and captured by the dark faceless men.

What happened after she fell into the blackness? A terrifying face, one she would never forget, the man the others called Devlin, had been livid when she kicked him in the groin and burned him. She had been rather pleased with herself right up until he stuck her with a needle. Now a dense fog clouded her mind, as she attempted to puzzle out the details of what happened and where she was.

Slowly and deliberately, Ash cracked one eye open ever so slightly careful not to alert her captors. She urgently needed to get a sense of her surroundings. The unmistakable itch of a woolen blanket scratched against her bare legs and arms. Bright florescent lights shone down on her and illuminated the entire space. A stainless-steel sink stood in one corner with a seamless toilet beside it. The walls looked like they were made of cinderblock and the floor concrete. No visible hinges, handles, or doorknobs appeared on the large gray metal door, only a small slot large enough to pass a book through. Two cameras hung from opposing corners on the high ceiling. A large vent was built into one of the walls close to the top. Someone had bolted a grate, like a cage, right over it.

Supine on a bed, dressed in a hospital gown instead of being nude, Ashlyn momentarily breathed a sigh of relief. Her comfort was short-lived. Her heart rate kicked up as the gravity of her situation began to sink in. She was alone in a cell. Ash attempted to wiggle her fingers and toes, but her body was not responding to her commands. With a deep measured breath, she endeavored to call her Flame to the surface, but that, too, was uncooperative.

A disembodied voice spoke to her, and her eyes ricocheted around the room searching for the person attached to it. "I can see you're awake, Firecracker. No need to pretend otherwise. The effect of the drug we gave you is still in your system. I see you still can't move, but I know you can hear me."

The voice sounded tinny and buzzed slightly which caused a ringing in her ears. It dawned on her the voice was being projected from the speakers above her bed, and he watched her from the cameras.

"You see, Firecracker, the drug has a progressive effect. Bursts of adrenaline can inhibit its effectiveness for short periods of time depending on how capable you are of fighting it. An antidote is required to restore your speech and motor abilities permanently. If you promise to be a good little girl, I'll consider giving it to you. It worked out quite nicely for your little friend. My boss considers her a bonus, so he doesn't really care what we do with her. She's very pretty by the way. And if you don't cooperate, I think I will enjoy hurting her in so many delicious ways."

The taste of bile rose in her throat. Where was Laurel, and what were they doing to her? A cold sweat broke out all over her body when she recognized the menacing voice of Devlin. Her Fire remained trapped, stymied. Ash couldn't fathom who these people were and what they wanted with her.

****

Hawk

The resonance of a thump-thump-thump followed by two more thumps in a rapid staccato had Hawk rolling his eyes as he stretched his long body. Quill and Kai had helped to invent the distinctive knock when they were children. He knew it must be Quill disturbing his peace. Hawk ambled to the door swinging it open to greet his best friend even though he was annoyed with the early morning visit.

"What's up, Quill? We don't have to be in the Square for a couple of hours yet." He glared at his friend.

"I figured you didn't hear your phone. That's why I'm here. The Elders have called a meeting in their chambers immediately. All of the Protectors and the entire Council have been summoned. No idea what it's about, so don't even ask. Let's just go and get it over with, so we can party at the festival later."

Hawk pulled on a pair of black work boots sitting

by the front door and followed Quill. He was dressed in a long sleeved snug fitting black T-shirt and dark jeans, his uniform, as Quill referred to it. Hawk knew he had a reputation as a badass, and he never did anything to refute it. He supposed the dark Native American looks he inherited from his father's family, combined with his brooding attitude, probably contributed to his intimidating image.

Quill, on the other hand, was quick with a joke and extremely gregarious. He was more of a colorful character in every way. Though every bit as tough as Hawk, he appeared lighthearted. Quill's looks were a total departure from Hawk's. Though he was also tall, measuring slightly above six feet, he carried lean muscle and not bulk on his frame. Short sandy colored hair and green eyes, not to mention the smile Quill wore as a permanent feature, made their differences even more apparent.

Their breath came out in soft clouds in the cold early morning air, and they walked at a quick pace in silence. Quill knew Hawk better than anyone. Preferring quiet in the morning, Hawk only spoke when he had something important to share. Quill enjoyed filling the empty spaces in any conversation with mindless chatter. It was amazing they shared such a close bond considering how opposite their personalities were. Somehow, these divergent traits simply worked for them.

Although they had very different perspectives on life, it was no surprise, at sixteen, both Hawk and Quill decided to enroll in the Protectors Trials. As the military police force of Aether, the Protectors trained in hand to hand combat, martial arts, and with weapons.

An individual, born a Protector, inherited a keen intelligence, tremendous strength, and the ability to influence one, or more of the Elements. Only a true Protector had the ability to pass all of the Trial's stages, but Protectors were not born marked with a symbol, like Guardians. Any man or woman at the age of sixteen became eligible for the Trials, but only a select few would receive the coveted tattoo. The Protector's symbol, marked on his, or her right shoulder blade, identified the individual as part of the elite force.

Hawk and Quill arrived at the Council Chambers and were instructed to go directly into the conference room. The Elders, including Hawk's grandfather, Bear, were all present. Hawk scanned the room sensing the immense power gathered together in one place.

Raven, the Fire Elder, opened the meeting. "Thank you all for coming so quickly. I'm afraid we have some rather disturbing news to share with you. Firstly, this evening's ceremony and festival have been postponed. We have sent representatives to spread the word to the community, and volunteers will begin to dismantle the preparations. Bear, why don't you fill them in on the details."

"Ashlyn Woods and Laurel Green went for a walk late last night in the woods beyond the North Tower. Laurel was found injured and unconscious by her parents at dawn. She had been hit by tranquilizer dart and Kai believes that drug is wreaking havoc on Laurel's system. She is in stable condition, but remains in a comatose state. Kai has been unable to ascertain much information from the dart itself. He is continuing his tests. We will pray to the God and Goddess for her speedy recovery and hope Kai can find us some answers quickly. It is imperative we obtain the information we seek with haste not only to save Laurel, but Ashlyn as well. Our Fire Guardian is missing."

Hawk's fists clenched tightly at his sides his knuckles whitening under the strain. He concentrated on breathing, but the air wouldn't flow. It felt like all the oxygen had been forcibly sucked from the room. He fought desperately to maintain his self-control. Quill turned to him with a knowing look of support. Silently, he urged him to hold it together. The ground beneath Hawk's feet vibrated, the air around him warped, and appeared distorted. Hawk, unsure if he caused the disturbance with his powers, stood shocked.

Bear's booming voice rang loudly through the room pulling him from his current state. "Hawk Crane! What in the name of the God and Goddess are you doing? We must all remain calm."

As oxygen filled his lungs once again, he shook his head back and forth trying to process what he just heard. Ashlyn was missing. "Sorry, Grandfather." He lowered his gaze to the floor.

"As I was saying, River, I would like you to set up teams to search the areas fanning out in all directions from the Green's house into the woods. Do not disturb the area, but search the ground, the trees, the road. Everything is important. Look for footprints, tracks, or anything that may have been dropped by the women or any possible perpetrators. Report back to me in two hours, and let me know if you find anything. Hawk, I want to see you and Quill when everyone leaves. You can catch up to the teams after. Let's move out!"

When everyone else had gone, Hawk and Quill waited for his grandfather to address them. Bear was red faced, and his brows arched downward making his face look harsh. Hawk could tell he was in trouble.

"Okay, one of you had better tell me what's going on with you, Hawk. I saw the look you gave him, Quill."

Neither of them spoke for a minute. Bear glared at them. Hawk's body continued to vibrate from his powers, even as he attempted to maintain control. He had never let his powers consume and dominate him before. Quill was uncharacteristically quiet, and Hawk knew it was up to him to explain. Finally, he resigned himself to the fact his grandfather was not going to let this go without an explanation.

"I'm in love with Ashlyn," he blurted out. "I think I have been my whole life. I'm sorry, Grandfather, I just lost control for a minute there. I promise it won't happen again." He lowered his head studying his boots.

"I see. Well, that explains a great deal. I have often said if love were a woman, she would be glorious, and wonderful, but sometimes a cruel vixen."

Bear often spouted words of wisdom to Hawk and his friends. He concocted sayings and quotes that were truly original to him. His stories were entertaining and full of life lessons they often took with a grain of salt. Bear was prone to embellishment, and sometimes it was hard to tell fact from fiction. Despite his colorful nature, Hawk loved and respected no one more than Bear.

"I have to find her, Grandfather, if anything happens to her…" He stammered, "I-I just don't know what I'd do. I need to tell her how I feel, now more than ever." Hawk placed his hand over his heart, and closed his eyes as he spoke, "It's strange really, it's as if she inadvertently projects herself to me. That sounds crazy, right?"

"No, it does not," Bear responded. "There is a little-known gift among the Guardians that pertains to such connections and communication. Every so often a Guardian may be born with the gift of selective telepathy. The power is awakened when the Guardian finds her true match. It is a form of telepathy so rare it is not often spoken about. It takes time for the bond to fully form. Although telepathy is strictly a Guardian power, once the link is opened, the telepathic energy can flow both ways between the Guardian and her partner."

"Do you think that's what this could be? I saw her in the Tower's Atrium yesterday, and I could've sworn I'd heard her thinking. My imagination went wild."

****

Completely overwhelmed, Hawk's heart raced. His heated skin tingled with a strange sensation. With his gaze fixed on Ashlyn in the Tower above, Hawk sensed her Fire. He felt her longing, and he was ensnared, captured by the beautiful Guardian. The intense urge to scale the side of the Tower, to take command of the woman holding his heart and his mind captive, filled Hawk. A trance-like state gripped him cementing his feet to the ground, and his gaze was riveted to vision before him. Hawk's lids suddenly grew heavy, and his eyes closed of their own volition. Before he could process what was happening, his stomach dropped, and he felt the sensation of being lifted from the very spot on which he stood. Floating on a current of air, he was transported to the top of the Tower. Or was his mind playing tricks on him?

When he opened his eyes once again, his fantasy was a whisper's distance away. She was close enough to touch, to smell, to taste. There was no hesitation on his part. Hawk's long strides had him in front of Ashlyn in seconds. Her wild red curls whipped in the wind gently blowing around her delicate features. Those intense amber colored eyes pierced him while her brow furrowed in confusion. Hawk didn't care how it had happened; he was alone with Ash feeling her need as much as his own.

As if fueled by compulsion, Hawk's hands reached out grabbing Ashlyn by the shoulders. He was silent deciding to let his lips, and his body do the talking for him. Swallowing Ashlyn's surprised gasp with a deep penetrating kiss, he devoured her. After her initial shock, she responded as he had always hoped she would. Licking her way into his mouth, she explored every inch. The taste of her lips, her tongue, so sweet, her intoxicating cinnamon scent drifted up, filling his nose. The moan he made sounded animalistic to his own ears, as he plunged further into the already ravenous kiss.

Ashlyn's arms wrapped tightly around his waist as she pulled herself closer to him. Her nipples hardened to sharp points abrading against his chest, driving his desire to new heights. Desperately needing more of Ashlyn, he gripped her perfectly rounded bottom lifting her to meet his throbbing erection. The contact had him nearly exploding from the electric jolt which zapped through him. As if by instinct, she used her legs to hold on, moving her hands from his waist and plunging them tightly into his hair. The sound of Hawk's ragged breathing combined with Ash's, formed an erotic sounding rhythmic chorus. The pounding of his heart in his ears added the beat of a bass drum to the symphony.

Hawk, spellbound, dreamily closed his eyes. In that instant, the loss of Ashlyn's nearness, her heat, overtook him. The floating sensation returned. When he had opened his eyes, he was back on the ground under the trees behind the South Tower. Looking up, he found himself in the exact spot from which he had risen to the Atrium.

****

Hawk snapped out of the memory when Quill interjected. "Listen to me. I've seen her looking at you the same way you look at her. You two look like you're going to go full volcanic eruption, like Pompeii, and you're going to take all of Aether with you. Just chill out, buddy, we're going to find her and then you can tell her everything. It's been a long time coming."

"I want you to go see Kai and find out if he has learned anything new. Report back to me and then you can join the others in the woods. We need clues and fast and not just to save your love life. Ashlyn is needed for the Guardian Ceremony to bond with the infant. And, Hawk, stay calm. Ashlyn needs you, we all do. Now hurry," Bear said.

Chapter Four

Kai

A spectrum of tones rang out from Laurel's monitors creating an odd sort of vibration echoing through her room in the Medical Center. Kai stood over her bed gazing down. Although he knew it was wrong, he reached out, running his fingers through the tangled strands of her hair. He enjoyed the feel even in its bedraggled state. Taking a step back, Kai huffed out a frustrated breath. "Damn it! What the hell is going on with you?" He gripped the dart in his tightened fist allowing it to dig deep into his flesh, welcoming the sting of pain.

"I wish you could talk to me, Laurel. I can't for the life of me figure out what's going on with you. Barely a trace of the substance contained in this dart is left. I don't even have enough to test. Your blood work didn't reveal much either." Rolling the dart between his fingers, he shoved it into the pocket of his lab coat so hard he felt it give way at the seam. The desire to save her consumed him, and he knew it was more than his commitment as a doctor; it was personal. Perhaps the time had come to admit to himself he still had deep feelings for Laurel. Maybe his parents were right in telling him he needed balance in his life; balance between work and a personal life.

"Look at you lying there. You're so beautiful. Even

after all these years, I've never stopped thinking about you and loving you. There isn't a day which goes by when I don't wish I could go back in time and change things between us. I know I hurt you, and I don't expect you to ever forgive me, but I am sorry." He swallowed the lump forming in his throat. Gently he gripped her delicate hand, warm and soft inside his much larger one. "Wow, am I pathetic or what? Instead of fawning over you, I should be helping you. Don't worry, I won't give up on you no matter what. I promise you that."

He heard someone clear his throat and looked up to find his two closest friends, Hawk and Quill, in the doorway. He wondered how long they had been standing there and how much they had heard.

"Kai, you confessing to an unconscious girl? Isn't there some medical law against that shit?" Quill joked. "It's been a big day for confessions around Aether. Isn't that right, Hawk?" Quill gave Hawk a playful jab with his elbow.

Hawk responded with what appeared to be a friendly shove back. "You really don't know when to shut up, do you?"

"All right, all right, but I've heard enough about you two and your feelings. I can't stand all this emotional crap. I think I'm going to be sick. Please just tell the man why we're here," Quill said.

Hawk turned to Kai. "Ignore Mr. Sensitive here. I'll get right to the point. My grandfather sent us for an update on the dart and Laurel's condition."

"As usual, I have no idea what you two are talking about. Seriously though, as you can see, she is still unresponsive, and I'm at a complete loss with regard to the dart. Obviously, it's some kind of tranquilizer, but I haven't been able to figure out much more than that. There simply wasn't enough left in the dart to test," Kai said. Shaking his head, he blew out a rough breath. Running his fingers through his hair, he tugged and pulled making it stand on end.

The sound of heavy footsteps and loud voices advancing abruptly paused their conversation. River poked his head in the doorway as two other Protectors loitered just outside.

"Can I have a word with you guys out in the hallway, please?" River asked.

Hawk and Quill withdrew quietly from the room, but Kai lingered for a moment and raked his eyes over Laurel's sleeping form. "I'll be right back, Honey. Don't you worry. I'll figure this out and you'll be back to your old self in no time." He leaned down gently pressing his lips to her forehead. Forcing himself to turn away, he stepped out into the hallway glancing back over his shoulder the entire time River spoke.

River reached inside his jacket pocket, produced a small cardboard box, and handed it over. "We found several darts in the trees and this, deep in the woods near some tire tracks. Go ahead and open it."

Kai took hold of the box and turned it over in his hands examining it. It was plain cardboard marked with a handwritten red *X* on one side. His hands trembled slightly, and he struggled with the flap. Finally, he ripped the edge free. Encased inside were a dozen ampules containing a clear liquid. He wondered if this was the break they were praying for.

He turned to River. "It's possible you may have just helped us find the answers we need with this discovery. Clearly, I won't know for sure until I conduct some experiments on these, but I'll get started right away. I'd also like to see the rest of the darts you collected for a comparison."

River reached into his other pocket, pulled out several more darts, and handed them to him. "Okay, we'll leave you to your work. Let us know the minute you have any information for us. I don't have to tell you time is of the essence here. Not only to save Laurel, but to find Ashlyn, too. Laurel is the key to finding out exactly what happened last night."

"Don't worry, I understand the importance of finding Ash to everyone in Aether."

Kai waited for the others to leave before entering Laurel's room. "I told you I'd be right back," he said, in a gentle tone. He proceeded to tell her about the Protector's findings. Even though he thought she couldn't hear him, it felt good to share the news. "Don't worry," he continued soothingly, "I won't leave you alone. I'll stay until your parents get back. They haven't left your side the entire time you've been here. I forced them to go get some food. They should be back any minute." Kai took Laurel's hand and tenderly stroked his thumb across the back. He mused how right it felt to hold her hand, to feel the warmth of her soft skin.

Zarina and Canyon walked in and noticed Kai caressing their daughter's hand. Zarina looked pleased, but Canyon cast a suspicious glare in Kai's direction.

"Hi there. I'm glad you're back," Kai said. Handing Canyon the box, he updated them as her father examined the contents. "I'm hoping it's the same drug that is affecting Laurel."

"What are the chances it's anything else if it was found in the woods near tire tracks?" Zarina asked.

"It seems logical that it's the same," Kai answered. "If it is, I suspect I'll be able to use it to develop a formula to counteract the effects. Listen, I know this may not be the right time, but a few of Laurel's students were here asking to visit her. I told them they had to check with you guys first. They're in the waiting room. It's up to you if you want them to come in. If you need me for any reason just come find me in the lab. As soon as I figure anything out, I'll let you know. I have a really good feeling about this, so you two hang in there," Kai said. Walking out the door he turned back, unable to resist a final glance at Laurel. Vowing to cure her, he hustled down to the lab hopeful for the first time since she was brought in.

Kai had a goal, a purpose, and he urgently wanted results. The recognizable smell of starch tickled his nose as he donned a fresh lab coat. Kai enjoyed spending time in the lab. The familiarity of the sleek black countertops with beakers and test tubes lined up in an orderly fashion gave him a sense of control. His laboratory was as well-equipped as any other hi-tech hospital lab.

He carefully opened the box with the mysterious X printed on it. It was like a treasure map; figure it out, and you find a bounty at the end. The box only contained a dozen ampules, so he needed to take care not waste any of the solution. With a gentle grip, Kai plucked one of the innocuous looking tubes from the box. He held it up to the light, and the yellow hued transparent liquid glinted at him.

Agitating the tiny vial in his restless hands, Kai continued to examine the specimen. He watched the substance flow back and forth checking its viscosity.

Although he delighted in the idea of discovering something new, of solving a puzzle, nothing was more important than figuring out what was happening to Laurel.

****

Laurel

It was pitch black when Laurel gradually became aware of a strange tempo resonating around her. Her head ached, and she willed her hand to move to her forehead needing to rub the pain away, yet she remained detached from her own body. She was mystified. With as much strength as she could muster, Laurel attempted to force her eyes to focus within the eclipse obscuring everything before her. It was to no avail. All consuming darkness continued to weigh her down. Desperately seeking to retrieve her last memories, Laurel strived to slow her racing heart and to think through this peculiar murky feeling.

As she concentrated, the memories clicked into place like a key in a lock. Snapshots flashed through her brain in a staccato formation. Walking in the forest with Ashlyn…masked men shooting at them…a prick in the back of her thigh…a dazzling flash of light in the distance. Emotions flooded her system, and her stomach swirled with nerves. Bits and pieces in a chaotic rhythm, a slideshow of images, continued to barrage her making her head spin. Stumbling…waking up in the dark of night…freezing…pain and then nothing except blackness.

After puzzling it out, Laurel had a pretty good handle on the events which had left her in this strange dark place. But, where was she? And Ash? For that matter, where was anyone? She called out tentatively at first, then grew bolder. *Hello? Can anyone hear me? Hello?*

A gentle hand stroked Laurel's hair startling her. *Hey! What the hell do you think you're doing?* The stranger in the darkness continued to caress her. It was oddly soothing, and she fought the feeling of this person providing her comfort in the midst of her confusion. *Will you stop that! Come on, turn a light on. I can't see a thing... Yo, are you listening to me? I said knock it off with the petting thing. You're freaking me out.*

A voice, evidently attached to the hand, shouted loudly making Laurel's heart jump in her chest. *All right, let's calm down, buddy.* She tried to soothe the angry man. As his tone gentled, the deep timber of the voice somehow sounded familiar. A warm grip softly clasped her hand. Shuddering from the contact, Laurel tried to pull back from the stranger. It was no use. The brushing of fingers across her tender skin did not relent. *Okay now, I've just about had it with you. Who are you and where the hell am I?*

The stranger continued to ignore her pleas. The repetitive sweeping motion of his thumb across the back of her hand persisted. Fear churned in her belly, and nausea took hold. Laurel attempted to draw in a deep breath, but even her chest felt constricted. Her panic swelled when she endeavored to sit upright and nothing happened. *I-I can't move. Oh, dear Goddess, what's going on here? Please help me.* Laurel wanted to weep as emotion swelled inside her, but even her tears refused to fall.

The voice, focus on the voice. When she concentrated hard enough, she realized the guy sounded frustrated not truly angry. The stranger said something about wishing she could talk to him. *Um, really? I've been talking to you this entire time. Clean your ears much?* Still no response. *Seriously, what is your damage?* Still no response. *Holy crap, you can't hear me, can you?* Still no response. *Wait a second... I can't hear myself either.*

Bile rose in Laurel's throat. If she couldn't hear herself, it dawned on her, perhaps she hadn't actually been speaking aloud this entire time. A really bad feeling nudged its way into her gut sinking deep. Then, true realization settled in. Blackness shrouded the world around her. She was unable to move and unable to speak. This monumental revelation caused a stampede of terror thundering through her making her heart pound.

Using the deep breathing exercises she learned from doing yoga, Laurel tried to slow her racing heart. *Okay, Laurel, get a grip. What's the last thing you remember? Think, Think.* Laurel's mind raced replaying snippets of memory over and over until it finally became clear to her. *The dart! That maniac shot me with something. Dear God and Goddess, please protect me. Don't let them kill me. I have to get out of—*An odor tingled her nose pulling her away from her current train of thought. The scent was divine, masculine, like a sweet-smelling ocean mist. Her olfactory nerves registered the intoxicating fragrance instantly. Kai.

Laurel breathed a sigh of relief that she wasn't with her attackers. *Kai, that's Kai's voice.* She attempted to absorb all he was saying, and a million thoughts scrambled her brain. *Get your act together, girl! Think about what the man just said to you. Something about a dart and blood tests. Wait a minute, I get it. I'm in the Medical Center.*

The sound of his voice made her want to cry. Laurel had never fully recovered from her painful break up with Kai. Part of her hated him for pushing her away, but part of her still loved him, still craved him. Just feeling him near, touching her, had her frozen body melting from the inside out. She knew with her whole heart, and even with the history between them, nothing would deter him from helping her find her way back from the darkness.

She focused on Kai; his touch, his scent, his tone. A picture of his handsome face ran through her brain. Intense aquamarine colored eyes and an adorable dimple in his left cheek winked at her whenever he smiled. In the midst of her memories, Kai's words slowly penetrated the forefront of her mind. Words like beautiful, love, and forgiveness floated in the air. *Wait just one damn minute! Is he kidding me? He loves me?* Anger and passion mingled inside her fighting each other. *That jerk broke my heart. Now, after all this time, when I'm incapacitated, he decides to tell me he's sorry. Well forget it, buddy!*

Kai's strong yet gentle hands continued to soothe her. Her body heated against her will. When he moved to her arms, brushing and rubbing her skin, Laurel's arousal began to rise. *This can't be happening. How can this man's simple touch still have so much power over me?* Tingles settled between her legs even as she willed them to stop. An ache grew inside her begging to be released. If she was being completely honest with herself, she'd have to admit forgiving Kai wouldn't really be that hard to do.

Laurel heard someone else enter the room, and suddenly Kai's warmth was gone. She recognized Quill's voice immediately. They had known each other forever, and his effervescence was unmistakable. There was another voice, deep and serious. Instantly, she realized it had to be Hawk. Those three were never far apart. They were asking about someone who was drugged and injured. *Ashlyn?* Momentarily stunned, it finally occurred to Laurel they were talking about her.

Wishing she could communicate aloud, thoughts continued to race through her mind. Stomping feet, that's what she noticed next. Her dad walked like that. Though it wasn't her father's voice Laurel heard, it was someone she couldn't identify. He called Kai and the others to join him out in the hallway.

She heard Kai's reassuring whisper and felt his soft lips press a delicate kiss on her forehead. "I'll be right back, honey. Don't you worry. I'll figure this out, and you'll be back to your old self in no time."

Her soul had been trapped in winter since Kai left her all those years ago. An ice age had passed, and her heart was frozen solid. The sweet things he was saying now were beginning to slowly melt away a glacier's worth of ice. Her heart's beat kicked up its rhythm, and she was surprised the monitors didn't pick it up. Yet, she remained conflicted. She simply couldn't let go of her pain. She still wanted to hate him, but the truth was, she never really did. Although her heart had been broken, Laurel never stopped loving Kai.

As she strained to hear what was being discussed just outside her room, Laurel recognized the deep murmur of male voices but couldn't comprehend the content of their discussion. What were they saying about her? Frustration suffocated her; if only she could open her eyes or move a little. Laurel, buzzing with anger, screamed inside her head. *Listen to me! Somebody hear me, damn it! I want to get up! I want to see!*

Exhausted, her seething slowed to a simmer just under the surface when she felt the warmth of Kai's hand and heard his voice once again. His touch felt natural, but she wished she could see his eyes. Laurel was grateful to have him near making promises to free her from this state of limbo. Confidence in Kai's abilities abounded. His tender confessions regarding their long-discarded love both frightened her and left her feeling hopeful.

She sensed her parents enter the room before she actually heard them. Zarina always smelled like flowers and sunshine to her, like home. It didn't matter how old she got, to Laurel, Canyon would always be the bravest, strongest man in the world. She listened while Kai updated her parents on what was found in the woods, and he left shortly after. She felt her parent's presence and was comforted by their closeness.

"Hey, baby, we're back," Canyon said. He placed a kiss on her forehead, and she could smell the fresh air on his clothes.

Her mother's soft hand smoothed her hair back away from her face. Laurel wished she could lean into the tender caress of her mother's love. "Kai's gone to figure this out, so you can come back to us," her mother encouraged, with tears in her voice. "He said some of your students wanted to visit. Knowing how close you are with them, we thought we'd let them spend some time with you. We're going to run across the Square to the South Tower to see how Rowan and Mica are doing. They're worried sick about you, and Ash of course. We won't be gone long, ten minutes tops. Wren, Briar, and Aidan can't wait to see you. We'll be right back, and they'll keep you company." She felt the press of her mother's lips on her cheek.

Laurel could instantly feel their absence. *Wait a minute, my parents said something about Rowan and Mica and how worried they are about me and Ash. Where is Ash? Why aren't her parents here in the Medical Center with her, too? What the hell is going on around here?* The outrage inside her started to crest again and her agitation built once more.

Just as she thought she would burst from all this confusion and lack of control, she heard three very familiar voices. "Miss Laurel? It's us, Wren, Briar, and Aidan. Your mom and dad said it would be okay for us to see you. They told us you were asleep but it was all right to talk to you." Wren's sweet little voice was music to her ears.

Although Laurel always made it a point never to show favoritism among her students, she definitely had a soft spot for these three. She called them the Three Musketeers because they had been inseparable since they started school. Kids like these were one of the many reasons Laurel loved teaching so much.

As Aidan spoke, she thought about how deep his voice had gotten this year. "This totally sucks! We've all been trying to think of what kind of jerk would want to hurt the best teacher in the world, and who would want to take Miss Ashlyn away from Aether. She's the coolest Guardian ever!"

Stunned, she considered what Aidan had just said.

No! No way! Those assholes took Ash! She wanted to howl with rage but still felt completely paralyzed.

Briar's voice brought her back to the children in the room. "When we were talking about how crazy this is, you know, like, someone wanting to hurt you and take Ashlyn. We started to think about the story you told us last month in history, you know, like, the whole deal with those bad guys, the Renegades. Like, we thought it had to be those big jerks, you know, like, who else?"

Laurel was so busy being angry she had only briefly considered the who and the why of their situation. *Who would want to hurt me and take Ash?* The kids were right. The Renegades made perfect sense. She had just taught the class the history of the people of Aether, and the Renegades were a huge part of that history.

The people of the Houses of Aether had always believed in balance and harmony with the God and Goddess. The world they occupied and all of its inhabitants existed together by divine decree. The four Elements: Fire, Water, Air, and Earth guided them through their destiny. All of the Elements and all life on the planet were of equal importance, each playing a specific role in the universe.

The story had been told and retold for many hundreds of years, about the unrest which began with one man.

****

Jet Thorn was born of The House of Earth with hair as black as ink and eyes as dark as the night's sky. He was handsome, intelligent, and gifted. As he grew to manhood, so did both his physical and supernatural

74

strength. His powers were greater than all the people from The House of Earth. Only the Guardian's astonishing gifts were a match for Jet's.

He seemed happy and lived in peace among the people of Aether until one day when everything changed. Jet and his brother were walking deep in the forest together when the young men heard a loud inexplicable boom. A deer shot out in front of them and dashed away farther into the woods. Suddenly, out of nowhere, two ordinary humans came barreling out from between the trees giving the deer chase. The hunters carried hand cannons, an early form of the modern-day gun. The men were not expecting others so deep in the forest and mistakenly shot Jet's brother in the head. The young man fell instantly to the ground. Jet shouted out his rage as he cradled his only brother, dead in his arms.

The ordinary humans, shocked and remorseful, tried to apologize, but Jet rose with fury in his dark eyes. He slammed his fists to the ground opening a hole in the Earth large enough to swallow the humans. Devoured by the crater, they fell deep into the Earth's core, disappearing forever.

After, Jet sat for a long time just holding his brother. His anger never receded. Eventually, he began the long trek back to the village. All of Aether deeply mourned the loss of such a young and beautiful soul. The Elders, however, were furious with Jet for killing the humans and taking matters into his own hands. They worried more humans would arrive to search for their lost brothers.

Jet grew more and more angry and disillusioned with the Elders. Charismatic and persuasive, he preached to whoever would listen. "Aether should dominate and rule the planet."

Soon others began to follow his ideology. While the majority of the community remained loyal to the Elders and Aether's origins, a division grew among the people. Thus, the Renegades were catapulted into existence. As their momentum built, tensions in the village mounted. The Elders felt they had no choice but to banish Jet Thorn and his supporters as they continued to persist in their vendetta against humanity. Consequently, Jet, his family, and his followers departed from Aether. He vowed to annihilate all ordinary humans and then come back to wipe out all of the people of Aether. It was at that time the Elders felt compelled to increase the training of their police force, the Protectors. In light of the threats from Jet and his people, the Protectors had evolved into a highly skilled, precision, military team. It was their destiny to safeguard the people of Aether from harm.

Chapter Five

Hawk

Covered in grime and too tired to care, Hawk collapsed onto his bed without even removing his boots. He couldn't stop thinking about Ashlyn and the day he spent looking for her. When River had reported the drug's discovery, Bear called off the search. The inky darkness of night would obscure their surroundings until daylight dawned. Hawk's fists clenched and unclenched over and over again as frustration settled inside him. The invaders could be anywhere by now.

Caked with dirt and sweat, Hawk had scoured every inch of the woods himself. The hard ground dug into his knees as he examined a scorch mark they found in the forest. It was as if Ashlyn had disappeared in a burst of Flame. He rubbed the charred cinders of earth between his fingers and had imagined with pride, his beautiful Guardian, enveloped in her Flame, fighting back.

All of Aether hummed with rumors of the Renegades returning to the village to finally seek their revenge. Hawk couldn't help but wonder; why now? Why Ashlyn? It had been hundreds of years since the banishment of the Renegades. If only they knew where the Renegades might have gone, the Protectors would have a place to begin hunting. Hawk was certain of one thing. When he found out who took Ash they were going to pay, and if they hurt her, they would surely die.

He closed his eyes and pictured Ashlyn safe in the South Tower gazing down at him. Her beautiful fire-colored hair surrounded her, as flames radiated from her fingertips. Hawk didn't often pray, but he couldn't help himself from doing just that. "Please, let Ashlyn be safe."

Exhaustion overwhelmed him. His head ached as he drifted off into a restless sleep. Images of Ash filled his dreams. She felt so real, her warmth seeping into his body. He could smell her intoxicating cinnamon scent. Shock and confusion slammed into him when an ethereal image of Ashlyn appeared before him. How was this even possible? Ashlyn was lost to him, yet here she was in front of him. Her beauty was still a radiant light. Then, all at once he was jittery. Cold sweat trickled down his back. A turbulent storm raged inside him. Ashlyn was filled with fear and fury.

Her voice floated through the air, and he felt her presence even though she was nowhere to be found. With a desperate plea she spoke, "Hawk, please help us. Save Laurel. They took us away. I'm scared, Hawk. I need to get out of here. I'm in a room with no way out."

Loud pounding ripped Ashlyn's image away from Hawk, and he was brought back to reality. It took him a minute to realize the banging was coming from his front door. He bolted upright in his bed and then raced to the door. Quill was standing there when he jerked it open. "What's going on?"

"Hurry! Kai thinks he found an antidote for the drug. He wants us at the lab as soon as possible."

Hawk grabbed his jacket, and they were running to the lab seconds later. Their footsteps echoed in the empty Clinic as they made their way to the lab. Kai held a syringe in his hand examining it under a bright light.

"I'm so glad you guys are here. I did a quantitative analysis of the drug using a spectrometer. It is a reverse engineering method we use to isolate the different parts of the drug. I'm pretty sure I have developed an antidote for the sedative. I'm really just hypothesizing about some of the ingredients because I've never seen anything like them before—"

Quill interrupted, "Kai, man, we don't need all this science crap. Just give us the bottom line."

"Sorry, I know my process doesn't mean anything to you guys. Sometimes I get a little carried away. Let me simplify this. I need you guys to inject me with the drug." He held up the syringe. "Then, the antidote I made." He pointed to a different syringe resting on the counter. "So that we can test it before I try it on Laurel."

"Wait a minute, Kai. You can't test it on yourself. We need you to figure this out if the drug doesn't work. You're the only one who has any idea how to fix this. Try it on me first," Hawk insisted.

"No way, I'm not using you to experiment on. What if I'm wrong? It's my risk to take, not yours. I have to help Laurel. You both know how I feel about her. That's why I called you guys. Please, just inject me." Kai handed Hawk the needle.

"Damn it, Kai! You are too important. Laurel needs you and so does Ashlyn." Hawk slammed the syringe onto the countertop.

While the two were arguing, Quill must have surreptitiously seized hold of the syringe and injected himself. Because the next thing Hawk knew, Quill dropped the needle at their feet and was shouting at them. "Would you guys shut up! The room is spinning and everything is in slow motion. I-I-I got it," he sputtered, just before he hit the floor.

"Quill! What did you do?" Hawk yelled. He dropped down at his friend's side.

Kneeling on Quill's other side, Kai reached up, grabbing the syringe, and shoved it in his lab coat pocket. "Oh shit! Let me get the antidote, and then we'll find him a bed." He and Hawk lifted Quill and carried him out of the room.

Placing their friend's unmoving form on the bed, Hawk asked, "Is he okay?"

Kai quickly moved into action assessing Quill's condition. "Don't worry. He's all right. I just want to allow the drug to reach its maximum potency. Laurel has been under the influence for two days, and I need to make sure the antidote is strong enough to pull her out of the coma."

"I can't believe Quill did that. What was he thinking? If he's okay after this, I may kill him." Hawk, unnerved, paced back and forth.

"He really is something, that's for sure. I guess he solved the issue for us about who was going be the lab rat. I just hope this works for everybody's sake. My father and the Elders are both going to have our heads if something goes wrong." Kai pulled at his already tousled hair. "Listen, I know you guys are my best friends, but this whole thing is just too awkward. I still can't believe you heard me confessing to Laurel. I'm sure you know I never stopped thinking about her. Everything that happened was totally my fault." He sighed loudly and lowered his head. "I was so filled with anger and grief that I pushed the best thing in my life away. I just pray I can make it right, you know, tell her how much I love her."

"Believe me, I'm in no position to judge anyone. In fact, when I heard you talking to Laurel, I nearly confessed something myself."

"What are you talking about, Hawk?"

"It's entirely possible... I'm in love with Ashlyn. Holy shit, I can't believe I just said that out loud."

"I've known you've had a thing for her, but love? Holy shit is right! You and Ash? How long has this been going on?" Kai asked, shocked.

"Um, well, never. I don't know what's wrong with me. I've been drawn to her since we were very young, but I never really understood my feelings. Somehow, I seem to abandon all rational thought around her. It's crazy. The connection is so strong between us; I can feel her thoughts. My grandfather told me about a rare telepathy some Guardians possess. And, well, I have to tell you something strange, but you have to promise not to think I'm completely nuts."

"Hawk, we've been friends our entire lives. You are one of the most rational people I know. Of course, I won't think you're nuts. Just tell me what it is."

"When I was sleeping earlier, I, um, I saw Ash in my dream. She called out to me and told me she was afraid. Ash also said someone took her and Laurel. I know that doesn't make sense because obviously Laurel is here. There was also something about a room with no way out. Then Quill woke me up, and she was suddenly gone. This has to work, Kai. I have to find her."

"Wow, you really saw her? You don't think it was just a dream, you know, wishful thinking?"

"No, I'm sure it was real. I could actually feel her fear and anger, too. I knew you would think I was crazy, but I'm not!" Hawk pounded his fist on the countertop in frustration.

"Calm down," Kai said. He held up a hand in surrender. "Of course I don't think you're crazy. Did she say anything else?"

"No, Quill woke me up, and she just vanished."

"Okay listen, let's just put this on the back burner for the time being. I do believe you. We should probably talk to Bear about this. Maybe it can help lead us to Ash. For now, we should concentrate on Quill and the antidote. I think we've let enough time pass to test my theory. I'm ready to administer the drug. Pray this works."

The tension in the room was thick as Kai rolled up their friend's sleeve to administer the antidote. He took a deep breath before piercing Quill's skin with the needle and injecting the contents into his body. Hawk and Kai focused on the powerful Protector's lifeless form practically boring holes into him. Finally, his eyelids fluttered a short while later. Quill's fingers twitched rhythmically as if he was playing an invisible piano.

Kai bent low. He spoke in a gentle tone, "Quill? Can you hear me? Try to keep your eyes open."

Quill blinked repeatedly as if he had something in his eyes. The twitching of his fingers slowed, and he moved his legs in a jerky motion.

"Do you think he's okay? He looks like he's

having a seizure or something the way he's moving around like that." Concern etched his face.

"The drug is working its way through his body, and his muscles appear to be reacting to it. Let's just give him a couple of minutes to adjust. His vital signs are all still strong."

At last the spasms subsided, and Quill's body movements ceased. He continued to blink his eyes, and it looked like he was trying to focus his vision. Hawk stood over him and smiled. "You really are a total asshole, you know? You scared the crap out of me. Can you talk?"

Quill answered, in a weak voice, "That was a really freaky trip. I couldn't move or see, but I could hear everything going on around me."

"You could hear us?" Kai inquired.

"Oh yeah, you two sounded like a couple of girls talking about love and your feelings. Made me feel sicker than that stupid drug I jammed into my leg. I felt really dizzy, nauseous, and it gave me a whopping headache. That's all starting to feel better already. Quite the wonder cocktail you whipped up there, Doc."

"I'm curious if everyone is affected by the drug in the same way," Kai queried.

"What you really mean is, does Laurel know you still dig her?" Quill answered.

"You know, Quill, you take subtlety to a whole new level. You're a dick. Can you give Kai a break? I think he just saved you from the land of the lost."

"All right, I'll give it a break, but I reserve the right to torture you both later," Quill teased.

"What's the plan now, Kai?" Hawk inquired.

"Well, I need to do a work up on Quill. Blood

panel, vital signs, and motor ability. Then it's back to the lab to make more of the antidote. I only made enough for one dose, because I didn't want to waste the limited supply of the drug the Protectors found. So sit back and rest, Quill, and I'll get started on all that. First, I need to call my dad and tell him what we've been up to. Wish me luck."

Hawk and Quill chatted while they waited for Kai to come back from talking to Rayne. Quill seemed to be feeling much better, and Hawk was more relieved than he wanted to admit. He didn't think he could handle anything happening to one of his best friends and the woman he loved at the same time.

Kai walked in ten minutes later with a scowling Rayne right behind him. "That was a pretty brave move, Quill, but also a really dumb thing to do," Rayne reprimanded.

"I've definitely heard the dumb part before. I just couldn't stand to hear those two bickering. Too much testosterone in one room gives me hives. It all worked out, so no worries."

Rayne smiled. "Quill, you are too much. I'm going to stay and do your work up. Kai is going to go to the lab and make more of the serum. Hawk, do you think you could give him a hand to make things go a little faster? We would love to be ready to revive Laurel first thing in the morning."

"Sure thing, whatever I can do to help." Hawk responded by quickly getting to his feet.

"After I'm done with Quill's work up, I'm going to update the Elders on our progress. Hopefully everything will go smoothly with Laurel, and she can tell us exactly what happened to her and Ashlyn the other night."

Returning to the lab, Kai handed Hawk a white coat. The Protector's wide shoulders and thick arms stretched the garment to its limit. Kai fumbled with the box containing the unknown drug; it flipped on its side, and the small glass vials rolled out. He scrambled to catch them, but Hawk swept his hand in an upward motion tapping into his connection with the Element of Air. His power lifted the vials on a current and combined with his quick reflexes, he was able to save the tiny containers from shattering to the floor.

"Thanks, man. I'm exhausted." He scrubbed his hands over his tired eyes. "I feel like I'm all thumbs. I better get myself together and quick if I want to do this right. We don't have any of those to spare. How many are left?"

"Don't worry, none of them broke. We have seven left. Will that be enough?"

"Should be plenty. Do you mind putting them back in the box?"

"Of course not. What else can I do to help you?"

As Hawk reached for the box to place the vials back inside, he noticed something at the bottom. He pulled back the flaps opening it further. His eyes widened as he looked into the box and spotted a label glued in place.

"Kai! Look at this! There's a tag, or something in here. It says, *CEB Laboratories*."

Kai practically leapt from his seat to peer into the box. "This is amazing! Our first real clue." His smile quickly faded. "When the hell is the new tech center going to open already?" He slammed his fist onto the counter. "I need to do some research to figure out the story with this lab. I guess it's another trip to the University's library."

"I got your back. I'm coming with you."

They worked side by side with Hawk assisting Kai for hours until he had several doses of the antidote encased in syringes. Rayne came in to check their progress and to tell them Quill's test results were normal. Kai told his father about the label they found.

Hawk wondered aloud, "What do you think the Renegades would be doing mixed up with a lab? Don't you think they would just attack us with weapons? Or at least Element against Element? Plus, it's been hundreds of years, why now? And why take Ashlyn? The whole thing just doesn't add up to me."

Rayne responded, "Hopefully, when Laurel wakes up she'll be able to shed some light on this entire mess, and we can start searching for Ash. I think you guys should try to get a couple of hours of sleep. We have plenty of open beds here, so no need to go home. We can wake Zarina and Canyon at first light. They're asleep in Laurel's room. Quill is sleeping, too."

Hawk followed Kai to an empty patient room with two beds. The florescent lights hummed overhead and gave the room a much too bright glow. Exhaustion penetrated his body as he lowered himself onto the bed with a creak. Pulling off his boots, he stretched out his long frame allowing a small moan escaping his lips.

"Hey, Hawk?"

"Yeah?"

"If you dream, I mean talk to Ash, keep it PG okay?"

"Very funny. I think Quill might be rubbing off on you, and that's not a compliment. Good night, Kai."

"Night, Hawk."

****

Ashlyn

Pure rage and a healthy dose of fear filled Ashlyn. Her Fire rippled along her nerve endings but could not escape the confines of her body. If Devlin was telling the truth, she needed to feign cooperation in order to protect Laurel. Ash's stomach tightened in knots. She was determined to endure whatever her captors inflicted even though she had never been more terrified in her life.

"Listen up, Firecracker. If you think you can behave, I'll administer the antidote. We have a lot of work to do. Blink your eyes twice if you agree to be a good girl. Otherwise I will be happy to make things as painful as possible for you, and your pretty friend."

Ashlyn blinked her eyes twice and prayed to the God and Goddess to give her strength. A strange hissing sound started coming from the vent with the cage. Thick white smoke billowed from the slats. Ash tried not to panic. Her breath caught in her throat as the clouds began to fall and form around her. Before long, she became lost in the dense fog as the entire room was filled. The air hung heavily around her and had a metallic taste.

Five or ten minutes passed before the vapor dissipated, and Ashlyn no longer felt consumed. Testing her body, she wiggled her fingers and toes. Her legs and arms were next, and finally, she felt strong enough to sit up. Still lightheaded, her stomach finally settled, and her nausea eased.

"There you go, Firecracker. Take it nice and slow. We don't want you damaged, too much, yet."

Ashlyn found her voice, "Who are you? What have you done with Laurel?" She could feel the heat of her Flame rising up her neck, her cheeks burning. Fire danced inside her. "What do you want from me?" she demanded.

"Whoa there, Firecracker, I'll be the one asking the questions around here."

"Stop calling me that! My name is Ashlyn, not Firecracker!"

"You're as feisty as I remember and even more beautiful when you're pissed off, Ash-lyn."

Already regretting giving him her real name, Ash reined in her temper. She was desperate to know what was happening with Laurel. Drawing Devlin in seemed like the only way to get some information. Playing scared and compliant would probably be more effective than enraged and obstinate.

"Please, what do you want from me?" she implored, with as much innocence as she could falsely muster.

"Oh, baby, I like the sound of you begging, and you will be begging me. That's a promise. For now, I don't want anything from you. Just rest for a while, and regain your strength. It may take some time for you to feel like yourself again. After that, we'll talk."

With his words still hanging in the air, the slot at the bottom of the door opened. A tray with a sandwich, an apple, and a bottle of water slid into the room. She ran her hands along the tray hoping it could be used as a weapon. Sadly, it was made of heavy cardboard not metal. Ash couldn't remember the last time she ate, and her stomach rumbled loudly reinforcing the point. How long had she been gone from home anyway? Her sense of time was severely jumbled. She didn't trust that the food on the tray wasn't poisoned, but it seemed she didn't have much of a choice.

As if he read her mind, Devlin's tinny voice droned from the speakers once again. "Don't worry, there is nothing in the food that will hurt you. When I want to hurt you, trust me, you'll know. Now eat and rest. We'll talk later. And, Ashlyn, I'll be watching you, always. So, don't try anything stupid. In case you were wondering, your room is fireproof, waterproof, windproof, and earthquake proof."

Well, her captors obviously had knowledge of her people and were quite well prepared. Though the question remained, who were they and what did they want? There was only one known enemy of the people of Aether; the Renegades. Jet Thorn and his followers had left the village many hundreds of years ago, and as far as she knew, no one had any inkling as to their whereabouts.

Why now? Why me and Laurel? What do they want from us?

Putting the thought aside, Ashlyn took hold of the tray and sat down on the bed with it. Thinking it would be safer, she decided to try the apple. The first bite was like heaven, juicy and crisp. She didn't want to enjoy it, but she was famished, and it tasted amazing. After eating it down to the core, she figured she may as well eat the sandwich too. If her captors wanted to kill her, they would have done it already. Sniffing in between the slices, she couldn't detect anything out of the ordinary. It was your basic ham and cheese on a doughy white roll. Gobs of bread stuck to the roof of her mouth, as she consumed the sandwich with lightning speed.

Ash guzzled down the entire bottle of water, then rose, and placed the tray next to the slot in the door.

Knowing she wouldn't be able to relax unless she relieved herself, Ash eyed the toilet in the corner with trepidation. Disturbed by the complete lack of privacy, she grabbed the blanket off the bed draping it over her shoulders. Self-conscious, her eyes darted around the tiny space. There was no seat on the metal toilet, so she squatted, balancing on her wobbly legs.

After she was finished, longing for the comforts and security of home, Ash curled herself into a tight ball on the bed and wrapped up in the scratchy blanket. *If I ever get out of this place, I'm going to proposition Hawk and tell him once and for all how I feel about him. I'm going to tell him, I think about him night and day. How I long for him to hold me in his arms and to kiss me senseless. Now if only he could find me.* Still feeling weak from the drugs, weariness overtook her, and she slept focusing her thoughts on Hawk.

Even in her sleep, Ashlyn could sense the air around her humming with energy. Her mind was consumed with Hawk, and she unwittingly connected to him. Reaching deep, her concentration intense, she begged him to help her. A feeling of warmth filled her, and her nose twitched when she caught a whiff of Hawk's woodsy, masculine scent. Without warning the door to their link was suddenly slammed shut, and Hawk was forcibly ripped from her mind. Waking with a start, Ashlyn bolted upright.

"Dear Goddess, I actually felt him!" she exclaimed, in shock. "But how?"

Ash sensed the loss immediately. There had always been a connection with Hawk, but this was something altogether different, something stronger, something, much more. Hope flickered inside her. Now, if only she could do it again. Maybe she could lead the Protectors to her.

Baffled and plagued by questions, too much had happened for Ashlyn to process. She breathed deeply in order to relax and concentrate, but she felt powerless. Strengthening her resolve she declared, "Get your shit together, girl! You're a damn Guardian! Sol always says, your powers are limited only by your own mind." Perhaps her mentor was right. Maybe her powers were not limited to her Fire. If she could somehow reach out to Hawk again, she could tell him about her theories regarding the Renegades. Also, she wanted him to know about the specially designed cell she was in which was impervious to all of their powers.

Ash wondered why they used drugs and not their magical gifts against her and Laurel. Conceivably, Devlin could be a descendant of Jet Thorn. Or, was he simply working for Jet? More questions than answers arose and nothing had crystalized for Ashlyn.

The walls of her prison appeared thick and impenetrable. If Devlin was telling the truth, her Fire would not free her from this unjust sentence, but Ashlyn was confident in the strength of her power. She closed her eyes, concentrating, until she felt the telltale heat of her Flame spreading. Ashlyn lifted her hands and projected her Fire at the imposing door. The metal glowed red but did not falter. She remained captive.

Chapter Six

Kai

Kai tossed and turned as he listened to Hawk's rhythmic breathing. His mind churned with a mountain of questions and concerns. Would his serum work on Laurel in the same manner it did on Quill? Kai wasn't sure if he was more worried about the serum working, or how Laurel would feel about his confessions. Beautiful and popular, Laurel never lacked for male attention, but he never noticed her spending time with any particular man, and he definitely would have noticed.

Fantasies of Laurel returning his feelings took shape in his mind. He pictured her standing before him. Her beautiful brown hair was burnished to a deep shine. Kai's hands itched to touch the silken strands. In his vision, the length obscured his view of her perfect breasts. Her gaze, focused only on him, disarmed him completely. She was bared to him, her bronze-toned skin silky and smooth. Memories of her pliant beneath him with their mouths and bodies fused together invaded his brain.

Stop it! Stop it! The woman has just been through an ordeal beyond which I can only imagine. It made his blood boil when he thought about anyone hurting Laurel. He would wait for her to recover fully, and then he would tell her about his feelings. That is, if she didn't already know. He prayed Laurel would find it in her heart to forgive him and didn't think he was some depraved stalker spouting his feelings to her while she lay unconscious. Though now, after Quill's experience, Kai suspected she had most likely heard everything. He was mortified feeling every bit the fool. He needed to redirect his focus. It was definitely time for some balance in his life. For now, he had a duty to his work and needed to lock away his fascination with Laurel.

Was Hawk right about the Renegades and their connection to this CEB Laboratories? What would they be doing with tranquilizers instead of attacking Aether? Hawk's perceptions were spot on. Ashlyn being taken was truly a mystery. Guardians were precious and rare. The Renegades might be motivated to try to destroy Aether by taking their Guardians. Kai couldn't help wondering if Ashlyn was still alive. Even though he had both experienced and witnessed some amazing magic, he had never heard of the telepathy Hawk described. He wanted to believe Hawk had actually spoken to Ashlyn, but the scientist in him was still slightly skeptical. Kai's inner scientist and his intense connection to the Elements were often divergent splitting him in two. He was constantly seeking balance between science and magic. Right now he needed to concentrate on the problem in front of him, to find and stop their unknown enemy. Waking Laurel was the first step in finding Ash; no pressure there.

It was still dark when Kai finally closed his eyes and allowed sleep to take him. He felt like he'd slept for only a few minutes when someone gently touched his shoulder and called his name. Slowly, he blinked the sleep out of his eyes trying to focus.

His father stood over him. "I'm sorry to wake you, but we should really get started. I've already woken Zarina and Canyon, and they're very eager to see if your antidote works on their daughter."

Early morning sunlight spilled into the room making everything it touched appear to glow. Kai noticed Hawk was already up. He hopped out of bed, captured his shoes, and haphazardly shoved his feet inside.

They made their way down to Laurel's room where Quill was leaning against the wall waiting. "Well, good morning, sleeping beauties. Share any good love stories last night?" His voice dripped with sarcasm.

"Really, Quill? It's way too early for your bullshit. Do we need to knock you out again? Just shut up, and let Kai do his job. We need to wake Laurel and find out what she knows. The more time we waste, the further away Ashlyn slips."

"Sorry, dude. Just trying to bring some levity to a really tense situation," Quill responded.

Rayne rolled his eyes. "Zarina and Canyon are waiting for us, so let's get on with this." Laurel's parents were standing together by the side of her bed when the men entered the room. Canyon held one of her hands while Zarina stroked Laurel's long hair offering comfort and whispering quiet words to her. Kai thought Laurel looked beautiful and peaceful, but he couldn't say the same for her parents. They looked exhausted.

Rayne handed Kai the syringe filled with the same serum he had administered to Quill yesterday. Kai swabbed her arm with an alcohol wipe, took a deep breath, and prayed with all his heart that this would work.

He spoke to her as if she could definitely hear him. "Okay, Laurel, this may sting a bit, but it's going to be all right. You may experience some muscle reactions to the drug, but that's perfectly normal. Don't fight the medicine; let it do its job. We're all here with you."

Kai gently pricked Laurel's arm with the needle, slowly depressing the plunger, and emptying the contents into her body. He said a silent prayer to the God and Goddess that she would return to them. Moments later, her eyelids fluttered and the same trembling Quill had experienced commenced. Everyone in the room looked on nervously, but Kai remained in clinical mode. He watched the monitors carefully for any signs of distress, but her vital signs remained strong and steady.

"What's happening to her?" Zarina asked, turning an anxious gaze on Kai.

"It's okay. It's normal. Quill had a similar reaction and he's perfectly fine," Kai reassured.

After a short time, Laurel appeared to be breaking through the effects of the drug. Her spasms slowed, she squinted, and he could see her eyes fighting to remain open. Kai leaned over her and spoke softly, "Can you hear me, Laurel? Try to keep your eyes open. You may feel a little lightheaded, that's also normal. Focus on my voice."

The rapid blinking subsided. Laurel's eyes remained open and fixed on Kai's. A faint smile emerged. She anchored her gaze up at him as he checked her pulse rate. The machines were monitoring all of her vital signs, but he couldn't resist the chance to touch her. Feeling the warmth of her skin, seeing her eyes open for the first time in days, Kai breathed a sigh of relief.

Zarina and Canyon wedged in together to see for themselves that Laurel was truly awake. Canyon sagged with relief and Zarina's eyes filled with tears as she spoke, "Laurel, sweetheart, can you speak?"

"M-m-mom," she said, in a barely audible tone.

Canyon pulled Zarina in close to his side. "Thank the God and Goddess. Our baby is back."

Reaching for the electronic controls, Kai elevated the head of Laurel's bed. Her gaze darted around the room, and Kai wondered if she was trying to make sense of the situation. "How are you feeling? Any headache? Nausea? Dizziness?" Kai questioned.

"I feel weak. A little light headed, too," she replied groggily, "my headache feels better, not so nauseous anymore."

"We tested the medicine on Quill, and he felt the same way. With a little time and rest he was good as new. You will be, too, you'll see," Kai reassured.

"Hey, Laurel, I'm so glad you're back with us. Do you feel up to talking about what happened?" Hawk probed gently. "It's all right if you need some time. We're just all very worried about Ashlyn. We were hoping you could tell us what happen to her."

"I know everyone is worried." Laurel took a deep breath and continued, "I couldn't open my eyes or move, but I could hear and feel. It was so strange."

Canyon held up his hand, halting her. "It's all right, honey, we can talk later when you're feeling stronger."

"It's fine, Dad. I know Ash was taken and I want to help. I'm really starting to feel better, truly." She turned to Kai with warmth and gratitude in her expression.

"Thanks to you, Kai. You saved me. I was so scared. It was the most frustrating feeling not being able to speak or move. It made me so angry that I couldn't communicate. There was so much I wanted to say."

"Yes, I bet there was quite a lot you wanted to say," Quill chimed in.

Simultaneously, Hawk and Kai sent Quill a silent reprimand. He backed off and smirked. Thankfully, nobody else picked up on Quill's little innuendo. Kai knew he wouldn't be able to avoid a conversation with Laurel, but he certainly didn't want it to take place in front of her parents and his dad.

"If you feel up to it, can you tell us what happened to you and Ashlyn the other night?" Kai asked.

"We were walking in the forest, like we do sometimes. It wasn't that late maybe ten or eleven. I'm not exactly sure. We walked for a long time, and the night was very still. We realized we'd traveled deeper into the woods then we usually do. We stopped to talk, and we both heard some rustling. I assumed it was an animal, but Ash was worried, so we headed back toward the house. It started getting louder and louder and closer and closer—" Tears ran down Laurel's cheeks.

Canyon held her hand tightly and interrupted her. "You don't have to talk about this now, honey. You need rest. This is too much, too soon."

"No! I'm okay, Dad. It was just so terrifying. Of course I'm upset. But those assholes took my best friend, and I'm going to do everything in my power to help find Ash. She's been looking out for me since we were kids, and now it's my turn." Laurel's voice broke as she recanted the details of her horrific night.

She was weeping now, and Kai took her other hand not stopping to think about anyone's reaction. His need to comfort her was instinctive. "It's all right now. You're safe. No one can hurt you here. The Protectors have double shifts guarding the forest night and day."

"I'm not worried about myself, it's-it's Ash. She led the other three away from me. She was so brave. I saw a bright flash, and I knew she must've done something with her Fire to save me. I can still hear Ash's voice in my head telling me to run and get help. So I did. A man shot me with one of those darts, but I just kept running and falling. I was so weak. I don't remember much after that. It was dark and cold when I woke up. I couldn't move, and my head was pounding. Everything was spinning, and I felt like I was going to throw up. I'm not sure what happened after that. I just knew I needed help. The sun was just beginning to lighten the sky, and I was freezing. I so scared no one would find me."

Laurel whimpered, and her tears flowed unreservedly. She looked at Kai and squeezed his hand, trembling slightly. Kai couldn't resist the urge to put his arms around her. Stroking her back in slow circles, he offered her silent comfort. With a deep shuddering breath, she turned to Hawk. "You have to find her, Hawk. I can't imagine what they might be doing to her. Please, I know you and the other Protectors can do it. You need to find those Renegade bastards and get our Ash back."

"Don't worry, Laurel, I intend to do just that. Quill and I are going to talk to my grandfather and the other Elders right now. We're going to find Ashlyn and bring her home." Hawk approached Laurel, bent down, and placed a kiss on her forehead. "You rest. We'll be back soon to give you good news." Hawk and Quill left the room and headed over to the Council Chambers.

"I'm sorry, Laurel, but I need to draw some blood and take it to the lab. We want to make sure all your levels are normal," Rayne said.

"It's fine, Rayne. Compared to everything I've been through, it really seems like nothing." She extended her arm to him.

"I'm going to need to do a full exam on you when my dad is done," Kai added.

"We'll let you do your tests. You make sure my baby is all right, Kai. We're going to run home, shower, and change. Then we're going to see Rowan and Mica. They're worried sick about you, Laurel. They'll want to come back and see you. Anything you can tell them about Ash will be helpful. They need something to hold onto right now. Hawk and Quill will keep us posted on the plan to find Ash and bring her home. Let's move it out people," Canyon ordered.

Chuckling at her father's bossy alpha male nature, Laurel said, "Take it easy there, Dad. I know everything is going to be all right. Hawk will bring Ash back to us. I just know it."

With that little statement, everyone left the room. Kai and Laurel were finally alone. Their gazes met, locked, and they continued to stare at each other without saying a word for several minutes. Kai knew he needed to address the elephant in the room, but he wasn't sure where to start. When he looked down he realized he was still holding Laurel's hand. It felt warm, soft, and right, touching her, but he started to pull back loosening his grasp. Laurel held tightly to his hand as he tried to release hers. "Don't let go, Kai."

"I won't." He looked deeply into her eyes. "You heard everything, didn't you?" Laurel simply nodded. "I should have told you how I still felt about you a long time ago. I guess I spent so much time using my logic, my science, and my skills striving to keep the people of Aether healthy, I forgot how to just feel. I know I pushed you away with my anger and grief and I'm so sorry I hurt you, Laurel. When I thought I might not be able to help you, something inside me snapped. You've been through so much these last few days, but I need you to know one thing… I still love you, Laurel, that's never changed, and it never will."

Laurel started to speak, but Kai gently put a finger to her lips. "Please don't say anything yet. I need to finish, or I'll never get this out. You are so beautiful, smart, and kind. I know you could have any man in the village you want, but I hope you'll give me another chance. Let me make this right. I know this may seem like it's coming out of nowhere, but it's not. I've longed to get back the connection we once shared." He released a heavy, breathy sigh. "Okay, please say something now." Laurel smiled up at him and stroked his cheek with her free hand. He couldn't imagine what she was staring at, probably the dark circles he knew were under his eyes or his scruffy unshaven face.

"If you think I'm going to make it easy for you, you've got another think coming. There will be plenty of time for fighting later, but for now how about you kiss me instead?"

Kai's eyes widened taken aback, but then a broad grin broke out across his face. He bent down and pressed his lips to Laurel's. The kiss was tender yet passionate, just like the woman. Taking the kiss a bit deeper, Laurel responded, matching each stroke of his tongue. Her hands were gripping his shoulders tightly, pulling him closer, seeking more of him. His hands fisted in her hair positioning her right where he wanted her. They were both breathless when he finally pulled away.

"I knew kissing you would still be as amazing as it always was. You taste so sweet just like I remembered. But we can't do this now. I really do need to check you over. Medically, I mean," he said, with a laugh.

Laurel was practically panting when she responded, "Okay, Doc, check me out, I mean check me over. More kissing later, I hope?"

Kai smiled. "You can count on that, baby." Then he turned serious. "But I have to admit I was pretty scared about what your reaction would be when I realized you could hear what was being said. I thought you were unconscious. By that kiss, I hope that means you've decided to forgive me."

"The jury is still out with regard to forgiveness, but the kissing verdict is definitely in, and it was a resounding yes. Kissing you was...electric. I've missed you, Kai. I miss what we had between us. I'm looking forward to exploring where this takes us, but I feel like I'm dreaming. The only thing missing is my best friend. Ash would be thrilled by this...development between us."

"We'll find her, and you can tell her everything." Kai gently ran his finger down her cheek to her neck. A delicate blush rose in her cheeks. He loved watching her respond to his words and his touch. He couldn't wait to really let go and hopefully be with Laurel the way she deserved. He vowed this time he would do everything in his power to cherish her and never hurt her again. Kai needed to find balance in his life, and he knew in his heart that Laurel was the key for him.

****

Laurel

Laurel was alone for the first time in days. Kai had barely finished his examination when her parents barged into the room with Rowan and Mica on their heels. With great difficulty, Laurel once again recounted the details of her evening with Ashlyn and the subsequent attack. She was certain Rowan and Mica were disappointed she couldn't provide much information, but they didn't show it. This had been so hard on her loved ones, Laurel realized, as she offered comfort to them. "Hawk is going to find Ash. He promised. And I believe him. Kai is going to release me in the morning, and I'm going to help. You guys all need to go home and rest. You'll be of no use if you are falling down on your feet. I love you guys, but please, go home. I'll see you in the morning." Those were Laurel's last words to them as they left, and she was alone at last.

Deciding a shower was in order, she grabbed the small duffle bag her mother had packed for her and headed into the bathroom. Laurel nearly shrieked with fright at her reflection. She reached out and touched the smooth surface of the mirror. "Oh my God, look at me!"

As she ran her fingers through her normally sleek hair, they kept getting stuck in the bird's nest of knots she bore. Her eyes drooped with dark circles. Her knees were covered with antiseptic looking white bandages she hadn't noticed before. Broken, chipped fingernails, small scrapes, and cuts highlighted the damage to her hands. She examined the rest of her body. Laurel's fingers wandered down her legs inspecting the fading bruises which remained tender to her light touch. Slowly, she unwound the bandages, releasing the smell of eucalyptus ointment. Her torn flesh already healing, itched and stung.

The hospital gown fell to the tile floor as she reached back and loosened the ties. She pulled shampoo, conditioner, and soap from her bag and placed them on the bench in the shower. Steam filled the tiny stall. Laurel stepped in, and the warm spray seeped into her body. Inhaling deeply, she let the familiar smell of her shampoo soothe her. Her jagged fingernails scratched along her scalp. She rinsed, moaning as the rush of hot water cascaded over her head and down her back. Her favorite vanilla scented body soap sat on the bench untouched. All the scrubbing in the world wouldn't be enough to wash away the memories of her attack. She grabbed the tube and squeezed it into her hands; it dripped down her arms, and pooled by her feet. She covered every inch of her body cleansing away the physical evidence of her experience.

She wished she could wash away her thoughts as easily. *Oh my God, where is Ashlyn? What are those animals doing to her?* She held her head beneath the forceful spray. *I have to help Hawk and the other Protectors find her.* Clearly, Hawk had some serious feelings for Ash. The distress and concern was written all over his face. If Ash could see how worried Hawk was, Laurel wondered what her best friend would think now. She knew the two had been dancing around their feelings their entire lives.

For that matter, what would Ash think about Kai and his apology? She was extremely protective of Laurel. Although Kai was her friend, too, Ash had never quite forgiven him for hurting her best friend. Laurel was still processing the gravity of Kai's words herself. She hadn't known how to respond, so telling him to kiss her seemed like the right idea at the time.

Talking to herself aloud, Laurel worked through her feelings. "I can't believe he still has feelings for me after all these years. The truth is, I never stopped loving him not even for one day. When Kai's lips met mine, it was as if the past, our history, didn't exist." His renewed passion made her question everything in her life. Why had she never gotten serious with anyone she had dated? Was she secretly hoping Kai would come back to her some day?

Fantasizing about a rekindled romance with Kai was one thing, but she never imagined she could have a real relationship with him again. Kai was so focused, so serious, always working. She rarely saw him out in the pub or at the café in the evenings unless Hawk and Quill were dragging him along. Laurel wanted romance. She wanted things to be the way they were when she and Kai were young, but he had changed, and so had she. Kai seemed like he was in love with his job, and she couldn't imagine the brilliant, logical, doctor letting go of his heart ever again. Her palms tingled with nerves, and Laurel wondered if she had changed too much as well. No longer a naive young girl, she had hardened her heart to protect herself just as Kai had. They were definitely going to have to talk and not just kiss if they had even a small chance of something working out between them.

The skin on her fingers and toes wrinkled from being in the water too long, so Laurel turned off the faucet. She pulled a couple of towels off the rack next to the shower, twisted her hair in one, and wrapped a second one around her body.

She found her favorite PJ bottoms, a tank top, and fuzzy slippers as she dug through her bag. After dressing, she found her toothbrush and toothpaste. She gloried in the familiarity of doing something so normal. When she felt fresh and clean, she brushed the tangles out of her long thick hair. The repetitive motion lulled her into a trancelike state.

A knock on the door pulled her out of her daze. Refreshed and feeling much more like her old self, she went to the door and opened it to find Kai standing there. The adorable dimple in his left cheek winked at her as he smiled, lighting up his masculine face. Laurel's heart skipped a beat. He made her feel too much when he smiled at her.

Flirting, she gently and oh so slowly ran her finger from his dimple to his full lower lip. "I like seeing you smile. You should smile more. That dimple is too cute for words."

Kai leaned in seemingly unable to resist touching her. He rubbed his hand up and down the length of her arm. "I'm happy to see you. You look like you again, and you smell amazing, too." He moved even closer bending to nuzzle her neck.

Laurel shivered in the best possible way from the contact. "Kai, we need to talk. I'm feeling a little overwhelmed by everything that's happened. I can't deny the spark between us still exists, but where did this come from after so long?"

Pulling back to look into her eyes, Kai choked up as if he were trying to find the right words, "I've wanted you back from almost the first moment I let you go. I know I hurt you, and I'm so sorry, but I've always loved you, Laurel." He took hold of both her hands in his. "I was young, angry, and stupid. I didn't think I deserved to be happy with Storm gone. Even after all these years, you're the only woman I've ever loved. I wish I had the courage to tell you sooner, but I was afraid you hated me. But now, all I can think about is the kiss we shared." Kai took her into his arms and lightly touched his lips to hers.

"Kai, I can't concentrate when you do that... Ahhh. Kai, please." A moan escaped her lips.

"What is it, baby? Anything you want. Just tell me," he whispered in her ear. Then he took her lips again, giving all of himself in the kiss. His tongue delved deep into her mouth. Her legs shook slightly as her core ached for Kai's touch.

Laurel thought they should be talking not kissing. But with Kai's big body pressed up against hers, she could do nothing but surrender to the feeling inside her. Laurel reached up and wrapped her arms around his neck turning up the heat between them. Kai's hands dropped down to grasp her bottom and pulled her closer to his arousal.

They were so lost in each other that they apparently did not hear the knocking on Laurel's door. It wasn't until Hawk and Quill stood in front of them coughing and clearing their throats over and over again that the couple finally broke apart. Laurel was breathing heavily and felt completely flushed, from both embarrassment and passion. She attempted to straighten her clothing while Kai barked at his friends.

"What the hell are you two doing in here? Don't you believe in knocking?"

"Um, dude, we totally knocked, more like pounded. Not to mention, we did call out to you a bunch of times. Guess you were a little preoccupied," Quill answered, with a snicker. He hopped onto Laurel's bed clearly making himself comfortable.

"Sorry, you two, but we have important information to share. By the way, Laurel, you look great. Glad to see you up and moving around," Hawk said.

"Yes, that really was some fine moving around you were doing there, Miss Laurel. Wonder what the student body would think about their hot teacher getting it on with the nerdy doctor. Kai, dude, seriously, didn't know you had it in you. Felt like I was walking into the beginning of a porn flick," Quill teased. He leaned back on Laurel's pillows and clasped his hands behind his head.

"Quill Robbins, you act as immature as my students, and they're thirteen years old." She grabbed his arm yanking him off her bed. "Seriously, I can't wait for you to fall for someone. Because when you do, I'm going to laugh my butt off. You'll probably be the worst sort of mush calling her nicknames like 'schmoopsy-pooh,' or 'cuddle bunny.' You just wait."

"Never going to happen. I enjoy my freedom way too much. Plus, I'm more of a sexy nickname kind of guy. 'Schmoopsy-pooh' and 'cuddle bunny' don't really fit my image."

Kai glared at Quill. "Honestly, Quill, I don't know why we put up with you. I'm ignoring you, or else I'm going to deck you." He turned to Hawk. "What's the plan?"

"We spoke to my grandfather and the other Elders. They agreed we need to do some research on CEB laboratories—"

"Wait a minute, what are you talking about? What laboratories?" Laurel interrupted.

"Sorry, I didn't get a chance to tell you we found a label on the box of drugs they used on you. It said CEB laboratories on it," Kai informed her.

"How the hell would you get a chance to tell the woman anything when you had your tongue down her throat and your hands all over her ass," Quill countered. He mocked Kai gesturing with a squeezing motion of his hands.

Simultaneously, Hawk and Kai yelled, "Shut up, Quill!"

"You guys are way too tense, just like the Elders. And you two have no sense of humor anymore," Quill chuffed.

Straightening to his full height, Hawk's faced reddened. "Stop your joking and whining, Quill, I need to find Ashlyn, now!" He sighed, lowered his head, and regained his composure. "I'm sorry."

"Hawk, I've never seen you like this before. Is there something you're not telling me?" Laurel asked softly. She reached out and touched the warrior's arm in a tender action.

"Duh, he's in love with Ash. But I'm sure you already knew that. Didn't you? You women have an intuition that we dopey males just don't possess," Quill blurted out, unrestrained.

"Actually, Quill, there is a bit more to it than that. I guess you probably overheard Kai and me talking the other night. I've been meaning to talk to you about this for a couple of days, but you're always such a clown that I didn't know how to bring it up. Discussing something serious with you, well, let's just say, you don't always make it easy," Hawk confessed.

Quill placed one hand up in surrender and the other over his heart. "Great, well now I feel like shit. I'm really sorry if I made you feel that way, buddy. You guys are my best friends, you can tell me anything, no judgment, and all joking aside. For now anyway," Quill said, appearing humbled.

"Well, that's the closest thing to an apology I've heard in over eighty years. Glad you're on board, Quill." Hawk turned to Laurel. "The story is, Ashlyn and I have formed some kind of telepathic bond. My grandfather told me about this rare Guardian power. She actually called out to me the other night when I was sleeping. I could see her, hear her, and feel her. It was surreal." Hawk shuddered. "They've locked her up. She's scared. She thinks they have you, Laurel, I'm not sure why. She begged me to save her, and I'm going to, if it's the last thing I do."

"Wow, I don't know what to say. Honestly, Hawk, Ash has always, always been drawn to you. Though she's never really understood it. She definitely has feelings for you, that I'm sure of. But is Quill right? Do you love her?"

"Yes, yes I do. With my whole heart. I need to find her, bring her home safely, and I need to tell her how I feel. Kai, let's leave first thing in the morning for the

University. I'm going to find out everything there is to know about CEB Labs. We're going to track down those Renegade bastards, and then we're going to save my girl."

"I think it's amazing that you have this connection, Hawk." Laurel gave him a quick hug. "You can find her. I know you can. Will you tell me if she reaches out to you again? I want to help."

"Of course, I will. Right now, there's nothing any of us can do until morning. Kai, can you meet me at my place around eight tomorrow morning?"

"Sure thing, I'll be there as soon as I release Laurel. Her parents are coming first thing to spring her from here."

"Okay, see you tomorrow. Come on, Quill, let's go."

"Aw, come on, I want to stay for the fireworks."

"Get out, Quill, you're not funny," Kai said. Laurel wasn't sure if he was totally joking or not. "Later, Hawk. I'll see you in the morning. Don't worry, we'll figure this out and get her back." They left closing the door behind them with a loud click.

Laurel's head was spinning from this latest development. *Hawk loves Ash, and they are bound by some kind of telepathy.* "Can you believe all this? You haven't really said much. Aren't you surprised? Love? Telepathy? It all seems so crazy," she said, in a rush.

"Yes, I was surprised, but Hawk told me shortly after he and Ash communicated."

"You believe him, don't you?"

"I want to believe him. Hawk is one of my oldest, closest friends. Obviously we grew up surrounded by magic. I, myself, can see inside people to their injuries and manipulate water. It's strange and overwhelming sometimes, but I accept my gifts as part of my being. But there is this other side of me, this overly rational side, a side that only wants to see logic. Sometimes I feel like I'm fighting a war within myself. Which is it, science or magic? And then, there's you, always lurking in the back of my mind. I thought I'd destroyed any chance I had with you, but since I've kissed you…we belong together. I feel it in my heart. Please give us another chance, Laurel." He reached for her taking her firmly by the shoulders.

Laurel allowed a small smile to spread slowly across her face. "Okay."

Kai's brow furrowed, his nose scrunched up adorably, and he canted his head to one side. "Okay?"

"That's what I said, okay. I want to give us a chance. I can't stop thinking about kissing you either or being in your arms"—she wrapped her hands around his waist—"I feel it, too. I want things to be the way they used to be. I want to share everything with you"— she stepped back and stared into his amazing blue eyes- —"but you can't ever push me away again. I don't think I would survive losing you a second time. What do you want?"

"I want balance, and love, with you. I want to kiss you whenever I feel like it. I want you in my bed every night." He stroked her hair and she could feel his warm breath as he leaned in close to her.

"Why me after all this time? All the women in the village talk about you, you know? They think you'd be a great catch. Basically, they think you're totally hot, but they think you're Joined to medicine. I see more in you, Kai. They see the surface. I know the man inside. I

111

want to see you smile more. Laugh more."

"Why you? Really? Even a scientist like me knows that somethings just are. You're it for me, Laurel. I've always known it, but I was just too blinded by grief, by my sense of obligation. I'm sorry." He leaned down and kissed the top her head.

"When things get back to normal around here we'll see what happens. This is a big adjustment for both of us at a very emotional time. In the meanwhile, let's just take it one day at a time, okay?"

"That sounds good to me. I'd like to stay with you tonight. I want you to feel safe in my arms. Will you let me share your bed?"

Breathless at the thought of sleeping next to Kai, Laurel could barely whisper a response. "I'd like that."

Kai stepped closer to her and directed her toward the bed. He pulled back the blankets, helped Laurel settle in, and then climbed in next to her from the other side. The bed was small, and their bodies were pressed tightly together. When Kai's front made contact with Laurel's back, she involuntarily thrust her bottom against him.

"Um, Laurel, honey, if you do that, I don't think I'll be able to control myself."

"Oh God, sorry," she said, embarrassed. Laurel pulled her bottom away from him and scooted over a bit.

Kai placed a few soft kisses along her jaw and neck. "Relax, baby, nothing is going to happen tonight. But when it does, I know I'll be the one who sees fireworks, not Quill."

Laurel responded breathlessly, "Goodnight, Kai... I can't wait...for the fireworks."

Chapter Seven

Ashlyn

Trapped, hidden away, her Fire alone might not save Ashlyn, but she could still fight. The bright overhead lights burned her tired eyes. She rubbed at them furiously trying to shake off the feeling of fatigue. Devlin wanted something from her, but what? She needed to escape, except they had weaponized drugs. Not to mention, she was outmanned and outgunned. Still, she pondered her fate with fortitude. Her need to reach out to Hawk tugged at her heart.

Ash couldn't remember ever feeling this tired. Her limbs felt as though they weighed a thousand pounds, and her eyes burned incessantly. She wasn't sure if it was the residual effects of the drugs, or if it was her emotional state. Exhaustion to took hold, and she gave in to it hoping that it would lead her back to Hawk. The tiny bed creaked as she settled herself on the flimsy mattress. Relaxing as much as possible, she let sleep take her. The vibration of heavy footsteps and deep, loud voices rattled her, eradicating any chance of slumber. Her body shook from the inside out. Terror washed over her and stole her breath. "Holy shit! They're coming for me!"

A keypad outside her door beeped distinctively several times before the echo of the lock disengaging reverberated through the small cell. Devlin's dark, menacing form pushed his way inside. He was accompanied by another man. They were flanked by two soldiers dressed in black with weapons strapped to their bodies. The stranger was handsome. He was of average height and appeared fit with salt and pepper hair. His dark eyes seemed cold and merciless, and Ash shuddered from the intensity. He was dressed impeccably in a navy blue suit with thin pinstripes and a deep red tie. His shoes were black and reflected the bright lights from above. He had an air about him that screamed authority and old money.

Ashlyn jumped up feeling way too vulnerable in her position on the bed. The strange man smiled at her, and goosebumps erupted all over her body. He exuded power and hostility. It radiated off him. Ash squared her shoulders and faced the men. "What do you want from me?" she demanded, attempting to appear unflappable.

"Mr. Devlin, it appears our young guest is curious to know of our intentions."

The stranger's voice sounded too calm, dripping with saccharine. She could feel her Fire looming near the surface wanting to be released. Ashlyn's entire body tensed. Her Fire had a will of its own sometimes. She reined in the heat pulling it deeper inside.

"Sir, I was waiting for you to do the honors of explaining all of this to Firecracker here," Devlin responded.

"My name is Ashlyn, you Neanderthal!"

"Well, Ashlyn, my name is Dr. Charles Barrington and I am delighted to finally meet you. I'm sorry I had other business to attend to and couldn't be here when you arrived. As to what I want from you, the answer to that is fairly simple. Everything." He stared, never taking his dark eyes off her. She took a subtle step backward keeping her sharp gaze in his direction.

The ominous way he spoke gave Ash chills. What did he mean, *everything*? "Let me go now, and I won't hurt you!"

"I greatly look forward to you trying, Ashlyn. I'm most anxious to witness, up close, the extent of your abilities."

"You may be able to keep me here for now, but my people will come for me. Then you'll definitely regret taking me." Defiantly, Ash put her hands on her hips and faced off with the men.

"We are most assuredly prepared in the unlikely event that your people ever find you here. You should know your new home is a veritable fortress. Even your people, with their abilities, would be no match for our security measures. I suggest you cooperate. Mr. Devlin here, has a bit of an anger management problem."

The telltale tingles of her Fire caressed her skin. Ashlyn realized she needed to tread carefully with these people especially until she knew exactly what they wanted. She called to her Fire sending it deeper inside. It struggled to be free to protect the Guardian. "I'm warning you. Let me go now."

"My dear Ashlyn, I have absolutely no intention of letting you leave here, now, or ever. I have worked long and hard to get you here. Why on earth would I give you up now? The fun is just about to begin. Isn't that right, Mr. Devlin?" He nodded his head in Devlin's direction. Devlin and the two soldiers stepped closer. Barrington glided back by the door, watching.

There was no stopping it. Flame surged forward. It

wanted out, now. Bursts of red and orange climbed up her arms and down to her hands with a low whooshing sound. Ash was doing her best to keep her Fire in control. She was talking in her head and telling her Flame to stay back.

"Marvelous! Just amazing. She's everything you said, Devlin. Well done." Charles was animated for the first time, a sick excitement on his face.

Devlin's hand, inches away from Ash's shoulder, retracted when she turned toward the bed. "Stay back!" she warned, her voice steadier than she felt. Her Fire swelled. Raising her hands, she hurled the blaze onto the mattress. "I mean it. You're next. If you so much as touch me, you're toast."

"Oh, Firecracker, you wouldn't dare. Because if you do, I'm going take it out on your pretty friend. What was her name? Laurel, right?" Devlin taunted, with a sneer.

Her Fire rose up her arms and down the top of her legs. Ashlyn's voice was laced with venom. "You better not touch her if you know what's good for you! I'll torch this place until it's nothing but cinder."

"Enough! Ashlyn, I expect you to cooperate or Mr. Devlin, and his men here, will kill your friend. I really have no need for her. We are merely keeping her alive as a courtesy to you. Now let us see if you can't put out this fire at once." Charles' voice was smooth and calm even as he demanded her capitulation.

"I want to see Laurel, now. You better not hurt her."

The men inched closer to Ashlyn with their weapons pointed at her. "Firecracker, you had better listen to the boss. He's a man accustomed to getting what he wants, and you definitely don't want to disappoint him. Put out the fire, now." Devlin signaled the soldiers to move in even closer.

Ash needed to protect Laurel until they could find a way out of this madhouse. She had no doubt both men were sincere when they threatened Laurel's life. Ashlyn's Fire fought her for control wanting to lash out again. *Later,* she vowed to the Fire inside her, *you can consume them once Laurel is safe.*

Taking several deep breaths, Ashlyn called back the Flames that devoured the mattress and bedding. The smell of the burnt material permeated the air. The mattress was crisp and blackened with a gaping hole in the center. She commanded her Fire back inside her body pacifying it with her promise of retaliation. Ash was biding her time until she had the opportunity to make Devlin, and now this Charles character, pay.

"Impressive, young Ashlyn. Very impressive. Take her down to the lab so we can get started. We have wasted enough time with this foolish bickering," Barrington stated matter-of-factly.

The two silent soldiers holstered their weapons. Grabbing Ashlyn under her arms they knocked her off balance. Her feet dragged behind her as they yanked her from the cell. Relieved to be out of her tight confines, a blast of fresh air hit her in the face. She still trembled with fear and fought her Fire for Laurel's sake. *Pay attention, where are they taking me?* Ash focused on her surroundings absorbing everything she could about her environment.

Their steps down the long corridor echoed in her ears. Gray door after gray door lined the hallway every few feet. More gray, the cinderblock walls all around felt like they were closing in. She had no shoes, and the tile floor chilled her already cold feet. Two more soldiers stood on either side of a door leaning against the wall where the hallway ended. They straightened immediately upon seeing them approach. Ash wondered if that might be the way out of this maze.

Was Laurel in one of those cells? Unable to resist the urge she called out, "Laurel! Laurel!" She was answered with a hard-stinging slap to her cheek bringing tears to her eyes. The metallic taste of blood filled her mouth.

"Keep your mouth shut, or we'll shut it for you," the soldier said.

Even though she was scared and in pain, she concentrated on memorizing her surroundings. This new hallway was longer than her prison block. The first room they passed on her right side was large with a glass front. There were at least half a dozen computer stations with empty chairs. The next room had only a small window in the door. She thought she caught a glimpse of a wall of television monitors, but she couldn't see what was being shown because they dragged her by too quickly. They passed a few closed doors until coming to a stop in front of a double set. The word *Laboratory* was stenciled across and broken in the middle by the seam between the doors. The soldiers' tight grips cut off her circulation. Her arms ached as they continued to drag her to her impending doom. The computerized beeping of a keypad droned in her ears as Barrington punched in the code.

Ashlyn's stomach tightened in knots as she took in her surroundings. The space was expansive. In the center of the room stood an operating table fashioned with metal restraints. A huge surgical light hung down above the table. There were tons of cabinets, some with glass fronts and others with solid doors. In the corner of the room there was a large stall that resembled a shower. There didn't appear to be any plumbing or a door. It was glass on two sides, and the remaining two sides were made of the same cinderblock as in her cell.

The fear she had been repressing came barreling into her system triggering her self-preservation and her Fire. The familiar sensation crept along her nerve ending sending signals of warning to her brain. Ash was no longer in command. Her Fire took over and dominated her thoughts. Flames shot out of the tips of her fingers and then spread all over her body, catching the men's clothing alight. She could feel the thin material of her hospital gown disintegrate. The soldiers rolled on the ground attempting to extinguish Ashlyn's Fire that now ravaged them. Fury and fear blurred her vision. She didn't see Devlin approach, but she knew it was him when she felt a tremendous jolt of electricity. Ashlyn went completely rigid and was knocked right off her feet. The floor came up to meet her sending pain radiating through her entire body. Her Fire instantly snuffed out, Ashlyn twitched on the ground making sounds she did not recognize. Every muscle and nerve in her body was reacting to the strange intrusion.

Ashlyn felt her body rise off the ground as if being carried. Her limbs hung uselessly and continued to convulse as she was placed firmly on the table. Devlin roughly grabbed her wrists and manacled her in place with the cold, steely cuffs. Someone took hold of her ankles, and Ashlyn kicked out fighting the whole way. Her Fire remained subdued by the shock. No matter how hard Ashlyn fought, without her Fire, she was defenseless against their strength. Powerful hands gripped her legs like a vise restraining her with ease.

"I warned you about misbehaving, didn't I? I suppose we'll have to sedate you to conduct the Doc's initial experiments. Then, I think I'll pay sweet Laurel a visit. Nighty night, Firecracker," Devlin said, in a sarcastic tone.

Silently, Barrington came up beside her with a syringe in his hand. Seething, bitter heat emanated from him. He grabbed her arm roughly and jabbed the needle into her flesh. Ashlyn felt the sting before darkness took her completely. She stretched her mind reaching for Hawk. The walls around her seemed to be melting away, and then blackness overwhelmed her, taking her.

****

Hawk

As Hawk paced, he glanced down at his watch for the tenth time. "Where the hell are you, Kai?" He was anxious to get on the road for their drive to the University. He stopped and bent over his stomach in knots. "Damn it! She's running out of time!" He had to find answers.

Kai knocked on the door and walked in. "Ready when you are."

"It took you long enough. Let's get going," Hawk snipped.

Kai didn't bother with a retort. He simply turned on his heels and headed right back out Hawk's front door. Hawk suspected Kai understood his state of mind, so he didn't bother apologizing. Hawk climbed into the SUV's driver's seat while Kai walked around to get in the other side. His friend only had one leg in the vehicle when Hawk started to pull away. Kai's right leg trailed along banging into the side of the car and the road until he managed to pull it back inside. When he was fully seated, he slammed the door with a loud thud.

"What the hell, man? I know you're worried, but you've got to get a grip." Kai bent down and brushed off his pant leg. "You're not going to be able to help Ash if you don't keep it together. Everyone is concerned about her. I know it's not the same as it is for you, but everyone in Aether cares about Ashlyn. The entire village wants to see her back home where she belongs."

Hawk let out a deep breath he hadn't realized he was holding. "I'm really sorry, buddy. You know I'm usually pretty levelheaded, but I can't stop thinking about Ash. If anything happens to her, I just don't know what I'll do. This not knowing where she is, what they might be doing to her, is killing me."

"I get it. I do. But try to keep calm. We're going to find her."

After they cleared the air, there wasn't much to say, and they rode for a while in a comfortable silence. Out of nowhere, Hawk's body suddenly went rigid. He convulsed violently, and the SUV screeched as it zigzagged across the road. Kai reacted by grabbing the wheel and wrenching the vehicle to the side of the road. Clouds of dirt rose up surrounding them as rocks pinged off the sides of the SUV's body and windows. Kai slammed the shift into park, and the car lurched to an abrupt stop jolting them both forward.

"Hawk! Can you hear me?"

Hawk panted heavily as his muscles continued to twitch uncontrollably. Kai reached over and reclined

Hawk's seat. He took his pulse and checked his pupils for responsiveness with a flashlight he found in the glovebox. As quickly as the episode began, it subsided.

"It's Ash," Hawk said. Grabbing the center console, he struggled to sit up. "They're hurting her. I felt it." He rubbed his temples. "It was like I got zapped or something."

"It appears your central nervous system was temporarily hijacked. Most likely from an electric pulse that was emitted. The pulse matches those used by your neurons which transfer information between your brain and your muscles. Your nerves were flooded with pulses similar to their natural frequency and strength. Normal signals get drowned out and muscles contract uncontrollably," Kai explained, in his typical scientific manner.

"Wait a minute. Are you saying I got Tasered?"

"Um, yes, sorry, I'm doing it again, aren't I?" Kai asked, sheepishly.

"Yeah, you could say that. How come I never noticed what a total nerd you are? Am I going to be okay? More importantly, do you think Ash is okay?" Hawk raised his seat back to its normal position.

"Yes, you both should be fine. The effects are temporary. I have to admit, I'm pretty amazed that you experienced the same physical reaction as Ashlyn. It's not that I didn't believe you about the connection, but this is an entirely different level. Tell me what you felt."

"I'm not sure really. We were driving along and then wham! I felt Ash. I felt her fear, her anger, and then her pain. Holy shit, Kai, what's happening to me?"

"I truly don't have a clue. What did Bear say?"

"He didn't have that much to share. I wish there was someone who could tell me more about this Guardian power, I feel so helpless."

"You better let me drive. The Taser can impair a person's ability to remember and process information for a short period of time after the jolt."

Reluctantly, Hawk stepped out of the truck. He went around to the passenger's side while Kai climbed over the console into the driver's seat. As the vehicle merged back onto the road, Hawk settled in and thought about Ashlyn. Without a doubt, the connection between them appeared to be building. He could only imagine how far it would go.

Hawk fought to keep his eyes open, but fatigue quickly consumed him. He was being pulled into a state beyond relaxation. A small part of him wanted to protect himself and sever the connection, but Ash's lure, like a siren, was too strong.

She called to him, "Hawk? Please hear me."

"I'm here, Ash. Can you feel me?"

"Yes! Yes, I feel you. Oh God, I thought I might never be able to reach you again." Tears slipped down Ash's cheeks.

Hawk's heart broke as he felt the warm moisture on his own skin. "This is the oddest sensation." Finally, he believed this connection to Ash was real. "Are you all right, honey? Where are you?"

"I'm okay for now. I've been moved to some kind of lab, and they've given me drugs again. I think I might be knocked out. It seems like the only way I can connect to you."

"Do you know where they've taken you?"

"I don't know where the lab is. When they first

took us, I was unconscious. They haven't let me see Laurel. I'm so worried about her."

"Ash, Laurel isn't there. She's home in Aether. She was in the Medical Center for a while. They drugged her, but Kai found an antidote. She's safe."

Hawk could sense Ash's relief as he felt her tears pour down her face unchecked. It was amazing when they opened the gates to Ash's gift, how quickly he was able to see the world through her eyes and heart.

"Thank the God and Goddess she's safe. The evil bastard who took me, his name is Devlin. He told me they had Laurel, and they would kill her if I didn't cooperate with them. They want something from me, Hawk. Something to do with my powers, but I'm not sure what. There was another man, too, his name is Charles, Charles something, oh shit, I can't remember his last name. My head feels so fuzzy…Hawk?"

"Ashlyn, listen to me. I. Will. Find you. Can you hear me? Ash?" Despair shattered Hawk. Ashlyn was gone, again. "No! Come back! Ashlyn! Come back to me."

Strong hands shook Hawk's shoulders repeatedly. Opening his eyes, he found Kai hovering over him inches from his face. "Hawk, you were screaming. Are you okay?"

Hawk slammed his fist into the dashboard. "No, I am not okay. I was with Ashlyn. She's in serious trouble. They want something from her, her powers, she thinks. She's been drugged repeatedly and is in some sort of lab. She's terrified, Kai, I could sense it; we're connected. The name of the prick who took her is Devlin. Also, a Charles somebody, she couldn't remember his last name. She faded and then the connection was gone, again." Hawk appreciated the gesture when Kai put a firm hand on his shoulder.

"We're here. So if you're up to it, let's do this."

The two entered the library using false student identification cards their tech guys made for them. Aether may not currently have internet access due to security reasons, but they were certainly not lacking in technological knowledge and training. Some of the Protectors were as well versed as any American government expert. In fact, they were days away from opening a tech center which would house a secured system capable of avoiding tracking of any kind.

Shortly, Aether would be equipped with the most advanced, untraceable computers in existence. The people would no longer be forced to go outside the village to obtain information. Aether could remain off the grid but would now have access to any and all information they required to monitor the outside world. Although the people lived a relatively simple life in balance and harmony with the four Elements, they were not naive. The outside world continued to develop, and the Aetherians needed to keep up in order to maintain their anonymity and ensure their people's safety.

Hawk lowered his large frame into a relatively small seat which creaked under his weight. Kai followed suit beside him and immediately began typing. They learned that CEB Laboratories was a massive corporation. They owned at least a dozen facilities in the Northeast and were beginning to branch out farther west. The company's primary focus appeared to be the development and sales of pharmaceuticals.

"All this information about the lab is great, but we still need to figure out the possible connection to the

Renegades and their involvement with this lab. I think we should try to expand our search to the personnel associated with CEB. I'll keep digging for more information on the research and development, and you check the human resources," Kai suggested.

"I just have a gut feeling there is more to this than meets the eye. I'm not convinced this is the work of the Renegades. It doesn't add up to me. To what end would it serve to take Ashlyn?" Hawk questioned, rhetorically. They both worked silently for some time, clicking on link after link. "Hey look, Kai, I found a list of the company's board of directors. The president and founder is a man named Dr. Charles Edward Barrington III. Ash mentioned a guy named Charles. Seems like way too big of a coincidence that it's not the same man. No mention of a man named Devlin though. Here take a look."

Hawk turned his monitor toward Kai so he could more easily read the information on the screen. He paused when he noticed an abrupt change in Kai's demeanor. "Kai? Are you all right?"

Kai paled as he gripped the desk in front of him tightly and gawked at the screen, speechless. He was acting as if this Dr. Barrington guy was boring holes straight through him. Kai was quiet for a moment before he spoke. "Print out everything you can on CEB and Barrington. We need to get back to Aether immediately. I can't believe this is happening. I know who has Ashlyn. You were right, I don't think the Renegades are involved. Dear God, this is all my fault."

Chapter Eight

Kai

Guilt swamped him along with shame and dishonor. How did Kai begin to tell Hawk about his history with Barrington? After all these years, he couldn't believe Charles Barrington was back in his life. Hawk was quiet on their way back to the SUV, and he wasn't sure what to make of his friend's silence.

Hawk held out his hand demanding the keys. "I'll drive. You start talking." He guided Kai to the car with a gentle shove. "I want to know what the hell is going on, Kai." The slamming of the vehicle's doors echoed through the parking lot as they climbed in.

Kai turned to him. "I know I owe you an explanation. I just want to say something before I say anything else. I'm so sorry, Hawk. Really, truly, sorry." He dropped his head into his hands and didn't look up. "I never in a million years thought my association with Barrington would have led to something like this."

Hawk took his friend by the shoulder making him look up. "What the fuck are you talking about?" He released him. "How do you know this guy?"

"I met him over forty years ago. Charles Barrington was my roommate in med school." Kai's first meeting with Charles had left an indelible impression on him even after all this time.

****

With a large duffel slung over one shoulder, a backpack, and two boxes that he had precariously stacked on top of one another, Kai stepped off the dorm's elevator. He exhaled forcefully and squared his shoulders ready to settle into his new home. After fifteen years, Kai finally received permission from the Elders to attend medical school. He felt both upbeat and uneasy at the same time. The door to room 515 stood ajar, and Kai shoved it open with his foot. One of the boxes crashed to the ground with a resounding thud.

"Damn it!" Kai grumbled, as he bent and grabbed the upturned box.

Directly in front of him, a pair of shiny loafers with pennies in them stared him in the face. Kai followed the line of the stranger's legs which were encased in pressed Khakis and topped off with an ultra-starched looking striped button-down shirt. The arrogance in the young man's tone was the first thing that struck with Kai even before his words registered.

"They assured me I would have this room to myself, so I'm certain you are in the wrong place."

"Oh, uh, sorry. They told me room 515. This is 515, isn't it?"

"It is indeed 515, but I arranged for a single," the young man insisted. He rolled his eyes at Kai with a look of irritation on his face.

"Okay, well, um, I'll just leave my stuff here for a minute and go back downstairs and check with the housing department. I'm sure it's just a mix-up."

"Yes, you do that."

Kai's upbeat mood evaporated and only uneasiness remained as he left the room. The very first person he met' seemed to dislike him on contact. Perhaps the

Elders had been right, maybe he was too different to fit in with the humans.

Kai returned with the housing supervisor who appeared flustered and jittery. They entered the room and an older man dressed in the finest suit Kai had ever seen was standing beside Mr. Penny Loafers.

The gentleman spoke with upper crust accent Kai was unable to identify. "There seems to be a problem here. I arranged for my son to have a private room. He is not sharing with some stranger."

The supervisor wiped his damp brow with a handkerchief. "I'm s-so-sorry, Dr. Barrington, b-b-but the dorm is overcrowded. No one is allowed to have a single room. As soon as we have an opening, your son is first on the list. Please accept my sincere apologies."

"Completely unacceptable answer. Your incompetence is astounding. I'm going to have to contact someone with actual power not some stuttering fool. You are dismissed," the senior Barrington reprimanded. His tone held an authoritative quality that was cold, calm, and menacing all at the same time.

The poor man exited quickly with his head down low. Kai wasn't sure how to react to the strange tension left hanging in the room like an entity all its own. As both Barrington's sized him up, he felt hesitant and lacking under their scrutiny.

He offered his hand as a way of introduction. "Hi, I'm Kai, Kai Sanders." Ignoring Kai's outstretched hand, the men continued to gaze at him with distaste. Not sure what else to do, Kai retracted his hand awkwardly. He crossed the room and began unpacking his belongings.

Dr. Barrington addressed Kai as if he were a small

child, or an idiot. Using a tone Kai was unaccustomed to hearing in his tight knit, respectful community, he spoke, "I am Dr. Charles Barrington and this is my son, also named Charles. I expect you to stay out of his way and not interfere with his medical education in any way. Charles has a legacy to live up to. If I find out you are distracting him in any way, I will have you removed from this medical school. I have many connections here, so you can take me at my word." Kai's mouth dropped open and his only response was to nod. Barrington then turned to his son. "Charles, John is waiting for me with the car downstairs. You know what is expected of you. I suggest you do not disappoint me. Nothing less than perfection. There is no number two in the Barrington household."

Kai sighed in relief as the door closed firmly behind Dr. Barrington. "Whoa, no pressure. Are you all right there, Charlie?"

"My name is Charles and if you know what's good for you, you will mind your own damn business."

****

Shaking off the memory, Kai had explained to Hawk about the pressure Charles' father put on him. "I had desperately hoped that Charles wouldn't be like his father and that we could be friends, but unfortunately, that wasn't the case."

"What happened?" Hawk asked impatiently.

"Charles was angry and tense constantly. He loathed my presence. No matter what I did, or how hard I tried to be friendly, or helpful, it made no difference. Of course, he had no way of knowing that I was twice his age and from Aether. Admittedly, my life experience and my gifts gave me numerous advantages in med school."

Although Kai had excelled academically, he longed for home and the warmth of its people. He had missed Laurel every day just as he had for the previous fifteen years. Even though they weren't together any longer, at least in Aether, he saw her regularly. His father had been right about what he said the day Storm died. Pushing Laurel away was the biggest mistake of his life. He didn't realize it at the time, but he would never love another woman the way he loved Laurel.

Kai continued, "Living among the ordinary humans, away from Aether, was beyond challenging. I despised hiding who I really was. Plus, Charles persistently stalked me. He was always lurking in the shadows. It was as if he knew I was concealing something." Kai rubbed at his temples. "That's when the threats began," he said with a sigh. "He told me he knew I was cheating, and he was determined to prove it."

Hawk asked his friend, sounding puzzled, "How come you never told me this was happening? I know we didn't get a chance to speak very often, but we always hung out every time you came home from school. You never even hinted something was wrong."

Kai hung his head. "I never told anyone how miserable I was. Especially the first year when I had to share a room with Charles. I didn't want everyone to worry, or worse yet, ask me to give up and return home to Aether. I felt it was my duty and my responsibility to our people to become a doctor. In hindsight that was another error in judgement." Sarcasm laced his voice on his last words.

"You couldn't have known, Kai. Barrington was

just a kid at the time. Who would have ever thought he would turn into such a nightmare for Aether, and Ash."

Kai looked up and let out a huge breath before he went on. "Charles' resentment toward me grew on a daily basis. He became increasingly obsessed with me, and he clearly interpreted my abilities and intelligence to be false."

Jumping in, Hawk said, "That's total bullshit! Everyone knows you're the smartest guy around. We both know it's not the case with everyone in Aether. You being smart has nothing to do with Aether, Kai. That's all you, buddy."

"Thanks for saying that. But you don't understand. His need to please his father was psychoneurotic, it was unnerving to say the least. Charles strived to be number one, but he was always one step behind me. It made him crazy, I should've seen there was something deeper. He grew more and more cold and merciless always sabotaging my work, wrecking my lab experiments, and endeavoring to turn the other students against me. He feed them lies about my alleged deceiving ways."

Hawk interjected, "No one could possibly believe such a load of crap about you. What happened after that?"

"Most of the other students became accustomed to Charles' overly competitive nature and stopped believing I was a cheater. I was unfailingly polite, helpful, and friendly to everyone but never formed any close bonds. The others were friendly in return, but I was forced to maintain my distance, keeping every relationship casual." Kai's shoulders dropped and he lowered his head shaking it back and forth. "I guess I felt pretty alone at the time."

Hawk glanced up from the road to look at his friend. "I'm so sorry I didn't know. Maybe I could've helped you somehow."

"I managed to get through it. After the first desolate year living with Charles, things improved for me. I secured a single room on the third floor far away from Charles Barrington. Though, my true solace was the water, floating, diving, it didn't matter to me. The feel of the cool water on my skin gave me the comfort and feeling of home. It was during one of my excursions to the water senior year that had likely confirmed Charles' suspicions about my gifts." Kai was lost once again in his memories of the past.

****

Kai crept along under the cover of darkness. At the time, he was unaware Charles had tracked him from the dorm. When he reached the lake, he removed his clothing and placed it neatly on the grass. Diving deep into the water to calm his ever-present anxiety, he swam gliding along the crystal-clear bottom. Surfacing near the floating dock in the middle of the lake, he brought forth his power connecting him to the water. Kai created a wave and the whitecap crested gently surrounding him to his waist. Slowly he coasted along allowing the force to guide him. When he neared the dock, the swell lifted his body until he was level with the edge, and he simply stepped off onto the rough wooden surface.

A thump against the dock startled Kai. When he turned, he gazed down at a small canoe bobbing in the wake. There, glaring back, was his nemesis Charles Barrington with his mouth agape. "Www-what the hell are you? How did you do that?"

"I have no idea what you're talking about, Charlie." Kai used the nickname Barrington despised. He knew he probably shouldn't provoke him further, but he couldn't resist.

"I saw you stay under the water for a really long time. And then…then you came straight up out of the water and onto the dock without using the ladder. I-I-I saw you. You're a freak, Sanders! I always knew there was something very odd about you, but I had no idea to what extent."

Stepping closer to the canoe, Kai relaxed his posture. "Listen, Charles, I don't know what you think you saw, but I didn't do anything." Retreating back a bit, his hands raised in surrender, Kai pacified Charles. "It's late, and it's dark. You've been working really hard lately, and perhaps your imagination is running away with you."

"I'm not sure exactly what I saw, but I know I saw something." Agitated, Charles rocked the canoe splashing water onto the dock and Kai's bare feet. "You're some kind of mutant! I may not be able to prove it to anybody right now, but in time I will. And you'll be sorry."

"Charles, I really don't understand why you harbor such resentment toward me. What have I ever done to offend you? Your family obviously has lots of money. You drive a Ferrari for God's sake. You're one of the top students in our class. You have a lovely girlfriend."

"I'm supposed to be number one, you fool, not you." Pointing back and forth between himself and Kai, Charles' voice became shrill. "My father and grandfather were both number one in their med school classes. It's expected of me. If it weren't for you, I would be. As for Olivia, I better not even catch you looking at her."

Olivia Royce was Charles' girlfriend. She was still an undergraduate, and all the guys were crazy for her. Olivia was beautiful, smart, and sweet. Kai never understood why she was with Barrington.

"I have no interest in Olivia. My only interest is to finish our last few months here and match with a top surgical residency. I'll tell you what, you stay away from me and I'll stay away from you," Kai proposed.

"I'm not bargaining with you, Sanders, you're a freak. You think you're better than the rest of us. Just stay away from me." Using his paddle, Charles pushed off the dock and had disappeared into the darkness, leaving Kai speechless.

****

"After our encounter I steered clear of Barrington," Kai admitted. "He didn't so much as acknowledge my existence after that night. I thought he might be scared of me and that was why he backed off. I guess I was wrong. I don't know how he knows about Aether. And I certainly don't know how he knows about Ashlyn."

"It seems crazy this guy could hate you so much after all these years. Why wait so long? And what the hell does he want with Ash?"

"I haven't seen the man since a mandatory conference when we were all residents. He was the same asshole then, too. He got drunk and was belittling Olivia in front of everyone. He went off with another woman. It was strange. There was a sadness in her eyes and a darkness. But I got the sense she didn't really care that Charles left with someone else. She wouldn't tell me anything, but I knew she was hiding something. I remember we sat at the bar for a long time talking and drinking. I was drunk and lonely. She was beautiful, soft, and lovely. We probably got closer than we should've, and I worried about her safety if Charles ever found out." Kai brushed off the memory of the intimacy. "They didn't show up the next day at the brunch the University hosted. I often wondered how Olivia fared, but I never saw either of them again after that night."

The console vibrated as Hawk's phone jumped around interrupting the conversation. Kai picked it up and listened for a few minutes before closing the phone. "Hawk, we really need to hurry. Apparently, there are some very odd things going on in Aether."

****

Laurel

Curled up on her couch Laurel felt safe if not a bit smothered by those who loved her. Her parents truly meant well, but their hovering was driving her insane. She couldn't really blame them after what had happened to her, and especially after Ashlyn was taken from Aether.

She nibbled on the corner of her thumbnail as nagging worry about Ash persisted. Laurel's self-condemnation consumed her causing her stomach to tighten in knots. Ash had sacrificed herself to save her. Debilitating nightmares plagued Laurel. Every time she closed her eyes, ghastly figures surrounded her with guns. Massive men dressed in black, with concealed faces, chased her through the woods. When she awoke, her heart was pounding and her palms were sticky with sweat.

A light rapping on her front door chased away the horrible images. Yanking it open, she revealed a serious looking Kai. "Hi, mind if I come in. I need to talk to you?"

Stepping out of the way to make room for him to enter, she closed her eyes for a brief second. "Of course, come in."

"I have to tell you something important."

"Oh my God, is it Ash?" she whispered, in a barely audible tone. Laurel all but dragged him to the couch and pulled him to sit beside her.

"Yes and no. We haven't found her if that's what you mean, but we did discover some very important information at the library." She noticed the rise and fall of his chest and his loud exhale before he seemed able to continue. "First of all, you should know Hawk made contact with her again and she's hanging in there for now. He told her you were home and safe. Hawk said she was very relieved and happy to hear you hadn't been taken. I think their connection is getting stronger, and hopefully we can use it to our advantage somehow. Hawk dropped me off and went to see his grandfather. Apparently, there are some odd things going on, in, and around the South Tower."

"Yes, I heard. The Vessel of Fire has been surging with flame one minute, and then the next moment, the flame has been barely visible. Also, Rowan told my mother the flame on their stove top seems to have a mind of its own. There were even some small fires breaking out in the Village Square in front of the Tower. Everyone is really nervous. Raven and Sol were up in the Atrium seeing if they could figure it out. It seems the balance of the Elements is off with Ashlyn in captivity. We need her back."

"Listen, Laurel, about that. I want you to hear this from me before everyone in Aether is talking about it."

"What is it? You're scaring me."

"I'm sorry, honey. I don't want to scare you, but I need to be completely honest with you. I can't stand the thought of giving you another reason to hate me, but it's my fault that Ash was taken." Kai looked down at the floor seemingly unable to make eye contact with her. He looked worried, and Laurel wondered what he was thinking. He had asked for her forgiveness, and she was really trying to let go of the hurt and pain of the past. There was obviously something else going on, something connected to Ashlyn.

Laurel took his hand. "Don't be ridiculous. I could never hate you, Kai. Well, maybe I hated you a little," she said, with a half joking smirk, "but how on earth could Ash being taken possibly be your fault?"

Kai gently tugged his hand away. Taken aback, she couldn't understand why he suddenly wouldn't touch her. He proceeded to tell her the entire sordid tale about his relationship with Charles Barrington. He included Barrington's connection to CEB laboratories, Charles' suspicions about Kai, and even about his one night encounter with Olivia Royce. "I want to be totally honest with you, and I don't want any secrets between us. I've kept my distance from you for far too long."

Laurel listened quietly allowing him to finish before speaking. "Kai, hear me, and hear me well. Just because Barrington resented you, does not, in any way, make this your fault. You had no way of knowing he would be so full of vengeance especially after so many years. How could you possibly know he found out about Aether?"

"What I just can't figure out is how he knew about the village. I mean, I know he was suspicious of me and my powers, but I didn't think he really processed what he saw that night on the lake. And after that, I was more cautious than ever, and I rarely used my gifts in even the smallest of ways. Why wait so long for vengeance? And what could his hatred for me possibly have to do with Ash?"

"I understand what you are saying. I do. Obviously, Barrington has some sort of sick plan in mind, and those men he sent, they meant serious business."

Kai dug into his pocket and pulled out his buzzing phone, indicating a text message. "Hawk is on his way over, he'll be here any second," he said. Abruptly halting their conversation, he moved to the door.

Hawk walked straight in as Kai stood with the door wide open as a way of a greeting. He went directly to Laurel and placed a kiss on the top of her head. "Hey, how are you feeling?"

"I'm doing a lot better, just a little tired still. The truth is my parents are driving me completely bananas. Can you say helicopter?" She chuckled, while twirling her finger in a circle.

"I'm sure you can understand how they feel. We all thought we might lose you. I know it was frightening for you, but it was pure torture for Canyon and Zarina. They love you with everything they have," Kai chimed in.

"Of course, I understand, but it doesn't make it any easier to deal with. Enough about me, what's up, Hawk?"

"The Elders want to see all of us. Are you feeling

up to it, Laurel?"

Laurel jumped to her feet ready to walk out the door immediately. Kai bent down dangling her shoes in front of her, laughing. "I know you're itching to get out of here, but maybe you want to put these on? I'm also going to send your father a quick text to let him know where we went. I don't want him to have a conniption."

Rolling her eyes, she yanked her shoes out of Kai's hands and shoved her feet in without untying them. "Happy? Let's get out of here before I go stir crazy."

The three walked in silence toward the Council Chambers. Laurel's knuckles brushed against Kai's. He grasped her hand tightly. The heat of his touch warmed her as he intertwined their fingers. Gently squeezing his hand, she offered her support. Charles Barrington was to blame, not Kai. Laurel was certain when Hawk and the other Protectors got ahold of Barrington, he would surely regret messing with the people of Aether and especially with Ashlyn.

The large wooden door to the Council Chambers gave a loud creak as Hawk pushed it opened. Bear was standing by the reception desk waiting for them when the groan of the old wood announced their arrival. Laurel swallowed a lump in her throat as the imposing looking Elder approached her. He enfolded her in his arms hugging her a little too firmly.

"Um, Grandfather, you want to ease up there? I think you're crushing her," Hawk said, coming to her rescue.

"I'm so sorry, Laurel dear. I'm just so happy to see you up and around. We have all been terribly worried about you."

"Thank you, Sir. I'm feeling fine now thanks to

Kai and of course, the Protectors for finding the drug."

"Please join me inside. The rest of the Elders, along with River, are waiting to speak with all of you. Hawk filled me in on what's been uncovered, but I want the others to hear it directly from the three people most closely involved in this situation."

Laurel seized Kai's hand offering a silent pledge she would stand by him regardless of the Elders reaction. She knew he would feel guilty in spite of what anyone else thought. Kai anchored her to his side seeming to not only accept her support, but truly need it. Even with all that was going on, her world felt right again with Kai at her side.

Power emanated through the Council Chamber. Laurel gasped as they entered the grand space. The room was cavernous minus the expected echo. Her belly fluttered, and she felt like an intruder being in the Chamber for the very first time. The room was dominated by a massive conference table. The highly glossed wooden surface reflected the pendent lights hanging above creating a magical luminescence.

Bear gestured toward a beautiful seating area large enough to accommodate a dozen people, and yet it still felt personal and cozy. "Please make yourselves comfortable."

Laurel ran her hand over the smooth leather. "We're sitting here?"

Bear faced them, turning serious. "This is not an inquisition, my dear. We are merely seeking detailed information so we may save our Fire Guardian and protect Aether."

They had yet to take their seats when the other Elders and River filed in. Kai turned toward Laurel and looked into her eyes the way she hoped he would have when Storm died. His gaze was intense as his steadfast grip tightened around her hand. He clearly needed her, and she squeezed back in response. They remained standing out of respect to their community's highest-ranking members. The Elders were indeed an awe-inspiring group, not to mention, quite an imposing collection of individuals. Together they could make even the strongest of people squirm.

Taking their seats, Laurel wedged herself in between Kai and Hawk. Inching closer to Kai, her leg made contact with his muscled thigh and her body tensed.

She focused on Bear instead of her racing emotions. Bear's broad shoulders filled the oversized chair he occupied. His strong presence made her sit up a little taller. "Welcome to the Council Chambers. We thank you all for coming. I know I speak for all of us when I say we are very grateful you have been returned to us, Laurel. Can you please tell us what happened the night you and Ashlyn were attacked?"

Laurel cleared her throat fearful nothing would come out when she spoke. She rehashed the horrible events of the night she and Ash had been pursued by the masked men in black. She praised Kai and the Protectors for saving her from the tether of the drug she had been subjected to. When she was finished speaking she blew out a breath, tears welled in her eyes but she did not let them fall.

"Thank you for sharing with us, Laurel. And may I say again, we are all very relieved you have rebounded from your frightening ordeal so quickly," Vale said.

Bear smiled warmly at Laurel and then turned to

his grandson. "Hawk, I'd really appreciate it if you could share with the others what you have told me about your telepathic connection to Ashlyn."

Unfolding his large frame from his seat, Hawk stood. Appearing edgy and fierce, he paced around the small area giving a brief history of he and Ashlyn. When he finished, Hawk leaned down with his hands on his knees breathing deeply for a moment. Then, straightening his powerful body, he concluded with a plea for action.

Raven spoke, "Hawk, thank you so much for disclosing this personal information. I want you to know your connection to Ashlyn may be paramount in locating her. The entire Council, as well as your brother Protectors, will leave no stone unturned until we find Ashlyn and bring those responsible for her capture to justice."

"Thank you so much, Raven." Hawk gave her a grateful look.

Next, Bear stood and approached Kai, placing his hands on his shoulders. "Listen, Kai, everyone here believes you are in no way responsible for any of this. So, relax. Please just tell us how you know Dr. Charles Barrington and whatever you think may help find Ashlyn."

Kai ran his fingers through his hair leaving it standing on end. "I'm so sorry I brought Barrington's personal grudge against me to Aether."

He dispatched every sordid detail and then slumped in his seat, drained. Laurel was genuinely proud of Kai. She had a feeling sharing his memories of that time was probably one of the most difficult things he ever had to do.

"Thank you, Kai. We appreciate how forthcoming you have been with this Council. Again, please be assured we support you," Bear stated.

Laurel was relieved for Kai, but he still looked miserable. She was aware it would take a great deal of convincing on her part before he was able to forgive himself. Ashlyn's return would certainly go a long way in helping him to recover and release his guilt. She addressed the Council, "What can we do to help? Ash is my dearest friend in the world, and I will do anything to ensure her safe return to Aether."

"We appreciate the sentiment, but right now the Council and the Protectors are going to meet to formulate a plan to rescue our Fire Guardian from these loathsome barbarians. We will most assuredly let you know if you can be of any further assistance. Laurel and Kai, we thank you for coming. Hawk, please remain for the meeting," Bear said, dismissing them.

Laurel and Kai said their goodbyes and left the Council Chambers. She gently tugged on Kai's hand steering them toward his house. Kai paused. "Wait a minute, where are we going? I need to get you home to rest."

"I know how hard that just was for you. I'm not leaving you alone right now. We'll go to your place and talk."

"I really don't think that's a good idea. I-I don't trust myself to be alone with you right now." Kai pulled his hand free of Laurel's grasp. "The other night in the medical center you were confused and feeling vulnerable. I took advantage of you. I'm sorry. I couldn't help myself; I wanted so much to be near you." Kai reached out and ran his hands up and down her arms. "I can't bear to hurt you again, Laurel, and if I'm with you, alone, I'm afraid all that is pent up inside may be unleashed." His smoldering stare burned her.

"What are you talking about?" Laurel's voice quivered.

"God, Laurel, I never stopped loving you. Every time I'm near you, all I can think about is stripping you bare. I want you underneath me calling out my name. But after everything I told you about my past with Barrington and Olivia, I know you probably don't want anything to do with me." He hung his head, shaking it back and forth.

"It was pretty shocking to hear, but I'm proud of you. It was really brave the way you told your story. And you're right, considering our past history, I may be the most gullible woman ever. But the truth is, fifty years hasn't changed the way I feel when I'm near you. I love you, too, Kai, but I am afraid of being shut out by you again, pushed away. I know I should still be mad at you, but I can't seem to help myself where you're concerned. I lose all rational thought." Laurel wrapped her arms around his neck and looked into his spectacular blue eyes.

Leaning in closer, Kai breathed hotly against Laurel's neck. "The way you smell drives me crazy, like vanilla and a sweetness all your own. Oh God, I know I don't deserve you, but please give me another chance. I've dreamed about being with you for so long. I promise to never shut you out again."

He bent down to Laurel lightly pressing his lips to hers. His were warm and soft. Deepening the kiss, he opened his mouth. His tongue invaded and she responded with a low moan. Laurel could feel Kai's need as he pulled her even closer. She felt him everywhere. Desire heated her body, and tingles of awareness danced from head to toe settling between her legs.

Panting, Kai broke their contact. "I think we should get out of the Square if we don't want all of Aether talking about us tomorrow."

Laurel yanked her phone from her pocket. "Let me just send a text to tell my parents I won't be home." After recent events, Laurel didn't want them to worry about her.

"Are you sure, honey? No pressure," Kai asked.

"All set. Come on, let's go. I can't wait to see your house. Last time we were together you were still living with your parents." Laurel leaned in close her lips brushing against his neck. She whispered in his ear, "Remember how creative we had to be to find a place to be alone?"

Kai took her hand and led her the short distance to his home. He stopped by the front door. "Are you completely sure you want to come inside with me? I'll understand if you've changed your mind."

"I want this as much as I think you do."

"In that case—" Kai tugged her inside. He didn't so much close the door, but push her against it, shutting it with a loud bang. Every ridge of his hard body made contact with hers. Their breaths were one. Kai's hands were everywhere at once. One tangled in her hair, the other snaked around her waist keeping her close. Finally, he tore himself away. "I'm so sorry. I seem to lose control when you're near me. I want this to be special. Please tell me you want this to happen, Laurel?"

"I'm scared, but I definitely want this. I've missed you. Please, Kai, make love to me. I've never wanted anyone more."

With that last statement hanging in the air, Kai swept her into his arms. Laurel squealed as he carried her to the bedroom. Using his foot, Kai forced his way into the room holding Laurel the entire time. He gently brought her over to the bed never losing contact. Laurel sank into the downy mattress when Kai's muscled form pressed erotically against hers. She saw the heat in his eyes and knew he was going to make her every fantasy a reality. Kai would definitely remind her of the passion they had once shared.

Chapter Nine

Ashlyn

Awakening gradually, Ashlyn fought through the haze clouding her mind. She winced as pain radiated through her entire body. Where was she? And why did everything hurt? Taking a quick inventory of her injuries, she gently probed the angry abrasions which burned her wrists and ankles. Mottled blues and purples marred the fair skin inside her forearms. She had several puncture wounds running along the length of the sensitive area. The damage stung under her touch.

Placing her hands on the floor, she slowly hoisted herself into a sitting position. Her arms screamed in pain, and she took a minute to catch her breath. Chilled to the bone, she rested against a cold, hard, cinderblock wall. Ashlyn closed her eyes calling deep inside to her Fire. Healing and warmth buzzed through her body, but her brain remained scrambled, fuzzy. The drugs they used against her were taking their toll, and she was getting damned tired of it.

Stretching her legs, her knees creaked. Ashlyn, confused, scanned the unfamiliar space. "What the hell is this?" Walls of glass, with no doors or visible seams surrounded her. "Hello? Can anyone hear me?" Her voice echoed bouncing off the empty enclosure. She craned her neck to look up at the high ceiling. It had vents just like in her cell. A large drain sat in the center of the concrete floor, and her stomach rolled as terrifying thoughts filled her head. Glancing around the room, she realized she was still in the laboratory with all the torturous looking equipment.

Slowly, she rose to her feet wrapping her arms across her chest protectively. The thin material of yet another hospital gown clung to her skin. Feeling utterly vulnerable, she wondered who kept dressing her. Though she was glad to be covered she shuddered at the thought of a stranger touching her. She prayed it wasn't Devlin or Charles what's his name. Repulsed, Ash pushed the thought out of her head.

Ashlyn preferred to fixate on her connection with Hawk instead. The link between them was evolving, and she could feel it building each time they united. She had inadvertently drawn him in when she was shocked by the Taser gun. Perhaps it was her fear driving her toward him. *Poor Hawk, I hope he wasn't hurt. I've got to learn to control this bridge between us.*

She could actually feel the deep timber of Hawk's voice when she concentrated. It was soothing, comforting, and it fortified her. He sounded so strong and confident. She needed to believe he would find her and free her from this nightmare.

The knots in her stomach loosened further when she reminded herself Laurel was most definitely safe in Aether. Hawk had assured her of that fact. Lava boiled in her veins. "That bastard Devlin is going to pay for taunting me with Laurel's life!" Ash placed her palms on the cool, smooth glass and looked out into the abandoned lab. "They need me for something, or I'd be dead already. But how long do I have?"

Minutes felt like hours to Ashlyn as she pondered

her fate. Yet, in the end, her thoughts always seem to go back to Hawk. It was strange allowing him into her mind, but at the same time it felt right. It was as if he belonged there. Her Fire rippled along her nerve endings. Heat surged through her as her Flame answered Hawk's call of rage and frustration. Ash had also gleaned his strength which radiated through their connection. His feelings, those of warmth and something else remote, sadness she thought, also traveled through her. Determined to spend all of her time working on developing the bond between them, she reached out with her mind. Seeking. Feeling. Longing.

Raised voices in the hallway just outside the laboratory caused Ashlyn to lose her concentration. The soft tone of a woman's voice and the deeper resonance of a man's had her on guard. She'd only had direct contact with Devlin and Charles thus far. Ashlyn worried about who else might be out there and what they wanted from her.

Straining to listen, she pressed her ear against the glass. The woman's voice was getting louder by the minute. "Don't you know who I am? I can assure you, nothing at CEB labs is off limits to me. I insist you open this door at once."

The man begged. "Please, Miss, I'm new here. You don't understand. I'm just supposed to bring this tray of food down and give it to one of the guards. I came to look for him. I guess he went to the bathroom or something. I'm just a lab assistant. I didn't realize you followed me. I'm supposed to make sure nobody follows me. I'll get fired. Please, I need this job. Plus, I couldn't let you in even if I wanted to. I don't even have the code to access the lab."

"Fine then, leave the tray with me and go back upstairs. I won't tell anyone you were here. I promise, it will be okay, really, just go." To Ash, the woman sounded authoritative.

The sudden silence indicated at least one of the people had gone. The drone of an electronic keypad buzzed as it denied someone entrance to the lab. Over and over this person attempted to gain access. Eventually, she heard several dings, and the door clicked open. Ashlyn stiffened, and her Fire hovered near the surface on full alert. Her Flame wanted to lash out and protect the Guardian. Ash fought to keep her Fire at bay as she waited for the stranger to appear.

Pushing the door open with her hip, a young woman with blond hair entered carrying a tray of food. Her eyes settled on Ashlyn freezing her in place. With her mouth agape, the tray slid from the woman's hands crashing to the floor scattering its contents.

"Oh my God! What have they done?" She brought her hand to her mouth. Then the blond slowly approached the glass, her posture tentative. Her voice came out in a whisper, "Who are you?" Her breath caught, but she managed to choke out the words, "Why are you in there?"

"My name is Ashlyn, and I don't know why I'm here. A lunatic named Devlin kidnapped me." A single tear ran down Ash's cheek. "Please help me. I just want to go home."

The woman paled before her eyes, and she appeared shaky and stunned. Looking to be in her early twenties in terms of human maturity, the woman was tall with bright blue eyes and golden blond hair twisted up into a neat bun. She wore dark colored slacks and a white blouse with a starched lab coat over it. Her shoes were sensible looking loafers. While very pretty, she kept her look plain and simple.

"Who are you? What do you want from me?"

"I'm so sorry. My name is Brooke. Don't worry, Ashlyn, I'm going to find out what the hell is going on around here and get you out of there." Brooke's eyes widened as she took note of the bruising on Ash's arms. "What happened to your arms? You're covered in bruises."

"I'm really not sure. They drugged me, and I just woke up in here. What is this place? Please, I'm begging you. Let me out."

The door to the lab burst open, and a guard with his weapon drawn came toward them. "What the hell are you doing in here? No one is supposed to be in here without permission."

"Lower your weapon, you imbecile. I'm the assistant director of CEB laboratories, and I can be anywhere I want to be."

"We'll see about that. I'm going to get Mr. Devlin." He hustled out of the room, and the door clicked shut behind him.

"What is CEB laboratories, and what exactly do you do around here?" Ash questioned.

"CEB Laboratories manufactures and sells pharmaceuticals. I am the assistant director. I'm a biochemical engineer and a pharmacist. Our goal is to cure a variety of diseases with new medicines we are working to develop. I help people."

"Well, from where I'm standing, you and your company aren't doing a very good job of helping. I'm being held prisoner if you haven't noticed. I'm no lab rat, and I want out of here right now before those two lunatics come back with the guy with the gun."

"I'm so sorry, Ashlyn. I don't know how to release you from there, or I promise you I would. I don't approve of holding anyone against their will. I will get to the bottom of this. You have my word," Brooke said, sounding sincere.

"That's all well and good, but your word means nothing to me. As you can imagine, I have some serious trust issues where you people are concerned. Please, before they come back, get me the hell out of here." Ash's fists pounded the glass uselessly.

The double doors to the laboratory swung open, and Charles Barrington entered with Devlin at his side. Three armed guards with weapons drawn came in just behind them and flanked them once they were fully inside. "What are you doing down here, Brooke?" Barrington asked. His face reddened, and his voice was harsh.

Brooke shrunk right before Ashlyn's eyes, when Barrington addressed her. "I-I was curious. I saw someone coming down here with a tray of food, and I thought it was odd. This area is supposed to be used for storage or so I thought. Please tell me this isn't what it looks like."

"This is none of your concern. You need to leave at once," Barrington commanded. Stepping toward her, he narrowed his eyes. "How did you even get in here? This is a secure area."

"I figured out your code on the keypad and let myself in."

"You are a little too smart for your own good. Now

be a good girl, and do as you're told. Go back upstairs, and pretend you never found this place," Devlin said, coldly.

"Please, don't listen to them. Don't leave me here. Please, Brooke, help me," Ashlyn implored.

"I'm sorry, Ashlyn. I can't help you. I have to go," Brooke said, regret filling her voice. She turned rushing out the door, seemingly frightened.

Devlin laughed cruelly as he kicked an apple across the room. "Guess your dinner is gone, Firecracker, hope you weren't too hungry."

Barrington, Devlin, and the guards left the room without so much as a backward glance. The door closed tightly behind them with the now familiar click of the lock engaging. Ashlyn sank to the floor, and her body shook with heaving sobs. Her tiny glimmer of hope left right along with Brooke.

****

Hawk

The Protectors gathered in their war room to discuss strategies for rescuing Ashlyn. The war room was located in Protector Headquarters, more commonly known as PH, which was housed in its own building right next to the Council Chambers.

The Protectors were fairly private. They only allowed trainees who had passed the first two years to enter PH beyond the training gym and classrooms. Established Protectors, of course, had full access to their base of operations. PH was comprised of many parts: an armory, offices, training rooms, gyms, a recreation center, and a brand-new technology center.

The new technology center had been completed only days ago, and their experts were finally finished installing and securing everything this morning. It was an impressive set up rivaling any government's. Thanks to Cadence, their head tech guy, it was now fully operational. He had found a way to block all outside tracking of their computers and other technology. Cadence was a genius, and Hawk had faith he would figure out something to help them locate Ash. Hawk handed over the information he and Kai had gathered at the University. He stared in awe as Cadence's hands flew furiously across the keys entering the data into their new system.

After reviewing all the material there was no question, Charles Barrington was the individual responsible for Ashlyn's capture. Cadence hacked into several classified files which revealed Barrington had affiliations with some underground government sectors. CEB was listed as the developer of a drug the government had sanctioned to create stronger soldiers. Barrington walked a fine line between ethical and inventive.

Even with all the information they had gathered, the problem remained, they still didn't know where their Fire Guardian was being held and why. CEB Laboratories had at least a dozen locations in the Northeast, and they were beginning to expand out west. Ashlyn's whereabouts were going to remain a mystery if they were unable to gather more intel.

Hawk's gut churned as a gnawing feeling persisted; time was running out for Ash. As their link grew stronger, it opened Hawk to Ash's lancing pain. Her fear and anguish tore away at his soul. Desperation to find her was becoming an urgent hunger to him with each passing day. Need surged through him to protect her, to rescue her, and to make her safe. Once that happened, Hawk was determined to make her his own in every way.

Every surface of the war room was covered with maps and floor plans of Barrington Labs. River appeared to be concentrating on a large monitor hanging on the wall with the schematics of CEB's original location and headquarters. The lead Protector answered only to Bear and the Council. River ran an efficient, well managed organization. He carried himself with the confidence of a strong leader and appeared every bit the powerful fighter. An expert on tactical maneuvers, the teams he led were among the greatest minds in all of Aether.

Hawk looked on and speculated whether Ashlyn was being held in the depths of CEB headquarters. His impatience growing, Hawk repeatedly ground his fist into his palm. The warrior in him demanded he fight to save his woman. Hawk wondered when had he begun to think of Ashlyn as his or had he always?

A select few Protectors hovered over the layouts of the Lab's other locations examining every detail. They were searching for weaknesses in security. In addition, they sought out the possibility of hidden portions of the Labs where the company would most likely be conducting their surreptitious experiments. The remaining soldiers milled about discussing what weapons they would be using, checking ammunition stores, and supplies.

River stood and held his hand up addressing the group halting the frantic energy in the room. "Listen up. We have a lot of ground to cover. Cadence tells me our best chance of finding Ashlyn is to start systematically searching the known locations of Barrington Labs." Walking to the monitor, River pointed to several areas on the map. "Some of the new ground they are breaking is less likely to be housing the type of facility we are looking for. Also, we feel some of the locations are not remote enough to keep clandestine experiments, and certainly not prisoners, secluded. Therefore, we have narrowed down the strongest possibilities to six locations. It is plausible the Labs have hidden underground areas which will not be visible from the surface. We will need to infiltrate the various facilities and search them fully. This will be a stealth operation. I am going to set up teams to scout these areas."

Bear stepped up and interjected, "I hope I do not have to remind you we need to remain under the radar for this operation. Finding Ashlyn, and bringing her home safely is our primary goal. However, we want Barrington brought in; alive if possible. He has many questions to answer for." Shaking a pointed finger in the air, he punctuated each word with a series of emphatic gestures. "And remember, no heroics and no unnecessary harming of humans. It is of paramount importance we continue to keep the existence of our people from the humans. So, no using your powers unless absolutely necessary."

"Thank you, Bear," River acknowledged. "There will be six teams heading out. I will be leading the team going to the headquarters. I'm sending the list of teams and leaders to your phones as we speak."

Scanning the list of team leaders with his finger, his name clearly missing, Hawk rose to his feet. Clenching his fists, low level vibrations emanated from him as his anger took control. Fighting the urge to take

M. Goldsmith and A. Malin

River down with a punch to his face, he squinted his eyes shut tight and pushed the violent thought away. Everyone knew Hawk was River's second in command. He always led a team. Moreover, everyone now knew he and Ashlyn had a unique connection. He should be leading not following someone else's orders to save Ash. She was his.

"Check to see if you are going on the first phase of this mission. Everyone else will help prepare weapons and communication devices. We will also continue with our stepped-up guard duty on the grounds and surrounding areas of Aether. That schedule is also posted. Hawk, can I have a word with you please? The rest of you, fall out. We have no time to lose," River ordered.

River approached him cautiously. Hawk figured he was reading the tension and vibrations in the air surrounding him. "I understand you're pissed and I don't blame you. Under normal circumstances you're always my first choice, but this thing with you and Ash. Well let's just say, the nature of your special bond complicates things. Face it, Hawk, you're both an asset and a liability." River placed his hand on Hawk's shoulder and looked him straight in the eyes. "We need you, Hawk. Ash needs you. I was hoping you would join my team along with Quill. My gut is telling me she is in CEB headquarters which as we know is in the original facility. What do you say? Are you in?"

Hawk took a moment to consider what River had said. If he connected to Ash and he was physically effected he could put the entire team in jeopardy, as well as Ashlyn. River was right he needed to help find Ash, and his bond with her might give them the extra leverage they needed. "You're right, River. I'm sorry. Ash means everything to me, and I'll do whatever it takes to find her and bring her back home."

"Great, I knew I could count on you. Aether needs our Fire Guardian back, and it appears you need Ashlyn just as much as the rest of us, if not more. We have a long trip ahead of us. Let's go find Quill and the others and discuss our strategy."

The group worked for a long while and Hawk was glad Quill would be by his side. Although he liked to joke around, when it came down to it, Quill was one of the best fighters Hawk knew. He was loyal to a fault and would put the other team members' safety above his own. Hawk knew Quill would do anything to save Ash including give his own life. He prayed River's instincts were correct, and Ashlyn was being held at the headquarters. Hawk needed to be the one to find her. He wasn't sure how he would handle it if someone else got to her first. River assured him none of the teams were going to attempt a rescue without backup. The lead Protector was calling this mission, Phase One, and its purpose was for intel only. Phase Two would involve a carefully planned rescue and hopefully the capture of Charles Barrington himself.

It was nearly midnight when they finished all the preparations for the Phase One mission. All the teams were prepped and ready to leave at first light. Bear and River dismissed everyone to go home and get a good night's sleep. Hawk was restless pacing the room. His mind was on Ash.

Bear reached out and touched his grandson's shoulder gently. "You need to go home and get some rest. Ashlyn needs you in top form when you find her.

And I know you will. I have always had faith in you. Now you need to have faith in yourself. And in Ashlyn. Your bond is extraordinary. It will bring you to her."

"Thanks, Grandfather. I don't know what I would do without you. It means the world to me to have your support. You've been both parent and grandparent to me since we lost my mom and dad."

Hawk's parents had died in an automobile accident when he was just twelve years old. They were on vacation celebrating the anniversary of their Joining. The couple was heading back to Aether, when their car, a 1940 Chrysler Saratoga, went over a cliff on a mountain side road. The weather had been clear and sunny that day, and it remained a mystery as to how the accident had occurred. The Protectors of the time, including Bear, had gone to search for them when they did not return home.

The charred remnants of their car had been found at the bottom of the mountain under a mass of rocks. No one knew if they were killed when the car erupted in flames or upon the impact of the crash. Their remains had been burned beyond recognition. Wolf's beloved Saratoga was unmistakable with its bright blue color peeking through the blackened wreckage. The Protectors had to use their combined powers to traverse the steep cliff in order to bring back the bodies of Wolf and Lark Crane.

Though his grandparents had taken him in and raised him with love and kindness, Hawk had never fully recovered from the loss of his parents. The inexplicability of the situation continued to haunt him. He knew his father to be an excellent driver. Wolf would never have risked Lark's safety by driving recklessly. His father worshipped his mother and would have done anything to keep her free from harm. Although Hawk was not with the rescue party, to this day, he was still plagued with nightmares of the car plunging down the embankment and bursting into flames.

"Your parents would be so proud of you, Hawk. You have grown into a fine man. I know your father would have been thrilled to see you become a Protector. And I am certain Lark would have loved the idea of you and Ashlyn together. Hold their memories in your heart when you go on this mission. We will all be with you. May the God and Goddess watch over you."

Hawk felt a lump in his throat. He didn't respond with words, he simply hugged his grandfather in an unusual display of affection. Bear returned the embrace and then released Hawk. "Come on. Let us take our leave. You have a big day ahead of you tomorrow. We will stay in touch throughout your journey. You go, and find our Fire Guardian."

The two exited Protector Headquarters and headed home in opposite directions. Hawk left his grandfather feeling positive for the first time in quite a while. Bear was right. Hawk could feel it. He was going to find Ash and bring her home where she belonged.

Chapter Ten

Kai

Kai woke before it was light shivering from the memory of the intensity he and Laurel had recaptured. During the night, her soft lips and delicate hands roamed every inch of his body, waking him from a sound slumber. He'd never seen this side of her before, wild and demanding. Sleeping soundly beside him, Laurel's arm was slung across his stomach with their legs intertwined. Though shadows shrouded most of her face in darkness, Kai could still see her beautiful dark hair spread across his pillow. It partially covered her face. Kai couldn't resist touching her and softly brushing her hair away so he could fully take in her beauty. Leaning in, he took a deep breath inhaling her intoxicating vanilla scent. He didn't want to wake her since he'd lost count of how many times they'd made love during the night. He wanted to be gentle and tender with her, but his control had snapped. Being with Laurel again was everything he fantasized about and more. She was so giving, and Kai had taken all of her. He gave of himself, too, coaxing her on, with unrelenting persistence and passion, until she screamed his name. He feared he would never get enough of her.

Slowly and carefully, he pried himself out from under her grasp. She stirred a little, and her nose twitched adorably, but then she snuggled herself back under the blanket. As much as he wanted her again, he had business to attend to. Hawk had texted him late last night telling him the Protectors were heading out at dawn.

Kai hurried to get to the Protectors before they left. He wanted to go with them to find Ashlyn. It was his fault she was taken, and it was essential he be a part of the rescue mission. After all, he knew Barrington better than anyone.

Laurel would never approve of him going on such a dangerous mission, and Kai knew it. He was a doctor not a Protector. Though Kai knew how to fight, as did most of the men of Aether, he was not a solider. Quietly, he grabbed a duffle and began haphazardly stuffing clothing inside. Sneaking into the bathroom, he relieved himself, then brushed his teeth, and washed his face. After, he tossed his toothbrush and toothpaste into the bag with the rest of his belongings. He dressed silently in jeans, a worn T-shirt, a hooded sweatshirt, and sneakers.

Creeping out quietly, he grabbed a pad from his kitchen drawer and wrote a note.

****

Laurel,

You are so gorgeous when you're sleeping. I just want to crawl back into bed with you and hold you. I'm so sorry I have to leave you after our magical night together. But you know I need to go with Hawk and Quill to find Ashlyn. Please understand, baby, I have to make this right. I will think about you every minute while I'm gone.

All my love,
Kai

The floorboards creaked under his feet as Kai snuck back into the bedroom and placed the note on his empty pillow. He stood there staring at Laurel sleeping so sweetly; her chest rising and falling. *Oh God, the feel of her soft skin, the taste of her kisses. The way we fit together, it's like she's meant only for me.* Reluctantly, he turned and left tossing his duffle over his shoulder. He quietly closed the bedroom door behind him and said a silent prayer that he would return to her soon.

Kai raced up to the lot where all the cars and trucks in Aether were kept just as Hawk and Quill arrived. Hawk, dressed head to toe in his customary black, a Kevlar vest, and fierce looking weapons strapped to his tall muscled frame, appeared prepared for battle. Stoic, strong, determined, Hawk looked every bit the warrior Kai knew him to be.

Quill asked in his usual teasing tone, "What are you doing here, Kai? Come to see us off? Is that a care package over your shoulder? I hope there is food in there. I'm starving."

"No, I've come to join you," Kai responded, matter-of-factly.

"Kai, I don't think that's a very good idea. This mission is for Protectors only. I know you want to help, but this isn't the way," Hawk said.

Bear and River walked over to join them. Their eyes focused on Kai standing with his friends. The ancient Protector's face was unreadable, but River wore a scowl as if he knew why Kai was there. As the lead Protector, River had been under a lot of pressure since Ashlyn's abduction. Everyone knew he felt responsible for what happened to both Ash and Laurel. The Protectors normally ran patrols nightly in the area where the women were attacked. Everyone was tired from the preparations for the Guardian Ceremony, so River gave them the night off. They had no known enemies with the exception of the Renegades. Their land was marked with signs warning people away claiming the area to be protected lands and a wildlife sanctuary. However infrequently, they were required to escort humans and their prying eyes from wandering into Aether. It never occurred to him something like this could happen.

River, hands on his hips, didn't waste any time with formalities. "What can we do for you this morning, Kai? We're pretty busy here as you can see."

"I want to join in the rescue mission. This entire situation is my fault, and I need to be part of the solution."

Bear's booming voice cut him off. "Kai, we have assured you, countless times, this is not your doing. You are in no way responsible for Barrington's actions. Your place is here in Aether."

"Please. You don't understand Charles the way I do. I know how he thinks. I'm sure I could help in some way. Plus, what if Ashlyn is injured and she needs medical attention..." Kai trailed off, wanting to consider Hawk's feelings. "I need to do this, Please."

Hawk jumped into the conversation. "He has some very valid points. Don't you think? And he can fight. He's trained with us in the past. Right, Quill?"

Quill looked to Hawk, and then to Kai, before answering. "Yeah, I've watched Kai kick Hawk's ass from time to time. He can definitely take care of himself. Who knows, maybe he would be helpful to have along."

Turning to River, Bear gestured with his hands. "It's up to you, River, you are in charge of this mission. What do you think?"

"I think you are going to be a pain in my ass, Sanders. You can come, but you two are in charge of making sure our only doctor doesn't get hurt. Go suit him up. There are more vests and gear in our SUV. And, Kai, don't make me regret this."

"You won't regret it. I promise. I know I can help you catch Barrington. We knew each other well in our time together, and a leopard doesn't change his spots."

Hawk, Quill, and Kai went around to the rear of the SUV. They assisted Kai in gathering the equipment for their potentially dangerous mission. He was determined to help in any way he could. Even if the others didn't blame him, he still couldn't help but blame himself.

Kai also worried about what Laurel would think when she realized he was gone. For the rest of his life he would imagine her sleeping peacefully in his bed where she belonged. She was the most beautiful woman he had ever seen, and touching her, making love with her, was a dream come true. Hopefully, when they brought Ashlyn home to Aether all would be forgiven.

As usual, Quill attempted to defuse the tension with his humor. He nudged Kai with his shoulder. "So, Kai, I saw you and Laurel leaving the Council Chambers together. I couldn't help but notice you two looked pretty cozy. She couldn't keep her hands off you. Do you care to elaborate so I don't have to use my very active imagination?"

"Really, Quill? You're kidding, right? You think of all the people in Aether I would tell you anything intimate?"

"Oh, so you admit you and Laurel were intimate huh? Details, I need details."

"You are a complete and total idiot. You know that, right? We're not fifteen anymore and anything that may, or may not have, happened with Laurel is none of your damn business. So, piss off."

Hawk laughed uncontrollably his eyes watering. Kai guessed he was fairly worked up over the impending search for Ash. Even though Kai wanted to deck Quill, he was glad he could help Hawk relax. Maybe the outrageous Protector knew what he was doing after all. The two had been his best friends his entire life, and he couldn't imagine them anywhere but by his side.

River whistled shrilly gathering the teams together one last time before they all headed off in different directions. The squads were traveling to six different locations and would be arriving at varying times. He would require constant communication from each group in case any one of them discovered Ashlyn's whereabouts. River reminded all of the Protectors of their obligation to Aether and their Fire Guardian. He reiterated the importance of bringing as little attention to themselves as possible.

With his hands clasped behind his back, River addressed the teams. "I don't have to remind any of you of the significance of this mission to all of Aether. Finding and securing our Fire Guardian is the most important operation we have ever undertaken." Pacing back and forth, he speared each of his soldiers with steady gaze. "Use your heads. Work as a team, and follow your leader's orders no matter what. While on this assignment they speak for Bear and myself. Make us proud, and let's bring Ashlyn home safely."

Bear advanced and stood at River's side. "May the God and Goddess be with you during this most urgent quest."

****

Laurel

Opening her eyes slowly as bright sunlight streamed in through slatted wooden blinds, Laurel stretched her tight muscles. Wait a minute, she had flowing curtains in her bedroom not blinds. "Oh my God! I'm in Kai's bedroom. I was with Kai last night," she whispered, not wanting to wake him.

Laurel groaned, her body tender in all the right places after her incredible night with Kai. He was beyond comprehension, full of passion, not to mention stamina. Rolling over she hoped to catch a glimpse of Kai's naked body, but the other side of the bed was cold with his absence. Burying her head in his pillow, she breathed in his delicious scent; masculine and decadent. Something crinkled under her cheek, and she realized there was a piece of paper hanging off the edge of the pillow. Laurel lifted the paper and read the note Kai left for her. He was gone. Not just from his bed, or his house, but he was gone from Aether. What the hell was he thinking?

She knew the Protectors were leaving at dawn. Glancing over at the clock on Kai's bedside table, she realized she had slept passed ten in the morning. Laurel never slept so late, ever. So immersed in their passion, they stopped only to catch their breath, to hold each other close, and to rest somewhere in between. It was no wonder she had slept so soundly. But why did Kai sneak away? Laurel knew the answer. He didn't want her to talk him out of going with the Protectors to find Ash.

"Damn him," she said aloud. She was going to give him a piece of her mind when he made it back, hopefully soon, and safely. Laurel knew Kai was consumed with guilt since finding out his medical school roommate, Charles Barrington, had been the one responsible for attacking her and Ash. Somehow, he felt he was at fault for bringing Barrington's resentment and anger to Aether.

How could Bear and River, not to mention his two best friends, let Kai go on such a dangerous mission? Kai was Aether's only doctor. He was not a Protector. What if something happened to him? Laurel's stomach tightened into knots at the thought of any harm coming to Kai when they had just found each other again. She knew it seemed silly, but she missed him already.

The sound of the front door bursting open made Laurel jump, and when she heard the sound of heavy footsteps, she didn't know what to think. Hoping Kai had come to his senses and returned to her, she quickly pulled on his T-shirt which had been tossed on the floor next to the bed. Thankfully, it was long on her petite frame and came down passed her thighs. It smelled like Kai and made her feel caressed by him even though he wasn't with her.

A loud, familiar voice thundered through the house chasing away her hope Kai had come home to her. "Kai? How can you still be sleeping at this hour? We have patients. Are you all right?" Rayne Sanders opened his son's bedroom door and froze when he saw Laurel standing beside the bed in nothing but a T-shirt. "Laurel?" Rayne quickly averted his eyes. "I'm so sorry. I-I-I didn't realize Kai had, um, company."

Laurel felt heat rush through her body and knew she must have turned crimson. "Kai's not here. He left me a note. He's gone with the Protectors to find Ashlyn. I'm sorry, Rayne. This is so embarrassing."

"No need to be embarrassed. You and Kai are adults. I shouldn't have barged in. It's my fault. Kai doesn't, um, entertain guests very often. Please forgive me for startling you." Rayne backed out of the door. "I'm going to wait in the living room so you can get dressed. Then what do you say you and I go find Bear and figure out what the hell Kai was thinking?"

"Thank you. By the way, I think your son is the most wonderful person. But right now, I want to kill him for leaving to do something so dangerous. I'll gladly go with you to speak to Bear. Just give me five minutes."

Closing the door behind him, Rayne gave Laurel some privacy. *I can't believe that just happened. I may die of embarrassment. Yet another reason I'm going to kill Kai when I see him.*

Slipping into Kai's bathroom, Laurel splashed water on her face and cleaned herself up as quickly as she could. She came out and scanned the room in search of her scattered clothing. Her panties dangled from the bedside lamp, her bra snagged on a doorknob, and the rest of her clothes were strewn about the floor. Waves of memories from last night flooded her, and she warmed all over. *Get a grip, girl. You need to face his father. Plus, you need to speak to Bear.* She repressed the thoughts she was having about her and Kai and went out to the living room to face Rayne.

Feeling more confident and slightly less

embarrassed now that she was properly attired, Laurel cleared her throat. "Okay, I'm ready when you are."

To his credit, Rayne acted perfectly natural as if finding a half-dressed woman in his son's bedroom was an everyday occurrence. Rayne held out his hand gesturing for Laurel to lead the way out. He closed the door behind him with a loud click. They walked in silence toward the Council Chambers to look for Bear.

They didn't get very far because Bear stood looming in the Village Square surrounded by a few Protectors. Water dripped from the end of a fire hose, and a pile of glowing cinders sat right outside the front door to the South Tower. Rowan and Mica were nearby talking animatedly. They approached the group. Rayne asked, "What's going on?"

"More fires, I'm afraid. Everything has been going crazy since my Ashlyn was taken from us," Rowan answered. Her normally sparkling eyes appeared dull and lifeless as she leaned on Mica.

Laurel instinctively went to Rowan and hugged her tightly. "Oh, Rowan, I'm so sorry. Don't you worry. The Protectors are going to find Ash. You'll see."

Bear approached the group. Rayne confronted him in an accusatory tone, "Bear, do you want to tell me why my son is on a mission with the Protectors?"

"Ah, Rayne, I see you are understandably concerned about Kai. I assure you the Protectors are looking after him. He insisted on going to lend a hand. He feels guilty. River and I decided the only way for Kai to move on is to participate in Ashlyn's rescue. He knows this Dr. Charles Barrington, and Kai is convinced he can aid the Protectors in bringing him in. He is also concerned that Ashlyn might need his skills."

Rayne sighed, shaking his head. "I get it. I just wish he would have discussed it with Cassy or myself before skulking off in the dead of night."

"Are you sure he'll be safe?" Laurel questioned. She nibbled on her thumbnail nervously.

Bear's eyebrows rose as if with sudden understanding. "Yes, Laurel, I'm sure he will be absolutely fine. My grandson and the other Protectors would never allow any harm to come to him. Additionally, I understand that he is quite capable of defending himself should that be necessary."

Rayne added, "Remember, Laurel, Kai is an excellent fighter. You know he trained with Hawk and Quill when they entered the Protector Trials, and I'm sure those two will make sure he stays out of trouble."

Laurel nodded in acknowledgment and then turned to Bear. She questioned, "Have you heard from them?"

"Not yet, they only left a few hours ago, so I do not expect to hear from them for some time. I promise I will let you know when I do."

"Thank you, Bear," Rayne acknowledged. "Laurel, I'll let you know if I hear from Kai and you do the same. Okay?"

"Of course, thanks for um, everything, Rayne. I'll speak to you later," Laurel said, feeling self-conscious. She turned her attention back Ashlyn's parents. "What can I do to help you? What's going on with the fires?"

Mica answered, "They are beginning to spread out. At first, they were contained to the living quarters in the Tower and just out front in the Village Square. But now they are starting to move farther from here. Fires have been breaking out in the woods and near the lake as well. Bear and the Protectors are doing a great job of keeping them contained and everyone in Aether is being especially vigilant."

Mica held Rowan close. "It will be fine. They'll find Ash soon, and everything will return to normal." He turned to Bear. "I still wish you would have let me join the rescue party. I belong out there helping to find my daughter."

"I'm sorry, Mica, but you are needed here with Rowan. We can't have her worrying about both you and Ashlyn, can we?"

Mica raised his hands in acquiescence. Laurel had known Mica and Rowan her entire life and couldn't remember a time when they both looked so tired and helpless. Mica's hair stood out in every direction, and his clothes were wrinkled as though they had been slept in. Rowan's normally composed manner faltered, and she leaned on her Kanti as if needing his support. Laurel wished she could do something for them. They all needed Ash back where she belonged.

"Come on. Let's go to the café and get some coffee. Looks like it's going to be another long day, and we could all use the jolt of caffeine. I'm buying," Laurel suggested.

"Thanks, Laurel. I think that's a great idea." Rowan put her arm around Laurel and turned in the direction of the café.

Laurel was so concerned about Rowan and Mica, she almost forgot how worried she was about Kai, almost but not quite. Desperate to hear Kai's voice, she felt for her phone in her pocket willing it to ring. Before all of Aether burned to the ground, Laurel prayed Kai would find her best friend and bring her home.

Chapter Eleven

Ashlyn

Gritty, her eyes itched, but Ashlyn couldn't even be bothered to rub them. She sat on the floor with her knees to her chest and wrapped her arms protectively around herself. Exhausted, she nearly tipped over. Even Ash's Fire called for a time out. It stayed hidden but hovered near the surface in case it was needed. She couldn't help but wonder about the woman named Brooke. She looked like the girl next door. But who was she really? It had been a huge blow when Brooke left her alone with those two psychos. At first, she had appeared self-assured and confident. Then, her entire demeanor changed when Devlin and Barrington entered the room. Ash thought she had been saved, but she was wrong. Hopelessness enveloped her. Extreme fatigue was the only thing pulling Ashlyn under into a fitful sleep.

Ash dreamed of Aether. Alone in the Atrium of the South Tower, her gaze lingered over her beautiful village. She startled as her name was called from behind. Turning to the sound of the voice, she breathed a sigh of relief. "Hawk. How are you here?"

Ash could tell immediately when Hawk recognized where she had brought him through their connection. "You're dreaming, honey, but I've been searching for you through our link. I wanted you to know I'm coming for you. The Protectors and I are on our way. Are you okay?" He ran the back of his hand down her cheek and she nuzzled into his touch.

"Thank the God and Goddess. Yes, I'm all right, but I can't take much more of this. How did you find me?"

"That's a pretty long story. Let's just say it's not the Renegades who've taken you. It's a man named Dr. Charles Barrington. Apparently, he and Kai have a history together. He was his roommate in med school. Obviously, he knows about us, about Aether, and what our people are capable of." Hawk gently stoked her hair and smiled sadly. "I don't know which facility they're holding you in, baby. They have dozens of locations, but we're searching all of them. Can you tell me anything about where they've taken you?"

Ashlyn lay her cheek on Hawk's muscled chest, tears pooling in her eyes. "I don't know, but I've met Barrington. He's really scary, cold, and there's something dark in his eyes that's chilling." Wrapping her arms around his waist, breathing in his masculine scent, she fortified herself with his inner strength.

"I know, honey. I promise I'm going to come for you very soon." Hawk rubbed slow comforting circles up and down her back. "You just need to hang in there a little longer. What else can you tell me about where you are?"

"Nothing, I can't tell you anything. I'm locked in a lab now not a cell. They keep knocking me out with drugs. When I woke up this time I had bruises up and down my arms. Looks like they've been taking my blood." Ash sensed the moment Hawk had drawn on the Elements, and then the air around them swirled like a subtle breeze. She could physically feel his power and anger boiling up inside her. She took a deep breath trying to calm herself and hoping to calm Hawk as well. Remembering something important, she suddenly pulled back. "Wait, there was a woman last night. Her name was Brooke. I felt like she wanted to help me, but then Barrington and his henchman Devlin came in and scared her away. She said she is the assistant director of CEB Laboratories."

"Good job, baby. I'll look into her and see what we can find out. Ash, there's so much I want to tell you when I find you. But right now, I need you to stay strong. Can you do that for me, honey?" Hawk leaned down and pressed his lips to her forehead.

"Yes, I'll try. But, Hawk, please hurry. I'm so scared. These men are dangerous. And crazy. This place is like a fortress. Everything has security keypads and tons of guards with guns. I'm worried they'll hurt you."

"Don't you worry about me. Those assholes are the ones who should be worried because I'm going to kill anyone who has put their hands on you. Nothing can stop me from finding you, Ash."

Without warning, Hawk was gone. Ash bolted upright. A strange hissing noise followed by a slight breeze lifted the thin material of her hospital gown. Her Fire sprang to action dancing along her fingertips and down her arms. Devlin stood before her grinning menacingly. He toyed with some kind of remote control, and the glass wall in front of her continued to rise several inches. He slid a tray of food and bucket underneath the opening. Ash's Flame shot out seeking its target. But it was too late, the glass quickly dropped back into place sealing her inside once again.

"Good try, Firecracker. Looks like you were having a nice dream. Dr. Barrington insisted I feed you, so I brought you a snack. The bucket over there is your toilet. So, enjoy," Devlin said, his eyes filled with cruelty. "You better eat up because the boss has lots of fun experiments in store for you today. Remember, if you don't cooperate I'm going to hurt your friend some more. I get hard every time she screams her pretty little head off." He adjusted his pants obscenely.

"You are a lying sack of shit. I know Laurel isn't here. She never was. She's home. She's safe from you sick, demented people, and you are never going to touch her." Ashlyn knew provoking Devlin was a really bad idea, but she couldn't help herself. She was nearing her breaking point. For once she wanted the upper hand with Devlin and his cruel sadistic ways. She needed him to know he couldn't use the threat of harming Laurel against her anymore. "So go fuck yourself!"

Appearing shocked, Devlin's mouth hung open. Quickly, he snapped it shut. Ashlyn reveled in the feeling, until his face turned beet red and his gaze darkened. "Why would you say that? Of course, she's here. She's my toy. Don't you forget it."

"You can't threaten me with Laurel's safety anymore. I know the truth, so give it up, asshole." The fury scalding her veins sent her Fire raging. Bright red and orange flames glowed as they surged forward. The steady burst directed at the glass hovered yet had no effect on it. Devlin stepped back several feet. Ash got her first hint that he may have genuinely been intimidated by her powers even if he tried not to show it.

177

Devlin's voice dropped low and threatening. His eyes narrowed looking fierce. "I'm going to make you suffer, Firecracker. I'm going to leave my mark all over you, and you will beg me to kill you." He pointed at her aggressively. Salvia foamed in the corner of his misshapen mouth reminding Ash of a feral dog. "Then, I'm going to tear the flesh from your pretty body. There will be nothing left of you to even bury." Devlin turned and stormed out of the lab.

Sagging against the wall, Ash let out a breath. Her Fire continued to rage. She closed her eyes calling to it, "It's okay. Back down. He's gone now. We're all right. Hawk's coming for us." Her Flame tapered off and buried itself just below the surface.

Ashlyn lowered herself to the floor crossing her legs. Sliding the tray in front of her, she grabbed a bottle of water. Tearing the cap free, she gulped down half its contents in one swig. Loudly, her stomach rumbled. She plucked the sandwich off the tray and tore off a chunk with her teeth. Barely tasting the turkey and cheese, she swallowed it down until there was nothing but crumbs.

She stood, brushed herself off, and eyed the bucket with distaste. Peeking inside, she saw a yellowed roll of toilet paper sitting at the bottom. "They've gotta be kidding me. They expect me to pee in that. Gross."

Hesitantly, she lifted the roll out of the bucket with the tips of her fingers, disgusted. "Well, I guess it's this or the floor." Cautiously raising her hospital gown, she squatted over the bucket relieving herself in a rush. Unrolling a couple of sheets of the foul looking paper, she did what she had to do, and then tucked the bucket in the corner of her tiny prison.

She opened the water bottle and poured a small amount over her hands, then scrubbed her face. Ashlyn felt dirty. Not simply because she hadn't bathed in who knows how long, but because these men made her feel filthy inside and out. She downed the remaining contents of the bottle in one huge gulp. Picking up a shiny green apple, Ash rolled it in her hands before taking a bite. She consumed it quickly and pitched the core onto the now empty tray. Endeavoring to relax and clear her mind of Devlin's threats, she closed her eyes and leaned back against the cinderblock wall. Stretching out her legs, she reached for her toes struggling to loosen up her aching muscles.

The now familiar beeping of the keypad and the click of the door lock disengaging broke her meditative state. She rose to her full height ready to face Devlin again as her Flame rocketed forth from its hiding place within her. Fire brushed her forearms, racing down her hands, and out through the tips of her fingers.

Brooke stood before her with her mouth agape, her eyes wide, and looking altogether bewildered. "Ashlyn? Oh my God. What's happening to you? You're-you're on fire!" Brooke squeaked out.

Thankful and relieved to find Brooke and not Devlin, Ash pulled her Fire back. She faced Brooke coldly. "What do you want from me, Brooke? You deserted me last night when I needed you. How could you have left me with those evil men? I thought you wanted to help free me, but I can see now you're a liar. Why don't you just go away?"

"Please, forgive me," Brooke begged, "it's complicated. But you're right. I shouldn't have left you." Edging closer to the glass barrier, Brooke stared at Ash's hands. "Please, tell me what they've done to you? The-the fire, oh my God! I'll find a way to fix you."

"There is no way to fix me. This is who I am. I am Ashlyn, of The House of Fire. This is the reason Barrington and Devlin took me. They obviously want my power for some purpose, but I don't know what it is."

"I can't believe this. This is insane. People can't make fire." Brooke paled and backed away from Ashlyn's enclosure.

"I assure you I can, as you have seen with your own eyes. Now why don't you run along like Devlin told you, before you get into trouble. Besides, I don't know you, and I certainly don't trust you. So just leave me here for them to torture some more since you have no intention of helping me."

"I don't even know how to process all of this, but I do truly want to help you whether you believe me or not. I can't say I blame you for not trusting me with the way I left you last night. I'm so sorry, Ashlyn. My relationship with Charles Barrington is…well, it's complicated. I doubt you would trust me even a little if I tried to explain who he is to me."

"Why don't you try me? It couldn't be any worse than what I've been imagining since you left last night." Ash gazed into Brooke's eyes searching for any hint of what her relationship with Barrington might be. "Your much older lover? Professor? Boss? Come on, Brooke, what is it?"

"He-he's my father." Brooke stared down at the ground seemingly unable to look at Ashlyn. "But you don't understand. I don't even understand it. I barely know the man."

Ashlyn was wholly dumbfounded. Brooke was that monster's daughter? She examined Brooke for any hint of a resemblance to the chilly, frightening, Dr. Charles Barrington. Brooke's hair was a lovely golden blond, and Charles' was dark, sprinkled with gray. His eyes were black and merciless; whereas, Brooke's were blue like the ocean and held warmth in their depths. Physically they appeared very different. Ash wondered if they were alike in other more nefarious ways. Brooke seemed genuine, but how could Ashlyn trust her? How could she trust anyone?

****

Hawk

After they outfitted Kai with a Kevlar vest and the rest of the gear he would need for the rescue mission, Quill started harassing Kai in his own unique style. Hawk belly laughed in a way he hadn't in a very long time. It felt good to let loose from all the tension and anticipation which consumed him. Leave it to Quill to lighten any mood.

The Protectors gathered together for River's final words to the teams. A dynamic leader, River was authoritative but fair, and Hawk had the utmost respect for him. There was no one whose judgement Hawk trusted more. Yet, nagging worry over the mission to rescue Ashlyn ate at him. Praying River's instincts were correct, Hawk hoped they were heading in the right direction. The need to find Ash was becoming more crucial to him than the air he breathed. After River's speech, and Bear's small prayer, the teams boarded their respective vehicles for the most important mission in Aether's history. Aether needed their Fire Guardian back, and Hawk needed Ash. The thought of anything happening to her was unimaginable. Just as Hawk was about to climb into the SUV, Bear pulled him aside.

"I know you will find her, Hawk. Use your bond to lead you to her. Trust your instincts. Use your connection to the Elements. I know I do not say it very often, but I want to remind you, I love you very much. I am incredibly proud of you. Go with the God and Goddess."

"Thank you, Grandfather. And I love you, too," Hawk said, with a smile. "I'll call you as soon as we find anything." Stepping up onto the running board, Hawk slipped into the black Hummer they were using for the mission. Quill, Kai, and Bracken were already seated in the back.

River started the engine with a roar. "Is everybody ready?"

The men all grunted in acknowledgment. River pulled away leaving Aether behind. The truck kicked up gravel from the parking lot leaving a cloud of dust in their wake. Hawk's mind reeled, crowded with a jumble of thoughts, and he couldn't seem to settle himself. *This is it. We are going to get my girl.* Hawk leaned back resting his head against the cushioned support of the Hummer. He reflected back on the previous night after leaving PH.

****

He had parted from Bear and was en route home aiming to clear his head during the walk in the cool night air. Except, when he arrived, he saw Raven, the Fire Elder, waiting for him on his front porch. He wondered what the elegant looking woman was doing sitting outside his home at midnight.

"Good evening, Hawk, I hope you do not mind me making myself comfortable on your lovely porch while I waited for you. I think you and I need to talk."

"Of course, I don't mind at all. It's one of my favorite places to sit, especially when I can't sleep. Unfortunately, that has been quite a lot lately. What can I do for you?"

"Actually, I was thinking it was I, who could be of assistance to you. I wanted to share with you my personal experience with the connection you and Ashlyn have discovered. I thought perhaps, if you were not too tired, I could share some of my story with you?"

"That would be amazing." Hawk pulled over a chair and settled himself next to the Elder. "I would love to have some insight into what's happening between Ash and myself. I've kept her at arm's length fighting what was meant to be between us. I know now I should've acted on my feelings and not run from them. Keeping everything bottled up has been the biggest mistake of my life," Hawk said, with regret.

"I completely understand. I, too felt overwhelmed by the connection when it happened to me."

The Elder wove a tale of love and connection intriguing Hawk with her wisdom and insight. Mesmerized by her power and knowledge, he inched to the edge of his chair absorbed in the moment.

Hawk lowered his head and ran his fingers through his hair. "I've never been able to process what this is between Ash and me, so I guess I deflected my feelings. Keeping my distance felt like the only solution. I can't help imagining how different things might have been if I'd explored this bond instead of avoiding it. Ashlyn would be here, safe, with me, right now." He finally felt like he was sharing his burden instead of enduring it alone.

Raven appeared lost in thought for a moment as if she were looking back in time. "I understand better than you might think. But the point here is, not what if, but what can you do now? I want you to know since Ashlyn has opened the link between you, it is now your gift to share with her. It will become a part of you both."

"I don't know how I did it, but I accidentally tapped into Ash's power. I wish I knew what I did."

"My young friend, you will see in time and with practice you will be able to reach out to Ashlyn with your mind, purposefully. You should be able to sense her presence when she is close by. Have you been sensing her emotions? Feeling her joy? Her pain?"

"Yes, yes I have. We have connected only a handful of times, but it seems to be growing stronger each time. This-this link between us is beyond belief. When her captors were hurting her, I was physically effected. I can feel her fear, her anger, and her pain. It's driving me crazy. I need to find her, to save her, and to correct my mistakes. I need to tell Ashlyn I love her."

The Elder smiled broadly. "Hawk, you remind me of my Kanti in many ways. You are so strong and confident. I miss him every day. I have no doubt you will find Ashlyn and Join with her. You will bring our Fire Guardian back to Aether where she belongs, by your side. Reach inside yourself, and use your bond, Hawk. Seek out her thoughts. Now go and get some sleep if you are able. May the God and Goddess be with you on your journey."

"Thank you, Raven. Thank you for everything."

Raven surprised him by kissing his cheek. He felt

the heat of her Fire as it gently grazed his skin. It was an odd feeling. It was as if she shared something with him through the small gesture.

****

A bump in the road jolted Hawk from his musings and brought him back to the present, in the Hummer with his team.

"Hawk? Did we lose you there? I was asking you if you've connected to Ashlyn." River raised an eyebrow.

"Sorry, I was thinking about last night. Raven came to see me and enlightened me about my bond with Ash. She had a similar connection to her Kanti," Hawk responded.

"Raven is really something, isn't she?" Kai chimed in.

"She's a scary old woman. I wouldn't mess with her. She would fry me alive," Quill joked.

"Lots of women in Aether want to fry you alive, Quill. Maybe if you could stick with just one woman, for more than one night, they wouldn't all want to burn you. Actually, come to think of it, if they had more than one night with you, they'd want to kill you even more," Kai teased.

"You better watch it, Sanders. I know things about you nobody else does, and I'm not afraid to share." Quill lightly punched Kai's shoulder.

"Boy you can dish it out, but you really can't take it. I was just kidding." Kai laughed, as he shoved Quill back.

"Guys, really, grow up," River reprimanded. "Hawk, did Raven tell you anything that would help us?"

"Yes, talking to Raven was amazing. Even though

the telepathy power belongs to the Guardian, once the bond is formed the connection goes both ways. I haven't intentionally tried to connect to Ash yet, but I want to try."

Bracken remained quiet during this entire exchange. He was a relatively new Protector and was initiated only about two years ago. Brack had been inadvertently entangled in a tragedy during the Trials just before inductions took place. River and Bear told Hawk they sensed Brack needed this opportunity to move forward. Apparently, he had never fully recovered. Although he was not at fault, guilt consumed him. Brack's gifts were unique. He needed to be able to let go of his pain and regret. Brack would have to learn to trust in his abilities in order to become the Protector he was meant to be.

Hawk thought he seemed like a smart, tough kid. The young Protector was tall and broad like most of the others. He gave the impression he was intelligent. Carefully observing everything around him, Brack didn't find it necessary to ask endless questions like some of his peers. He was also enormously gifted and had the ability to manipulate anything botanical. Plants bent to his will.

"Well, now appears to be as good a time as any. Why don't you give it a try? We'll be quiet and let you concentrate. Right, Quill?" River prompted.

"Who me?" Quill pointed to himself. "You won't even know I'm here. Just like always. I'm such a wallflower. I have to work on that."

"Ignore him please. Go ahead, Hawk, give it a try," Kai encouraged.

Closing his eyes, he concentrated on Ashlyn. He

imagined her standing before him; her beautiful red hair, her amber colored eyes, her gorgeous body. Blocking out everything else around him except for thoughts of Ashlyn, he suddenly found himself in the Atrium of the South Tower. Hawk lost his breath when he saw her standing there with the wind blowing her curls around her beautiful face. They were both highly emotional. Ash shared what she could with him. Hawk's heart broke at the desperation of Ashlyn's tears as she uncharacteristically begged him to help her.

The connection broke abruptly, the air crackled around him, and Hawk found himself seated back in the Hummer instantly feeling Ashlyn's loss. He sprang up in his seat. "It worked! Raven was right. I did it. I initiated the connection."

Hawk was encouraged. If Cadence could use his skills to find out where this Brooke woman worked, it could lead them straight to Ash. He had something concrete to hold onto now. Hawk immediately told them everything he learned from Ash. River was on the phone with Cadence almost before Hawk had finished telling them the details of his conversation.

Hope. Hawk had hope. His instincts were finally telling him he was going to find Ash and bring her home to Aether. From now on he would keep her safe. Never again would she wonder how he felt, because he would tell her everyday how much he loved her. They were going to be happy together, forever.

Chapter Twelve

Ashlyn

Studying Brooke, Ashlyn cocked her head slightly. She looked her up, down, and sideways. Brooke exuded something Ash couldn't put her finger on. An innocence and kindness radiated off her. Logically, she knew she shouldn't trust her, but her instincts told her there was something special about Brooke Barrington. She wasn't anything like her father, but trust sometimes had a price, and Ashlyn didn't want to pay with her life.

Brooke seemed desperate as she implored Ashlyn. "Please, won't you let me try to explain? I really want to tell you a little bit about my childhood, so maybe you can understand where I'm coming from. I know I can't change the fact I'm a Barrington, but I'm nothing like my father." Brooke advanced to the enclosure placing her hands on the glass. "I promise. Please, listen to me. I want to help you."

"Okay, I'm listening." Ash acquiesced, crossing her arms over her chest, standing tall.

"I'm thirty-four years old, and I have spent all of those years trying to get my father to notice me. I desperately wanted to please him and to make him proud. He's always put his work before anything else in his life including my mom and me. When I was little, he was busy building his medical career. I remember my mom begging him to come home for Christmas when I was about six. He refused saying he had patients who needed him, and my mom was selfish."

"Why didn't you and your mom leave him?"

"I'm not really sure. They slept in separate bedrooms for as long as I can remember. He was always so abrupt with her, so cruel. He expected us to be perfect, but it was impossible to live up to his standards. Believe me, my mother tried. When I turned eight, he forced her to send me to boarding school. I was never smart enough, or pretty enough, and certainly not good enough to be a Barrington. In case my shortcomings weren't enough, I am scarred, damaged goods. As a baby, I was burned in an accident. I have no memory of it, but to this day I still have discomfort and tingling in the area. That's why I wear this compression glove on my hand." Brooke lifted her hand and turn it around to show Ashlyn. "It's a constant reminder I'm imperfect and no matter how hard I try, I'll simply never be good enough for Charles Barrington." Brooke wiped a tear which had escaped from the corner of her eye.

"I'm sorry, Brooke. It must've been really hard growing up with a father who was so heartless. You must have been so scared when he sent you away at such a young age."

"It was hard, and I definitely was scared. My mom cried for weeks. One time, I overheard them arguing about it. He told her he didn't need the distractions of a small child around, and it was bad enough he had her to contend with." A few more tears leaked silently down Brooke's cheeks as she shared the memory. Then, as if collecting herself, she paused a moment before continuing. "Even though I was afraid, I was also relieved to be getting away from my father. Despite my age, I knew there was something very wrong with our relationship. When I wasn't being ignored, I was belittled at every opportunity. He never hit me, but he had this terrifying manner which made me cower when he got too close. And his words cut like a knife. I guess he still holds more power over me than I realized. I'm so sorry I left you. I was a coward."

Ashlyn believed Brooke was telling the truth. She couldn't imagine someone who was supposed to love you making such a strong statement with such cruelty. Even though her experience with Charles Barrington had been limited, it wasn't really hard to believe he was capable of such harshness, even to his own daughter. He appeared a cold and merciless man.

"Anyway, that's how I grew up. It was as if I didn't exist to him. My mom, her name was Olivia; she was amazing. She was warm and kind whereas my father was aloof and cutting. Mom thought everything I did was brilliant. He thought everything I did was a childish waste of time. After a while, it got to the point I didn't even come home for holidays anymore. My mom would pick me up at school. We would travel to some far away, fun, or exotic place together instead."

"Sounds like you're lucky to have her."

"Was. I was lucky. She died last year. I miss her every day." Brooke's voice trembled. "My mom was possessive of me. She tried to keep me away from him. Most of my memories of my father are from photographs. I rarely saw him in person. When I did, he acted like a stranger to me. His attitude ranged from dismissive to out and out cruel." Backing away from the glass wall, Brooke slowly paced back and forth in front of the enclosure. "The more apathetic he was, the more determined I was to please him. I got my degree in pharmacology. I graduated first in my class but still no acknowledgement from him." Shaking her head back and forth, she continued. "So I got a Master's in chemistry and a PhD biochemical engineering thinking I'd impress him and finally make him proud. No such luck. He stuck me here, gave me a powerless title, and treats me like an interloper." Brooke stopped, approached the glass again and looked Ashlyn directly in the eyes. "Last night was the first time I've seen him in months. I used to beg my mother to explain to me why she was with him, their history, anything, but she shut me out. My mom and I could talk about anything, except Charles Barrington."

"The way he treated you was cruel. I'm sorry, Brooke. I feel bad. I do. But none of the things you told me explains any of this." Ash gestured with her hand around the lab. "What can you tell me about this place? Why am I here?"

"I really wish I knew. Honestly, I'm in the dark here. My father is a complicated and brilliant man, but I never, ever, imagined he was capable of something this heinous." Brooke placed her hand over her heart. "Please, Ashlyn, you have to believe me. My mother and I were never enough for him. He built CEB Labs in order to fulfill some need. Now it seems, this company isn't enough either. I don't know what he's up to or what he wants with you. But I promise, if it's the last thing I do, I'm going to find out."

"I need to get of here now. I don't want to help your father with whatever crazy scheme he has going on. And Devlin is pure evil."

"You're not kidding about Devlin. Don't provoke him, Ashlyn. He's ruthless and crazy. He was in the military for a long time, and I think that's why he's not quite right." Twirling her finger next to her temple, she continued. "He's been my father's right-hand man for a long time. He makes my skin crawl, always has. I don't know how to get you out of there or how to keep you safe from them," Brooke admitted softly. Her shoulders dropped and she let out a deep breath.

"I believe you, Brooke, I do. We need that damn remote to open the glass. If you can't find it, I'm stuck here. But you can help me in another way. I need to know where we are. My people are coming to rescue me. Will you help me?"

"Yes, yes of course I'll help you. You are in CEB's main headquarters in a subterranean level that's supposed to be used for storage. But how can you be so sure they're coming?"

"There's no time to explain. Trust me, I know they're coming. Right now, you need to get out of here. Devlin told me Barrington has plans for me today. They could be back any minute. You can't get caught here with me. My best chance is if you go now. Please, Brooke, I know you want to help, but go. Think of a plan to help my people get passed all this security. That's what we need. I'm counting on you."

"I can't leave you here. God knows what they'll do to you, Ashlyn. I can't let them hurt you anymore."

Ashlyn held up her arms. They had been covered heavily in bruises just last night, but today there was barely a mark remaining. "They can only hurt me so much. I have the ability to heal myself for the most part. Only a catastrophic injury can kill me. I'm not sure your father knows that yet. I'm not sure what he knows. Please, I'm begging you. Just go. Keep my secret safe. Make a plan, Brooke. Help me."

"This entire thing gets more insane by the minute. I hope you'll explain all of this to me when we have more time. I'm not happy about leaving you to the wolves, but I'll go for now. I'll come up with a plan and be back for you with or without your people's help. Don't fight Devlin and my father, Ashlyn. It will only make whatever they have planned worse."

Brooke slipped out quietly. Ash didn't have the heart to tell her it wouldn't matter if she fought them or not. Devlin was going to bring her pain. Ashlyn had seen it in his glacial eyes. She mentally prepared herself for whatever they had in store for her. She would fight with everything she had inside her and so would her Fire.

Not long after Brooke left, the telltale beeping of the keypad outside the laboratory doors sounded. Ashlyn's entire body tensed. Charles Barrington entered with his guard dog Devlin at his heels. The synchronized beat of military boots echoed through the lab, as four men dressed in strange suits marched in. They carried what looked like giant plastic shields of some kind. Sweat dotted her forehead, and her stomach tangled in knots. Ashlyn had a really bad feeling about this.

"Hello, Ashlyn. I hope you are ready to cooperate with some experiments I have planned for today. Your attitude has been less than exemplary. We will get what we want from you one way or another. I do hope you will not give Mr. Devlin and these other men a reason to cause you unnecessary pain," Barrington commanded, in a condescending tone.

Devlin simply smiled at her with the promise of vile things to come written all over his face. Fearsome looking, Devlin was tall with black hair cut in a severe looking military style and his skin was tan, as if he spent many hours outdoors. Built thick with bulging muscles, his body was ultra-fit. Eyes the color of a midnight storm seethed, boring straight into Ashlyn. A raised, jagged scar ran from the middle of his forehead, along the outside edge of his eye, and down his right cheek ending in the corner of his mouth. It was apparent to Ash, Devlin carried many scars and not just physical ones. How else could a person hold such anger and rage?

Ash knew Brooke's advice not to fight them was sound, but she was strong willed with a passionate nature. Ashlyn Woods was of The House of Fire. She had an instinctive drive to fight rather than submit.

With moxie, Ash stood up tall thrusting her shoulders back as she faced off with her enemies. "Go fuck yourself, Dr. Barrington. I have no intention of cooperating with you in any way, and I dare you to try to make me."

"I am certainly looking forward to seeing you in action, Ashlyn," Barrington mocked, arrogantly. He gestured to the men dressed in the odd-looking suits. "Go set up on the other side of the lab. Ashlyn and I still have much to discuss before we get started."

"I have nothing to say to you. Except let me out of here before I make you regret this. You really have no idea what I'm capable of." Ash narrowed her eyes feeling her Fire stir.

"You're right, young lady, but that is why you are

here. I intend to discover the full extent of your oddities. We have studied your blood, your organs, and your bone structure. I have even done scans of your brain. We have learned a great deal from our medical studies, but now I wish to see the full force of these strange powers of yours. I will need all the data I can obtain to make my new drug. It will be sold to the government with the highest bid to enhance their soldiers."

"You are sicker than I thought," Ash said, losing a bit of her bravado.

Barrington ignored her statement. "Tell me about the brand you have on your palm. Who marked you? And for what reason?"

Ashlyn instinctively traced the outline of her Guardian symbol with the tip of her finger as she often did when she was contemplating something. She knew she shouldn't tell him anything about her Guardian mark. "None of your damn business."

"Ah, I see you are still not feeling obliged to comply. Well, let us begin with an experiment instead. I have a feeling you will change your mind rather quickly."

The men in the strange suits approached her glass prison surrounding it. Barrington and Devlin backed away behind the plastic shields, as Devlin used the remote to raise the glass wall. Ashlyn faced them. Her Fire hovered near the surface, and her hands and fingers tingled. One of the men grabbed her roughly, and her Fire erupted surging toward him. To her dismay his grip remained firm still biting into her flesh.

"The suits are fire retardant. Didn't think we were dumb enough to face your flames without defenses, did you? These shields also screen us from you and your temper, Firecracker," Devlin taunted.

Dragging her, the soldier deposited her about five feet in front of three tables with concrete tops. The cavernous laboratory had been cleared on one side except for the tables. The first one was piled high with logs which smelled like Aether's forest. The second was covered with thick metal sheets and the third held a shimmering cluster of amethyst colored crystals. Flanking her, two of the men stood with guns pointed at her. Ash's heart pounded when she realized they were tranquilizer guns. Her gaze flickered anxiously between two men behind her holding imposing metal sticks tightly in their thick grips. Her Fire perceived danger and drifted up and down her arms and hands.

"Are the heat sensors connected, Devlin? I want to register how high the temperature rises on the samples, as well as the room temperature," Barrington questioned.

"All set for our little Firecracker here to strut her stuff."

"Now, Ashlyn, if you would please demonstrate for me the capacity of your power by setting the contents of each table alight. One at a time please." Barrington made his request as if he were asking her to pass the salt at the dinner table.

"Sure thing. I'll get right on that, as soon as hell freezes over, you asswipe," Ashlyn said, unable to stop herself.

Crossing her arms over her chest, defiant, Ash stood firm. Devlin signaled the men behind her with a nod of his head. Searing pain shot through Ashlyn's left shoulder blade. Groaning, she grabbed for it. The burning sensation subsided quickly. But before she even fully recovered, another zap shot through her buttocks jolting her forward. The pain was intense, but Ashlyn remained upright thinking this wasn't as bad as the Taser they had used.

"We can do this all-day, Firecracker." Devlin mocked her, rubbing his hands together. "You ready to show us what you've got yet?"

"Drop dead, you sadistic pig!" Rage overtook her, and Ash knew her face must have been as red as her hair. Her Flame rocketed toward Devlin melting his shield. The heat forced him to drop it to the ground and back away.

Devlin signaled his men. Rapid, unrelenting jolts of electricity continued to pierce random parts of her body. Ashlyn fought to remain upright to no avail, and she sank to her knees from the pain, panting. One of the goons yanked her back to her feet. The onslaught continued lasting for what felt like hours.

"What do you say now, you little bitch?" Devlin ridiculed.

"G-g-going, to, to, to, f-f-ry you, prick." Ashlyn sputtered, fighting off the effects of the electricity.

Weak, she raised her hands. Her Fire, suppressed by the unyielding voltage, remained buried. Approaching her, Devlin pulled his arm back and drove his fist directly into her face. Agony ripped through her eye and cheek. The metallic taste of blood filled her mouth. Three more jabs to her ribs followed, taking Ashlyn back to the ground. Finally, a series of electric shocks had her curling into a protective ball.

Standing over Ashlyn, with the scrape of metal against leather, Devlin unsheathed a long, serrated blade from his belt. "Are you done being a pain in the ass? Or should I carve up that pretty face of yours?" With practiced hands, he menacingly spun the knife around. Then slowly, he began running his fingers along the edge of the blade. He sneered; his scar twisting his features further.

Ashlyn couldn't move. Her survival instinct battled with her need to fight. Her Fire fought a battle all its own, reaching for the surface, yet unable to protect the Guardian. Devlin yanked her to her feet, roughly taking hold of her shoulders, and spinning her around until the knife grazed her throat.

"Enough of this bullshit! You do as the boss says, and light the goddamn fire!" Devlin roared directly in her ear making her wince. Dragging the knife across her neck, he sliced her with the blade.

Warm and sticky, blood trickled down Ash's neck and chest. Trembling on shaky legs, she felt the fight leave her. With her head down, Ash watched her blood flow steadily, staining the front of her hospital gown scarlet.

Devlin released her and pointed her toward the three tables once again. "Now do it! Or I'll cut you like I mean it next time."

Desperately fighting off the effects of the electric shocks, Ashlyn took a deep breath. She winced from the pain to her damaged ribs calling desperately to her Fire. Flames emerged traveling up her hands, arms, and fingers, answering her call. Facing the first table, she raised her hands throwing her Fire onto the pile of logs. They burst and crackled blooming with vibrant colored flames. Next, she turned to the table with the metal sheets. Targeting her Fire onto the pieces of metal, they gradually began to melt. Blue flames skimmed the surface, and the puddle bubbled like a pile of molten lava. Focusing her attention on the third table, sweat beaded along her forehead, and her arms shook from the exertion. Ash closed her eyes as she concentrated on the beautiful crystals. They took all of her energy to burn, but they did not erupt in flames. They simply melted into a pile of oozing liquid.

Ashlyn dropped to the floor depleted of energy. She nearly gagged. The air smelled toxic from the mixture of blood and the charred remnants of Barrington's experiment and Devlin's torture. Taking advantage, Devlin swooped in and delivered several kicks to her already damaged ribs as well as her arms and legs. "Take that, Firecracker."

The next thing she knew, Barrington was beside her and pressed the plunger of a needle into her arm. He chuckled maniacally. "Well that was quite helpful. You will rest now, and we will address your injuries. Sleep well, young Ashlyn. Our work here has just begun."

Ashlyn's last coherent thought was of Hawk. She had to believe he and the other Protectors would free her before these madmen finally killed her. She said a silent prayer as darkness took her. *Please, Hawk. Find me. Save me. I need you.*

****

Hawk

As the endless stretches of highway buzzed by, Hawk stared blindly out the passenger side window and relived his time with Ash in the Atrium. She took his breath away; so beautiful, so strong, so brave. If he didn't get to Ash soon he feared he would lose control of his powers, or worse yet, his mind. He needed to show her how much he loved her and not with words. He wanted to use his hands, his lips, his body. Ash had a seductiveness about her without even trying. Her allure was as powerful as her Fire. River's voice roused him from his musings, and Hawk's body hummed with tension and frustration.

River mumbled through the phone to Cadence, "Yeah...okay...no...just a sec." He handed the phone to Hawk. "Put this on speaker, and grab the laptop under your seat." Hawk balanced the phone in the console and reached under his seat for the laptop. The computer sprang to life when Hawk raised the top. River spoke again, "Go ahead, Cadence, send it through."

The computer screen flashed images in rapid succession, like a strobe light in a dance club, as the downloaded information appeared on the screen. Hawk noticed a company logo he quickly recognized as Barrington Laboratories. It was followed by a series of articles and then tons of photos whizzed by. The barrage of information screeched to a halt stopping on the face of a young woman. The caption underneath the photo read; *Dr. Brooke Barrington, Assistant Director of CEB Laboratories.*

Hawk couldn't hold back his reaction, and a slight breeze picked inside the Hummer. "Holy crap! The Brooke, that Ashlyn met is Brooke Barrington. *Barrington*! As in Charles Barrington. I've got to warn her not to trust that woman."

"Calm down, Hawk. Ash told you the woman wanted to help her," Kai said. He leaned over the seat inclining the laptop with Brooke's photo into his line of vision. "Plus, look at her. Does she look like someone capable of hurting anyone? In fact, there's something in her eyes, maybe she truly wants to help Ash," Kai said.

Quill grabbed the laptop right out of Hawk's hands. "Let me see." Hawk glared at his friend as he brought the screen close to his face and froze. Quill appeared fixated on the woman's image. Hawk noticed her spectacular blue eyes and wondered if Quill might feel some kind of connection to this Brooke Barrington. Hawk shivered at the thought.

His friend deposited the computer back into his lap as if trying to break Brooke's spell. "Kai's right. Look at that face. She wouldn't hurt a fly. I think she looks, um, sweet, you know, innocent." Quill dropped his butt back down onto his seat. "Does it say anything about her in there? Maybe she's a distant relative of—"

"You two are kidding, right? Innocent looking, my foot. Her last name is Barrington. You can't think that's a coincidence. The bastard must have sent her to Ash to deceive her into thinking she can trust her. The cagey prick is up to something. We've got to get to her now, River." Low level vibrations made the Hummer shimmy a bit as Hawk's powers took control.

River responded in an even tone, "Hawk, I'm doing the best I can to get us there. You need to get in control. Ash has held her own so far, I'm sure she can hang in there a little longer. She's tough. She's a Guardian. She's going to be all right. Now hand the laptop to Brack and let him do the search. You three are as emotional as a group of woman at a PMS convention."

"Holy shit, River, you actually cracked a joke. Hey, I wonder what Lily would think about your PMS convention comment. How's about I give her a call and we'll see if she thinks it was really funny?" Quill joked. He whipped his phone out and held it up.

"Don't even think about going near my woman, Robbins. She may be small, but she'll kick your ass. And when she's done, I'm going to kick it even harder," River answered, with a chuckle.

"You wish, man," Quill bantered back. Then he twisted in his seat to face Brack. "Enough of this BS, I want to know more about this Brooke woman. What you got there, Brack?"

Quill seemed captivated by Brooke's picture, and Hawk wondered if he would need to save two people from the Barringtons. Bracken smiled and relieved Hawk of the computer. "It says, Brooke Kylie Barrington was born on March 5, 1982. She is the only child of Dr. Charles Edward Barrington and Olivia Claire Royce-Barrington. She attended boarding school in England from the time she was eight years old until her graduation. She holds a degree in Pharmacology, has a Master's in Chemistry, and earned a Doctorate in Biochemical Engineering. Graduated top of her class from Princeton. It also says Brooke became the Assistant Director of CEB Labs five years ago, and her office is located in their main headquarters."

"I knew we were on the right track. We're heading straight to her now. It's going to be okay, Hawk. We're going to get Ash back," River assured.

Still on the line, River spoke to Cadence, "Hey, buddy, call in the two teams closest to our destination, and tell them to meet us at the rendezvous point tomorrow. Also, book a few more motel rooms. We're pretty conspicuous, so spread out the locations; we don't want to draw any unwanted attention. Recall the remaining teams back to Aether. Tell Bear we're pretty sure we've tracked down Ashlyn's position, and I'll be in touch soon. Got all that?"

"Got it, River. Bear's right here listening in on the speakerphone so he's all caught up. Don't worry, I'll take care of everything. I'll recheck the schematics of the CEB location you're heading to. I just want to make sure we didn't miss anything. Let me know when you get closer, Cadence out."

As they neared their destination Hawk grew more hopeful, but his anxiety kicked his powers into high gear. His hair lifted in a current of air and swirled around his head. Small tremors continued to rock the Hummer. He couldn't wait to get to Ash, but at what cost? Would Ash ever be the same person again after enduring her captivity and abuse?

Quill grabbed hold of the seat in front of him; it seemed, he was trying remain upright. "Hawk, dude! Get your shit together. We're going to drive off the road."

Unable to keep his thoughts from her, Hawk soon sensed something creeping in, despair, hopelessness. Caught off guard, pain bombarded him in a rush, doubling him over. Repeated electric shocks wracked his body. Thrashing, he slid down to the floor in front of his seat groaning loudly.

Quill dove over the seat. "What the hell? Hawk, what's wrong with you?" Grabbing River's sleeve, he panicked a bit. "River, pull over, quick! He's having a seizure or something. "Kai, get over here!"

Kai leaned over the seat, and Hawk felt his fingers pressing on his neck. "His pulse is normal, and he's conscious. My guess is, it's Ashlyn. I've seen this before, but it is even more intense than the last time. Their telepathic link is growing stronger." Kai closed his eyes. He looked as though he were concentrating to bring forth his gift. Placing his hands on Hawk, Kai reassured everyone their friend was in no physical danger.

Hawk heard faint whispers all around him. Quill got down on his knee squeezing in next to his friend. "Hawk, buddy, talk to me."

He opened his mouth, gasping, only able to mumble faintly. "Hurting her. Need to stop them…" His voice trailed off as another round of violence assailed him. Hawk's head shot back into the seat just as Devlin's fist made contact with Ashlyn's face. Reaching up, he touched his throbbing eye and cheek, wincing. He received a jab to his ribs and expelled a loud, "Ooof." The punches were followed by several more shocks, and Hawk crumbled.

Quill hoisted him under the arms and back up onto the seat. Hawk floated between Ash's pain and his own physical body. As he tried sit up, his stomach tightened with fear.

Hawk's words caught in his throat. "Someone has a knife to her neck," he managed to choke out. Blood trickled down, and Hawk instinctively reached up to wipe it away, but his hand came back clean. "They c-c-cut h-h-her," he stammered, "I feel the blood." He looked down at his hands, turning them over. "Nothing here though."

A surge of power rammed into Hawk throwing him more off balance. Ash's Fire. The heat of her Flame coursed through his veins. She was fighting back. "That's my Guardian. Fight back, Ash. I'm almost there."

"Have you gone mental? What the hell are you talking about?" Quill yelled out.

Slumping down lower in the seat, Hawk felt defeated. He thought Ash fought back with her Fire, but he encountered something altogether different, her surrender. Before he could even process the idea, the bond between them ignited in a burst of intensity. As both bodies absorbed blow after blow, Hawk's ribs protested, his arms and legs convulsing. Ash's Fire was squelched. Hawk curled into himself as Ash absorbed wave after wave of pain. Helpless to save his Guardian, Hawk collapsed in a heap. Even as she called out to him, he remained powerless. "Please, Hawk. Find me. Save me. I need you." Gone in an instant, their link severed, no more pain or fear, and no more Ash.

Chapter Thirteen

Laurel

The smell of smoke tingled inside Laurel's nose. Thick, gray clouds filled the blue sky, and glowing fires blazed all around Aether. Even the Grand Lake protested the capture of Ashlyn. A layer of flames skittered along the surface like an oil spill set on fire. The Aetherians utilized their partnership with the Elements to keep the fires at bay. Even with their union, they barely maintained control and balance in Aether. The Elders feared the disharmony would soon affect the human world as well.

As fires glowed incandescently all around the village, Laurel said a silent prayer. *Please bring Ash back safely. Aether needs her. I need her.* The longest Laurel had ever gone without seeing or speaking to Ashlyn was about two days while she was on a trip. Not only did Laurel worry about Ash, now she worried about Kai and the others, too.

As if he knew she'd been thinking about him, Laurel felt the vibration of her phone. Her stomach knotted, and she hesitated before tapping the screen. "What if it's bad news?" she whispered to no one.

Squaring her shoulders, Laurel took a deep breath as she unlocked the screen on her phone. Kai's words filled the screen. *—Hey, baby, I'm so sorry I had to leave you this morning. Forgive me? If it helps, I miss* *you already.—*

Laurel stared blankly at Kai's message. She understood completely why he had needed to join Ash's rescue team, but the timing could not have been worse. Her fingertips moved to her lips which still tingled from Kai's passionate kisses. Squeezing her legs together, she reminded herself of the delicious soreness that settled there. The night before had been magical, but she woke alone in his bed after their first night back together. In spite of herself, Laurel smirked as she thought of her response. *—I may consider forgiving you if you grovel appropriately. I've always wanted a sex slave.—*

His retort was almost instantaneous. *—Oh, baby, I'll be your sex slave anytime. I'm all yours, my love.—*

Her smile wide, Laurel held the phone to her chest and wished Kai was back with her in Aether.

The phone sounded again, and she pulled it away to read what Kai had written now. *—Good news about Ash. We know where she is being held, and we should be there in 8 or 9 hours with the way River is driving. They're sending two more teams to help us. Hopefully, by tomorrow night we will have Ash back with us.—*

She let out a breath she didn't realize she was holding. *—That's the best news! How is Hawk holding up?—*

Kai replied. *—He had an encounter with Ash, and he was really thrown by it. He'll be okay as soon as we have her back.—*

Certain that Kai was keeping something from her, Laurel wondered, what kind of encounter they could've had? *—What aren't you telling me, Kai Sanders?—*

It took a minute to receive an answer. *—There is*

too much to explain in detail through a text. I'll call you tonight when we can talk privately. I'm squished between Quill and Bracken. I keep catching Quill trying to read over my shoulder. I'm going to slug him.—

She laughed loudly. *—That I would love to see. I'm still laughing at the image of you sandwiched between those two. And Quill snuggling up to you. Ha, Ha, Ha.—*

Her phone dinged with his response. *—Nobody used the word snuggled but you! You are the only one I want to snuggle, baby. Anyway, thanks for making me laugh. I really do miss you already, Laurel. I'll call you tonight. But it's going to be really late, probably not before one or two am. Why don't you stay at my house? I like the idea of you in my bed.—*

There was only one response she could think of.

—Okay and I miss you, too xoxo—

Stowing her phone in the back pocket of her jeans, Laurel headed for the South Tower. She was worried about Rowan and Mica and wanted to check in on them. The majestic South Tower jutted up in front of her blocking the sun and casting a mammoth shadow over her path. It made her think about Ashlyn. A vision standing in the Tower's Atrium, Ash exuded beauty, strength, and power. Pausing, Laurel looked up. "I miss you so much, Ash." She dabbed the corner of her eye with her sleeve. "I know what you would tell me, sister of my heart, tap into the Elements." Laurel planted her feet firmly and brought her fingertips to her temples. Opening her connection to the House of Earth, Laurel let the power fortify her. Taking a deep breath, she focused on the task at hand. "One day, one hour, one minute at a time, that's what I'm going to concentrate on." Determined to think positively, Laurel pointed herself straight toward the Tower.

****

Kai

Watching helplessly as Hawk convulsed and thrashed from Ashlyn's assault, Kai felt powerless. Once again, his two worlds collided in dramatic fashion. Science and Aether were diametrically opposed. The unfolding of this phenomenon before his eyes still left him bewildered. Hawk had suffered Ash's pain previously, and Kai knew there had been no lasting effects. This time, the connection appeared stronger and even more physical. Kai was completely convinced Hawk and Ashlyn were now linked empathically not just telepathically. Kai drew a deep breath into his lungs and blew it out. He needed to stay calm and find a link between science and the Elements. Squinting his eyes tightly, Kai dug deep searching for his own gifts. Hesitantly, his power came forth revealing his true nature.

Kai leaned over Hawk. "It seems you have tenderness to the touch on several areas of your body yet no bruising or swelling of any kind." He suspected it was phantom pain laced with emotional distress that had Hawk reeling. Kai could see it written all over his friend's face. His gift kept him in tune with what was happening inside Hawk's body. He could sense the increased rate of Hawk's heart and respiration. He wished he could help his friend, but he knew only time would help Hawk recover. And Ashlyn.

Hawk turned to River who was still at the wheel. "If you stop this truck, I will kill you. Just keep driving. I'll be fine in a little while but Ash won't. She's hurt badly, and I lost communication with her. I'll try again when I'm feeling stronger. Please, River, just hurry."

It seemed Quill could not stay quiet another minute. "Hawk, buddy, listen to me. Some serious shit just went down here. You need to let River stop so Kai can get a better look at you. It was like some invisible guy was pounding the crap out of you, but there was nobody there."

"I'm fine, Quill, really. I'm much more worried about Ash then I am about myself. They tortured her and she did something, something I never thought Ash would do in a million years... She surrendered. We can't afford to stop for any reason."

Kai leaned over Hawk. "Can you straighten up? I know the areas are tender, but you have no residual damage." Hawk winced but pulled himself upright in his seat. Relief was evident on everyone's faces. "Do you want to talk about it?" Kai asked.

"No... Yes... They wanted her to do something for them, but Ash refused so they shocked her with cattle prods. I guess the jolt temporarily knocked out her Fire. This one bastard, with a scar running down his entire face, punched her in the eye." Sweat streaked down the side of Hawk's temple as he described Ash's experience. Hawk reached up and touched his cheek where Ash must have been hit. "Then, they shocked her again. She was hanging tough until he held a knife to her throat and cut her." Hawk ran his hand over his throat, and pain was evident on his face. Whose pain was it though, Hawk's or Ash's?

"I could feel the blood on my own neck but when I touched it, nothing was there. It's like hovering between two places at once. It's so strange."

210

Not only was Hawk's anger palpable, but his powers lingered in the air around the Hummer. Currents swirled around the massive vehicle, and vibrations jostled everyone in their seats.

"Really, Hawk? Again? Give it a rest with the powers, man," Quill said.

"You don't understand. They forced her to use her Fire. She was so strong, but finally, she acquiesced. They gave her no other choice. I'm going to kill the son of bitch who put his hands on her." Hawk brought his hand to his forehead rubbing his temples with his thumb and forefinger. "I felt her fall to the ground. Then she was gone, and our link was severed."

"Listen to me, Hawk. Ash can definitely handle those types of injuries, and she'll be able to recover pretty quickly. Most likely within a few days. Please don't give up hope," Kai encouraged.

"I get the medical shit, Kai, but why the hell should she need to recover at all?" Hawk's fists tightened, and his voice developed a dark edge. "The prick with the scar is dead. I'm warning you guys right now. Don't even think of stopping me." Hawked cautioned, vibrating with tension.

River sounded steady and even when he interjected. "All right, this is what's going to happen. For now, Hawk, you will cease and desist all talk of murder please. You need to get some rest and get your strength back. We're going to need you in top form. Everyone, unless it's an emergency let's just stay quiet. Get in touch with your true Protector. We will fight to the end to get Ashlyn back. I need all of you to focus on our common goal, to save our Fire Guardian."

They drove in silence for many hours on the

winding mountain roads. The scenery hummed by as they sped along mesmerizing Kai as he stared out the window. Quill slept beside him dropping his head to Kai's shoulder every once in a while. Jabbing Quill repeatedly as he attempted to use him as a pillow, Kai was sure Quill's ribs were going to be bruised tomorrow. The buzz of his friend's loud snores permeated the vehicle's interior furthering Kai's irritation. He couldn't help but think how amused Laurel would be with the image of Quill resting on his shoulder. He was anxious to hear her voice tonight when he called her from the motel. Part of him still worried she would be angry with him. With the way River drove, they would be there in no time so Kai closed his eyes and dreamed of Laurel.

Bouncing out of his seat, Kai woke with a start. The Hummer lurched forward as River hit a giant pothole in the motel parking lot. "Up and at 'em, men." River chuckled under his breath as he hit a second divot in the lot. Kai thought he was having a little too much fun. "We're here at the motel. The other two teams are staying at different locations in the area. We have a rendezvous point where we will meet up tomorrow. Brack and I will take one room and you three take the other. Sorry for the triple. Kai, you were an unexpected bonus. I'll be right back. I'm going to check us in and get the keys." River disappeared into the motel office while the rest of them waited.

Quill broke the silence, "Hawk?" He paused, stared, and said nothing else until Hawk replied.

"Yes, Quill?"

"Are you all right? You kind of scared the crap out of me with the whole Exorcist, possession thing you

212

had going there. Thankfully, your head didn't spin around cause that would've totally freaked me out."

Hawk smiled faintly. "I'm fine now, but I appreciate the support, buddy." Hawk's smile faded, hard lines creasing the corners of his eyes. "I'm pissed though. Seriously pissed. I'm going to—"

River swung the door open, abruptly ending Hawk's mini tirade. The lead Protector expertly maneuvered the massive vehicle through the cramped parking lot and found a spot near an exit. He backed in and left space on both sides of the SUV in case they needed to make tracks in a hurry. "Let's all get some shut eye. Come to our room in the morning at 0700. We're in room 115, and you guys are next door in 116. Grab the gear, and let's move out."

They yanked their bags and other gear from the cargo hold and headed for the room. A green light flashed when Kai inserted the key card and pushed his way in. Looking around, he stepped aside to make room for Hawk and Quill to join him. The room was time worn but clean. Two full sized beds with yellow and white flowered bedcovers took up most of the room. Across the way, sat a long dresser with an old-style box television bolted to it.

After surveying the place, Kai took a deep breath letting it out slowly. His entire body felt stiff. He desperately wanted two things, a steaming hot shower and to hear Laurel's voice. They were all completely wiped out from driving for nearly twenty hours straight only stopping for gas and to use the bathroom.

"I'm going outside to call Laurel. When I come back, I'm jumping in the shower. Then I definitely need to crash." Kai headed toward the door looking over his shoulder.

"Dude, you should probably call from the bathroom. I'm sure the other motel guests don't want any part of your phone sex. Hawk and I can play some music real loud, you know, to drown out your moaning and shit," Quill teased.

"You never quit, do you?" Kai said, with a smile. "I'll be outside if you need me for any reason. And, Quill, I mean a real reason. None of your bullshit tonight, please, I'm tired." He swiped the keycard off the dresser on his way out the door.

Sweaty palms had Kai wiping his hands on his pants. Pacing in circles, his stomach tangled in knots, he couldn't remember being this nervous in a long time. But when he thought of Laurel, of being with her again, he knew he needed her desperately. Truthfully, if he was being honest with himself, he never stopped needing her. When he couldn't endure it another second, he slid his finger across the screen scrolling through his contacts. Laurel's name lit up. With his finger hovering over the button, he took a deep breath and touched it.

Laurel answered on only the second ring not a hint of sleep in her voice. "Hello."

"Hi there, beautiful, hope I didn't wake you."

Kai's heartbeat picked up its rhythm. He could picture Laurel; lips swollen, sheets rumpled, waiting for him. The feel of her silken hair pulled tight in his fist as he held her exactly where he wanted her. He had to get a grip, or Quill might be proven right about the phone sex. Just the thought of Laurel talking dirty to him had Kai adjusting his pants. The sweet sound of her voice snapped him out of it.

214

"No, I was waiting for your call. How are you?"

He could hear the worry in her tone, and the heavy weight of guilt clutched him. Words flew from his lips seemingly of their own volition, "I'm so sorry I left. You know I had to come and fix things. Please, I need you to understand. I have to stop Charles."

She laughed. "It's okay. I knew you were going as soon as Hawk told you the plan. Of course, I'm not happy. I'm worried about you. But being with you again kind of makes me want to forgive you." He could hear the smile in her voice as she continued. "It was even more amazing then I remember. It was like a dream."

"I love you, Laurel. I wish you were here and could feel my heart racing. Leaving you sleeping in my bed nearly ripped me in two. But I need to correct my mistakes and to help save Ash, then everything will be in balance again, including us."

"None of what happened to Ash and me was your fault. I know you guys will get her back. But listen, I have to ask you something, and be honest with me. You were very cryptic earlier. Please, is there something you're not telling me? I have a right to know."

"I'd never keep a secret from you. I'm just trying to protect you, honey; it's upsetting. Are you sure you want to hear this?"

Laurel took a moment to answer. "Yes. Yes, I really want to know. I want to be prepared to help Ash with whatever she's had to face. When she gets back to Aether, she'll need me. It's better if I know now."

"This needs to stay between us. You can't tell a soul."

"Kai, you're talking in riddles. Just tell me

already."

"A woman who works in the lab, named Brooke, found Ash and said she wants to help. The problem is, she's Charles Barrington's daughter."

"Oh my God!" Laurel squeaked out.

"Ashlyn believes Brooke is genuine, and I trust her instincts. She's smart and tough not some gullible young girl. Ash is the Guardian of Fire after all. I think we need to have faith in her."

"Wow, that's a lot to take in. I hope you're right about this Brooke woman. Why would she go against her own father to help Ash?"

"I don't know for sure, but maybe it's because her father is an evil, psychotic kidnapper. But, Laurel, there's more..." Kai choked up, as dread filled him. He knew what he had to tell Laurel next would destroy her.

"Go on, Kai, just tell me. I'm going to find out sooner or later. I'd rather hear it from you."

"They hurt her, honey. Those animals beat her and cut her." Laurel gasped loudly. "Listen to me, Hawk was linked to her at the time, and none of the injuries were serious. It seems they were trying to coerce her, teach her a lesson, and get her to submit. I'm so sorry, Laurel."

She sniffled softly. "I'm glad you told me. No wonder you don't want me to tell anyone." Her crying got a little louder, causing her words to stick in her throat. "Oh God, Kai, poor Ash."

"It's going to be okay, baby. We're going to get her back. And I'm going to stop Charles Barrington for good. I may have inadvertently started this, but I'm going to end it. I'm going to help restore balance."

"You better be careful, Kai. These men are

ruthless. I need you to come home to me. You don't think I waited 50 years to get you back just to lose you again, do you? I stayed in your house tonight like you wanted me to. I'm in your bed right now, and I'm not wearing anything. I can still feel your hands on me, Kai. My lips can still feel yours. Please, promise me you won't do anything to will risk your life."

"Laurel, baby, you're my everything and always have been. I promise to be careful. You know Hawk and Quill won't let anything happen to me. Plus, with the visual you just gave me of you in my bed, I know what I have waiting for me when I get back. I was going to go in and take a hot shower, but I think now I'll make it a cold one. I'm not sure when I'll be able to speak to you again. Strategies tomorrow morning, and then we free Ash tomorrow night. I'll be in touch as soon as I can. Sweet dreams."

"Kai, Dream about me."

Chapter Fourteen

Ashlyn

Despair clung to Ashlyn like Velcro. It had evolved into a mighty force and embedded itself deep inside her. Her entire body throbbed with pain; it even hurt to breathe. Gathering her strength, Ash realized she was back in her cell. She never thought she would be glad to see the gloomy gray walls again, but anything was better than the lab. She used the metal bed frame as an anchor dragging herself into a semi-upright position. Swaying, she placed her hands on both sides of her head attempting to steady herself. She still felt fuzzy from the drugs in her system. This last round with Devlin and Barrington had left her weak and demoralized. She fumbled with the bandage at her neck. The memory of Devlin's cold, steel blade against her throat made her shiver. Ashlyn sagged on the bed, all of her fight vanishing.

She was worried that when they finally killed her she would remain in a state of limbo, unable to move on to Arcadia without a Passage Ceremony. Ash ached to see Hawk one last time. Stretching out her battered body she winced, but then closed her eyes tightly and explored the depths of her mind. Her soul yearned to link with Hawk's one last time before she would consider her end, a welcome friend.

Hawk's presence and strength washed over her like

a gentle breeze. It infused her with warmth and something else, something inexplicable, intangible. Invisible hands held her up, supported her, and guided her to him. Only moments ago, she had given up on any chance of ever getting free from Barrington Laboratories, but then she united with Hawk's aura.

Her voice sounded strange even to herself. She spoke in barely a whisper, "Hawk?"

With their link in place, Ashlyn could feel the combination of Hawk's relief and fury. "Ash, thank God. You're alive. I've been so worried about you. I don't know if you realized it, but I was with you when that scarred faced prick hurt you. Are you all right, honey?"

Ash had promised herself she would never perform for Barrington like a monkey in a circus, but in the end, it was exactly what she had done. Devlin had hurt her, and her courage faded away to nothingness. Emotion choked her, and tears spilled down her cheeks. Ashlyn had never cried so much in her entire life as since she'd been kidnapped. Determined to hold it together for Hawk's sake, she spoke calmly. "I tried, Hawk, but their weapons and drugs are too strong to fight. I had no choice. They were going to kill me if I didn't do what they wanted. Devlin is a crazy sadistic maniac. I'm trying, but I don't know how long I can keep this up. Just in case, I wanted to tell you goodbye and thank you for being with me when nobody else could. You've kept me going. Please, tell my parents and Laurel, I love them."

"No, I will not let you give up and say your goodbyes. I'm here. Just a few miles from CEB, and we're going to get you out of there tonight. Promise me you won't quit yet. Please, Ash. There's so much I need to tell you. I've been so stupid keeping you at arm's length. We have this connection for a reason, a very special reason. And I refuse to allow even one more day to go by without you. Tell me you hear me." Ashlyn couldn't help chuckling. "Ash? Are you laughing at me?"

"You have no idea how long I've hoped you would say something like that to me. I feel like such a fool. I should've told you about the connection I sensed between us a long time ago, but I couldn't seem to reconcile it with myself. It was so completely overwhelming I blocked it out. And you. I'm sorry."

"Stop apologizing. You've done nothing wrong, and you've certainly done nothing to deserve this. We both made mistakes, but tonight I'm coming to get you and this will all be just a bad memory. I know you've been through so much, but please, trust me. I need you to hang in there a little longer. You'll be free very soon. You have my word."

Ash felt the prickle of tears, but this time, they were tears of joy. They were linked, and they both responded to the deep connection. She knew with her whole heart he would give everything to rescue her, but she was worried about him and the other Protectors. "You don't understand what this place is like. It's a total fortress. You're asking me to trust you and I do, unconditionally, but I need you to trust me, too. The only way you're getting in here is with Brooke's help."

"No, Ash, *you* don't understand. Your friend is Brooke *Barrington*. Her father is Charles Barrington. You can't trust her."

She appreciated Hawk's skepticism. At first, she

herself had been very suspicious of Brooke's motives. Then she had opened up to Ashlyn. She shared some details regarding her horrible childhood memories and about her relationship with Charles. Ash believed the sincerity of Brooke's words and her true desire to help. "I know who she is. But I'm asking you to have faith in my intuition, faith in me. I'm telling you she can be trusted. She hates her father. She's not safe here with him and especially not with Devlin. There's something special about her. I can't put my finger on it, but it's as if part of me recognizes her somehow. She's going to help save me, and then we're going to save her, too."

"I don't like it, but I do trust you. So I guess I'll just have to trust her, too. Tell Brooke to meet me at noon, at The Park Lane Diner on Route 25. You better warn her there are a lot of us, and we can be a bit intimidating as a group. I don't want to scare her away. Does she know about our connection to the Elements? Our Powers?"

"Brooke knows I can create fire and self-heal but little else. She doesn't have any idea about the other Elements, or about Aether, but I'm going to tell her today. I want her to come home with us, and she needs to understand and appreciate what she is going to be up against. I believe her father and Devlin will be a danger to her if they discover she helped me escape. I know I said this before, but she is not like them. She's genuine and honest. You'll see when you meet her later today. Thank you for trusting me. I'll make sure she meets you this afternoon." Her body sagged in relief. Hawk's unequivocal support meant everything to her.

"You are aware the Elders are never going to allow an outsider into to Aether, let alone permit her to stay there. They're very suspicious of ordinary humans, let's not even mention who her father is and what he's done to you."

Ashlyn knew Hawk was right about the Elders. They had always been wary of typical humans, and Ash was convinced Brooke's presence could certainly be interpreted as a threat to Aether. In order to get the Aetherians to accept her, Brooke would have to prove her trustworthiness. If she helped to secure Ashlyn's safety it would go a long way in demonstrating her loyalty. Ashlyn planned to argue, even defy the Elders if necessary, in order to shelter Brooke. She belonged in Aether with Ash and her people, at least until they no longer felt threatened by Barrington.

"Why don't you let me worry about the Elders? You know I can be pretty convincing when I want to be. They need me, and I need to protect Brooke. It's really that simple."

"Okay, honey, we'll cross that bridge when we come to it. I wish I could stay with you, but I think you should rest. Heal yourself. I need you to be strong. I wanted to tell you this when I saw you in person…but I need you to know something… I love you, Ashlyn, I've always loved you."

Hawk's confession hung in the air and wrapped around her like a passionate embrace.

Then he was gone, and Ashlyn didn't even have the opportunity to tell him she loved him, too. Their link had been severed again. He would come for her tonight, and she wouldn't have to tell him how she felt, she would show him.

Keeping her breathing even, Ash allowed her eyes to flutter closed. Drawing on her powers, she concentrated allowing her internal Flame to shoot through her. Her body began the gradual process of healing her various injuries. As the magic inside of her took hold, Ashlyn drifted off into a fitful sleep.

She was pulled from her restful state as Brooke's tinny and slightly distant voice reached her ears. "Ashlyn? Can you hear me? It's Brooke."

Furrowing her brows, Ashlyn's gaze darted around the room. "Brooke? Where are you?"

"I'm in the control room which monitors the entire facility including your cell. I bribed the guy on duty to let me have a few minutes alone with you," Brooke answered, pride evident in her voice.

"You should be more careful. I'm worried about you. What if your father finds out you've been down here asking to see me?" The images that came to mind if Barrington or Devlin found Brooke with her were too horrible to imagine.

"It's super early and none of the regular employees are here yet. Don't worry; I know the guy I bribed won't say anything. He was pretty happy with the money I gave him. Plus, Charles Barrington is way too arrogant to think I would ever defy him." Brooke's voice was strong and confident.

Ash hoped she was right about her father. She knew from her own experience Dr. Charles Barrington possessed a highly exaggerated self-opinion.

"There are so many monitors in here, I just have to find the right one… Okay, there's the camera focused on you… My God, Ashlyn, what have they done to you?" Her voice squeaked and cracked, and Ash thought she sounded near tears. Brooke continued, "I never should have listened to you. I shouldn't have left you to their devices. I'm so sorry. Tell me how to help you."

"I'm going to be okay, Brooke. I promise. I've already begun to heal myself. You should've seen me last night. I'm sure I look much worse than I feel."

"Well, you look terrible. You're covered in bruises. Your eye and cheek are totally swollen, and you have a giant bandage on your neck. Are you hurt anywhere else?"

Pain lanced through her. Ashlyn grimaced holding her ribs but managed to sluggishly sit up. She wished she could spare Brooke the truth about her father and Devlin's abusive treatment. But, there was no hiding her injuries from Brooke. She could see everything through the cameras, and Ash wanted to continue to build their trust. "Other than what you see, they shocked me with these long stick things. I think Devlin broke a couple of my ribs, too. They wanted me to use my Fire for their experiment. You were right. I guess I shouldn't have fought them because I ended up doing it anyway. But really, I swear, I'm okay. I feel much better than last night. Anyhow, we have more important things to talk about especially since you don't have much time."

"All right. What do you want to talk about?"

"My people are here, Brooke. They've come to rescue me, and I need your help." Ash swung her legs back and forth as they dangled over the edge of the bed. She wiped her sweaty palms on the itchy woolen blanket.

"Anything, absolutely anything. I'm not going to let that man who calls himself my father, and that brute Devlin, hurt you anymore. I've always known my father was a cruel man, but this goes beyond anything I ever imagined. I'm done being afraid of him. I'm ready to fight for what's right. Just tell me what to do."

"Would you be willing to meet my people and work with them? Share your knowledge of the facility?"

"Of course," Brooke said.

"They want you to meet them at noon, at the Park Lane Diner, on route 25. Do you know where that is?"

"Yes, it's very close to here, no more than ten or fifteen minutes away. I go there sometimes on my way home from work. I can definitely be there at noon."

"Great, you'll meet Hawk and the other Protectors. They are like a military police force, sort of. I want to warn you they can be a rather intimidating group. Mostly men, all very large, fit, and armed. Hawk is…Hawk is special to me. He'll take care of you."

"Special, huh? What does that mean exactly? Is he your boyfriend?"

Ashlyn searched for a way to explain things to Brooke in simple terms. "It's more complicated than I have time to explain in detail right now. Let's just say he and I are connected in a very special way." Ash thought her explanation was vague but got the point across. "You know if you help me, you can't stay here. Your father and Devlin won't let you get away with being disloyal. You'll be in danger, Brooke. There is a lot about my people I need to tell you. I want you to understand because I want you to come home with me, and you need to know what you'll be up against."

"Is this about your Fire? Can all of your people create fire?" Brooke asked.

"Yes and no. It's more complex than that. We are

225

from a place called Aether—"

"Wait a minute. Are you saying you are from outer space or something? You know I'm a scientist, right?"

"I assure you I am not from outer space. Aether is the name of our village. We're from Earth, the same as you. For reasons that should now seem pretty obvious, we live in isolation for the most part in order to protect ourselves. Aetherians are different from typically functioning humans. We are linked to the four Elements: Fire, Water, Air, and Earth. We work in unison to maintain balance on the planet and with its inhabitants. Many of my people have some sort of control over one or more of the Elements. There are four corresponding houses and each has a Guardian. I am the Guardian of Fire. My gifts are stronger than most. The role I play in my community and on this planet are crucial to its survival."

Brooke was quiet for a moment, and Ash couldn't blame her. Even from another room, she could almost feel Brooke shaking her head in disbelief. "My head is spinning right now. It just doesn't sound real. If I didn't see your Fire with my own eyes, I'm not sure I would believe it. Now you're telling me there are more of you. This is too much, but I have to admit, I'm both curious and kind of freaking out at the same time."

"That's certainly understandable, but think about what I said, Brooke. My people have gifts. They're good people. We may be different from you, but we have compassion and love, just the same. We can keep you safe from your father and Devlin. I know it's a lot to absorb, but please consider it. It may not make sense right now, but I believe we were destined to meet. I can feel it, and I think you can, too."

"As overwhelmed as I am right now, I do believe you. I agree we were fated to meet. I feel as if I've known you forever. But I'm not sure about coming home with you."

Ash understood Brooke's hesitation. After all, Ash was a stranger to her. Witnessing her Fire power must have been shocking for an ordinary human.

"You don't have to decide this minute. But, I want you to know what I love about Aether and why I think you belong there. We are one people. The strong do not pray on the weak. There is no crime in Aether. We live as one, in harmony. Can you say that about humankind? Trust me, Brooke. Go meet Hawk and the others. Help me. I need you. I don't think they can do this without you. My people will be indebted to you."

"I don't care about debts. I care about saving you. I'll go meet them, and we'll get you out of here. I promise."

Ash lifted her gaze to the camera and placed her hand over her heart. "Thank you, Brooke. Thank you for everything."

****

Hawk

Hawk kicked at the covers wrapped around his feet in the motel bed. Flipping from his side to his back and over again, his loud exhale echoed around the quiet room. Hawk's jaw tightened as he thought about Ash's suffering. Shaking his head, and rubbing his stubbled chin, he let his jaw go slack. Emptiness filled Hawk. His chest ached. He dug his fingers deep into his flesh and rubbed at the tightness which remained. Ash's surrender nearly tore a hole in his heart. Hawk's powers pulsed near the surface itching to be released. Slow measured breaths helped him regain his control.

Finding out if she was alive was the only thing that mattered right now. But time sped by like the hand on a stop watch, another enemy, like Barrington and Devlin. Violent thoughts raced through his mind: Devlin, bloody and dead at his feet, and Barrington on his knees, begging for mercy. Hawk wanted vengeance not justice. There would be no trial for Devlin or Barrington. The Protectors would decide their fate.

He punched his pillow fluffing it for the tenth time. Sinking his head into the foamy disc, he pulled the sheet to his chin. No matter how hard he tried he couldn't get his brain off Ash. As much as he trusted her intuition, he still worried about Brooke Barrington. What would happen if she betrayed Ash? The more he thought about it, the more he realized his belief in Ashlyn remained absolute. Everything would unfold as it was meant to, and anyone who hurt Ash better say their prayers.

Turning to face the digital clock on the nightstand, Hawk groaned. He whispered under his breath, "What the hell time is it anyway?" He spun the dated looking timepiece toward him and watched as the red glowing numbers flip to 5:46. They weren't meeting River and Brack until seven, and he gave up any hope of sleep.

The bed creaked as Hawk inched his way out to go to the bathroom. The light from the parking lot shone through the thin curtains creating a spotlight effect. Hawk bit his cheek to keep from laughing when he noticed Quill and Kai lit up in the beam. They were spooned together, and Quill was snoring a boisterous melody. The three had done rock-paper-scissors for the single bed just like when they were kids. Kai protested adamantly when he lost, complaining he and Quill had been more than close enough in the car. Even in his sleep, Quill managed to lighten any dark mood.

Hawk flipped on the lights as he stepped into the bathroom shutting the door behind him with a soft click. He blinked rapidly while his eyes adjusted to the bright light. Cranking the hot water, steam filled the small, stark space. If he could just wash away the jitters. Hawk held out his hands and watched as tiny tremors shook them. After about three seconds he retracted them abruptly, clenching them into two tight fists staving off his agitation. His boxer briefs hit the floor, and he stepped under the warm spray. It seeped into his aching muscles, tight from tension. The water cascaded down his back, and he moaned at the sensation.

Vibrations hummed through his body when he sensed the first tingle of his link with Ash. Her voice was soft and shaky. Where had his beautiful, feisty, Fire Guardian gone? Seeing her severely injured and in pain had set his powers into motion again. Waves of anger settled inside him when he thought about her suffering. The need to have her safe in his arms and away from those madmen took over his rational thought. No way he would allow her to give up hope when he was so close.

Thunderous hammering shook the flimsy bathroom door pulling Hawk out of his stupor. "Hawk? What the hell are you doing in there? The entire room is shaking. You better not be jacking your hammer. I'm serious. I know you need to get some, but this is ridiculous," Quill scolded, from the other side of the door.

Protector training had taught him to control his

powers, but lately, Hawk exhibited nothing of the sort. The relentless onslaught of emotions had been taking its toll on him. Hawk prided himself on discipline at all times, and he had failed miserably at maintaining it. Quill's infernal knocking picked up a rhythm Hawk was having a hard time ignoring. He twisted the handles in the shower stopping the misty spray. With a tug, he yanked a towel from the rack, patted himself dry, and then wrapped it around his waist. *Time to face the music.* He stepped out of the quiet serene space to face his friends.

"Wow, man, you must've broken some kind of world record," Quill teased.

"Shut the hell up, Quill! It's Ash. Devlin, the psycho with the scar I told you about, hurt her badly." Words erupted from his mouth like lava, "I'm going to tear that prick to pieces with my bare hands!" Hawk backed up to the edge of the bed and lowered himself to the saggy mattress. He ran his hands through his dripping hair. "Her ribs are broken. She's got bruises everywhere, and he cut her... I don't know what to do, guys. I'm not sure how much longer she can hang on." His shoulders slumped as he let out a broken sigh. "Ash arranged for us to meet Brooke at noon. I hope we aren't making a mistake trusting Barrington's daughter. But Ash's faith in her is absolute. So, I guess we don't have much of a choice but to go through with the meeting."

"She looks pretty innocent in her photo, and Ash obviously knows her enough to trust her. I'm sure it's going to be okay," Kai supported.

Quill pulled out his phone. As it sprung to life, Hawk could see Brooke's image fill the screen. *Holy crap! What is he thinking?*

His friend continued to stare down at the photo when he spoke. "Look at her. There's a sparkle of innocence in her eyes. Ash says she's nothing like her father, and I believe her."

Looks could be deceiving, but everyone was on board with the Brooke scenario. The part which shocked Hawk the most was Quill's defense of a woman he had never met. His friend, an easy-going guy with a keen sense of humor, behaved like a different person every time Brooke's name came up. Hawk had the distinct feeling sparks were really going to fly when they finally met in person. He hoped for Quill's sake, and of course for Ashlyn's, that Brooke abided by her word to help.

Just before seven they headed next-door to River and Brack's room. According to River, the other Protectors had arrived some time during the night and planned to meet them at a rest stop just outside of town. Since Hawk didn't want to talk about the details of his latest link with Ash, he asked Kai to update River. His avoidance of the subject certainly didn't ease the tension which lingered inside him. Even his skin felt too tight. Hawk paced around the small room alternating between clasping and unclasping his hands, and then clenching them into fists.

Hawk screeched to a halt and faced River. "Damn it! We need to get out of here. What if they're hurting her again? We need to meet the others and formulate our plan. If Brooke can't help us, then we better be prepared for anything tonight."

River nodded to the others, and silently they grabbed their gear shutting the musty motel room behind them. The Hummer rocked when the five substantially sized men climbed in. Seven miles zipped by Hawk's window, and his body buzzed with apprehension. It took hold and affixed itself to the whole group. When they reached the rest area, two Hummers were parked only visible once inside the small lot. River backed into a space with his usual finesse. Before the vehicle even came to a complete stop, Hawk jumped out.

As his boots hit the ground, gravel crunched under his size twelves. A dense row of tall trees obstructed his view of the highway. The rest area was set back and made an ideal location for their meeting. Good thing the place appeared to be deserted. His brother Protectors were sprawled out on every available surface. Muscled limbs and broad shoulders filled the benches and tables. Dressed head to toe in black, the group could intimidate a squad of Marines. No weapons were visible, but Hawk knew, as he felt his own weapon at the small of his back, they were all heavily armed.

After all the handshakes and backslapping, River launched the meeting. "Thank you all for driving through the night to get here. Ashlyn has been injured by her captors, and it has become abundantly clear time is of the essence. I texted Cadence regarding the man who beat Ash. She told Hawk his name is Devlin. Cadence sent me a profile on this bastard, and we're dealing with a professional, a mercenary. Apparently, he's worked for Barrington for many years. You can all read the details when you have a chance, but let it suffice to say he is an extremely dangerous individual. Devlin is a former Army Ranger who was dishonorably discharged, and his mental health status is highly unstable—"

Hawk interrupted, "I'm telling you all right now that prick is mine. I'm going to end him, painfully."

Powerful tremors shook the ground beneath their feet. A couple of the guys sat up straighter and held onto the tables. Quill must have slipped in behind him, because he felt his friend's firm touch on his shoulder. Hawk whipped his head around to look at Quill, and the ground settled. Everyone had the good sense not to say anything.

River continued, "We all understand how personal this is for you, Hawk, but we want to come out of this with as few casualties as possible. The plan right now is to use stealth to enter CEB and extract Ashlyn. When we've cleared the facility, we'll blow the entire complex. Our goal is to make it look like an industrial accident. Before anything happens, we need to retrieve any and all information they have on Ashlyn, including medical samples they may have obtained. Hopefully, when we meet Brooke Barrington later today she can fill in some of the gaps in our intel."

Hawk leaned back against an ancient oak his arms crossed over his chest. He gazed up at the open sky and thought about Ash. He knew River had already assigned him to Ashlyn's extraction team, and his mind was consumed with getting her out. Using his bond, he planned to pinpoint Ashlyn's location once they were closer.

One of the teams outlined their idea to use CEB's own chemicals to blow up the entire facility. Any files in their system pertaining to Ashlyn would be corrupted. Their tech experts were looking forward to planting a virus designed to crash CEB's entire network. After, they were prepared to search the laboratories for any medical samples and destroy them. River didn't want to leave it to chance the explosion alone would eradicate the specimens. Hawk and the rest of River's team would take out the guards on the subterranean level, locate Ash, and get her to safety.

They worked for several hours before River dismissed the other Protectors. "Go and get some lunch, then make the final preparations for tonight. After we meet with Brooke Barrington and she shares her intel, I'll update you."

Hawk had another goal in mind. He wanted Brooke to lure her father and Devlin to the facility so he could end them both.

With River behind the wheel once again, the Hummer bumped its way into the lot of the Park Lane Diner. Checking his watch for the umpteenth time Hawk saw it was 11:45. They weren't due to meet Brooke until noon. Kai and Quill flanked Hawk as they followed River up the wide walkway leading to the restaurant. Heads snapped left and right in their direction the minute they entered. Hawk immediately recognized Brooke from her picture. She sat alone looking small in an oversized booth in the corner.

Strong fingers gripped and dug into Hawk's flesh. Quill had taken hold of his arm, halting his progress toward the table. "I'm warning you. You better take it easy on her. I've seen that look in your eyes before. Just remember she's risking everything to help Ash. And, I have no problem knocking your lights out if you scare her with your snarly Protector's ways."

Hawk yanked his arm back from his friend. "What the hell, Quill? You've been acting nuts ever since you saw this woman's picture. By the way, I am house broken you know. I would never threaten a woman no matter who her father is. Now back off."

Quill ignored Hawk shoving his way in front of the others to greet Brooke first. As he extended his hand to her, she placed her much smaller one inside of his. Fear and intimidation were plainly evident on her pretty face. "I'm Quill. You must be, Brooke." Hawk noticed the light in her eyes change as Quill held onto her hand a little longer than was necessary. "Don't worry about these guys." Quill winked and added his charming smile. "They're perfectly harmless."

Brooke managed to find her voice. "Somehow, I highly doubt that." She sat up a little taller and met Hawk's piercing gaze. "You're, Hawk, right? Ashlyn told me about you."

Broad shoulders and long legs squeezed their way into the cramped booth. Quill introduced River and Kai to Brooke. Kai stared at Brooke with a strange look in his eyes, putting Hawk on edge. What was it about this innocent looking blond that had his friends all mesmerized?

All except River, who was strictly business. "We appreciate you coming to meet with us, Ms. Barrington."

"Please, call me Brooke, and I'm happy to be able to help Ashlyn anyway I can. I'm truly sorry for what my father and Devlin have done to her. She's a very special person. Tell me how I can help you."

River explained in detail the information they required from Brooke regarding the holes in their intel. Impressed by how candid and forthcoming she was, Hawk's opinion of her promptly rose. He knew Ash had

235

obviously been right in placing her trust in Brooke. As much as he didn't want to admit, there was a light in her eyes gleaming with innocence and kindness.

Hawk watched as Quill fixed his gaze on Brooke seemingly spellbound. His best friend licked his lips, as his eyes focused on her mouth when she spoke. Quill was more subdued than Hawk had ever seen before. No jokes. No wisecracks. Kai, only marginally better, gaped at the poor girl. *What am I going to do with these two idiots?*

"Brooke, are you sure you want to do this? Once you help us go against your father I mean, there will be no turning back. Do you think you're ready for those consequences?" Quill questioned.

"Yes, I definitely am. I don't blame you for having doubts about my sincerity, but I know what I'm doing here. I haven't had any sort of real relationship with my father my entire life and I don't expect that will ever change. What my father and Devlin have done to Ashlyn is horrific."

"We appreciate your candor, Brooke." River handed her a small black duffle bag. "This device will block all the camera feeds in the building. I've enclosed instructions for installation in the bag. Do you think you'll be able to get in without being detected and take care of it?"

"It won't be a problem. It's very quiet in the lab at night. I've figured out how to get down to the lower level where they are keeping Ashlyn. I'll take care of it, I promise." Brooke pulled her shoulders back and sat up straighter.

Without looking at River, Hawk addressed her directly. "There is one more important detail I'd like your help with. Do you think you can come up with an excuse to bring your father and Devlin to the lab tonight? We would like to…question them."

Chapter Fifteen

Ashlyn and Hawk

Ashlyn's body slowly recovered over the next several hours. Testing her ribs, she poked her fingertips gently into her still purple flesh. Wincing a little, she inhaled deeply and then let out her breath slowly. *Well, I'm definitely better than last night. Now let me see what's happening under this bandage.* Ash slowly picked at the tape and unraveled the length of gauze from around her neck. Small strips were taped vertically along the wound holding it closed. Gingerly, she pried each piece free revealing a thin scar. She wished she had a mirror to see it properly, but instead she explored it with her fingers. After, she gently probed her eye and cheek. *Oh great, that still hurts, too.* She squinted as waves of anger washed through her. *As soon as their guard is down, I'm going to fry those two psychopaths.*

She continued to seethe, and the anticipation of Hawk's arrival weighed heavily on her. Ash knew she was helpless. Her Fire itched under her skin as she waited. It brought to mind a quote from one of her favorite books, The Handmaid's Tale by Margaret Atwood. "Time is a trap. But that's where I am, there's no escaping it. Time's a trap, I'm caught in." How apropos the quote seemed to her at the moment. Not only was she trapped in her cell, but she felt trapped by time itself as if it were a living breathing entity. Now that she knew Hawk and the other Protectors were so close, the hours flattened her like a heavyweight holding her down. She had no idea how long she had been held captive. The days, hours, and minutes blended together. With no real concept of time, being cut off from the normal sights and sounds of the outside world, Ashlyn was left feeling bereft. *Is it morning still? I can't tell if it's the middle of the day, or the middle of the night.*

The whoosh of the slot in her door startled Ash. Her now standard issue cardboard tray slid in. One of the water bottles teetered until it landed on her sandwich squishing it a bit. Mindlessly going through the motions, Ash stared off into space groping her way through the items on the tray. Her stomach rumbled in response to the smell of food, but Ash didn't even feel hungry. She tore off pieces and forced them past her lips, tasting only sawdust. When she finished, she brushed the crumbs off herself and paced the confines of her tiny cell. She kept it up until her ribs started to protest, and her whole body ached. Ash's Fire continued to hover close as she curled up on the mattress with a creak. *I'll just close my eyes for a few minutes.* The weight of her lids could not be fought as if they were being forced shut. Still weak, she dozed off into a restless sleep.

****

Darkness fell shrouding the area where the Protectors concealed themselves. They gathered together on the fringe of CEB Laboratories' property. Woods surrounded the building on all sides, and they hung close to the edge, watching and waiting. Dressed in black, the rugged warriors were cloaked in the shadows. Clouds hung low in the sky obscuring the glow of the moon, giving the air a hazy aura. The night felt ominous and eerie for more than one reason. Encased in his own murkiness, Hawk's hand remained poised on his weapon. With every snap of branch or rustle of leaves, he choked up on the gun's grip, his knuckles whitening.

River addressed the teams, "I know we've been over our plan numerous times and you are all impatient to get inside, but we need to wait a while longer to make sure the building is clear. I just want to review it one more time since we have to wait anyway." There was some eye rolling and moaning from the group, but when River gave them a dissatisfied look, the Protectors ceased instantly.

"Thank you for your cooperation," he said, sarcastically. "Brooke is going to signal us when the last of the regular employees have left for the night. And at some point, she's also going to open a side entrance. After which, she'll install the device to knock out the cameras. When we're certain the feed is blocked, we'll enter the facility. You all know what you're supposed to do. Skye, after your mission, I'd like you to remain as a lookout. We don't want any unexpected interruptions."

Skye, one of the few female Protectors, was the best sharpshooter in Aether. "Of course, River, whatever you need. You can count on me. I'm your man, or woman as the case may be," Skye responded.

The other Protectors chuckled at her joke. Skye was the perfect combination of toughness and beauty. Her long dark hair was pulled back in two braids giving her an innocent look. But none of the men fell for the guise. Skye was a lethal Protector. Her vivid blue eyes pierced through every target in her sights. Even the group of alpha males, which dominated the Protectors, were no match for her skills.

"I'd like everyone to please check your communication headsets." River ordered.

The voices of the others testing the com system echoed through Hawk's ears and filled his mind with static. He scrubbed his hands down his face and then ran his fingers through his hair. Ash remained just out of his reach, and Hawk was unaccustomed to feeling helpless. His muscles tingled in anticipation of the battle, and his powers were beginning to hijack him again.

River's voice drowned out the other Protectors' and Hawk regained his focus. "You were told the lives of the people inside the building would be spared, but I conferred with the Elders this morning, and they don't want any witnesses. The innocent guards in the main part of the building will be shown mercy as we previously planned. We think the mercenaries that have tortured and held our Guardian captive need to be taken out. I know this goes against everything we, as Aetherians, believe about the value of all living things. But this is a necessary evil in order to ensure the safety and anonymity of our people. Please tell me now if anyone has a problem with this." River paused, looking each team member in the eye before continuing.

Everyone in Aether respected River, but none more than the Protectors who worked with him. Hawk and Quill had especially looked up to him when they were teenagers. River had always been fair and

241

understanding of other's opinions and differences, which is probably what made him such a great leader. The badass Protector exuded a cool, calm demeanor even in a crisis. River's influence and support was one of the reasons the two wanted to participate in the Protector trials.

When no one responded, he continued. "All right then, I'll take your silence as an agreement. We will attempt to be quick and merciful unlike these people who have hurt Ashlyn. It is still our plan to capture Charles Barrington and Robert Devlin alive so we may interrogate them. However, if you feel at any time your life, or that of one of your fellow Protectors, is in jeopardy, do whatever you have to. Are we clear?" Rumbles of affirmative responses were grunted out among the group.

With his hands clasped behind his lower back, River slowly walked back and forth. "After our goals on the main floor have been achieved, my team will head down to the lower level where Ashlyn is being held. This is where we expect it to get rough. Brooke's intel has helped us to be more prepared, but these individuals are highly trained and extremely dangerous. Don't take any unnecessary chances and everyone, and I mean everyone, must stay alert and on guard. Are there any questions—"

Quill interrupted, jumping to his feet, a hint of anger in his eyes. "Wait a minute. What about Brooke? She's risking everything to help us. We need to keep her safe and away from the fighting."

"Brooke promised she would remain locked inside the lab until we come to get her," River responded.

Quill's fist hit the table with a thud. "For the

record, I don't like it, not one bit! What if something happens to her?"

Stopping in front of Quill, River looked him directly in the eyes. "I'm sorry, Quill. While I appreciate your concern, I'm afraid no matter how prepared we are, things can always go wrong on a mission. Of course, we'll do everything in our power to ensure her safety. But remember, Brooke knows what she signed up for. She's well aware of the potential risks."

Quill's jaw clenched and his face flushed, but he remained silent. Hawk could feel the tension radiating from his friend. This protective streak of Quill's was really beginning to worry him. They had only met Brooke briefly, and he acted as if he were duty-bound to protect her. *Clearly, he's drawn to her. Wait until he finds out Ash wants her to come home to Aether with us. Laurel predicted Quill would fall hard someday, guess she was right. The charismatic fighter and the beautiful scientist, this should be fun.*

No one had anything else to add. The plan was memorized by everyone, inside out and backward. Tension vibrated through the Protectors. They all wanted to get the mission underway already, especially Hawk. He leaned back against a tree closing his eyes concentrating on blocking his link with Ash. He wanted to keep her from worrying until they were ready to free her.

****

Ashlyn woke jumping up off the flimsy cot in her cell. The hair on the back of her neck prickled with a strange sense a storm was coming. She rubbed the sleep from her eyes and wondered how long she had been out. Placing her hands on her lower back, she stretched her aching muscles. Then, she took a slow deep breath and concentrated on Hawk. Nothing. Something was blocking their link. "Not now! Where are you, Hawk?"

She paced back and forth around her small cell, like a tiger in a cage. A million thoughts swamped her making her feel dizzy. *I wonder if Brooke met with the Protectors?* The image of sweet Brooke with the group of alpha males normally would have made Ashlyn laugh, but she worried they might have intimidated her. Although, with Charles Barrington as her father, Ash was sure Brooke could handle herself.

Her new friend still needed convincing coming back to Aether with them was her safest option. Persuading the Elders would be an entirely different story. Their wariness of typically functioning humans was understandable, but Ash knew without even the smallest doubt Brooke was different. She was special, of that Ashlyn was sure. Although she couldn't possibly explain the reasons behind her belief, it didn't make it any less true.

With no idea of the Protectors' plan, Ash hoped there wouldn't be too much blood shed, with the exception of one person, Devlin. It went against her character to wish harm to come to another individual, but Devlin was a true monster. The mercenary personified the type of evil villain born from the nightmares of both children and adults alike.

Barrington was a different kind of horror altogether. He used his intelligence, not his brute strength like Devlin. Cruelty and coldness radiated off him like steam rising from Aether's Lake on the first cold days of Autumn. She shuddered, shaking off a chill which had nothing to do with temperature in the room. Her fingernails dug into her palms leaving little crescent shaped marks.

Ash knew Brooke had only expressed a fraction of how much she struggled growing up with Charles Barrington as her father. The more Ash had gotten to know him herself, the more she got a glimpse inside of what her friend's childhood must have been like. Manipulation was his weapon of choice, and he displayed an arrogance which could not be measured. His quiet, matter-of-fact demeanor and callousness alarmed Ashlyn almost as much as Devlin's savagery. Regardless of what happened tonight, Ashlyn would make sure Brooke was free of her father, and of Devlin, too.

****

The Protectors took turns pacing, sitting, and staking out the facility. Finally, after several hours of waiting, River announced the all clear from Brooke. Once the camera feeds were down, they would be ready to move in. Hawk and Quill were assigned positions on either side of the door to provide backup.

Hawk heard the subtle vibration of River's phone ten minutes later when a text message came through. Brooke indicated the device had been installed as instructed, and the cameras were down. Wasting no time, River gave the signal and the first team moved into action. The side door made a low whoosh when Quill opened it for Skye and the others. Staying low they entered in stealth mode. The guard didn't turn to the sound, and Hawk noticed wires hanging down from his ears. Peering in through window he smiled as he watched Skye in her element. She crouched low to the ground and slyly crept along until she was positioned directly behind the guard. The young man bopped his head and clicked away on the keyboard in front of him, clueless. Skye brought the tranquilizer gun up to her sights, closed one eye, and shot the guard directly between his shoulder blades. His head hit the desk with a thump causing him to slump over in his seat.

Weapons at the ready, the Protectors stayed close to the walls. Single file, they edged their way to the stairs. Two guards remained, and Hawk hoped the rest of the mission went as smoothly as Skye's first shot. As he watched River, Hawk realized their fierce lead Protector seemed not only worried about saving Ashlyn, but like the true commander he was, he appeared anxious for the safety of his teams.

Hawk's stomach tightened as they waited for the first group to return. Ten minutes later the stairwell door burst open, and Skye appeared. She held the door wide to make way for the others dragging the unconscious guards. They were lowering the men to the shiny tile floor, just as the remaining Protectors entered the building. The teams followed River's orders quickly and efficiently. The soldiers, all moving with silent precision, worked like a well-oiled machine.

Skye clipped the tranquilizer gun into a holster at her hip and pulled out an automatic rifle. She winked at Hawk. "Just in case." She was a crack shot, and Hawk felt relieved she would be standing guard.

He stared at CEB Laboratories. An innocuous looking building, no one would ever suspect it held a prison within its depths. He could hardly wait to see it explode and crumble to the ground. With the Protectors on the job, hopefully there would be irreparable damage to the lab's computer system. It was imperative they destroy any chance of Barrington, or anyone else, continuing with his inhumane and vicious experiments. Barrington and Devlin needed to be stopped permanently, or Hawk was afraid they might possibly find a way to pick up where they left off. Even though River wanted them alive for questioning, Hawk was going to make sure after their interrogation they would never be a threat to anyone again.

River commanded everyone's attention, "Okay, you all know what to do. Let's move out and go get our Fire Guardian!"

The Protectors' determined gazes darted around scoping for potential threats. Each individual was hyper focused on their mission goals. River, weapon drawn, signaled the team to move into position. Hawk knew which stairwell led to Ashlyn, and his powers vibrated with awareness. Soon he would have her safe in his arms. Like a whisper, they descended the stairs, weapons ready for battle. According to Brooke, two guards kept watch on either side of the door, and Hawk braced himself. River raised his mammoth sized boot kicking the door and shooting at the same time. And then, all hell broke loose.

****

Blasts rocked Ashlyn's cell and she surged to her feet. She ran to the door and pressed her ear to the thin seam running down its length. All she could make out were faint shouts and the roar of rapid fire gunshots. *What in the name of the God and Goddess is going on out there? Who is shooting and who is being shot?* Nausea curdled her stomach, and her Fire reached for the surface. Flames so hot they burned blue, danced up her arms and down again. Then, turning orange, her Fire coasted down her body with a crackle, engulfing her in Flames. Her ever-present hospital gown singed and crumbled to the ground falling at her feet. She called to Hawk, but the wall which had been erected between them remained firmly in place. Sparks flew, and Ashlyn directed her Fire and rage toward the door of her cell.

"I melted the crap out of Barrington's stupid experiment. Why can't I…get…this…damn door to yield!" She closed her eyes and visualized the door giving way. It glowed red but refused to budge. Winded, she called her Flame back. It lingered on her arms and hands for a moment before receding. She collapsed on the bed with a heavy sigh.

Ash prayed Hawk and the other Protectors were all right and they were the ones doing the shooting, not getting shot at. "Please, let Hawk be okay. I can't lose him before I even really have him." Tears rolled down her cheeks. "What the hell is the good of being the Guardian of Fire if I can't do anything!" she yelled, "Damn it! Get me out of this cell now!"

She rose from the bed and pounded on the door with her fists, shouting until she ran out of steam. Ashlyn slumped over breathless, her body sliding down against the cold metal door, and landing on the floor in a heap. Curling herself up into a tight ball, her tears continued to fall. "I'm going to die here, and I'm never going to get to tell Hawk how I feel. Never going to feel his touch, his kiss." Ashlyn remained contorted on the floor of her tiny prison and wept for all she had lost.

****

"What a freaking cluster fuck! Everyone stay

down!" Hawk yelled over the roar of bullets. They crouched low as the gunfire continued to blast them. "Two guards my ass!"

Everything had happened so fast that it took Hawk a minute to realize River was down. Bright red blood poured down his neck just above his Kevlar vest. River gripped his thigh, and Hawk watched on, momentarily frozen, as blood spurted up between River's fingers. Suddenly, Hawk burst into action seizing their lead Protector by the shoulders and yanking him back behind the heavy metal door.

Turning his head, Hawk saw one of the other Protectors practically sitting on Kai holding him in place. His friend was yelling like a lunatic. "Get the hell off me, man! I've got to get to River right now." He watched as Kai swung and landed a solid punch to the warrior's bicep. The doctor slipped out of the Protector's hold and raced over to River.

The poor guy rubbed his arm and bellowed back at Kai. "You're going to get your damn head blown off! Come on, man, River wanted you to stay back."

The rat-tat-tat of automatic weapons clanged off the door. Broken, it remained ajar either from River's kick or gunfire. Bullets kept making their way through the small opening and pinging around the tight stairwell. River's blood covered hand came up and took hold of Hawk's vest pulling him down so he could speak in his ear. He coughed and blood dripped down the corner of his mouth. His voice came out in wheeze, "Hawk…you're lead now…save Ash…save them all…tell Lily I love her…" River's eyelids fluttered and then closed.

Sitting up, Hawk lifted River gently by the

shoulders. "Don't you dare leave us! Do you hear me?" River's eyes opened again, and to Hawk's relief Kai was suddenly by his side. He pulled opened a backpack and pressed a thick bandage to River's neck to stave off the bleeding. Kai continued to apply pressure to the neck wound and ordered Brack forward to do the same to River's leg as well.

"Hawk, if he has any chance, I have to get him out of here and I mean now," Kai told his friend.

"Hey, kid, help Kai get River up to the surface. My com link is a goner. Call for backup. Tell them to hurry. We need more weapons and explosives pronto."

Brack and Kai lifted River carefully and rushed up the stairs with him. He watched them disappear and prayed River would be all right. Though he was reluctant, he knew the time had come for him to take command. "I think we need to show these bastards what happens when you mess with Aetherians. I'm going to use my powers to shake things up around here. Quill, I want you to make some heavy wind for us. Let's see what these pricks think of the power of the Elements. I'm going to open the door a little more. The rest of you keep your weapons up and don't stop shooting until I say. Okay, let's do this on the count of three. One…two…three."

Cracking the door open a bit farther, Hawk focused his power. The ground shook violently. Refusing to hold back anything at this point, he needed to get to Ashlyn quickly. Quill's hands were up with his palms facing outward toward the opening in the door. He directed great gusts of air at their enemy. The gunfire from the other side of the door ceased. Hawk heard the mercenaries' shouts as they struggled against the forceful blast of air and the tremors they were creating.

Backup arrived with more guns, ammunition, and some explosives. "We brought whatever we could carry," one of the men said. "The others stayed up top to continue setting up the chemicals for the explosion. How about I give these guys a little gift they'll surely remember?" He dropped a duffle bag and held up a handful of grenades with a devious grin.

"By all means, give them a nice blast. We need to get through this door. We have to get to Ashlyn," Hawk directed.

As Hawk and Quill let up on their assault, the wind ceased to blow, and the rumbling of the ground stilled. The Protector's large hand was wrapped around three grenades at once. Pulling the pins, he tossed them through the door in rapid succession. Hawk reached out and yanked the guy back behind the door. Eight seconds later, the walls around them shook, pieces of the ceiling tiles rained down, and the floor vibrated under their feet. The silence that followed was deafening. No shouts. No gunfire. No movement.

The heavy steel door squeaked on its broken hinges as Hawk pushed it open a bit farther and peered around it. Three unmoving bodies sprawled out on the floor caught Hawk's eye. He shoved at the door with his shoulder trying to open it fully. It protested, metal scraping metal like fingernails on a chalkboard. With one final burst of Hawk's power and strength, the door finally gave way. Another body lay unnaturally twisted covered in blood. A fifth man was dragging himself along the floor on his belly leaving a smeared trail of red behind him. With a growl Hawk bent down and seized the solider. Forcefully, he pulled the man up and held him off the ground. Blood oozed from a gash on the mercenary's forehead and his tattered shirt revealed a deep abdominal wound. He sagged unable to support his weight, and Hawk slammed him against the wall. Wrenching out his gun, Hawk jammed it forcefully under the man's chin.

He stood nose to nose with the soldier. "Point me in the direction of the cell block where they are holding the prisoner, or I will decorate the walls with your brains." The man shook violently, and his blood pooled on the floor beneath Hawk's boots. Lifting a shaky finger, he pointed down the hallway, and Hawk dropped him to the ground with a snarl on his lips. "You guys, make sure all of these sons of bitches are permanently out of commission. Then spread out and remove any remaining threats. I'm sure there are more where this lot came from. Stay sharp. Stay focused. According to Brooke, the computer room is down this hallway on your right. Find it. Get to work quickly. Be vigilant. Quill, you and I are going to get Ash. We'll meet back here as soon as we can. Now move out."

The thunder of boots echoing through the hallway was all that could be heard as they raced toward Ash. Suddenly, Hawk stopped. He braced himself against the wall, took a cleansing breath, and lowered the barrier he had erected to block Ashlyn. He closed his eyes and opened his mind to her. His heart pounded when he called out to her, both aloud, and through their link. "Ash? Can you hear me? I'm here, honey."

****

The ground shuddered violently. Chill bumps rose on Ashlyn's skin as the metal legs of her cot screeched along the floor. The sound of debris flying around

252

outside her cell compelled Ash to uncurl herself from the fetal position she had taken up. Her eyes burned from crying, and she could feel her dried tears staining her cheeks. Three loud blasts jarred her where she sat. "What the hell is going on now?"

Instantly, everything went quiet, very quiet. She held her breath and waited. Ash felt Hawk before she heard him. Trembling, she rose to her feet. His voice echoed in the hallway nearby, as well as in her head. Approaching the door, she put her forehead against the cool metal. "Am I dreaming? Are you really here?"

Energy flowed through her as Hawk answered her telepathically. "No, honey, you're most definitely not dreaming. I can feel you. We're right outside the door. I'm going to get you out of there. Stand as far from the door as you can. We're going to blast it. Is there anything to hide behind to protect yourself?"

"Yes, there's a bed. Give me a minute, and I'll get behind it in the corner of the cell." Ash lifted one end of the bed, and it scraped loudly across the floor as she dragged it to the corner. She hoisted it on its end and then tucked herself behind the flimsy mattress and the frame. "Okay, I'm ready."

"We've got some C-4 here, and we'll use a small amount to control the blast. Hang tight, it will take us just a minute to set the detonator." Quill stuck a small amount of the plastic explosive to the door and attached the detonator. "Okay, honey, hang on. Here we go." Hawk nodded to Quill and he flipped the detonator's switch. They ran back down the hallway holding their hands over their ears and taking cover. The blast peeled the door away from its frame and hung gnarled and jagged.

Ash jumped to her feet sending the bed flipping on top of the rubble. Hawk was already through the twisted metal opening, and Quill was stepping in behind him. Ash didn't think; she just flew straight into Hawk's outstretched arms. Quill must have moved to where the bed lay in a heap and grabbed the blanket. Ash didn't see him cover her, but she felt the weight of the woolen blanket as he draped it over her naked body.

Hawk's strong arms held her close, and she buried her face in his chest. He smelled amazing, like fresh air and man. The floodgates burst open, and she wept in the warm comfort of his embrace. "It's going to be okay, honey. I've got you now, and I'm never going to let you go again."

"Guys, I hate to interrupt this Hallmark moment, but we need to get out of here." Quill commented, affectionately.

"Calm down, Quill, give her a second. Will ya?"

Ash pulled away slightly without letting go of Hawk. Her gaze reached up to meet his. "I'm okay. We need to get to Brooke before those two maniacs find her. Let's go." While still clinging to Hawk, she secured the blanket with one hand tucking it tightly around herself. Quill climbed out of the opening first, and then Hawk lifted Ash through.

Only the sound of boots clomping and Ash's bare feet slapping along the tile floor could be heard. As they came around the bend, Ashlyn wrinkled her nose from the strong smell of blood and gunpowder. She gasped audibly as she witnessed the carnage in the main hallway. The Protectors were lining up bodies like books on a shelf. Some of the other soldiers stood alert with weapons drawn. Hawk pulled Ashlyn in closer to his side. "Is that all of them?" he asked the men.

One of the guys looked at Ashlyn before answering Hawk. "Hi there, Ash. You okay?"

Ash smiled. "I will be, thanks. Thanks to all of you for coming for me."

He flashed her a smile before turning back to Hawk. "We think so. We found one in a central monitoring room and two more in the computer room. Our team on the computers has already set the virus in motion. The others are searching for the medical samples. We'll be ready to move out when you give the word."

"Okay. We are heading to the lab to get Brooke Barrington. Stay sharp. We'll be back shortly."

Ash pointed down the hall. "The lab is this way. Come on."

Hawk remained glued to her side, and Quill followed. The door to the lab was open. As they stepped inside, Ashlyn gasped. Devlin stood with one arm banded around Brooke's waist while he held a large hunting knife to her throat which dripped with blood.

Chapter Sixteen

Kai

Adrenaline coursed through Kai's blood making River's bulk feel like nothing, and River easily weighed over two hundred pounds. He was pure muscle and had to be at least six feet two or three. Still, sweat ran down Kai's back as he and Brack carried the now unconscious Protector to the edge of the woods. Gingerly, they placed him on the ground, and Kai wiped his brow with his sleeve. Skye, who had been on lookout, came jogging over. Her face fell when she took in the sight of their lead Protector bleeding and unconscious.

"What the hell happened?" Skye pointed down at River.

"We were ambushed and took on heavy fire. River was the first one through the door, of course." Brack held his hand out to Skye. "Give me the tranquilizer gun. You go down and help them. I'll stay here with Kai and River. Go on. They need your skills down there more than mine."

Kai hated the way Brack made himself sound so dispensable, but it was the most he had ever heard the young Protector utter at one time. Skye didn't say anything. In a highly uncharacteristic gesture, she leaned down and kissed River's forehead. Kai tried not to react, but he felt a knot tighten in his throat. "I'm going to do everything I can for him, Skye. Go down there and get those bastards for River." Skye nodded, and jogged back toward the building.

Turning back to Brack, Kai nodded toward their downed man. "I need to keep pressure on his leg. Check inside the bag for me. We need something to use as a tourniquet to slow down the bleeding. The bullet went through and through, but he's going to bleed out any minute. We have to hurry."

Without any hesitation Brack stood and closed his eyes. He directed his hands with a unique waving motion toward the woods. A vine slowly crawled along the forest floor toward River. The climbing plant snaked its way around River's upper thigh several times and tightened firmly in place. Blood still oozed from the wound, but it slowed considerably.

"Uh, thanks, well done. The bullet tore through his femoral artery, and it has retracted up. Your tourniquet will help to slow the bleeding, but it won't stop it completely. Grab the medical bag, and get me a liter of ringer's lactate."

Brack, furrowing his brows, looked at him like he had six heads. "I have no idea what you are talking about, Doc."

"Oh, sorry, I always forget people don't understand my medical jargon. It's a clear plastic bag with liquid IV solution. We're going to do what we call fluid resuscitation. Hopefully, it will buy him some more time. I also want to wrap a new bandage completely around the wound as tightly as we can."

Brack pulled three IV bags out of the medical pack and handed one to Kai. He placed the others on a cloth he found in the bag and dug out some more bandages.

Kai inserted a needle into River's arm, attached the tubing to the bag, and looked around as if he was searching for something.

"What are you looking for?"

"I need to suspend this so it hangs above him. I was just looking for something to attach it to."

Once again Brack stood and called upon his powers. A branch hanging high above them grew downward before Kai's eyes. He took hold of it and attached the IV bag to the limb. "You're a handy guy to have around. Thanks." He gave Brack a sad smile.

"For now, I need to leave the bullet in his neck. It nicked his jugular so I want to pack the wound off. We'll apply a pressure bandage which should control the bleeding. Once we get some fluid into him, hopefully, he'll regain consciousness. Then I want to call Bear. River may only have a small window of time in which he'll be able to speak, and I want to give him a chance to talk to Lily."

"Give it to me straight. Is River going to die?"

"Very likely. I can see with my powers the damage is severe. I'll do all I can, but I don't have any equipment, and I certainly can't operate out here. There appears to be too much damage for his natural healing abilities to repair his body. Aether is a twenty-hour drive from here. The chances of us making it back in time are nearly impossible. And as much as I would like to, we can't go to a human hospital." Kai huffed out a frustrated breath. "He's losing too much blood, and I don't have anything to clamp off his wound. I'm sorry, Brack. I'm not giving up hope, but it doesn't look good." Kai packed the opened wound on River's neck with tons of white gauze which quickly turned red. He firmly placed a pressure bandage on top of the gauze. "Keep the pressure steady on his neck while I make the call." Kai pulled out his phone and dialed Bear's cell phone.

Bear answered on the first ring. "Kai? What's happened? Is everything all right?"

"It's River. He's been seriously injured. I need someone to get Lily, quickly. It might be her only chance to speak to him." Kai could hear rustling in the background and raised voices.

"I sent someone to get her. It shouldn't be long. There is a large group of friends and family in the Council Chambers' Gathering Room. They are waiting to hear any news about the mission. What in the name in the God and Goddess happened? River was so confident this morning when I spoke to him."

"Everything went smoothly tranquilizing the regular guards, but when we got to the lower level, we were ambushed. They knew we were coming and were prepared for us. River was hit in the leg and neck. It's extremely serious. I don't think his body's natural healing gifts will be enough to stop the bleeding. There isn't much I can do for him, except maybe buy him some time. Can you please explain it to Lily as simply as possible? I don't want to do it over the phone. I need someone there with her in person. I want Lily and River to be able to say goodbye, in case I can't save him. I'm so sorry, Bear."

"I know you will do everything you can, Kai. Give me a few moments to speak to Lily. I hear her coming now. Hang on."

Kai heard mumbled voices through the connection, but he couldn't make out exactly what was being said.

A familiar voice penetrated all the rest, Laurel. She was there waiting for news of the mission's outcome. Hearing her voice warmed him. He felt as if he had been gone for two weeks rather than two days. Kai had to admit he had fallen hard again for the beautiful teacher.

The news of River's demise was a harsh reality which would devastate all of Aether, but his heart truly went out to Lily. The two had been joined longer than Kai had been alive. The hardened Protector became a completely different person when Lily stepped into the room. His features softened, and his stiff demeanor visibly relaxed.

A sweetheart, Lily taught kindergarten. Petite with wavy light blonde hair, a snowy complexion, and eyes as blue as the sea, she possessed the gentlest soul he had ever encountered. Physically, she and her Kanti were complete opposites. River, a no-nonsense person, was tall, dark, handsome, and brooding. Kai was sure the tender-hearted Lily would be left completely heartbroken when Bear told her about River's condition.

At this moment, Kai wished more than anything he could save River. All of his training as a doctor, and all of the magical gifts bestowed upon him by the God and Goddess would not be enough. Even the abundant power of all the Elements combined would not bring about the result he prayed for.

****

Laurel

Everyone in Aether worried about the Protectors' mission to rescue Ashlyn. People had been coming in and out of the Council Chambers constantly for the past two days. Laurel was sure she had dark circles under her eyes since she'd barely slept since Kai left her alone in his bed. She didn't dare leave the Council Chambers for fear of missing even a scrap of news. Her family and friends stuck close the entire time.

Others in the community brought food and supplies multiple times per day, but Laurel couldn't eat. Following her ordeal with Barrington's men in the woods, she'd been having some trouble eating and sleeping. She needed to focus on Ashlyn, Kai, and the Protectors. She hadn't heard from Kai since the night he arrived in the town near CEB Laboratories. Although she understood, she wished he would text or call her.

Her longtime friend, Lily, took a seat beside her and smiled brightly. "Try not to worry, Laurel. River will make sure Kai stays safe. They're just busy. That's why they haven't called. You'll see, any time now we're going to hear they have Ashlyn and are on their way back home."

"I'm sure you're right, Lil. This is kind of new to me. I don't know how you do it. Waiting around, worrying, it's awful."

"Thankfully, River hasn't had to go on too many missions which have taken him away from Aether. But you're right. It is awful." Lily reached out and took hold of Laurel's hand and gave it a gentle squeeze. Laurel appreciated the unwavering support of her friend. It was nice to have someone to pass the time with.

One of the Protectors came into the room and it went completely quiet. He walked straight up to where Laurel and Lily were sitting. "Lily, Bear would like to talk to you. Can you please come with me?"

"See." Lily turned to Laurel. "Bear probably wants to tell me they are on their way back home. Come with me."

Getting to her feet quickly, Laurel followed Lily and the Protector into the Council Chambers. Just days before she had met with the Elders in this very room, and it felt strange to be back. Bear rose from the sofa on which he had been seated when they entered. A giant knot in her stomach twisted and ached. Laurel had a bad feeling about this. Her palms tingled, and perspiration beaded along her hairline.

Bear spoke to Lily in a gentle tone that ratcheted up Laurel's anxiety. "Please have a seat, Lily dear. And you, too of course, Laurel." They took seats next to one another. Lily gave Laurel a knowing look which made her realize Lily also sensed something was very wrong. Her friend was stoic and silent.

Laurel spoke, "What is it, sir? Please just tell us."

"There is no easy or gentle way to tell you this. Things on the mission did not go as we hoped, and River has been seriously wounded. Kai is with him and doing everything in his power to aid him, but I'm afraid it might not be enough. He has been shot in his leg and in his neck. The wound to his leg is extremely serious. Kai wanted you to be able to speak with River."

Lily went pale and visibly shook. "Is he going to die?" she asked, her voice breaking.

Bear took hold of her hand and stroked it gently. "I'm afraid only the God and Goddess know that, my dear. But Kai is worried this may be your only chance to speak with River. I'm so sorry, my dear. Do you think you are ready?"

Putting her arm around Lily's shoulder, Laurel

could feel a slight tremor just before her friend began to shake uncontrollably. Bear placed the phone on speaker and set it on the coffee table in front of them. Laurel didn't know where Lily found the strength, but she thrust her shoulders back and spoke. "Kai, It's Lily. Bear explained to me what's happened to River. I need to hear his voice. Please."

"Okay, Lily. I'm going to wake him up. He's been resting. Give me a second." Kai's voice was gentle and tender.

River's raspy whisper came through the line. "Hi, babe... Sorry to be so much trouble... I'm going to be okay... Kai is taking good care of me...so try not to worry."

Tears streamed down Lily's face, but she kept her tone steady and positive. "Of course, you're going to be okay. You are the strongest man I know. I was saving a great surprise to share with you when you got home, but I want to tell you now, okay?"

Weakly, he spoke, "What is it, babe?"

"We are going to have a baby, my love. You see, so you have to come back to me because we both need you." Lily's shaking persisted, but her voice gave nothing away.

The room spun in a dizzying motion as Laurel absorbed the impact of Lily's announcement. River and Lily were going to be parents. But River may never get to meet his child or hold him or her. He would never be able to share this joy with Lily. Laurel swallowed down a lump in her throat. Folding her arms over her stomach, she bent at the waist trying not to vomit. Her eyes filled and once the first tear had leaked out, she couldn't hold them back. She sat up, her face wet with tears. Even Bear looked like he might lose his tightly held control. Poor Lily, it was truly heartbreaking.

"Oh, babe, that's the best news ever," River said, in a hushed and sluggish tone. "I'm fighting with everything in me, babe…but…just in case… I want you to know that I love you more than anything in this world…and if I don't come back…I need you to move on with your life…you deserve love in your life, my beautiful Lily."

Lily lost it with River's loving words, and she was racked with heaving sobs. "I love you, too, River. You're the best thing that's ever happened to me. You fight…you hear me…fight. Come back to me, my love."

Kai's voice was the next one they heard. "Lily, he's exhausted and he needs to rest now. But I want you to know that I won't give up on him no matter what. He's strong, and I'm doing everything I can for him. Try to hang in there and if anything changes I promise to call you right away."

"I know you'll do your best, Kai," Lily said, between sobs, "you're a good man. Stay with him no matter what, promise me."

"Of course, I will. Hang in there, sweetheart. I'm going to go see to River now. Take care of yourself and we'll see you soon." Kai sighed dejectedly, as he rang off.

Laurel wrapped her arms tightly around Lily and held on while her friend collapsed with grief. How could this be happening? River was the strength of Aether, the lead Protector; he had to make it. Didn't he?

Chapter Seventeen

Ashlyn

Once the trio crossed the threshold, Ash's fingers dug into Hawk's arm, and she froze in place. Devlin's slashed jaw curled up in a sneer as he held a knife to Brooke's throat. Small droplets of blood ran down her neck, and Brooke's eyes were filled with tears that did not spill. None of them made a move, worried what the unhinged man might do.

"Well, there you are, Firecracker. I wondered when you would show up to collect your friend. I've been watching Brooke here since the day she stumbled upon you and our little experiment. Charles, my arrogant friend, insisted Brooke would forget all about what we were doing down here. I, on the other hand, was much more skeptical. And rightly so it would seem. When my men alerted me about the camera feeds going down, I was nearby, and I just knew this little backstabbing bitch had something to do with it. I headed this way and sent extra soldiers to the entrance. I hoped you enjoyed our little welcoming committee."

Hawk's posture changed when Devlin made his last comment. Ash could feel the anger radiating off him through their link. She didn't need a bond to see Quill's reaction. His fists clenched tightly at his sides, and his gaze turned hard. Quill eyed Devlin with daggers the likes of which she had never witnessed from the easygoing Protector.

"Ashlyn, you need to get out of here right now," Brooke squeaked out. A single tear leaked out of the corner of her eye and ran down her cheek.

"I'm not leaving you with this lunatic. Let her go, Devlin, and I won't hurt you. You know what I can do," Ash said. She straightened her spine. Then squinting her eyes with as much venom as she could muster, Ash stared down her tormentor.

"Now, Firecracker, is that any way to talk to me? If you, or your bodyguards make one move, I will take great pleasure in slicing Miss Barrington from ear to ear," Devlin retorted. He laughed, and his scarred face, with its distorted features, made him look like he stepped out of a horror movie. A chill ran through Ash's entire body. "Charles is on his way here, escorted by more of my men. And when he arrives, we will all have a nice chat. I'm sure your friends have some skills Dr. Barrington would be interested in."

Hawk stood erect, his gaze piercing the mercenary. "That's never going to happen, Devlin. We have this place surrounded by sharp shooters who have orders to kill anyone who approaches. I suggest you let the girl go, and stand down immediately."

"Listen up, Tonto. I don't take orders from you. Your people will never see my men coming. There's more than one way into this facility. And if you freaks make one wrong move, I will kill Brooke before you can say Firecracker." Devlin harshly yanked Brooke making her lose her balance. He kept her upright with a vice-like hold and to prove his point, he dug the knife into her neck a bit more. She winced. Then he put his mouth to Brooke's ear, and Ash watched her friend cringe from the contact. "You've always been a giant pain in my ass; you and your whore of a mother. I warned Charles you two were a burden he didn't need, but he liked the image he portrayed as a family man. Best thing that ever happened was when your mother died. And when a horrible accident befalls you all the better."

"You are sicker than I ever imagined, Devlin. My father isn't going to let you get away with this," Brooke spit out. She struggled against his hold.

"You really believe that, don't you? He doesn't care about you. He never has. He only cares about his image, success, and making money. And when he finishes developing the drug synthesized from Firecracker's blood, we are going to make billions."

To Ashlyn, it felt like a standoff in an old western movie. Then on Devlin's emphatic statement, gunfire erupted in the hallway. There was shouting and the sounds of thunderous footsteps. Ash heard the whoosh of the door opening, and as she turned her head she saw Charles Barrington slip into the room. Ash watched Brooke heave a huge sigh of relief and hoped her friend would not be disappointed by her father once again.

The Protectors both tensed, and Hawk shoved Ashlyn a little bit behind him. "What on earth is going on here, Devlin? Who are all these people? And why in God's name are you holding my daughter at knife point?" Charles questioned.

Charles stared Devlin down. It was the first time Ashlyn had seen the two men at odds. She wasn't sure if it boded well for her and her friends or not. They had always presented as a united front; the calculating mad scientist and his evil mercenary.

Devlin's face flushed bright red, and his voice was abrasive and harsh. Spittle flew from his scarred lips when he spoke. "I'll tell you what they're doing here. Your stupid bitch of a daughter helped them to enter our secure facility. And I lost some very valuable men in the process. I told you not to trust her, but your arrogance has overridden your common sense once again."

"Don't be ridiculous, Robert. Brooke had nothing to do with their presence here tonight. Isn't that right, Brooke?" Charles questioned.

"Go ahead. Tell him the truth. You only care about helping your friend Firecracker escape from us. You don't care about what your father and I might lose in the process. You, and this saint act you've got going." Devlin shoved the tip of the knife into Brooke's chin, drawing more blood. He was shouting now. "Go on. Tell him! You nosy little bitch, you're just like your mother."

A flood of tears ran down Brooke's cheeks. "What you've been doing to Ashlyn is wrong. You can't just take people and experiment on them. Hurt them. Keep them prisoner. I had to help her. You were going to kill her."

"They are not people, Brooke. They don't deserve to live. I knew when I met that self-righteous know it all Kai Sanders back in medical school. He tried to take everything from me. He may have beat me in our rankings, but no one beats Charles Edward Barrington III."

Brooke's body shook as she wept openly. "That's what this is all about? Some guy beat you at being number one, and you want Ashlyn and her people to pay. Oh my God…you're as crazy as Devlin."

Poor Brooke's defenses cracked in two. It seemed she finally understood her father was as off balance as Devlin. A plan formed instantly in Ash's head, and Hawk's body became rigid next to her. Telepathically he connected to her. "*I know what you're thinking. Don't you dare do it. I mean it, Ash. These two are completely nuts.*"

She responded in his mind. "*Please, I need you to trust me. I know what I'm doing. Just be ready to move quickly.*"

Before Hawk had the chance to react, Ashlyn closed her eyes and concentrated all of her focus on her Fire. Slowly, she raised her palms and directed a burst of flame toward Devlin. His sleeve ignited with a whoosh of blue flames. He dropped the knife, and it clattered to the ground echoing through the room. Enraged, Devlin roared inhumanly snarling as he tamped out the flames while still clutching Brooke. Ash barely caught a glimpse of Quill. He moved like the wind that was his power. Swooping in, he freed Brooke from Devlin's deadly grasp.

Devlin lunged seizing the knife. He grabbed Ash by her ankle before she knew what happened, pulling her off her feet. Startled, she slammed hard to the concrete floor. Jolts of pain radiated through her shoulder. Momentarily stunned, and with nothing to grip onto, Ash's hands skidded along the floor. She tried to brace herself attempting to fight Devlin's rage-fueled strength. He gained purchase and drew her to him. Before she could even call to her Fire, Hawk flew at him like a flicker of light. Devlin's eyes opened wide, and his grip on her loosened as Hawk attacked.

Ash yanked her leg back and rolled away. With the power of the Elements behind him, Hawk pounded Devlin. The Mercenary's eyes glazed over, and he fought back viciously slicing deeply into Hawk's forearm. His blood splattered from the considerable sized wound.

Ashlyn didn't hesitate. Her Fire raced down her arms. She targeted Devlin and sent a barrage of Flames straight at him. His pant leg caught alight, and once again he lost his hold on the knife. Dropping to the floor, he rolled around dousing the flames. Then quickly arching his back, Devlin landed on his feet in a move that was almost acrobatic. He followed up by planting a solid punch to Hawk's nose. It responded with a resounding crack making Ash shiver all the way down to her toes. But Hawk did not slow down, in fact, it appeared to provoke her man further. Even as blood flowed into his mouth and soaked his sleeve, the Protector kicked and punched Devlin mercilessly. Fury permeated his every pore, and Ash could sense it to the point of pain. Hawk unleashed the full strength of his powers revealing them to all those present. The ground beneath them quaked. Strong gusts of wind whipped through the air sending debris flying around the room. Devlin fought him off, but Hawk was too fierce and relentless.

He screamed in Devlin's face as he continued his assault. "How dare you take her! How dare you hurt her!" Each blow was punctuated by another word or phrase until Devlin lay motionless unable to fight back. "I will kill you...you...son...of...a...bitch!"

Ash stared open mouthed at Devlin who was curled up in a protective ball. Bloodied and unmoving, she couldn't believe the terrorizing mercenary had been rendered helpless. Hawk crouched down grabbing Devlin by the chin. He pulled him up off the ground and with a twisting motion, Hawk snapped the man's neck. The nauseating crunching sound rang in her ears. Dumping his lifeless body with a thud, Hawk stood over Devlin. Ashlyn heaved a sigh of relief. Devlin was gone. The monster of her nightmares was dead, and she felt no remorse whatsoever. She scrambled across the floor until she reached Hawk. He lowered himself to his knees to catch her as she threw herself into his opened arms.

"You're hurt. You're bleeding," Ash said. She wiped his face with the blanket she had wrapped around herself.

"I'm okay, honey. It's not bad, don't worry. Everything is going to be all right now," Hawk reassured her. "He can't ever hurt you again. You are so brave, my Guardian." He stroked her hair holding her tightly. "But you and I are going to talk later about you being so reckless."

Hawk pulled back just enough to gaze directly into her eyes. She saw so much love reflected in their depths, it melted her heart. He threaded his fingers through her hair drawing her close to him. His mouth crashed down on hers, and he kissed her deeply, passionately, the way she always dreamed about. It was better than any fantasy she could have ever imagined. His lips were strong yet tender. His tongue swept into her mouth, and a moan involuntarily escaped.

Quill cleared his throat. "Um, guys? You know there are other people in the room, right?"

They reluctantly separated and Hawk shot Quill a

death stare which made Ash chuckle. Leave it to Quill. Ash wondered if he would ever change, but then she noticed he still held Brooke snugly to his chest.

Hesitantly disengaging herself from Hawk's strong grasp, Ash stood and approached her friend. "Brooke? Are you okay? Are you hurt?"

Brooke's sobs had subsided, but every now and then she shuddered in the aftermath of her emotional state. She removed her tearstained face from Quill's chest yet continued to keep her arms wrapped around his waist. "I'm okay, Ashlyn. I guess I'm just in shock. I can't believe that happened. Is…is Devlin dead?"

Hawk got back up on his feet. "Yes. That sadistic psycho will never hurt anyone again. I'm sorry you had to see that, Brooke, but he left me no choice."

Ashlyn's gaze scanned the expansive room searching for Charles Barrington, but he was gone. She also noticed, the hallway, which had been filled with the sounds of gunfire, was now eerily silent. She clasped the blanket more securely around herself. "It's quiet out there. Do you think the other Protectors are safe? And where did Charles go?"

"I have no idea where Barrington went, but we will definitely find him. Quill and I will check on the other Protectors and see if they have him in custody," Hawk said. "But, Ash, honey, um, where are your clothes? What did those animals do to you?" He questioned, with a mix of anger and worry in his voice.

Her eyes met Hawk's and heat rose to her cheeks. "It's nothing like you're thinking. My hospital gown burned up when I used my Fire to try to break out of my cell. I haven't had clothes since I was taken from Aether. They've been providing hospital gowns. Every time I get angry my Flame seems to take over. Let it suffice to say, I have been burning through quite a lot of them. I'd give anything for a pair of jeans and a T-shirt." She re-secured the blanket around herself.

"Ashlyn, I brought you some clothes to wear. I didn't think you would want to leave here in a hospital gown," Brooke offered.

Quill added, "I think the blanket is a strong fashion statement. It really works for you, Ash. I like it, and I definitely think Hawk likes it. Right, buddy?"

The two women laughed, but Hawk rolled his eyes. "You know I'm going to tell you to shut up, right?"

"Yeah, I figured, but I couldn't resist," Quill joked.

Ignoring Quill, Hawk addressed Brooke. "Why don't you grab those clothes for Ash, and we'll check the hallway and make sure it's safe for you ladies. Try and be quick, we need to get out of here." Hawk leaned in and touched his lips to Ashlyn's. "We'll be right back. Come on, Quill."

Appearing hesitant, Quill released Brooke from his firm hold and began brushing his hands up and down her arms in a comforting gesture. Ash wasn't sure what it was, but something definitely passed between the two.

Hawk cracked the door open and stuck his head out glancing both ways before he and Quill exited the lab. Ash's eyes were glued to him until he disappeared from sight. Devlin was sprawled out on the floor his head canted to the side. Ash watched on as Brooke shivered and then quickly looked away. "Brooke, are you sure you're okay?"

"Yes, I'm sure. I've just never seen anyone killed before. It was awful, and I was so worried about Hawk.

He is one, tough, scary guy, that man of yours. I'm glad he's on our side." She grinned at Ash but then sobered quickly. "My father... I-I don't even know what to say about him. I always knew he was horrible, but I can't believe how far reaching it is. He's petty and vindictive, not to mention completely irrational. How could my father have so much hate in him? I don't want to talk about it anymore right now. Are you okay?"

"I'm fine. I want to thank you for everything you've done for me. You've been a true friend. Now you have to let me help you. You know you can't stay here right? Please come home with me. Aether is the only place you'll be safe. Every instinct I have is screaming you belong in Aether. Please, trust me. Also, I think Quill may not have it any other way," she joked. "I've known him my entire life, and I've never seen him react to a woman the way he's reacting to you."

Brooke smiled. "He is really something. The way he moved and saved me from Devlin. Plus, he is the hottest guy I've ever laid eyes on." She fanned herself. "Do all the men look like Quill and Hawk where you come from? Because if they do, I don't think I'm going to be able to speak when I get there."

Ash laughed loudly. "Yes. The people of Aether are all quite beautiful to look at and very diverse as well. You can see for yourself...hey, wait a second, you said *when* you come to Aether. Does that mean you've decided to join us?"

Brooke moved to the corner of the room where she produced a large suitcase on wheels and a small duffle bag. She beamed brightly. "I decided before any of this went down. I don't belong here. I think I've always known it. My mother used to call me "my gift." She said I was special and meant for great things. And one day, when I was ready, I would believe it was true and follow my heart. Well, I think the time has come. I'm finally going to follow my heart. I'm coming to Aether with you."

****

Hawk

Power pulsated off Hawk in waves. He did it. He actually succeeded in freeing Ashlyn. The pain and longing for her which had become his constant companion didn't dissipate though. Even having her in his arms and kissing her, didn't ease the tightness in his chest. The heat of their passion ran hotter than Ashlyn's Fire, and he knew he would never be able to get enough of her. Tearing himself away even for a few minutes was one of the hardest things he'd ever had to do. However, he needed to ensure her safety and that of the other Protectors.

With River injured the role of lead Protector had fallen upon Hawk, a responsibility he took very seriously. This mission's completion was his obligation, his duty. River's admiration and respect meant the world to Hawk. He didn't just want to make River proud; he needed to.

The hallway appeared clear from the threat of Devlin's men. Only the dead remained. Dragging two more bodies along the floor, the Protectors left a smeared trail of blood in their wake. The deceased were arranged side by side in a morbid queue. Hawk addressed no one in particular when he said, "What happened? And where the hell is Barrington?"

One of the men responded, "They came from another direction and caught us by surprise. We haven't seen Barrington. Glad we got these two, but there are two more somewhere. The others are searching for them. We have all the samples. The computer virus has been uploaded and is running as we speak. The explosives are all set to go on your command."

"You probably scared off the other two. I'm going back to the lab for Ash and Brooke. We need to get them out of here. Let's call the others and start moving these bodies. I can't wait to blow this place sky high."

Hawk poked his head back into the lab catching a glimpse of Ash slipping a sweatshirt over her head. He knew he shouldn't, but couldn't help admiring her beautiful breasts as the sweatshirt fell into place covering their perfection. Her creamy skin practically called out to be touched. *Whoa! Better get my head on straight, this mission is far from over.* He cleared his throat. "You ladies ready to go?"

Ash beamed at him. "More than ready to get out of this place."

Brooke followed pulling a large wheeled suitcase behind her. Hawk relieved her of the huge bag. "Here let me take this for you." Just as they stepped into the hallway, two men screeched around the corner guns drawn. A spray of bullets pinged off the walls sending shards of tile everywhere. "Get down!" Hawk yelled.

Quill barreled toward them diving in front of Brooke shielding her with his much larger body. Hawk watched as his best friend was pierced in the bicep by a bullet. A gush of blood ran down his arm, and Brooke screamed. "Oh my God, Quill!" Hawk heard him whispering words of reassurance to Brooke as he continued to cover her body with his own.

Before Hawk could even un-holster his weapon,

Ash's hands blazed with Fire. She discharged her Flame and directed it at their two attackers. Their clothing ignited. Shouts of terror rang out as they jerked about struggling to squelch the flames. Skye stepped out of the shadows bringing her weapon level with her line of sight. She planted her feet and in rapid succession precisely placed a single bullet directly into each man's head. Skye cocked her head to one side then rolled it on her shoulders. She appeared nonchalant as the soldiers dropped to the ground instantly. The world around them became quiet once again. She holstered her weapon and leaned back against the wall in a casual pose.

Brooke's entire body shook violently, and Hawk could see his friend steadying her with his hands on her shoulders. "Look at me, Brooke." Quill commanded her in a way he'd never seen before. Hawk watched on as her big blue eyes met Quill's. "I've got you. You're safe now." He pivoted slightly without losing contact with Brooke. "I guess we know where they are now." Arching his brow, he turned to Ashlyn. "Hey, Ash, nice pyrotechnics. You're a little badass. If the Guardian gig doesn't work out, maybe you should think about becoming a Protector."

Ash smiled at Quill and then faced Skye. "You were amazing, Skye. Thank you. I was actually scared to death. The Fire is just a natural instinct. You saved us all."

"All in a day's work," Skye said, humbly. "Everybody good?"

"No! Everyone is definitely not good! Quill was shot. Hawk was sliced with a knife and had his face bashed in. Ashlyn has been held prisoner, beaten, and tortured. And if you haven't noticed there are dead bodies everywhere!" Brooke's voice was high pitched and laden with panic.

Quill enfolded her in his arms and gently stroked her hair. "Shh, it's going to be okay. We heal really fast, remember? Look at Hawk's arm. It's hardly even bleeding. And Ash's bruises are totally fading." Brooke looked over at Hawk and Ashlyn while still holding onto Quill. His reassuring words continued. "I don't want you to worry. We're going to take care of everything. Trust me."

Hawk saw Brooke's eyes light up when she looked into Quill's. He knew at that moment his best friend's life was about to change forever. Right now, he had more important things to think about than Quill's love life. Hawk shifted into command mode. "Quill, you and I will take Ash and Brooke to the surface. Everyone else, start bringing the bodies up. Don't forget about Devlin. He's in the lab. Now move out."

Ash piped in. "Wait a minute, Hawk. What about Charles? We need to find him." She spun to face Brooke. "Does he have an office or someplace he might be hiding down here?"

Brooke pointed down the corridor. "I did see an office down that hall the other night when I was looking around. Come on. I'll take you to it."

"Are you two in charge now?" Hawk questioned, wryly. "We need to get you both to safety. I'll send someone to find Barrington's office and search it. Agreed?" The woman both nodded in silent agreement.

Hawk directed Skye and one of the other men to conduct the search for Barrington's office. Then he clasped Ash's hand firmly and headed toward the stairwell. River's blood splattered on the door looked like a gruesome Jackson Pollack painting. A crimson puddle glistened near the entrance. Hawk hoped Ashlyn and Brooke wouldn't ask about it. His grip on Ash's hand remained steadfast as they ascended the stairs. Quill grunted when he hefted Brooke's suitcase up with one hand. He had his other arm around her waist never losing contact with her.

Two more Protectors met them on the steps, and Hawk gave them their orders. "Get down there and help the others move the deceased. We're going to get the ladies to safety. Everything else on schedule?"

"Yes, and the explosives are ready to go whenever you give the word. We'll see you topside in a few."

The wind whistled, and Ashlyn's hair whipped around her beautiful face. Hawk knew with certainty he would never tire of drinking in her delicate features. Gravel crunched under their feet until they came to the end of the path and reached the edge of the wooded area. Hawk's gaze connected with Kai's. The doctor shook his head indicating things with River looked grim. Ashlyn pulled free of his grip and ran full force to River who was stretched out on the ground. Hawk addressed Brack. "Go help the others, we'll stay here with Kai and River." Brack walked toward the building but glanced back a few times before he finally entered.

Ash's eyes flooded with tears. "River, oh dear Goddess," she said to Hawk, "what happened? Why didn't you tell me?"

"I'm sorry, honey, there wasn't time to discuss it. Devlin had extra men at the entrance, and River was the first one through the door." Looking at Kai, he inquired. "How is he doing?"

Kai's tone was quiet and solemn. "I'm afraid it's not good. The bullet to his leg caused irreparable damage to his femoral artery. The blood loss is too great, and I obviously can't operate to repair it. I've been trying to keep him comfortable with IV fluids and painkillers. But I'm sorry to say, he's running out of time." Kai hung a fresh bag of IV solution. "This is the last of the IV bags. He spoke to Lily already. It was heartbreaking. Apparently, she is with child and was waiting to tell him when he got back from the mission."

Ashlyn ran the back of her fingers down River's face in a tender gesture. His eyes fluttered open and focused on her. With his voice weak and shaky he spoke, "Ashlyn…you okay?"

"I'm fine, River." Tears ran down her face. "This is all my fault. If you hadn't come to get me… I'm so sorry, River."

River reached up and found Ash's hand. He brought it to his lips and placed a gentle kiss to the back. "Not your fault, sweetheart…my job to protect…so glad to see you free… Aether needs you… Hawk, too…go home, be happy, live well…tell Lily I love her and the baby…help her. Ash…. don't let her be alone…tell her to let love in her heart…tell her I will always be with her…" His voice trailed off and when Hawk looked around everyone had tears in their eyes.

River's head lolled to the side. Kai checked his pulse and then reached over, closing River's eyes. "He's gone. I wish I could have done something to save him. Damn Charles Barrington and his vendetta! It should've been me, not River, I brought this to our people." His head dropped into his hands and then Hawk was at his side.

He placed his hand on Kai's shoulder. "This is no one's fault, not yours, not Ash's, no one but Barrington and Devlin. River wouldn't want you to blame yourself. He was a Protector of Aether. It's a risk we each knowingly take. We need to bring him back home, to Lily. Can you prepare him?" Kai didn't speak; he nodded. Slowly he slid the needle from River's arm removing the IV and then Brack's handy work.

The other Protectors began to emerge from the building carrying the dead soldiers. One by one they lined them up in the wooded area. *What a waste of life. And for what? To make a drug to sell to the highest bidder. Barrington needs to be stopped.* Hawk interrupted his own thoughts to ask Skye for a report. "No sign of Barrington I take it?"

"No, unfortunately not. We did find his office though. There was an open wall safe, but it was empty and also a hidden door that led to an underground tunnel. We followed it, and it came out about a quarter of a mile down the road hidden among some rocks. There was no sign of Barrington. He must have used it to escape."

"Shit! We need to find that son of a bitch. I'm going to end him." Hawk turned toward Brooke and then quickly diverted his gaze to the ground. "Sorry, Brooke. That was insensitive of me. I know he's still your father."

"The fact is, he's never really been a father to me. And in light of everything that's happened here, I completely understand how you must feel. You know, he might have gone back to his house. It's not too far from here. But it's very secluded. There are no roads signs in the area. I'd have to show you the way."

Quill rushed to Brooke's side wrapping an arm around her shoulder. "I'm coming with you," he asserted.

Ashlyn stepped around her other side. "Me, too."

"Well, I guess I have my new team," Hawk said, with a small smile. He turned to the others. "Are those all of the guards?" One of the men nodded. "Okay, I want all of these bodies burned. Everyone, use your powers to distribute the ashes with, water, wind, and earth." The Protectors worked quickly. The acrid smell of burned flesh lingered in the air until it was whisked away by water, wind, and soil. Brooke buried her face in Quill's chest while the Protectors did what was necessary. Ash never turned away. Hawk continued to be amazed by her strength. With her shoulders pulled back, she did not waver. She watched as the last of her enemies faded with the power of the Elements. Hawk took her hand and squeezed it in a silent show of support. Ashlyn looped her arm around his waist and rested her head against his shoulder.

After the Protectors finished, they gathered solemnly around River's body. Hawk addressed the group, "Let's all take a moment, to pray to the God and Goddess. May they protect our leader's spirit until he can be returned to Aether for the Passage Ceremony." Everyone bowed their heads in a silent benediction.

"I'm sorry we can't take more time, but River would want us to get on with our mission." One by one the Protectors turned away from River and focused their attention on Hawk. "After the chemicals are detonated, we need to move out pronto. The three surviving guards have been removed from the building. They will recover from their various injuries, and the human authorities will be none the wiser. The rest of you will head back to Aether. Quill and I are going take Ashlyn and Brooke to search for Barrington. We won't be far behind you."

Kai turned to Hawk. "I promised Lily I wouldn't leave River, no matter what happened. I need to bring him home to her."

Hawk replied, "Of course, Kai."

With the final remnants of the guards and Devlin eradicated, Hawk nodded to Brack. The young Protector gripped the detonator in his fist and tipped his head back to Hawk in response.

Brack counted down. "In three, two, one."

The ground shook violently, and flames burst upward lighting the night's sky. The group stood in solidarity watching as the structure erupted in a series of explosions. Smoke wafted through the air. Charles Edward Barrington Laboratories had been reduced to a pile of rubble. Hawk hoped this would be the end of Ashlyn's nightmare, but somehow, his instincts told him this situation was far from over.

Chapter Eighteen

Ashlyn

Consumed by fire, CEB Labs crumbled before Ashlyn's eyes. Her heart leapt as the flames burst and crackled, leaving her feeling cathartic. She was truly free. Fire seemed an appropriate end to this place where Barrington wanted to extract her power and leave nothing behind.

Grief hung like a heavy curtain in the air. Hawk and Quill gingerly lifted River's shrouded body into the cargo area of one of the Hummers. Kai climbed into the back and refused to leave River's side. The departing Protectors split up between the other two vehicles and drove off heading back in the direction of Aether.

Hawk took hold of Ashlyn and gently pressed his lips to hers. Then pulling back, he smiled at her. "Let's get the hell out of here."

After opening the passenger side door of the Hummer for her, Hawk's strong hands encircled her waist lifting her into the vehicle. He placed her gently on the seat. When he reached over to buckle her seatbelt, she breathed in his intoxicating scent. Hawk smelled like the outdoors on a spring day and something altogether masculine, like leather, she thought. Sweeping her hair to one side, he placed a kiss on her neck heating her entire body. He went around to the driver's side and hopped up while Quill and Brooke climbed into the back. Ashlyn couldn't resist the urge twist around in her seat and steal one more glance at the burning wreckage that was CEB labs. Gravel flew up around the vehicle as Hawk zipped away from the scene.

He handed her a cell phone. "You better give your parents a call. They've been worried sick. You should let them know what our plan is, and that we'll be home soon." Ashlyn took the phone and placed the call to her folks. Her mother's voice shook as she sobbed. Her father had a million questions which she promised to answer when they returned to Aether. Her parents wished she was coming straight home, but they understood her need to see things through with Barrington. She rang off and placed the phone in the console between her and Hawk.

"My parents wanted me tell you the fires around Aether came to an abrupt halt a short while ago. What fires?"

Hawk sighed loudly and Ash read the relief on his face. "Fires had begun to break out all around Aether when you were taken captive. It seems now that you have been freed things are back in balance."

The sky, alight with golden hues as dawn broke, looked as though the heavens came down and touched the Earth. *Freedom,* Ashlyn thought. But her stomach was still tight with knots as they drove along. The thought of confronting Barrington again had bile rising up in her throat. She closed her eyes and swallowed it down trying to clear her mind.

Brooke guided Hawk through the winding mountain roads toward Barrington's house. According to Brooke, Charles owned several homes and this location was one of four she knew of. They pulled onto a paved brick drive after following several small dirt roads. Barrington's house seemed to rise up in front of her and Ash's mouth hung open.

"Wow!" Ash turned to Brooke. "Do you live here?"

"No, I live in a small apartment just outside of town. I've only visited this home on a few occasions since I moved here. As you can see, my father likes his privacy."

The grand home stood two stories tall; its facade a mix of brick and stone. Windows abounded framing a centered entryway. Stately looking columns rose up like giant trees on both sides of the large double doors. It even had a turret at one end, and on the opposite side a three-car attached garage dominated the space.

Hawk removed his holstered weapon. "You two should stay here until Quill and I assess the danger."

"No way, Hawk, we're all in this together, and I can take care of myself. Plus, we need Brooke to gain access to the house. Right, Brooke?"

"Yes, we can get in through the garage door. I know the code for the keypad on the outside and the alarm pad just inside the door, too," Brooke confirmed.

"You know you can just share the information with us and wait here," Quill piped in.

"Nice try, but you're not going anywhere without me and Ashlyn," Brooke retorted.

"All right, I guess it's all for one and one for all," Quill said. Then he pulled his gun out from the back of his jeans clicking off the safety.

"You know that's the Three Musketeers, genius?" Hawk mocked.

"Well, I guess we're the *Four* Musketeers now," Quill answered back, with a smile.

The keypad beeped as Brooke punched in the code for the garage door. Quill swept in tucking her behind him as the automatic door rose. Hawk seized Ash by the shoulders and had her safely out of the way as well. The garage was pristine with painted walls and a shiny floor made of tile. No tools, bicycles, or other such clutter hung on the walls or lined the perimeter. However, two cars occupied the bays; a silver Aston Martin sparkled in one space, a regal looking black Bentley filled the other, and one remained blatantly empty.

"Is there a car missing, Brooke? Or does he just have these two?" Hawk inquired.

"Yes, he has a black Lincoln Navigator, also. Though he never drives the truck unless he has cargo of some kind."

"Well, let's go and see if he's home. Shall we?" Quill asked.

Brooke opened the door into a large mudroom and turned to the alarm pad but no sound chimed from it. "That's strange. He always sets the alarm, even when he's home."

"You ladies stay behind us until I give the all clear. Understood?" Hawk ordered. Ashlyn and Brooke both nodded in agreement.

The two Protectors raised their guns, and the foursome entered the kitchen. The ceiling was vaulted and classic cherry wood cabinets lined the walls. The room boasted high-end, stainless steel appliances and gleaming granite countertops. A large center island dominated the space, and crystal pendant lighting hung down over the massive piece. A surprisingly cozy breakfast nook sat in the corner. The room had all the modern amenities one could ask for with the bonus of old world charm. It seemed odd to Ashlyn that this was where Charles Barrington drank his coffee every morning and ate his meals each night. Ash wasn't sure what she was expecting, but it was definitely not this warm and beautiful place.

As if Brooke read her mind, she said, "He had an interior designer do the entire house. He didn't even see it until it was completed about eight years ago."

"Come on let's check the rest of the house. From the size of this place, it may take couple of days," Quill joked.

Ashlyn and Brooke stuck close behind Hawk and Quill while they explored the rest of the house looking for Barrington. Ash, amazed at the grandeur and opulence of the home, felt strange as they wandered through its expanse. There was no sign of Charles Barrington anywhere. In the master bedroom every drawer had been opened, and the contents spilled out as if someone had packed in a rush. The massive walk in closet was mostly empty with hangers scattered about on the floor.

"Looks like he left in a hurry. I can't imagine why?" Quill said, acidly.

"The only room we haven't checked is his office. It's down here. Come on. I'll show you." Brooke led the way.

"Brooke, you get behind me. Hawk and I will go in first." Quill pushed her completely behind his much larger body.

"He's not going to hurt me, Quill. He's still my

father." Even as Brooke said it, Ash could hear the skepticism in her voice.

"Well, I hope you don't mind if I have my doubts about Daddy Dearest's intentions where you're concerned. He slipped away while Devlin held a knife to your throat. I'm sorry, Brooke, but you can't trust him. He clearly doesn't have your best interests at heart. I don't want to hurt you by being so blunt, but you need to be protected. You're way too trusting."

Brooke's head dropped and her shoulders fell. "I know you're right. It's just so hard to believe all of this. It seems like a surreal nightmare and I keep thinking I'm going to wake up any minute. But I do appreciate your concern for me."

Quill lifted her chin with his finger forcing her to look at him. He gave her a warm smile. "I understand, but you deserve so much better. I'm going to see to it personally things are different for you from now on. If you're going to trust anyone, please, trust me." He gave her a quick hug. Ashlyn and Hawk looked at each other and wondered what was happening between these two.

After Quill's little pep talk to Brooke, Hawk led the way into Charles' office his gun clenched tightly and his eyes sharply focused. The space had rich dark paneled walls except for one, which consisted entirely of windows. A set of French doors led out to a small patio and overlooked the wooded area behind the house.

A large wall safe stood open and noticeably empty. There was a substantially sized desk which held a computer. Its drawers had been pulled open, and papers littered the top overflowing onto the floor. Brooke approached the computer and jiggled the mouse to wake it from sleep mode. The screen lit up, but it was password protected.

"Darn it! I don't know the passcode, but I know if I put in the wrong one too many times, it will lock us out." Brooke blew out an aggravated sounding breath.

"Don't worry. We know someone who can easily break into the system. Cadence is our resident technical genius. He can hack any system. I'll give him a call and explain the situation. Everyone just sit tight." Hawk took out his phone and placed a call to Cadence who answered on the first ring. He warned them it might take some time to break in, but he promised to call them as soon as he hacked into the system.

Ash's vision clouded, and the room spun. Her body felt heavy and her eyelids drooped. She slid down into one of the guest chairs across from the desk. Hawk was by her side in an instant. He dropped to his knees next to her taking hold of her hand. "Whoa there, honey. You okay? When's the last time you ate something? Or rested?"

"I'm not sure. I haven't eaten much, but I haven't been hungry either. And as far as rest goes, I was constantly drugged. I'm not sure if that counts as resting." She laughed it off, but Hawk was having no part of it.

"Well, now that we know the house is empty, and we have to wait to hear from Cadence, let's get you something to eat." As Hawk helped her to her feet, she swayed and her knees buckled. Just when she thought she'd hit the floor, he scooped her up into his arms and carried her to the kitchen. He gently placed her on one of the bar stools at the island. Strutting to the fridge, he grabbed a container of juice and poured her a large glass. "Drink. Now," Hawk ordered.

Ashlyn sipped the sweet, tangy liquid slowly, and it tasted like heaven as it slid down her parched throat. Brooke and Quill took seats next to her fussing over her. Hawk worked like a pro pulling out eggs, assorted veggies, cheese, bacon, and English muffins. In no time at all, he had several pans going. A glorious smell filled the air making Ash's stomach rumble. Brooke got up and grabbed plates and silverware for everyone. Quill poured juice for the others and refilled Ashlyn's now empty glass.

Hawk served the group and took a seat next to Ash. "Feeling a little better now that you've had some juice?"

"Yes, much better, thanks. This looks amazing, Hawk. I had no idea you had such skills."

It seemed Quill couldn't resist the urge to comment. "Apparently he has lots of other skills I'm sure he'll want to share with you in private later."

Tell-tale heat rose in Ashlyn's cheeks. She and Hawk said in unison, "Shut up, Quill!" They all broke out laughing, and Ash realized it was the first time she had laughed in way too long.

They chatted casually while they finished their meal. Quill had them all cracking up as he shared stories of their youth in Aether. Ashlyn couldn't help but sense envy in Brooke as they regaled her with tales of their happy childhoods. Brooke was endlessly curious about Aether and its people. She wanted to know about the power of the Elements, the people, the Houses of Fire, Water, Air, and Earth. Brooke asked question after question, but then she paused for a moment as if something had occurred to her.

"You know, I was thinking about something that has me a little confused. Your friend said something which didn't make sense to me. He was upset about River, and he said that he brought all this to Aether. He also mentioned a vendetta regarding my father. I don't understand what that was all about. Why would my father have an issue with this guy? Where would they have even met?"

"Um, Brooke… It's kind of hard to explain…this may be a little shocking. You see, the people of Aether live an extraordinarily long time. Many years ago, your father and Kai were roommates in medical school," Hawk explained, gently. Brooke just kept shaking her head, as if in disbelief. He continued, "It's true. Your father inadvertently stumbled upon Kai using his powers. He became obsessed in discovering the entire story. I'm afraid that's what led him to Aether and to eventually taking Ashlyn. It appears he wishes to harness our power to create a drug to sell to the highest bidding government to enhance their soldiers."

"No, no, that's not possible. Your friend Kai can't be more than twenty-five years old. My dad went to medical school before your friend was even born."

"Kai may look twenty-five, but he's actually eighty-three years old. As am I, and Quill. Ash is a year younger than us."

"That-that can't be true. You're teasing me, right?" Brooke stuttered.

Ashlyn reached out and touched her friend's hand. "It's no joke. Everything Hawk said is the truth. Most people in Aether live for hundreds of years. That's only one of many reasons we stay hidden from human society."

"Oh, my, God! You're all...old? But-but you look so young... Oh, my, God. I can't believe this. Does my father know about this?" she asked.

"We don't believe he does. He didn't see Kai at the lab, but I suppose it's possible that he saw him in Aether when he was gathering information for his quest," Hawk answered, honestly.

Tears streamed down her face. "You don't know him. He'll never stop. We have to go. We have to find him. What if he has other samples of Ashlyn's blood besides the ones you found in the lab?" Brooke said, her voice shaky and uneven.

Quill got up from his chair, stood behind Brooke, and put his arms around her. "We'll find him, baby, don't you worry. Cadence will hack into his computer, and we'll soon know everything he knows. It's all going to be fine, trust us." Quill soothed her rubbing his hands up and down her arms and back.

"I need some air. I've got to go take a walk or something. My brain feels like it's going to explode." Brooke pushed away from the counter and started for the mudroom door.

"I'll go with her and try to calm her down. Just leave the dishes. I'll clean them up when I come back. Ash, you need some rest. Oh, and a shower might be in order. Have you looked in a mirror?" Quill smirked, before sprinting out the door after Brooke.

"I do feel disgusting. I would love a shower," Ash admitted.

"I'll go out to the truck and grab our bags while you find a room upstairs. I'll bring you some more of Brooke's clothes to change into, so you don't have to put these back on. Can you make it upstairs by yourself, or do you need help?"

"I'm okay now that I've eaten and sat awhile. Go ahead. I promise I'll be fine." Ash headed upstairs while Hawk went out to retrieve the bags.

She found a lovely room that overlooked the back of the house with an adjoining bathroom. Ash kicked off the sneakers she borrowed from Brooke and wiggled her toes. The shoes were a bit tight, but she was relieved not to be barefoot any longer. She peeled Brooke's snug-fitting black yoga pants down her legs and yanked her bulky sweatshirt over her head.

Entering the bathroom, she caught a glimpse of her reflection in the mirror. "Oh, dear Goddess! Is that really me?"

Her usually vibrant red curls were dull and matted to her head. She could finally see the faint scar on her neck where Devlin had cut her. Running her finger along the mark she winced at the memory. Light yellowish patches were all that remained of the bruises on her face. A few angry looking black and blue marks marred the skin of her ribcage. Touching the tender flesh caused her to draw in a deep breath. She turned on the water and allowed steam to fill the large shower stall. Though her body was healing, she wondered if her heart and mind would ever heal. A booming knock sounded at the door, and she flinched. Reminding herself that her enemy would never knock, Ash grabbed a towel off the rack wrapping it around herself. She opened the door and took in Hawk's magnificent form. His broad shoulders filled the doorframe and when he entered, the space seemed to shrink with the powerful Protector so close. "Sorry, I just wanted to bring you some clean clothes for after your shower. I'll, um, just leave them here on the vanity. Do you need some help or anything else before I go?" Hawk stammered.

Ash reached up and ran her hand down the side of his face. "Please don't go. I want to thank you for saving me, in every way. I wouldn't have made it through my captivity without you in my head, supporting me."

Taking her hand, he placed a kiss on her palm. "You're everything to me, Ash. I've always known it. I've been such a fool for not telling you. I love you. I've always loved you. I plan on spending the rest of our lives proving it to you."

His strong hands were suddenly on her hips. Pulling her close, he captured her lips in a gentle kiss which quickly grew more urgent. Hawk broke away panting and rested his forehead against hers. Their breath mingled as one. Ash tugged on the bottom of Hawk's shirt freeing it from the waistband of his pants. He helped her by lifting it over his head and tossing it on the floor where her clothes were piled. She flattened her palms on his muscled chest then allowed her hands to drift downward. As her fingers danced across his tight abs, Hawk sucked in a deep breath.

Part of her recognized from deep within that this incredible man was her true match. Ashlyn was nervous. There had been so much anticipation leading up to this moment. She just wanted it to be perfect. He was so incredible, and she had dreamed about him her entire life.

Hawk reached for the towel she had tucked around herself pulling the end free, leaving her bare in front of him. "You are so beautiful, Ash."

She took hold of his belt and unbuckled it. When

she reached for his button and zipper, he caught her wrists halting her action. "We don't have to do this now. You've been through so much. I never want to hurt you, honey. I can still see the bruises on your gorgeous body. Just say the word and this ends right now."

"I don't want to stop. I want to feel... Alive... Free... Loved. Please, Hawk, I'm more than okay. I swear."

Clearly, Hawk didn't take much convincing as he toed off his boots. Shoving his pants and boxer briefs down in one swift motion, he stepped out of them and tossed them aside. Ashlyn gasped at the sight of the sexy man before her. Tanned skin covered ripped muscles everywhere she looked. He smiled, and Ash melted. He opened the shower door ushering her inside. Turning her under the warm spray, he reverently washed her hair and every inch of her body. All of her nerve ending tingled with anticipation, and her body hummed. Hawk swiftly washed himself and then turned off the facets. Opening the door a crack, he snatched her discarded towel. Lovingly, he patted her dry and then took his own towel wrapping it around his waist.

Stepping out of the shower, Hawk gathered her close. "Let's get the tangles out of this incredible hair." He picked up the hairbrush he brought her and gently brushed every last knot from her hair then toweled it dry. Then sweeping it to one side, he ran heated, wet kisses down her neck. He worked his glorious mouth upward. His lips and tongue played with the delicate shell of her ear. Whispers of promises and passion made her knees weak. Ash couldn't believe this was actually happening, finally.

"I want this to be special, Ash. I never want to forget our first time together. Let's go into the bedroom where I can worship you properly."

Ash could barely think. Hawk was going to claim her. Leave his mark, and make her his own. The way he looked at her made her gait unsteady, the heat in his eyes like melted chocolate. He took his time backing her into the bedroom. All she could do was surrender to her feelings for this breathtaking man. His lips and hands never left her body, except to tease her, building the anticipation to near maddening.

She reciprocated unable to get enough of him. Pressed even more tightly against him, she could feel his arousal, hard and needy. She moaned her pleasure. Ash never wanted any man more in her entire life. Never had she felt anything like this. Hawk's passion ignited her own. They were simply made for each other. The back of her knees hit the bed, and they both tumbled onto the mattress. She giggled even though she was burning up. Everywhere their bodies met she was on fire, and not her usual literal Fire, but the fire of true passion.

****

Hawk

Sweat ran down Hawk's back as he pounded into Ashlyn's tight heat over and over again. Barely able to form words, the link between them growing, Hawk couldn't tell if the visions in his brain belonged to him, or Ash, or both. He ran a finger down between her breasts, and she tightened around him. Kissing her delicious, supple skin, he bathed the pale smooth flesh with his tongue. His beautiful Guardian writhed beneath his touch.

297

But prevailing thoughts edged their way into Hawk's mind forcing him from their intense passion. He pulled back gazing into her eyes. His control hovered just within reach and as much as he wanted her, he had to know she was all right. "I just want to lose myself in you. But I'm afraid of hurting you. I can't stop thinking about what those bastards did to you."

Ash simply stared up at him for a moment; her marked palm stroking his stubbled cheek. The stark contrast between his deeply tanned skin and her milky white complexion looked perfect to him. She reached out to him telepathically. *"Don't let them take this from us, Hawk. I need you, please."*

When he searched deeper within their link, all he felt was love and passion and Fire. Warm hands wandered down his back touching him everywhere making him grow harder than he thought possible. Wrapping her legs around his back, she dug her heels in urging him deeper. Hawk couldn't help but to oblige, thrusting harder, stroking her inside and out. The upper swells of her breasts lifted to his mouth from their erotic motion. He licked and nipped softly at her delicate flesh. Ashlyn's moans turned to whimpers. Overcome, he devoured her mouth. With every swipe of his tongue, he tasted her love and her fire. Each sound she made, each response, each touch deepened their bond and his passion.

Breaking their kiss, he moaned. "Baby, I'm afraid I'm not going to last long." As a Protector, control, restraint, and discipline ruled him, but with Ash, that fell to the wayside. Every inch of Hawk's body pulsated as he fought against his aching need for release. He wanted Ash with him. Reaching down, he slowly ran his fingers through her hot, wet heat. The sounds Ash made only heightened his desire. He thrusted into her faster, deeper. Ashlyn's tight channel contracted around him sending sparks through his entire body. As they fell over the edge together in a mind-bending climax, he was certain no two people were ever more connected than he and Ashlyn. Joined as one; body, mind, and spirit.

Depleted, they held each other in a tangle of limbs neither wanting to separate from the other. Hawk couldn't stop himself. He stroked her damp hair enjoying the feel of her soft, wild, red curls. The lush strands were even more silky than he had imagined in his many fantasies about Ash. He placed gentle kisses on her neck as she clung to him tightly.

Finally, she broke the silence. "Wow. I mean, just, wow. That was wild."

Hawk laughed, loud and heartily. "I'm glad you thought so, too. I love you, Ash. Being with you was even better than I imagined. And I have a pretty good imagination."

Ash squeezed him around the waist and kissed his chest where her head rested. "I love you so much, Hawk. Can I ask you something silly?"

"Of course, you can ask me anything," he answered, tenderly.

"I feel a little ridiculous asking you this. But can I look at your Protector tattoo? I've always wanted to see it up close, but I didn't want you to think I was stalking you," she joked.

Hawk chuckled and rolled over onto his stomach. "I belong to you now, Ash. You can look at, or better yet, touch any part of me whenever you want," he teased, playfully.

When Ashlyn combed her fingers through his hair, Hawk had to fight a moan from escaping. He didn't want Ash to think he was a sex maniac. The truth was, he wanted her before she even touched him. But the moment her gentle hands brushed his hair aside to explore his back, he had to shift his weight to keep from crushing his arousal. She used her fingers and hands to caress his entire back. He could feel her gaze directed on his right shoulder blade where his Protector tattoo covered a four-inch space. Hawk knew every detail of his proud marking. A perfect circle, approximately four inches in diameter, divided into four quadrants, and each quadrant contained a different abstract depiction of one of the four elements. Bisecting the circle in bold, black letters the word Protector was scrolled in a flowing script. It was truly a beautiful work of art.

The Fire section had detailed orange and yellow flames which seemed to dance about like real fire. The representation of Water flowed in shades of blue which almost looked like waves. Air displayed three swirls of purple illustrating the image of swiftly circulating currents which appeared to move like a breeze. Lastly, Earth had the appearance of an actual green leaf from a tree, reminding him of the forest back in Aether.

Ashlyn's warm hands froze in place, and it took her a few minutes to speak. "It's incredible. The colors, the details, it's amazing. I love touching it. Actually, I love touching you."

Hawk turned over and pulled Ashlyn on top of him. "There are lots of parts of me to explore and touch, my love." He smiled before his lips met hers in a mind-blowing kiss. The ringing of his phone forced them to separate way too soon as far as Hawk was concerned. "Sorry, honey, I better get that." He sprinted into the bathroom. Digging through the pocket of his jeans, he finally yanked his phone out. He answered with an abrupt sounding, "Yes?"

"Hawk? It's Cadence. Is everything okay? You sound strange."

"Sorry about that. Everything's fine, but, I'll call you back in about 5 minutes." He hung up the phone and returned to the bedroom where Ashlyn now slept soundly. *Poor thing must be exhausted. I hope I wasn't too rough on her.* He grabbed clean clothes and dressed quietly before slipping out of the room.

Hawk went down the stairs two at a time and headed straight into Barrington's office. Before he even took a seat at the desk, Quill walked into the room alone. "Where's Brooke?" Hawk asked.

"She went upstairs to take a shower and a nap. She's doing better, just a little overwhelmed. We took a long walk and talked about everything. She'll be okay. Where's Ash?"

"She's sleeping. Cadence called when I was…um…upstairs…um helping Ash, so we need to call him back," Hawk replied, awkwardly.

"Helping Ash, were you? You actually knocked the poor girl out. I'm impressed, buddy," Quill gibed.

"I can say the same for you and Brooke. That was a really long walk you two took. Did you knock her out? Or did you just bore her to sleep with your incessant chattering?" Hawk retorted.

"Touché, my friend, touché! But it's not like that between me and Brooke. I just met her. Plus, she is going through some pretty hefty shit right now."

"You can deny it all you want, but I see the way you look at her. Dude, you took a bullet for her. There is definitely something there. I guess we'll just have to wait and see. Let's get Cadence on the phone."

Their tech expert stayed on the phone with them, walking them through Barrington's various computer programs and notes. It held a wealth of information regarding Aether and specifically Kai. The man was clearly obsessed. They were able to access his emails and found dozens which mapped out his plan to take one of Aether's residents. It became obvious, Ashlyn and Laurel were attacked by opportunity not design. The most disturbing fact was that Barrington had drawn numerous samples of Ashlyn's blood. The specimens destroyed at the laboratory were merely a few of those he had obtained.

One thing they were now certain of, Barrington would surely set up shop somewhere else. He planned to continue his relentless pursuit of the Aetherians and their powers connected to the Elements. Hawk had a sinking feeling. Dr. Charles Barrington would not stop, unless the Protectors stopped him. They needed to get back to Aether to regroup and to plan with the others. Their Fire Guardian's return was also essential.

Hawk informed Quill. "Let's get a few hours of shut eye. Then we'll wake Ash and Brooke and head back home. Start unplugging this computer, and load it into the truck. We're taking it back to Aether. This way, Cadence can have at it. I want to leave by noon. There's nothing more we can learn here. I'm not sure where that cagey bastard went. But if it's the last thing I do, I'm going to find him and stop him, permanently."

Chapter Nineteen

Kai

As the Hummer rolled to a stop, Kai jerked awake. Even though he'd fought his body's need for sleep, he realized he must have dozed off during the long ride back to Aether. Looking out the back window he caught a glimpse of Bear. With his massive arms crossed over his chest, his expression was unreadable. Laurel stood beside Lily, her arm draped over her friend's shoulder. Lily's complexion was more pale than usual. She bore dark circles under her beautiful blue eyes which lacked their usual sparkle. Her long blond hair was swept up in a haphazard looking ponytail. Stray wisps escaped, blowing in her face, but she didn't seem to notice. Bear approached, lifted the tailgate, and Kai breathed in the instant gust of fresh air. Stretching his cramped muscles, his knees cracked audibly.

After so many hours confined in the Hummer, Kai's legs protested. Tingling, they left him a bit unsteady when his feet finally hit the ground. He didn't care though; his only thought was racing to see Lily. A rush of words and emotions poured out. "Lily, I'm so sorry. I tried everything to save him, to bring him home to you. I hope you know that." Kai took a deep breath. He met Laurel's gaze and then slowed himself down. She gave him a small smile encouraging him to continue. "I also want you to know his last words were about you...please, forgive me, Lily." He finally paused as his chin dropped to his chest.

Lily spoke softly but with conviction in her voice, "Listen to me, Kai. I don't need to forgive you, because you did nothing wrong. I know you. And I know you did everything you could to save my Kanti. River understood the risks he took being a Protector of Aether. Bear told me he got to see Ashlyn before he passed on. I know in my heart he believed his sacrifice was worth her freedom. His oath meant the world to him. River always said the needs of the community were more important than needs of any one individual. I'm proud of him, and I will tell our child about what a brave and noble man his or her father was." As tears streamed down Lily's face, Kai could see Laurel's grasp tighten on her friend's shoulder.

Bear gently approached. "Lily, my dear, why don't you accompany the Protectors in bringing River to the medical center so he may be properly prepared for the Passage Ceremony. Ashlyn will return soon, and then we can help your beloved move onto Arcadia where he belongs."

Laurel whispered to Lily loud enough for Kai to hear, "Would you like me to join you? Or would you rather be alone?"

"Thank you for everything, Laurel, but I'd like some time alone with River, to say my goodbyes." Tears continued to pour down Lily's cheeks.

"Whatever you need, Lily. I'm here for you. I'll call you later to check on you." Laurel said, tears filling her own eyes.

Bear escorted Lily to the Hummer, helped her into the vehicle, and then climbed in himself. The truck pulled away leaving a cloud of dust in its wake. Alone in the parking lot, Kai faced Laurel. It was the first time he had seen her since leaving her alone in his bed. Their gazes locked, and he tentatively opened his arms.

Laurel sighed, shook her head, and stepped into his embrace. "I'm still mad at you."

He held her close absorbing her warmth and breathing in her addicting vanilla scent. "I'm so sorry. Please, don't be mad. I had to go. God, I can't believe how much I've missed you. I feel like I've been gone for months, not days."

"I've missed you, too. I'm just glad you're safe and Ash is free. I was so worried. Are you really okay? I know it must've been a really rough few days."

"Of course, everyone is devastated about River. But if you don't mind, I don't want to talk about it right now. I really just want to be alone with you. I need you, Laurel." Kai lowered his head and touched his lips to hers tenderly. The kiss turned more urgent, heated, passionate. He used all of his willpower to pull away from her before he took her right in the parking lot. "Let's go to my house. I can't seem to keep my hands off you. I'm afraid we'll give the gossips even more fodder if we stay here a minute longer."

He held tightly to Laurel's hand as he led her back toward his house. They walked in a companionable silence, though Kai quickened his pace the closer they got to his home. He practically dragged her from the halfway point until they finally reached his front door.

When Kai gazed down at her, Laurel just smiled at him. "Well, Doctor, are you going to invite me in, or what?" He pushed the door open, ushering her inside.

****

Laurel

Laurel's heart pounded as Kai rushed her through the door. His hands were everywhere at once, and she thought she might combust any minute. Right in the middle of the living room Kai stopped, lifting her up in his arms. "Wrap your legs around me, baby." She had always loved when he called her baby and she immediately obliged wrapping her legs tightly around Kai's waist. His hands dug into her bottom as his lips found the sensitive spot behind her ear. Carrying her to the bedroom, his mouth never lost contact with her heated skin. He lowered her to the bed and lifted her shirt over her head. Wearing her favorite pink bra and matching thong made her feel sexy, but Kai's intense gaze had her cheeks burning. He ran his hands over the lacy cups, his fingers teasing and caressing her nipples through the thin material.

"Baby, you may kill me. You look so sexy. Did you wear this for me?"

Unable to form words, she nodded and smiled coyly. Kai reached back and unclasped her bra with one hand exposing her breasts. His eager hands and mouth feasted on her sensitive flesh.

Laurel moaned as he continued to torment her. Her body throbbed and tingled. She was on fire. Her internal muscles clenched and a climax began to build from his maddening assault. "Kai, wait, please... I-I can't stop," she uttered, breathlessly. Kai smiled mischievously as he lingered, focused on her pleasure. She detonated on the spot screaming out his name as her release took over any rational thought. Coming down slowly from the euphoria, she blurted out, "I'm so embarrassed. That's never happened to me before.

When you touch me...I just seem to lose control... I'm sorry."

"Are you kidding? Don't be sorry. That was the hottest thing ever. I love the way you respond to me. And by the way, I'm just getting started, baby."

As Kai's words seeped in, Laurel's need was triggered anew. She lunged for his pants forcing them down to his ankles. He kicked them away. As he stood bare before her, she drank in his muscled physique. Laurel needed to touch him, to make him feel the way he made her feel. He divested her of her jeans and thong along with the rest of his clothing in a flash. The feel of his body as he came down on top of her, hot and aroused, sent waves of excitment through her. They rolled, entwined, a tangle of arms and legs. Ecstasy played out on Kai's beautiful face. Locked together in the heat of rapture, he kissed her fiercely not letting up on his bombardment of her senses. The climax which built in her reached a crescendo. Her orgasm crashed over her with such force it took her a moment to realize Kai, too, was swept up, shouting her name along with his release. With their slick bodies still coiled around one another, catching their breath, the couple's hearts beat in unison. No one ever made her feel the way Kai did. Cherished. Desired. Owned.

They held each other for a long while. The entire time Kai stroked her hair, arms, and back. Finally, he broke the silence. "I want you to know something. I died a little that day with Storm. And even though you didn't know it, your love brought light to my darkness. I pushed you away, and I'm sorry. I thought I didn't deserved love, but you make me feel alive again. I never want to be without you. Please, say you'll move in here with me. Sleep in my arms every night. And when you're ready...I want to be Joined with you, in front of all of Aether."

Gazing into Kai's ocean-like eyes made her feel like she was drowning. He was everything Laurel wanted and everything she feared. "Kai, I do love you, too, but I feel like we're moving a little fast here? We've barely had a chance to spend any time together...well, other than here in your bedroom." She smiled. "We just reconnected, and I don't know if I'm ready for such a big step yet. I know I want to be with you, but can we back up a little? You know, slow it down, maybe go on a date, or something, I don't know...normal, maybe? We were so young when Storm died and after everything happened between us... I'll admit, I'm afraid. I don't know if I can go through losing you again. I need to be sure about our feelings and not just in the heat of passion. Obviously, we still have some really intense chemistry, but ever since I was attacked everything's moved so quickly. We've gone from zero to one hundred in no time at all. I'm crazy about you, really, I am. But I think we both need some time to let this whole thing, I don't know, marinate, I guess. Please understand, I just want to take our time, not do anything too rash. I hope you're not mad at me, but I need to be honest with you."

"I'll do whatever it takes to make you trust me again. I know I hurt you, and I'd do anything to go back in time and do it over. I want you to be able to believe me when I say I'll never push you away again. I never want to lose you again either. I can promise you one thing, I am very sure about my feelings for you. I know I didn't act like it in the past, but I've always been sure of you. And my feelings have nothing to do with passion…well, that's not entirely true. They definitely have something to do with passion." He grinned like a Cheshire Cat. "But it's much more than that. Your kindness, your compassion, your devotion; I love all of those things about you and more. I'll give you all the time you want. Whenever you're ready, you let me know. How about I start by taking you to the café for something to eat? What do you say? That's normal, right?"

"Yes, that sounds very normal. I'd love that. I think we better get dressed first or those gossip mongers you mentioned will really have something to talk about."

"Okay, baby, whatever you say, but I really like you like this," he joked.

Laurel poked him playfully in the ribs. "Well…um…how about a shower first?" she said, feeling her face heat.

"Baby, I need you to stop being embarrassed. After everything we've shared, I want you be able to tell me whatever it is you want, whenever it is you want it. Taking a shower with you is top on my priority list. The café may have to wait a while though. Once I get you in there, all nice and wet and soapy…well, you get the idea." He leaned down and kissed her again gently.

"Come on, gorgeous. Let's go get clean. You can wash my back and then I'll wash yours." He waggled his brows suggestively.

After spending the next hour, *getting clean,* as Kai called it, they dressed and headed to the café. Laurel's stomach rumbled loudly. She couldn't remember the last time she had been this hungry. It must have been all the incredible sex with Kai. She felt energized, and her body still hummed with excitement just from being near him. Uncertainty drifted in and out of her mind. Being with Kai was everything she'd ever dreamed of. Handsome, smart, and sexy, he had it all. Part of her worried, perhaps saving her life was the reason Kai wanted her. Laurel needed to be sure, it was she, herself, he craved and not simply an image in his head. Now that she had opened up to him, she feared Kai might change his mind after the dust settled. In no time at all, he had suddenly become the most important person in the world to her again. And more than anything, she just didn't want to screw it up.

As they walked to the café to be, *normal*, as she called it, Laurel realized maybe being normal wasn't all it was cracked up to be. After all, wasn't that part of being from Aether, being a bit extraordinary? Kai held her close and they walked in step with one another without even trying. Maybe, just maybe, this would all work out the way that it was meant to. Laurel couldn't wait for Ashlyn to get back so she could share everything that had happened with her. Well, maybe not everything.

Chapter Twenty

Ashlyn

Aether felt like an oasis in a desert. The colors all around Ashlyn appeared more vibrant than she recalled. Mossy green hills, the roughened brown hues of the trees' bark, and the brilliant blue sky filled her vision, as well as her heart. Off in the distance, she could see the Grand Lake its water glistening like a giant mirror reflecting the magnificent landscape. *Home,* Ashlyn thought to herself. She was finally home. The moment Hawk had appeared in her cell she knew she had been saved. When their gazes met, some of her fear slowly dissipated. To Ash, Hawk *was* Aether and represented all she held dear. She didn't need a ceremony to join them; she knew she was already one with him in every sense. He was her soul, her breath, her life. Once her feet were firmly planted on Aether's soil, the worry and despair which had overwhelmed her during her captivity began to fade. While imprisoned, Ash believed she would never see those she loved and her beautiful Aether again. As much as she attempted to bury her feelings, nervousness itched under the surface of her skin like rash. Ash needed to let the warmth of Aether shelter her and release her anxiety completely.

Ashlyn wished Brooke was as happy to be in Aether as she was. Her friend gnawed on her fingers, her eyes darting around nervously. "It's going to be okay, Brooke, I promise. When I spoke to my parents, they were thrilled to have you staying with us here in Aether. As soon as you get to know everyone else, you'll see, you'll feel right at home."

Brooke let out a deep sigh. "I just keep thinking they'll all hate me because of who my father is. Coming here might've been a mistake. Maybe I should just leave now."

She started to walk back to the Hummer they had just exited when Quill gently took hold of her arm. "You're not leaving. It's not safe for you out there. Plus, we all want you here. You belong with us, Brooke. We never would've been able to save Ash if it weren't for you. Everyone in Aether will know you're a friend to us. It doesn't matter who you were born to. It only matters who you are now. And, personally, I think you're…amazing."

Ashlyn couldn't believe what she heard come out of Quill's mouth. He never displayed that kind of serious tone, and the way he looked at Brooke, well, that, too defied comprehension. Brooke looked back at Quill with the same kind of light and wonder in her eyes. Ashlyn chuckled to herself. "Oh, how the mighty have fallen."

"What did you say?" Quill asked.

"Nothing, nothing at all." Ash hadn't realized she'd spoken out loud, and Hawk smirked right along with her.

No one was in the parking area to greet them. Ashlyn didn't want a big production over her return. She'd encouraged Hawk not to call his grandfather with the exact time of their arrival. Coming back home felt incredible, but she wasn't eager to discuss the details of her ordeal just yet. Ash knew the Elders wouldn't allow her much of a respite before they started to probe her for information. Brooke would not be immune to the scrutiny and barrage of questions either. Perhaps her friend had a right to be nervous after all. The Elders were an intimidating bunch under the best of circumstances. Ashlyn held off sharing that titbit of information. For now, she just wanted Brooke to be able to relax and see Aether the way she did; a place of warmth, comfort, and wonder. But Ash had to admit, the complete sense of security she'd always felt in Aether remained just out of reach. She wondered if she would ever feel completely safe, anywhere, ever again.

The four walked together toward the South Tower, and Ashlyn watched as Brooke's mouth hung open. "Oh my. It's incredible," Brooke said, breathless. "I can't believe no one knows all of this is here…well, not everyone…my father knows."

Quill put his arm around her tenderly. "Brooke, I don't want you to worry. We'll find Dr. Barrington and put an end to this. You have my word."

Hawk held Ash's hand as they strolled along like they were on a double date or something. It felt very natural to Ash as if they had been a foursome of friends forever. The group walked the rest of the way in silence, but Ash noticed Quill kept his arm wrapped tightly around Brooke the entire time. As they drew near the South Tower Ashlyn's pace grew more frantic, and butterflies danced in her stomach. She couldn't wait to surprise her parents and walk in the door as if she had never been gone.

Ash knew her parents had been terrified by her abduction. She wanted to reassure them she was all right. Well, at least she was all right physically. Ashlyn feared her scars on the inside may never fully heal. *Poor Hawk,* she thought. *You may very well be stuck with a lunatic forever.*

The noiseless group filed into the Tower. Voices rose from the kitchen the moment Ash stepped one foot in the doorway. Rowan's melodic tone rushed through her like a beautiful song, drawing her in. As Ashlyn opened the door she witnessed a very familiar sight. Mica sat at the family's table with a large mug of steaming liquid. Her mother scrambled around the vast space busying herself with multiple pans on the stove.

The door stood open and Ashlyn stepped inside. "Mom? Dad?" Before Ashlyn even knew what happened, she was swept into a three-way hug. Her mother's body shook, and her tears soaked Ash's shirt. Her father squeezed her so tightly she strained to breathe.

Rowan cried quietly as she stroked Ashlyn's hair. "My baby, you're really here. Thank the God and Goddess. Are you okay? Let me look at you." Rowan took hold of both of her daughter's hands and moved her backward to drink in her appearance.

"I'm okay, Mom, really. I'm just glad to be home. I missed you both so much."

Rowan released her grasp on Ash and enveloped Hawk in loving hug. "Thank you so much, Hawk, for bringing our girl home to us." She dropped her hold on the Protector, as if she just noticed there were other people in the room. "Oh, Quill! And you, too of course. I'm sorry. It's all too much to take in." Rowan dabbed the corner of eyes with her sleeve.

Mica turned to Hawk and clasped his hand in a

314

hearty handshake. "Thanks to all of you, our Ashlyn is home where she belongs." He faced Brooke, addressing her. "I'm sorry to be so rude, you must be, Brooke. Ash has told us so much about you. It seems we owe you a world of gratitude. You're a very brave young woman from what I hear. Welcome to Aether. We're so happy to have you with us. I'm Mica, by the way and this is Rowan, we're Ashlyn's parents." Mica extended his hand to Brooke.

As Brooke took hold of Mica's hand her eyes widened. Shaking her head back and forth, she appeared rattled. Suddenly, she blurted out, "You can't be Ashlyn's parents. You look almost the same age. I'm sorry, I think I need to sit down if that's okay?"

Quill led her to the nearest chair. "Brooke, sweetheart, you remember what we talked about? Aetherians age differently than typical humans. Rowan and Mica are most definitely Ash's parents. I know this must be quite an adjustment for you. As soon as you get used to things around here, I'm sure it won't even phase you."

Rowan handed Brooke a glass of water. She sipped it slowly and Ashlyn thought she looked a bit steadier. "Hey, Mom, it smells great in here. What did you make? I'm starving, and I'm sure everyone else is, too. How about some breakfast? We barely stopped on the way here."

"Of course, sweetheart. I was praying you would be here soon so I made tons of food, all your favorites. Everyone, please, sit and eat."

Rowan piled everyone's plates high with bacon, eggs, pancakes, and more. Hawk and Quill dug right in. Ash watched Brooke moving the food around her plate but not actually eating anything. Brooke's eyes darted around the room as if she were lost. Ash got up from the table and grabbed her by the hand.

"Come with me for a couple of minutes. I want to show you something. Please, excuse us. We'll be back soon. Save me some bacon, Mom."

Ashlyn didn't wait for anyone to respond as she led Brooke up the stairs to the Tower's Atrium. Ash closed her eyes for a moment and took a cleansing breath. She aligned the Guardian symbol on her palm with the one on the entry to the Atrium. Beams of light shone brightly between her fingers. Then, the door swung open revealing the wonders of the Vessel of Fire. Brooke's lips parted slightly. She seemed stunned and was absolutely silent as Ashlyn approached the Vessel. Red and Orange flames surged up from its confines dancing high in the air when Ash approached the Vessel. When she made contact with the rough surface, she closed her eyes. A sense of completeness filled her, and the world felt right again, like the last remaining piece of a puzzle fitting into place.

Brooke stammered, "Wh-what on earth is that?"

"This, is the Vessel of Fire. Each of the Elements I told you about has its own corresponding Vessel. I am the Guardian of Fire. It is my destiny to be linked to this Vessel and what it represents."

Ash traced the symbol on her palm and then turned it toward Brooke. "I was born with this mark. It is a sign of great power in Aether. A new Guardian is born approximately every one hundred years. We pass our power and our knowledge onto the next generation when they come of age. A new Guardian was born just before I was taken. Soon you will witness the Fire

Guardian Ceremony. It's very special, and unique, and I can't wait for you to be a part of it. I will pledge my devotion to the child and teach her all I know. It is my job to mentor her, nurture her, and guide her. This is the cycle of nature and the Elements by which we live. I'm not sure by what design you were meant to be here with us, but I know with my whole heart you belong here."

Brooke paled on the spot. She looked completely shocked. "I-I don't know what to say. My head is spinning. I just have so many questions."

"Shortly, all of your questions will be answered. Right now, I just wanted you to see for yourself, something very few others have ever seen up close. This Vessel is the heart of the Guardian. It links us to the Element for which we possess an exceptional connection and control. Some things are simply meant to be. I was born with the symbol of the Guardian of Fire. It is my fate. In time, we will discover what divine decree is yours."

"Thank you for sharing this with me. I can sense the power. It's amazing. Your world is truly special. My mother would've loved this. I wish she were here with us."

"I'm sure she is looking down on you with pride. Now, enough of this seriousness. I'm starving. Let's go get some breakfast before the guys eat it all."

Allowing Brooke to go down the stairs first, Ashlyn noticed she gripped the railing white knuckled and her legs were shaking. She tried to put herself in Brooke's place. It wouldn't be easy to absorb all the intricacies of Aether and the power of the Elements. *Time, it's going to take some time, that's all.* She thought to herself.

When they returned to the kitchen no one seemed phased by their short disappearance. They took their seats, and Ashlyn savored the delicious meal moaning her pleasure with each bite. Brooke's food remained untouched. Ash watched in confusion as her friend repeatedly rubbed her hand up and down her pant leg. Perhaps it was a nervous habit Ash hadn't noticed before.

Always attentive to her, Quill picked up on Brooke's odd behavior. "Brooke, try to eat something. It's been hours since you've had anything. After, we can go for a walk if you want. I'd love to show you around Aether. The Elders called, and they want to speak with Ash and Hawk after breakfast."

"Okay. Thanks, Quill, I'd like that. I guess I'm just not very hungry. To be honest, I'm a bit overwhelmed. The food is delicious. I hope you're not insulted, Rowan?"

"Of course not, sweetheart. Anyone in your situation is bound to feel affected. How about I wrap up a few of my blueberry muffins for you to take on your walk?" Rowan asked, in a maternal tone.

"That would be really nice. Thank you so much."

Rowan got up and put a few of muffins in a brown paper bag and handed it to Brooke. "Here you go." She turned to Quill. "I put a bunch in there for you, too."

He smiled. "Thanks, so much, Rowan. Are you ready, Brooke?"

"Yes, I'm ready," Brooke answered. Then she diverted her attention toward Rowan and Mica. "I'd like to apologize if I don't seem appreciative. I'm not really myself right now. But I want to thank you for making me feel so welcome in your beautiful home."

Rowan didn't say anything. She simply got up and hugged her warmly. Brooke casually wiped away a few stray tears.

When Rowan released her, Quill took Brooke's hand and led her to the door. "We'll catch up with you guys later. I'm going to take Brooke back to my place to rest and relax after I give her a tour. So, give me a call when you're done. Good luck with the Elders."

Once they were gone Rowan sighed. "Poor sweet girl, she's so overwhelmed. This must be a lot for her to take in." With a big smile, she said, "Quill seems to be completely smitten with her."

Mica laughed. "Yes, that's quite a change for our ladies' man. And I have never seen him so serious before. He's always cracking jokes."

Ashlyn jumped in. "And do you see the way they look at each other? There's definitely some kind of spark ready to ignite."

Hawk was very quiet and his right leg bounced up and down continually. He was always so confident. She wondered if he was worried about talking to the Elders. Or maybe the loss of River was hitting him even harder than she thought. She planned on talking to him about everything as soon as they were alone.

Just as she pondered Hawk's state of mind, he broke his silence. "Um, Mica? Can I please have a word alone with you in the living room?"

Ashlyn didn't comment on the request. Perhaps he needed another man to speak to about everything that had happened. In addition, she really wanted a little time alone with her mother. The two were extremely close, and she wanted to tell her all about her new-found connection to Hawk.

Mica led the way into the living room with Hawk at his heels. When Rowan and Ashlyn were finally in private, Rowan walked over to Ash and handed her a cup of coffee. "So?" Rowan asked.

"What do you mean, so?"

"Oh please, I can always tell when you have something to share with me, so out with it. No point tiptoeing around it." With her mother's intuition, sharp as ever, she took a seat at the table across from Ashlyn.

"I missed you so much, Mom. I don't want to talk about what happened during my captivity just yet. But you're right as usual. There is something I want to talk about. Rather, someone, actually—"

"Hawk of course. Ash, I've known about the connection between the two of you since you were quite young. In fact, Lark and I often joked about it. It was very plain to us you two had a unique communication even when you were toddlers. I wish she were here to see what a wonderful man Hawk turned out to be. We were such close friends, and I still miss her every day," Rowan confessed.

"How come you never said anything to me? I mean, if you knew," Ash questioned.

"Lark and I both knew one day you and Hawk would realize what a special link you were destined to share. We agreed you would each have to come to terms with it in your own time. I'm just sorry we lost her so young, and she didn't have an opportunity to watch this magical bond blossom. I've watched you watching him for so long. I feared you two might be too afraid of the strength of the force which drew you to one another, and you would fight it forever." Rowan choked up. "But when you were taken from us…Hawk, he fell apart. He was so determined to find you. I guess you being gone triggered the telepathic link for both of you. I knew this day would come, but I'm sorry that it was at your expense, sweetheart."

"I'll be okay, Mom, really. It was awful, but I just want to put it behind me. I know with Hawk's help, and with Dad's, and yours of course, I'll come through the other side. Hawk is amazing, Mom. It's as if gravity is pulling me to him. I feel complete when he's near, and when he touches me, it's electric. I never imagined it could be like this. I love him so much."

"Sweetheart, I'm so happy for you both. Dad and I talked about it and we think you and Hawk need to be alone together, to grow and to bond further. I hope we weren't being premature, but we moved some of our stuff over to the old house. If you're not ready, we'll come back."

"Mom, I'm not kicking you out of our home. We can all stay here together. You don't need to leave," Ash quickly reassured her.

"You're not kicking us out, Ash. We're moving forward, and you need to do the same with the man you love. It's the way of things. Progressing through the many stages of life. It is the will of the God and Goddess. But as powerful as the Elements are, there is one thing even more powerful, love. Love is the greatest power of all."

****

Hawk

Hawk could feel his stomach tighten from nerves. He needed to tell Ashlyn's father about his intentions concerning his daughter, but that was easier said than done. Even the seasoned Protector felt intimidated by

321

Mica's protective nature toward his only daughter. Hawk certainly felt protective and possessive of Ash after all she had been through. He understood Mica's desire to keep her safe. Ash had become Hawk's entire world in such a short period of time. Though the more he thought about it, the more he realized he had always felt this way about her. Now that things with Ashlyn were out in the open, he wanted to spend every minute possible with her. After taking her to bed, he wanted to spend most of that time with her beneath him. To Hawk, nothing compared to the feel of Ashlyn's skin, her curves, her heat.

Mica took a seat on the couch and stretched his long legs out in a comfortable manner. "So, what did you want to talk to me about?"

Hawk had to focus on Mica and not on the idea of Ashlyn spread out for him, or he was going to have to do some serious explaining. He took a deep breath and centered himself. "I'd like to speak to you about Ashlyn, and me...you see, sir...well...the thing is, I love her." Hawk dropped down into the chair across from Mica. "What I mean to say is, I'd like your blessing in asking her to Join with me. There is something deep and special about our bond. She is a part of me, part of my soul. Our telepathic link has only made our feelings for each other stronger."

"I see. Is that so?" Mica said, with a teasing smirk. "I have to be honest with you, Hawk. Rowan and your mother, used to tell Wolf and me, you and Ashlyn were destined to be together. Your dad and I joked about it on many occasions. You and Ash always looked at each other in that special way, part enamored, part terrified." Mica smiled. "We've known this day was coming for a very long time. We've just been waiting for the two of you to realize it. I guess Ash being kidnapped was what it took for the link between you to spark to life."

Hawk responded, "I've never been more scared in my entire life; or more lost, or more determined. She's everything to me. I'm sorry it took me so long to recognize it. Our connection was so intense it actually petrified me. But after losing Ash, I realized nothing could scare me more than something happening to her. I promise you, I will never allow any harm to come to her again."

"Of that I have no doubt. I want you to know, both Rowan and I wholeheartedly give our blessing for your union with Ashlyn. Your parents were our dear friends, and I am certain they would've been as proud of you as all of Aether is. You're a fine man, Hawk. I can see the way my daughter looks at you, and it's obvious that you adore her as well. You'll make an excellent Kanti to Ash."

"Thank you for saying that, Mica. Your faith means the world to me. No Adara will ever be loved more than Ash. Making her happy is my number one priority from now on."

"When are you planning to ask Ashlyn to Join with you?"

"As soon as we're done talking to the Elders. I hope we'll be able to find some quiet time alone. I plan on asking her then." Hawk reached into his pocket, pulled out a locket, and let it dangle from his fingers. "I've been carrying this with me since Ash was taken. It was found on the ground beside my parents' car the day they were killed. It belonged to my mother, and her mother before her, and her mother before that. This locket was very special to her and now, in turn, to me. I pray Ashlyn will cherish it as much as my mother did."

"I'm sure she'll absolutely love it. And by the way, Rowan and I have moved the majority of our belongings to our old house. I believe my Adara's intuition has been working overtime. She foresaw this bond between you and thought you two should live here in the Tower, alone. Of course, we'll be close by in case either of you needs us. Ashlyn will be fragile for a while. I'm trusting you to see to it she feels safe, protected, and above all loved. Ashlyn is special, and not just because she's the Guardian of The House of Fire."

"I think I've always known that, sir. She is my light in the darkness. She carries my heart...and I carry hers. Nothing is more important to me than her happiness," Hawk confessed, sincerely.

With that last statement hanging in the air, the kitchen door swung open. Ashlyn and Rowan walked in. "We better not keep the Elders waiting any longer. Are you ready to go?" Ashlyn asked.

"Yes, I'm ready." Hawk turned to Mica. "Thank you for everything, Mica. I won't let you down, I promise."

Mica offered his hand to Hawk, and he shook it warmly. "I know you won't, son. Now you two go ahead and speak with the Elders. We're going to head over to the old house to finish unpacking. We'll see you later." Mica hugged Ashlyn one more time and kissed the top of her head.

Rowan hugged Hawk and then Ashlyn. "I'm so proud of you both. We'll see you later."

The front door shut with a loud click and Ashlyn

turned to Hawk. "Wow, that was really weird. What did you and my father talk about? I feel a little out of the loop. Both of you are acting very strangely."

"Let's go see the Elders, and I promise I'll tell you all about it later." He leaned into Ash, taking her hand, and touching his lips to hers, kissing her sweetly. Ash's hand felt delicate, warm, and soft inside his. His need to touch her, to remind himself she was real, and safe, seized him. He held onto to her all the way to the Council Chambers. Before he opened the door Hawk stopped and turned to Ashlyn. Then taking her in his arms, he kissed her urgently. Breaking away, he was breathless. "I'm sorry. I just needed to feel you. Are you all right? I'll be by your side the entire time, okay?"

"I'm okay. I just want to get this over with, but I'm really glad you're with me." She smiled up at him and squeezed him tightly around the waist.

With its familiar creak, Hawk pushed their way in through the large wooden door. He was relieved to be back here with Ashlyn at his side this time. It was where she belonged, with him, together always. They would face this challenge and everything else life would send their way.

Bear, as usual, waited for them near the reception desk. "Ashlyn, my dear, welcome home." To Hawk he said, "You have done well, grandson. I could not be prouder. Come inside, the others are waiting."

As they followed Bear, Hawk kept Ashlyn close to his side. The other Elders were seated on the leather couches and were chatting casually, until they saw Hawk and Ashlyn enter.

Raven stood first and greeted them both.

"Welcome home, children of Aether. We have missed you both greatly. We prayed to the God and Goddess for your safe return, Ashlyn. And, Hawk, we prayed you would find the strength to successfully complete this most important mission."

Bey stepped forward placing her hand on Ashlyn's shoulder. She looked directly into her eyes. "First and foremost, how are you feeling, Ashlyn? We have all been terribly worried about you, my dear."

"I'm feeling much better now that I'm home. Thank you," Ash replied.

Bear invited them to sit. "I want to lead off by saying, Hawk's actions, as well as all of the Protectors, was paramount in bringing our Fire Guardian home where she belongs. We are all devastated by the loss of River. He will be missed, not only as lead Protector, but by all of Aether. Hawk, the Elders, as well as the entire Council, would appreciate it if you would accept the position of lead Protector. We know it was River's wish for you to assume the role when he stepped down. Unfortunately, that has come to pass much sooner than any of us anticipated."

"I'd be honored to take over as lead Protector, but River's shoes will be impossible to fill. I'll try my best to make him proud and pay tribute to his memory." Hawk bowed his head and placed his hand over his heart.

Caro spoke, "We will have his passage ceremony early tomorrow morning. And if you think you are ready, Ashlyn, we would like to have the Fire Guardian Ceremony tomorrow night."

Ashlyn answered, "I would very much like to put this entire experience behind me and move on with my life. My vow to the infant must be declared through the ceremony in front of all of Aether. Nothing has changed in that regard, but I must warn you, I have been changed by this nightmare. If it were not for Brooke Barrington, I'm afraid I would not be here right now. I implore you to accept her as part of our community. I cannot possibly describe my feelings, or explain the reasons behind them, but Brooke is special. I'm asking you to trust me. Brooke is meant to be here with us. She is extremely vulnerable right now and needs our protection. Her role has not yet been revealed to me, but I am certain, in time, her destiny will be known to us all."

Hawk was moved by Ash's bravery. Standing up to the Elders thwarted even the most confident Aetherians. Yet Ashlyn defended her friend's right to remain in Aether. He knew Ash wholeheartedly believed Brooke had a greater purpose which remained a mystery to them all. Holding his breath, he waited for the Elders to respond.

Vale's emerald green eyes shone with respect. "Ashlyn, we have discussed the situation with regard to Miss Barrington. Although we have never before permitted an outsider to live on our land, we believe in you. The foreordination will reveal itself in due time. Until then, we will protect her as if she was one of our own. We should like to meet her, soon."

"Thank you for your trust in me," Ashlyn said, slightly choked up. "I know Brooke will be pleased to meet you. But as I'm sure you can understand, this is all very new and strange to her. I would appreciate if you could give her a little time to adjust. She'll be staying with Quill Robbins for now. You can contact her there if you don't cross paths soon."

Vale nodded. "Very well. Now, my dear, I am afraid the time has come to share the story of your capture and imprisonment with us. It is necessary so we may gain an understanding of the threat our people are facing. Please, begin."

Ashlyn painstakingly shared every detail of her ordeal, many of which Hawk was also hearing for the first time. It took all his strength to control the force of his powers when his anger began to bubble to the surface. Ash needed his support not his fury. He interjected during her recount, when necessary, filling in any gaps. When she finally finished with the entire sordid tale she slumped down in her seat, her eyelids heavy. Hawk pulled her closer to him, and she rested her head comfortably against his shoulder.

Bear spoke up, "You are truly brave and strong, Ashlyn. We are all so sorry you had to endure such conditions. We will make it our business to track down this Dr. Charles Barrington. We will stop this insanity. You have our word as the Elders of Aether."

"I'd like to take Ashlyn home to rest now. We'll see you in the morning for the Passage Ceremony." Taking Ashlyn's hand, Hawk gently pulled her to her feet.

With their arms wrapped around each other, they walked back to the South Tower in silence. Concerned for Ash's state of mind after her disclosure to the Elders, Hawk kept a firm grip on her. Ash leaned into to him seeming to need his support. When they entered the South Tower, Hawk finally spoke. "I think you should rest for a while. I know that wasn't easy for you."

"I know it wasn't easy for you either, but at least you know everything now." Ashlyn's body visibly relaxed, her shoulders dropping back down. "I can't believe my parents actually moved out. They wanted us to be alone together, and they know my place is here in the Tower. I hope that's okay with you."

"Of course, it's okay with me. I want to be wherever you are, Ash."

"My mother told me both of our parents knew about the link between us even when we were very small. How is it possible we didn't realize what was between us?"

"I think deep down we both did know, at least I did. Every time I looked at you, Ash, I dreamed about being with you. The pull, so strong, it felt like a force beyond control. When you were taken, I thought I might die from the pain. I realized then, that you were the one for me. I'm so sorry it took a tragedy to make me wake up. You deserve everything, and I want to spend the rest of my life proving to you just how much I love you. You asked what your father and I talked about...well."

Hawk got down on one knee in front of Ashlyn, reached into the pocket of his jeans, and removed his great grandmother's locket. "Ashlyn Woods, I love you more than anything in this world. You are my heart, my soul, my breath, my life. Please say you'll Join with me, become my Adara, make me the happiest man in Aether."

"Oh, Hawk," Ashlyn cried, with joy. "I love you, too, so much. I've dreamed of being Joined with you for as long as I can remember. Yes! Yes, of course."

Hawk brushed his hands down her soft, red curls.

Then tugging her close, his lips crushed hers in a heated kiss. He nipped and licked at her beautiful mouth unable to get enough of her. Breathless, he eased back from her delectable taste. "I need to take you upstairs…to a bed…right now." Ashlyn chuckled and led him up to her bedroom.

When they got to the doorway he swept her into his arms, carried her across the room, and placed her gently on the bed. "Ash, you are the most beautiful woman I have ever known. I feel like I'm dreaming."

Ash pinched him and he yelped. "What was that for?".

"I wanted you to know you weren't dreaming. This is very real." Then she spoke to him telepathically, *"Please touch me, Hawk. See how real I am."*

"You don't have to ask me twice, honey. All I can think about is touching you. Tasting you. Being inside you."

Hawk lowered his mouth to Ash's in a tender kiss. As she opened to him his tongue swept in, tangling in a passionate duel. Fingernails scratched along his scalp as she plunged her hands into his hair. The bite of Ashlyn's enthusiastic grip shot straight to his arousal, amping up his need. In a rush, they began tearing at one another's clothes, pulling, yanking. In their frenzy, articles flew across the room, landing haphazardly, giving the space the look of a dorm room.

The feel of her flesh, warm and soft, had him growing harder as he caressed every inch of her. His lips and tongue followed the path of his hands leaving goosebumps in their wake across Ashlyn's tender, milky, white skin. His fingers danced along her rib cage seeking out her incredible breasts. Slowly, he circled with his tongue, first one nipple, then the other. Drawing one of the luscious peaks into his mouth, sucking and licking at the sensitive tip, until she writhed and moaned from his ministrations.

Ashlyn's hips bucked up in invitation, but Hawk was not done playing yet. As frantic as he felt, he just wanted to enjoy every minute with his Adara-to-be. She was finally going to be his, and Hawk wanted to make sure Ashlyn never forgot that. He grazed his teeth lightly across her puckered nipple making her shudder. Slowly, he lowered his mouth so his lips lingered a breath away from her most intimate flesh. Dipping his tongue in deep, he tasted the honey of her arousal. Ash held tight to his shoulders moaning his name. Leaving her still wanting, he inched his way up her thighs, back to her belly, and finally reaching her mouth again, kissing her deeply.

"Baby, you make me lose my mind with want and need. When you're near me, I just can't control myself."

Restraint was no longer an option for Hawk. Taking himself in hand, he joined their bodies plunging into her heat. The feel of Ashlyn meeting his thrusts, forcing him deeper inside her tight channel, had him pounding into her at a furious pace. Her hands fisted the blanket as she continued to meet his every stroke with a counter of her own.

Grinding his pelvis hard against her, he slammed home, over and over again. If the sounds that ripped from her throat were any indication, he had sent her soaring. The harsh cry of his name, as she found her release, had Hawk following with his own. He kept a firm hold on her as he rolled to his side, taking her with him. They held onto each other as if no one else existed in the world. Neither of them spoke until their breathing slowly returned to normal.

"*Finally,*" Hawk thought, "m*y beautiful Fire Guardian, we are one.*"

"*Yes, my brave Protector. My hero, I am yours forever.*"

****

Ashlyn

Feeling sad when they had returned from the Passage Ceremony earlier, Ashlyn and Hawk found comfort in each other's arms. After everything she had endured, this bond with Hawk seemed surreal to her. The sound of his rhythmic breathing filled the room. Her fantasy personified, Hawk's eyes were closed. His long dark hair hung over his handsome face. She could not resist the urge to run her fingers over his finely defined abs. Soft, bronzed skin covered his firm muscles, and Ash had to physically restrain herself from licking his toned flesh.

"*Please don't hold back. I'd love for you to lick me,*" Hawk joked, inside her head.

"Hey, cut that out. That was a private thought. No fair being inside my head. Besides, I thought you were asleep?"

"I was, until you touched me and starting thinking about other things. By the way, I'm wide awake now." A suggestive smile curled his lips as he rolled on top of her.

"Hawk," she moaned.

"Yes, my love? Is there something you wanted?" He teased her as he kissed his way down her neck.

"I'm afraid we don't have time... we have to get

ready for the Fire Guardian Ceremony..."

"We have plenty of time, and I plan on putting it to good use." He pressed his lips to hers until she gave up any resistance. He urged her mouth open spearing his tongue inside. His taste and scent were intoxicating, overwhelming her senses.

They moved in sync with one another reaching new heights in their mutual pleasure. Satiated, they held each other, even their breathing in time with one another. Hawk stroked Ashlyn's curls and rubbed his hands up and down her body.

"You're going to be the end of me. People will talk if we never leave the Tower. I'm sure the rumors are beginning already," Ashlyn teased.

"Let them talk. I don't care one bit. I'm sure every man in Aether is jealous that you've agreed to be mine."

"That I am, my hero. Yours, always. But I'm afraid if I don't call Laurel she's going to stop by here any minute. I haven't seen her yet. It seems we both have some special news to share. I can't believe she and Kai are together again. And I still can't believe I get to call you mine."

"I love the sound of that, Ash. I love being yours." He kissed her again, groaning when he pulled away. "Go call Laurel, and then we can get cleaned up and ready for the Ceremony."

Ashlyn pecked him on the lips and reached for her phone to call Laurel. They caught up for a while, and Ash had to promise to share more with her later. After she hung up the phone, she realized just how much she had missed her best friend. She'd missed everything about Aether. Now that she had returned home, things had come full circle. Once again, she was facing the Fire Guardian Ceremony. Only this time, she would have Hawk at her side just as she had always dreamed.

When she entered the bathroom, Hawk's long muscular body was stretched out in her tub. Steam rose up from the hot water, bathing him in a mist of billowy clouds. His head was back with his eyes closed, but she knew he wasn't sleeping. Ash called upon her powers, lighting the various candles scattered about the tub surround. Switching off the lights, she slowly lowered herself into the luxurious water. Hawk's arm snaked around her waist hauling her against his hard body.

"I love your tub. And I love it even more now that you're in it with me." He turned her to face him and settled her on his thighs straddling his lap. Their lips met and no more words were uttered aloud.

"I fantasized about you in this tub with me on many occasions. Reality is even better than fantasy. Oh God, Hawk, you are amazing, perfect, my dream come true."

Water sloshed over the sides of the tub as they moved together. *"I'm glad to hear you dreamed about me as much as I dreamed about you. I can't get enough of you, Ash."*

Even their thoughts were quiet as they were swept away by the feel of each other moving in harmony. Intimacy which should have taken years to build had them climbing to the highest heights of ecstasy. Neither one of them wanted to break the spell of their spiritual joining, but the Fire Guardian Ceremony needed to be faced. They reluctantly left the warmth of the tub.

They readied themselves quietly, and then walked hand in hand to the center of the Village Square.

Ashlyn stood on the lovely mosaic of the compass rose and looked around her. All of Aether was gathered and Ashlyn thought, *How beautiful Aether is. And the people, oh the people, they are the most beautiful people I have ever seen.*

Forgetting for a moment that Hawk could read her thoughts, he was in her head. *"None are as beautiful as you, my love. Are you ready for this?"*

In preparation for the Ceremony, a fire circle had been created using large stones. Wood was piled high in its circumference. Groups of people were gathered all around, and she saw her parents waving to her. Laurel stood close by with Kai at her side. Dignified as usual, the Elders stood proudly next to the new Guardian's parents, who held the infant in their arms. The baby, swaddled in a special blanket which had been used for generations of Guardian Ceremonies, cooed loud enough for Ashlyn to hear. On the very edge of the crowd, Ash noticed Brooke. She stood solemnly with Quill's arm draped around her.

Ashlyn spoke aloud, "I'm ready."

Raven stepped forward and addressed the crowd. "Welcome people of Aether. As you know, our Fire Guardian has been returned to us. We are all grateful to have Ashlyn back where she belongs. The Guardian Ceremonies are a long-standing tradition in our world. Tonight, we are blessed by the God and Goddess to witness the dazzling display of the Fire Guardian Ceremony. Ashlyn, if you please."

Ashlyn advanced to the circle. "I, Ashlyn Woods, Guardian of The House of Fire, connect with the Elements and the people of Aether. I pray to the God and Goddess of the Earth." Ashlyn waved her hands, and the wood in the circle ignited with loud hiss. Bright red and orange flames surged, rising high into the air above the circle.

"I offer my gifts to the people, so I may protect and serve. With the stars above and all the people here to witness, I pledge my Fire to this beautiful baby."

The parents moved forward with the infant in their arms. "I vow to teach her the ways of our people and the gifts of Fire magic, so she may take her place when she comes of age. In this sacred place, where the history of our people was born." Ashlyn took the baby from her mother's arms and held her up. "I name this child, Ember, future Guardian of The House of Fire."

Ember's mother wiped away a few stray tears, and her father beamed with pride. Ashlyn held the baby close to her and looked down at her adorable face. Ember's golden colored eyes connected with Ash's. Electricity rippled through her body as the bond between them came to life.

"Oh, great God and Goddess, I call upon you and the Fire that burns within me. Give this child strength, knowledge, and peace, so she may she guard the people and the Flame. Fire is life. Water is life. Air is life. Earth is life."

Handing Ember back to her mother, Ash stood over the swirl of flames which rose above the circle. Lifting her hands toward the heavens, sparks ascended and soared upward. Bursts of blue, red, and orange flames exploded above the crowd. Gasps of astonishment echoed across the Village Square.

She took several paces backward and extended her arm above her head with her palm facing outward toward the assembled. "Behold, the symbol of the

Guardian of The House of Fire."

Ember's mother handed the baby back to Ashlyn. Together they unwrapped the blanket, and Ash lifted the child high in the air. "Ember, you were born with the symbol of Fire, and therefore you will take your place as the new Guardian when you come of age." The powerful symbol on Ember's palm was presented to the people of Aether. Then, Ashlyn slowly turned in a circle so all present could witness the power of Fire.

The ritual transformed her, releasing all of her unwanted energies and attachments. She was profoundly moved. "May all who are present be blessed by the Elements and the God and Goddess, who watch over our people. This is a time for celebration. Let us rejoice."

Ashlyn placed a kiss on Ember's forehead and returned her to her parents. They each hugged Ashlyn and thanked her. She smiled brightly and turned to face Hawk.

"You were incredible, Ash. I'm so proud of you. How did I get so lucky as to call you mine?"

"We were destined to be together. Selected by the Elements and the God and Goddess to be one. I love you, Hawk."

"And I you, my beautiful Fire Guardian, always."

She placed her hands-on Hawk's shoulders and gazed at him longingly. He lowered his head until their foreheads were touching and stared right back into her eyes. Ashlyn and Hawk blended together so seamlessly that neither could tell where one began and the other ended. They were truly one. Body. Mind. Spirit. Forever joined in love.

Epilogue

Brooke

The Grand Lake glistened in the sunlight as Brooke neared the water's edge. "Simply magnificent," she murmured to the peaceful surroundings. Aether was truly a place of beauty and wonder. How would she ever fit in with all these gorgeous people, amongst all their power and greatness. Their gifts were incredible, and she was just ordinary. Plain old, nerdy, Brooke Barrington, the scientist, she was no one special.

Quill came up behind her and placed his hands gently on her shoulders. Warmth spread through her. Relaxed by his touch, not startled, she'd sensed his presence as he'd drawn near. There was definitely something about the impressive Protector and not just his looks. Kindness and caring, which he masked with humor, radiated off him. Not to mention, he was the most handsome man she had ever seen. His sandy colored hair was on the shorter side making his striking green eyes stand out. Deep red lips which called out to her to be kissed made her melt when he was close.

Although she couldn't deny her intense attraction to Quill, Brooke remained leery. She didn't have much experience with men, at least none which were positive. Deeply in love with her first and only boyfriend, she gave him the gift of her virginity. He threw it back in her face telling her she was cold and horrible in bed. It turned out he had only dated her until she finally slept with him. Heartbroken, Brooke stayed clear of romantic relationships of any kind. She never wanted to feel rejected like that again. She sighed. *Maybe my father is right after all and I am unworthy.*

Quill would have to remain a naughty fantasy. He couldn't possibly want a plain Jane like her. Plenty of women in Aether probably sought his affection. Kind, funny, and extremely sexy, any woman in her right mind would want Quill.

"Are you okay? You checked out all of a sudden." Concern marred Quill's features.

"It's the water. I've always loved being near the water. It relaxes me, and sometimes I have a tendency to get in my own head a little too much."

"That's funny because I have a tendency to say or do whatever's on my mind. Sometimes it really gets me in trouble. Like right now, maybe? Because all I can think about is kissing you." Quill spun Brooke around to face him.

Heat rose to her cheeks instantly, and she didn't know how to react. My God, did he mean it? Did beautiful Quill actually want to kiss her? "I'm not sure it would be a very good idea, Quill. I'm not very good at that kind of thing…kissing I mean."

"There's only one way to find out." Quill gently touched his lips to hers and electricity jolted through her entire body. He licked along her the seam of her mouth encouraging her to open to him. She responded, on fire for this incredible man. His taste was intoxicating, and she felt consumed by him. No one had ever kissed her with such passion before, and she feared no one ever would again.

She pulled away breathless. "Quill, please, we can't."

"Why not? I thought it was amazing. And by the way, you're very mistaken, you are very good at kissing." He waggled his brows and smiled suggestively.

"I'm sorry... I just don't know how to navigate this. It's not you...you're perfect...it's just I haven't been very successful with all this, and with relationships in general. I wouldn't want to disappoint you."

"Stop right there! You could never disappoint me, Brooke. I think you're perfect, too, just the way you are. How about this? Let's just take things slowly and see what happens. Okay?"

"That sounds good," she said, with a smile.

Leaning down, Quill brushed his lips against hers once more. She could tell he held back, keeping things light.

"The sun is starting to go down. Let's go back to my house and get ready for the Fire Guardian Ceremony."

"Okay... And, Quill... Thanks for being patient with me."

The sexy Protector didn't say anything more, he simply took her hand and placed a kiss on the back. Then, he led her up the path toward his house.

Later, when they arrived at the Village Square, a crowd was already beginning to form. Brooke didn't have any desire to squeeze in for a close-up view, so they stood together on the periphery. Ashlyn and Hawk arrived hand in hand and Brooke thought they looked amazing together. Ashlyn was tall, shapely, strikingly beautiful, with her wild red curls, and Hawk was handsome, with dark Native American looks, muscled, and sexy.

Quill kept his arm around her making her feel safe and warm. The Fire Guardian Ceremony began with a dazzling display unlike anything she had ever seen before. Brightly colored flames of red and orange shot up from a circle which looked like a bonfire to Brooke. The stunning pyrotechnics lit the cloudless night sky, like fireworks on the Fourth of July.

As Ashlyn turned the mark on her hand toward the crowd, Brooke's stomach twisted in knots. A tingling and burning sensation pulsed through her scar when Ashlyn lifted baby Ember's hand to the assembled group. Slowly, Brooke pull backed the compression glove she always wore. Staring up at her was a raised red mark on her own palm. Her heart pounded, and she gasped when recognition set in.

Quill looked down at her as if he could sense her confusion and fear as it mounted. "Brooke?" He turned her wrist in his hand so that her palm faced him. "What the hell is that?"

"My scar… I was burned as a baby… I've had this my whole life." On Brooke's palm a bold triangle pointed downward toward her wrist, with a dot placed prominently in the center. It resembled a brand. Deeply embedded in her skin, the impression gave the appearance of having blistered and healed in a blush tone.

"My God, Brooke… Do you know what this symbol means? You, Brooke Barrington, are the Guardian of The House of Water."

A word from the authors...

M. Goldsmith and A. Malin (aka Mel and Anita), have been close friends for many years. As a writing duo, we love all kinds of romance, but especially exciting paranormal adventures. Avid romance readers and now writers, we have joined creative forces to create the world of Aether, where the Elements rule.

Thank you for purchasing
this publication of The Wild Rose Press, Inc.

If you enjoyed the story, we would appreciate your
letting others know by leaving a review.

For other wonderful stories,
please visit our on-line bookstore at
www.thewildrosepress.com.

For questions or more information
contact us at
info@thewildrosepress.com.

The Wild Rose Press, Inc.
www.thewildrosepress.com

Stay current with The Wild Rose Press, Inc.

Like us on Facebook

https://www.facebook.com/TheWildRosePress

And Follow us on Twitter
https://twitter.com/WildRosePress